Against the Odds

Nick Udall

Copyright © 2024 Nick Udall

All rights reserved. No part of this publication may be reproduced, stored in a retrieval system, or transmitted in any form, or by any means, electronic, mechanical, photocopying, recording or otherwise without the prior permission in writing of the copyright holder, nor be otherwise circulated in any form or binding or cover than in which it is published and without a similar condition being imposed on the subsequent publisher.

This is a work of fiction. Names and characters are the product of the author's imagination and any resemblance to actual persons, living or dead, is entirely coincidental.

ISBN: 978-1-916981-74-4

For Dodo. My life and inspiration.

Chapter 1

It was Sunday afternoon. The end of April 1956 and it was raining. Doreen lifted the net curtain that was covering the kitchen window and looked up at the grey Manchester sky. She was bored; desperate to go outside and play. Turning away, the little girl went over to her mam, Emily, who was sat darning her daughter's cardigan.

"Mam, when will it stop raining?"

"I don't know. It's no good asking me."

"But I want to go out."

"I'm sorry, Doe. I can't make it stop. Sit down and read one of your comics. Stop mithering. I need to get finished."

Having fetched a copy of the *Dandy*, the little girl sat at the table. It wasn't long before she started to fidget, periodically tapping her fingers and letting out an occasional sigh. Unable to concentrate, her mam would have to leave what she was doing. Yet Emily didn't mind. It was seven years since her daughter had been born and she and her husband, Jim, idolised her. Arriving ten years after her brother, Doe was a welcome surprise. After so long trying, Emily had become resigned to not having another child.

"Come on," said Emily, putting down the cardigan. "Let's go and sit in the front room and listen to the wireless."

Snuggled up next to her mam on the sofa, Doreen began to feel drowsy as she listened to the strains of the music and the drone of the voices. Finally falling asleep, Emily covered her with a coat and went back into the kitchen.

Sometime later, Doe was woken by the sound of men's voices. Slowly opening her eyes, she could see that it was her dad, together with some of his friends. There was Denis, who owned a photography shop on Stockport Road. Terry the coalman, Bert, a decorator like Jim and George, who was her friend Peter's dad. A crate of Guinness was on the front room table around which the men were gathered.

Naturally inquisitive, nosy according to her parents, Doe quickly closed her eyes, pretending to be asleep in order to stay and hear what the men were saying.

"Em, can you fetch us a pen and paper?" asked Jim.

Doreen heard the sideboard drawer being opened and sensed her mam moving past her towards the table.

"It'll be easy, believe me," continued Jim, speaking to the men.

"How do you know?" asked Terry.

"Because I've been working there all week. I've been watching them and I've checked everything out. Denis, you know the alarm. You can handle it."

"But Jim, maybe there's a second alarm you don't know about. One on the safe itself," said Denis.

"No, there's only one alarm. I checked."

"But how can you be so sure?"

"Because I stayed every night until the last man left and all he set was the alarm for the doors and windows."

An appreciative murmur went around the table.

"So, the best time to do it has to be a Saturday night. Do we all agree?" asked Jim.

The men voiced their assent.

Emily's voice suddenly cut through the air of optimism. It was clear that she was concerned.

"Jim. Don't. Think about it. You'll all get caught. It's not worth it."

"Don't worry," said Denis. "Jim's got it all worked out. It won't go wrong. You can trust us."

"And what happens if it does?" asked Emily.

There was a pause. Silence. It seemed as if no one wanted to answer. Finally, Jim responded.

"Em, I'm sick of having no money. This is going to make things better. It'll be all right. Honest."

Emily didn't reply and not hearing her voice again, Doreen assumed that she had left the room. For a while, she continued to listen as the men carried on with their planning. Slowly losing interest and tired of lying on the sofa, Doe yawned loudly, pretending to wake up so that the men wouldn't suspect that she had been listening to them.

"Oh, hello sleepy head," said Jim, turning to smile at his daughter.

"Has it stopped raining, Dad?"

"I think so."

"Oh, good. I can go and play out then."

Doreen rose from the sofa, went through to the kitchen and out into the back yard and across to her friend Alison. The two girls then played with their dolls in the small 'garden' at the front of Doe's house in Bright Avenue, Ardwick. A couple of hours later and somewhat heartened by the crate of Guinness and Jim's plan, the men came out of the house and set off home, cheerily saying goodbye to Doreen.

Chapter 2

"Mam? Dad?"

There was no answer. All Doreen could hear was the mumbled sounds of faraway voices.

Doe blinked her eyes through the dark of the night. The outside street lamps had been turned off long ago. She had been asleep in her bed, which was in the front bedroom she shared with her parents. Doreen was confused. Where were they? What were the voices downstairs? The little girl felt afraid. She didn't know whether she should hide under the covers or get out of bed and investigate. Finally, after what seemed like an age, she tentatively pulled back the eiderdown and blankets and swung her legs over the side of the bed, leaving them dangling as she struggled to overcome her fear. Doreen hated the dark; it terrified her. She never liked to be alone. Sliding off the bed, she inched quietly towards the door, felt for the handle and slowly turned it towards her. As it started to open, the light from downstairs slipped around the doorcase and welcomed her on to the landing, as the sound of conversation gradually became louder.

Listening intently, Doreen made out the distinct tones of her dad's voice. Relieved, she left the landing and went downstairs. Seeing that the kitchen door was open, Doe walked through it. There was no one there, just the sight of empty cups and plates of old sandwiches that had been left on the table. Turning back to the stairwell, Doreen headed towards the front room. From behind the door came the sound of animated voices, all of them talking at once. Suddenly, her mam could be heard above them all.

"Oh Jim, there must be thousands of pounds worth here!"

Her dad laughed.

"We're rich Em! We're rich!"

Opening the door, Doe saw several men, together with her mam and dad, gathered around the table in front of the window. Unable to see past them, she wondered what they were looking at. In their excitement none of the adults had noticed her come in. Unexpectedly, one of the men looked round. It was Bert.

"Jim!"

Doreen froze as the others turned towards her. Quickly, Emily took control.

"Doe! What are you doing out of bed?"

Jim moved towards her and swept her up in his arms.

"Back to bed, young lady."

"But I don't want to."

"What you want and what you'll do, are two different things."

Tired and somewhat surprised by her dad's unusually firm tone, Doreen capitulated, threw her arms tightly around his neck and rested her head against his chest. She felt safe and secure as Jim carried her up the stairs. Like so many young girls, Doe idolised her dad. Back in bed, she was still trying to find out what was going on.

"Why can't I stay downstairs?" she asked. "What was everyone looking at on the table?"

"Nothing. We're just talking and it's of no concern to you, Doreen."

Jim rarely used her full name. To family and friends, she was known as Doe. Doreen understood that his word was final. It was pointless asking any more questions.

"Will you light the candles please, Dad? It's dark."

"Of course."

Jim struck a match, lighting the two candles in the holders on either side of the mantelpiece. Moving back across the room he sat on the edge of Doreen's bed, gave her a hug and kissed her on the forehead.

"Don't worry, me and your mam will be up in about half an hour. You get back to sleep now."

Her dad having returned downstairs, Doreen lay listening to the low hum of voices and occasional bouts of laughter that drifted up from the front room. Tired and relaxed in the soothing light of the two flickering candles, she fell asleep.

Chapter 3

A fortnight later, at the beginning of a new school week, Doreen was woken by her mam and made her way downstairs for breakfast. It was seven o'clock, but Jim was nowhere in sight.

"Where's Dad?" asked Doreen, as her mam put out the cereals.

"He had to get off early. He's working away for a few weeks. It's a big job in Liverpool. It's too far to travel every day, so he'll be staying over until it's finished."

"But I didn't get a chance to say 'bye to him."

"I know, but your dad didn't want to wake you. Don't worry, he said he'll bring you a nice present when he comes home."

Sad that she wouldn't see Jim for a while, but satisfied with her mam's answer, the young girl finished her breakfast.

That evening, after tea, Doreen was sat with Emily in the front room. She was listening to the wireless before going to bed, whilst her mam was engrossed in a story in the *Manchester Evening News*. Unconsciously, Emily tutted as she read the article.

"That's not true. The owners are trying to bump the insurance. The crafty beggars," remarked Emily, not realising that her daughter was listening.

"What's that mam?" asked Doe, intrigued by her comments.

"Oh, nothing."

"What are you reading?"

"Nothing that's important, love."

"But it must be something."

Emily realised that she would have to answer.

"It's just a story about the jewellers on Stockport Road that got robbed recently."

"I've heard about that. Lots of the older kids were talking about it at school and Alison's mam said the police thought that it must have been a local gang that did it. She said they got away with thousands and thousands of pounds."

Although she wasn't sure what a local gang was, Doe felt grown-up repeating the phrase to her mam.

"Don't take any notice. People talk a load of nonsense," said Emily. "It's nothing for you to be bothered about. Anyway, I think it's time for bed."

"You're coming too, aren't you?"

Now that Jim was working away, his daughter was fearful of being upstairs on her own.

"Of course, love."

Emily folded the newspaper, placed it on the table and the two of them went upstairs. Now that Jim was away, Emily allowed Doe to sleep with her. Doreen felt safe; her mam would protect her and soon her dad would be back and life would return to normal. Content, she drifted off to sleep thinking about the present her dad would be bringing for her. She could hardly wait to see it.

Chapter 4

Another month had passed and Jim still hadn't returned. Doreen's constant question, asking to know when her father would be back, was met with the same response.

"He's still busy, Doe. The man he's working for is pleased with him and he's got your dad decorating all the other houses he owns. Your dad wants to come home, but he can't afford to give up the money. You have to remember that he's doing it for our benefit, so we're going to have to be patient and wait for him a little bit longer."

Sensible for her age, Doreen accepted what Emily said. She had learned that her family was relatively poor and that her dad worked for those who were much better off. In the school holidays he would often take her to work, teaching her the basics of painting and decorating. She found the 'posh' ladies of Didsbury and Gatley quite nice and they all seemed taken by the pretty, precocious and forthright little girl, with her sparkling green eyes and light brown hair. Doe gazed in wonder at the quality of their homes. The beautiful furniture, carpets and curtains and the range of modern electrical appliances. It was a completely different world, but not one in which she felt inadequate. Doe would never regard herself as less worthy than anyone else.

Returning home one afternoon from school, Doreen just had time to make herself a piece of bread and jam before a loud knock came to the kitchen door.

"Can you answer it, Doe?" asked Emily, who was working at the sink.

Doreen opened the door to see a policeman. Tall and imposing, he smiled reassuringly at her.

"Hello, love. Is your dad home?"

"No. He's at work."

"Where does he work?"

"I don't know," replied Doreen, holding the door close to her.

At that moment Emily reached above her daughter's head and opened the door wider.

"Don't worry, Doe. I'll see to it now."

Emily looked at the policeman.

"Can I help you?"

"I hope so. I'm looking for James Brodie."

Doreen noticed that the policeman's tone had changed now that he was speaking to her mam. He seemed more serious. There was no sign of the friendly face that she had opened the door to.

"I assume you're Mrs. Brodie," continued the policeman.

"Yes, that's right."

"Could you tell me where your husband is?"

"He's at work, like my daughter told you."

"Where's that then?"

"I'm not sure," replied Emily. "He's a decorator; self-employed. He works all over the place. Some small jobs; some bigger ones. He doesn't tell me exactly where he'll be on any given day."

Doreen felt uneasy. Her mam sounded tense and she could see her hand tightly gripping the edge of the front door. Something wasn't right.

"Well, obviously he'll be back later," said the policeman. "Someone will call tonight to see him."

The policeman left. Agitated, Emily grabbed her coat from the bottom of the stairs, put it on and moved towards the back door. In her haste, it seemed that she had forgotten about her daughter.

"Where are you going, Mam?" asked Doe.

"I won't be long," replied Emily, before she dashed outside.

Not wanting to wait on her own, Doreen went to call for Alison. After about twenty minutes the girls decided that they would play outside with their dolls, so Doe went home. Opening the back door, she shouted for her mam, but there was no answer. Emily's absence seemed strange, given that when her daughter wasn't at school, she rarely left home for more than a few minutes. Nevertheless, Doreen wasn't too concerned. She was sure that Emily would be back soon and so collected her dolls and went back to Alison's. The pair played happily until her friend went in for tea. Back home, Emily still hadn't returned, so

Doe went next door to call for Linda. Linda's mam invited Doreen inside and the two girls played 'school'. Doe always loved to be the teacher, telling her friends what to do, but now she was ill at ease. She was worried. Where was her mam?

"I'm going to see if my mam's back," said Doe to Linda. "I might see you in a bit."

As she reached the step to her back door, Doreen could hear voices. Her mood lifted and she slowly started to open the door, eavesdropping on the conversation within.

"I told him, but he never listens to me. He thinks he knows it all," said Emily.

"What are you going to do now?" came a woman's reply.

"Oh Lord, I just don't know. I've been racking my brains all afternoon. I told him he mustn't come back here."

"Shush!" said the woman. "Someone's at the door."

"It's only me," said Doreen, pushing open the door and then closing it behind her.

Emily and Mrs Warrington, one of her mam's friends, were sat at the kitchen table. Both turned towards her. Doreen didn't know Mrs Warrington very well, but was aware that she was married to Bert. He had been present on the night when she had woken up and gone downstairs, just before her dad had started working away. Doe looked at her mam and could see that she had been crying.

"What's up, Mam?" asked Doreen, concerned.

"Nothing, love," replied Emily. "Where have you been?"

"Only playing next door with Linda."

"Well, can you go to Horseman's to get the *Evening News*?" asked Emily, grabbing her purse off the table and giving her daughter a shilling. "You can buy some sweets with the change."

Doreen was surprised by the offer. Normally her mam wouldn't reward her for such a simple errand. It convinced her that Emily was worried about something. Doe suspected that her mam wanted her to go to the newsagents so that she could resume her conversation with Mrs Warrington.

Without comment, Doreen set off to the corner of Syndall Street and bought the newspaper. On her return, Mrs Warrington had left and Emily had started cooking the tea. Doe noticed that her mam had set an extra place at the table.

"Is Dad coming home? You've set three places."

"No, love. It's for Jimmy. He's coming round for his tea tonight."

As her brother hadn't been to the house for several days, Doe's eagerness to see him made her temporarily forget about her dad. At six, when Jimmy arrived, she rushed over to greet him. Jimmy, smiling, lifted her up and squeezed her tightly against him.

"Hi, Doe. Are you alright?" he asked, cheerily.

"Yes, Our Kid. Are you?"

"Of course, I am."

Jimmy lowered his sister to the floor and walked over to the table to sit down.

"What's he gone and done now, Mam?"

"Leave it till later. Remember. Doe."

Emily motioned towards her daughter.

"Sorry, Mam."

"Are you going out tonight?" asked Emily, quickly changing the subject.

Jimmy had come in his 'Teddy Boy' gear. He was wearing a grey suit. A long jacket with a black velvet collar, a skull robe tie and beetle crusher shoes. Although Our Kid was much older than his sister, the two siblings were very close. Doreen missed him being at home, but Jimmy had fallen out with his dad and had recently moved in with his girlfriend's family.

"I'm taking Val out dancing," said Jimmy.

"Can I come, Our Kid?" asked Doreen, excitedly.

"No, not tonight Doe and anyway, you need to stay with Mam."

Disappointed at her brother's response, Doreen sat quietly at the table as Emily put out the tea. As they ate, Jimmy asked his sister about her friends and school. Doe could tell that he wasn't really interested in her replies, but was far more eager to talk to her mam. Her suspicions seemed correct when, at the end of the meal as she began to clear away the plates, Emily told her to leave them.

"Don't worry, I'll do them. Why don't you go out and play for a bit, love."

"Yes," replied Doreen, deciding to comply with Emily's wishes. "I'll go and call for Alison."

"Don't be gone too long though," said Emily.

"No, Mam."

Determined to find out what Jimmy and her mam were talking about, especially as she believed that it concerned her dad, Doreen had no intention of going to Alison's. Closing the door behind her, she stood quietly on the outside step, waiting to eavesdrop on the conversation. Yet she hadn't reckoned on her brother who, shortly after, opened the back door.

"I thought so!" said Our Kid, looking at her and breaking into a grin. "Don't be so nosy and run along. Mam and I have private, grown-up things to talk about."

Her plan thwarted, Doreen shrugged her shoulders and reluctantly set off to Alison's. When she returned, Jimmy had gone. It was quarter past seven and Emily was wiping up the last of the tea pots.

"I'll be finished in a minute and then we can sit down."

Doreen sat at the table and watched her mam working. Suddenly there was a loud, pronounced knock at the door. Emily walked over and opened it. Without any invitation, two men in suits pushed past her and into the house. The men appeared intimidating. To a small girl like Doe, they seemed absolutely huge.

"We've come to talk to James Brodie. Is he here?" barked one of the men.

"I'm sorry, but he's not back from work yet," replied Emily.

"Well, we'd still like to take a look around please," said the second man.

Softly spoken, he seemed quite friendly, especially as he gave Doe a reassuring smile.

"There's no one here except us. You'll only be wasting your time," replied Emily.

"Well, if that's the case, you won't mind then, will you?" observed the first man.

Doreen couldn't understand what was going on. This was their house and it was clear by her mam's reaction, that the men weren't welcome. Yet they had forced their way in and one of them was being loud and aggressive. Doe was angry. If her dad had been there, she was sure that he would have given them a good hiding and thrown them out of the house. It was clear to the young girl that her mam needed help and it was up to her to give it.

"We don't want you here. Get out!" she shouted. "Go on. Get out!"

Walking over to the cupboard, Doreen opened it and took out her mam's wooden rolling pin. Brandishing it in front of her, she took a couple of steps forward and glared as fiercely as she could at the intruders. Shocked by her bravery and hostility, the two men hesitated. They looked at each other, unsure of what to do next.

It was Emily who broke the impasse. Doreen's actions had taken her by surprise and although immensely proud of her daughter, she had no desire for her to get hurt.

"Quiet, Doe," said Emily, calmly. "Put that away. These men are from the police. You can't go hitting them now, can you? We have to try and help them."

"That's right," said the nicer man. "We're from the CID. We didn't mean to frighten you. We'll be as quick as we can."

The men walked through to the front room and then went upstairs to check the bedrooms. Stood at the bottom of the stairs, Doreen heard the two of them talking, clearly unaware that they could be overheard.

"You're such a soft touch, aren't you? These people are scum. They don't deserve to be treated decently."

Doreen recognised the voice of the aggressive officer.

"Well, it's not the kid's fault, is it?" came the reply. "I'm not sure that the wife knows too much about it either."

"Well, I am. I'll tell you what though, it might be worth coming back when the old man's banged up. The missus is a bit of all right, isn't she?"

Doreen felt an arm on her shoulder. It was her mam.

"Come on, Doe. Let's go and sit down."

"What were the policemen talking about? What did they mean, Mam?"

"Oh, nothing. They're just being silly; talking nonsense."

When the men had finally left, Doreen settled down with her mam on the front room sofa, the two of them relieved at the return of some kind of normality. Doe could see however, that Emily looked tired and upset and the young girl had a sense of foreboding. The events of the day had made her realise that somehow, for some unknown reason, her life had begun to change. The happiness and security she had always felt at being with her parents, now seemed to be ebbing away. An uncertain and daunting future beckoned.

Over the next few weeks, the detectives kept returning. Each time they insisted on searching through the house. It seemed to get worse as they began to rifle through drawers and cupboards, claiming that they were looking for evidence. At first upset, Emily became determined to face them down, pulling out the drawers ready for them to look at and triumphantly laughing as they left empty-handed. By now, Doe's friends and their parents were beginning to talk. They were wondering what was going on at number seventeen. Doreen had no knowledge of what her father had been involved in, yet her friends constantly asked her where he was and wanted to know why strange men kept visiting the house. Their parents knew that they were CID, yet they didn't share this information with their children. Emily had told Doe that she must not talk about the visits to anyone and for once, she knew that she must not question what her mam had asked of her.

Chapter 5

The school year had finished and the long, lazy days of summer had arrived. On the first afternoon of the holidays, Doe returned from playing out to find her mam waiting for her at the back door.

"I've a surprise for you," said Emily, smiling. "You must promise me though, that you won't tell anyone."

"I promise," replied Doreen, wondering what the surprise could be.

Emily pushed open the door and as the little girl entered, she could hardly believe her eyes. There, shaving at the kitchen sink, was Jim. Excitedly, she rushed over to him. He picked her up and playfully rubbed his face against hers, covering it with shaving soap.

"Ugh, Dad!"

Jim grinned and hugged her tightly.

Doreen didn't know whether to laugh or cry. She was happy that her dad was back, but couldn't believe that everything was back to normal. She was right to be concerned. Sitting with her parents on the sofa in the front room, Emily explained to Doe that she would see Jim daily from now on, but that it would only be for a short time.

"Why?" asked Doreen.

"Well," explained Emily, "you know the policemen that have been coming?"

"Yes."

"Well, they want to take your dad away and so he's got to stay hidden."

Doe didn't understand. She turned towards Jim.

"Why can't you tell them that you're not going away with them?"

"It's not that easy love," replied Jim. "I know it's difficult to understand, but you have to listen to me and your mam and do exactly as we tell you."

Doreen paused, confused by the situation. Nevertheless, she realised that she had no choice but to accept it. Having been without her dad for so long, the chance to see him, even for just a short time every day, was preferable to not seeing him at all.

"Where are you going to hide, Dad?" she asked, fascinated to know how he could possibly stay undetected by the police when they came to the house.

"If we show you," said Emily, "you mustn't tell anyone."

"I won't."

Jim took his daughter up the stairs where a ladder was stood on the landing. It led up to the hatch to the loft.

"Can I have a look please, Dad?"

"All right, but go steady on the ladder."

Doreen climbed carefully up the rungs of the ladder and popped her head through the loft access, her dad having moved aside the cover. Inside, Jim had lit some candles and their flickering light showed that he had placed some blankets on top of an eiderdown that had been laid out on the loft boards. Well prepared, she saw that he had packs of cigarettes, bottles of beer and tins of food. A can opener, buckets and books completed the picture. Doreen wondered how her dad would be able to stay up there all day, but it seemed quite exciting; it was just like in the movies.

"Remember," warned Emily. "You mustn't tell anyone."

"Don't worry, Em. You don't have to keep telling her. You won't say anything, will you love?" asked Jim.

"No, Dad. Never."

For several weeks, Doreen kept the secret. She never let on to her friends that Jim was back home, even though she wanted to let them know how happy she was. The police however, were not giving up and continued to return. As they always came at different times, Jim became concerned that they may catch him unawares. He started to see his daughter upstairs. If necessary, he could nip quickly up his ladder, withdraw it and replace the loft cover. Emily now kept the doors locked when Jim was out. It would give him just enough warning if the police had to break the door down, to be able to retreat to safety. As time passed, Doe began to wonder just how much longer the situation could continue; her dad seemed just like a trapped animal. Jim had also given up shaving. It was too difficult in the loft and too risky to come down to the kitchen. Doreen disliked his beard. It was a sign of change and a visual reminder that her family was falling apart.

Still, Emily continued to put on a brave face. The last time the police had visited, they'd thrust a search warrant in her face and proceeded to hunt through the house. They'd never bothered to secure a warrant before, just entering the house and doing as they pleased. It was all aimed at increasing the psychological pressure. The police had gone over the back yard and outside toilet with a fine-tooth comb. Inside the house they had tipped over the sofa and beds to search underneath and emptied the contents of all their cupboards and drawers on to the floor. Yet when they had left, Emily just couldn't stop laughing. Seeing the state of the house, Doreen was confused.

"What's funny, Mam? What are the police looking for?"

"That's just it, Doe. They don't have a clue."

Doreen wasn't sure that her mam was really as unconcerned as she made out. Several times she had returned home from playing out, to see Emily with red and swollen eyes. It was clear that her mam had been upset.

It was in early September that Doe's world finally collapsed around her. Arriving home from school, she found Emily sat at the kitchen table crying.

"What's the matter, Mam? Why are you crying?" asked Doreen, concerned.

"Oh Doe, it was awful. The police brought a dog and it ran up the stairs and started barking up at the loft. One of them fetched the ladder from the back yard and they opened up the hatch and found your dad. They brought him down but then he tried to run away. One of the coppers hit him with their truncheon and cut his head. They handcuffed him and took him away. They wouldn't let me go with him, but they've said that I can see him at the police station later."

Doreen was shocked. She didn't know what to think.

"I've been waiting for you to come home so I can go and see him," continued Emily. "Mrs Cooper says that you can stay there and play with Sandra whilst I'm gone."

Doreen quickly grabbed a couple of her dolls and Emily took her straight round to Sandra's. Sandra's mam smiled as Doe and Emily entered the house.

"Don't worry, Em. You don't have to rush back. Just make sure Jim's all right and try to find out what's happening. It's okay for Doreen to stay the night if you don't get back before nine."

Doe was worried by the offer. Sandra's mam was always nice to her but very strict and so she didn't want to sleep there. She wanted to go with her mam; desperate to see her dad. He'd been away for so long, had finally come back and now, he was gone. Doreen felt that she was never going to see him again. She was worried that he was badly hurt. After all, her mam had been in tears; had told her that he had been hit on the head. When Emily had gone, Doreen found it hard to concentrate on playing with Sandra. She kept looking at the clock on the mantelpiece, desperate for her mam to return before nine, when she and Sandra would be sent to bed.

At eight-thirty, her wish was granted. There was a knock at the door. It was her mam. Emily went through to the front room with Mrs Cooper to talk privately. Re-emerging, she took Doreen's hand and the two went home. Inside the house, Doe wanted to know why her dad hadn't come home. Emily tried her best to explain, realising that she wouldn't do Doreen any favours by hiding the truth. Nevertheless, Emily was well aware that her daughter idolised Jim and would find it hard to accept what she was about to tell her.

"Your dad has to stay at the police station because they've charged him with breaking and entering and stealing thousands of pounds worth of jewellery."

Doreen didn't know what 'breaking and entering' was, but she did understand the word stealing. She was confused, especially as Jim had stopped her from seeing the items of jewellery on the table, when she had gone downstairs to investigate the noise in the front room.

"But why are they saying that Dad has stolen some jewellery?"

Emily knew that she would have to make things clearer.

"Doe, you mustn't tell anyone else this, but the police are right. Your dad did rob the jewellers on Stockport Road. The one that was in the newspaper, that everyone has been talking about."

Doreen took time to consider what Emily had told her.

"But why did he do it, Mam?"

"Because he was fed up of us having to struggle. He wanted to give us a better life."

Doe tried hard to understand, but it was all so confusing. Why would this have led him to steal? She had always been taught to believe that it was wrong and worst of all, because of what he'd done, she now couldn't see him.

"Will I be able to see Dad again?"

"I'm hoping that you can come with me to see him in a few days," replied Emily. "Anyway love, we need to go to bed now. You've got school tomorrow and your dad has to appear before the magistrates. I don't know when that will be, so I have to get to the court early to make sure that I don't miss him. Tomorrow morning I'm going to drop you off at Sandra's and her mam will watch you until it's time to go to school."

"What are magistrates, Mam?" asked Doreen, eager for more information.

"Not now, Doe. Let's go to bed. I'll tell you what happens tomorrow when you get back from school."

Returning from school the next day, Doreen found Emily at the kitchen table preparing some sandwiches for tea.

"What happened with Dad?" she asked, eagerly.

"The magistrates refused him bail after he pleaded not guilty. They've remanded him in Strangeways prison. The case has to be heard at the crown court."

Doe didn't understand what her mam was saying. Emily had used words that she had never heard before. Her mam tried harder to explain, saying how Jim had told the court that he hadn't stolen the jewellery, but that they wouldn't allow him to come home before they decided if that was true, as he had hidden from the police when they had wanted to talk to him.

"But last night, you said that Dad had done it," said Doreen, surprised.

"Well, it's not quite that simple," replied Emily. "You'd like your dad home again, wouldn't you?"

"Yes."

"Well, that can only happen if the court think that he didn't do it."

Slowly, Doreen began to comprehend the significance of what her mam was telling her; the awful realisation that her dad would only escape his predicament by telling lies. It was the first time that her faith in the goodness of her father had been tested.

"Remember, Doe. You mustn't repeat any of this, to anyone else. We don't want to get your dad in more trouble, do we?"

"I know, Mam. You don't have to keep telling me. I wouldn't do anything to hurt Dad."

"Anyway love," said Emily, changing the subject. "The good news is that we can both go and see your dad tomorrow. He can't wait to see you."

Doreen's spirits lifted. If she was going to be allowed to see her dad, then perhaps things weren't quite so bad after all.

Next morning, Emily and Doreen set off to see Jim. Doe was wearing a two-piece suit that her mam had made before Jim had gone into hiding. It was green. The jacket had two breast pockets and ordinary ones to match. It had unusually large cuffs and three big green buttons to fasten it. A pretty pleated skirt reached to just below her knees and she had on her white ankle socks and best shoes. Completing her outfit was a little beret that Emily had set on her head at a slight angle. As they rode on the bus into town, Emily was proud to hear the old ladies remarking on how cute her daughter appeared. Doe however, wasn't so pleased. She was a tomboy and liked to wear pants when she played out and wasn't at school. Nevertheless, she knew that today was important and she had to look smart when she went to see her dad.

For the young girl, the journey was something of an adventure. She'd only been to town on a few occasions and she gazed in wonder as they passed through Piccadilly, with its bustling crowds moving in all directions. There were people waiting or getting onto buses and sat on the benches at the edge of the gardens. Travelling on down Market Street with its host of busy shops, their bus turned into Victoria Street, passing the train station before continuing on to Great Ducie Street and their destination.

"Come on, Doe. Time to get off."

Grabbing her daughter's hand, Emily walked with her to the back of the bus.

"Next stop, love?" asked the guard.

"Yes, please."

Smiling, he pressed the bell and shortly after the bus slowed to a halt.

"Are you able to get down, young lady?"

Noticing that Doreen was quite small, the guard knew that it would prove a big step down from the platform to the pavement.

"Yes, thank you," replied Doreen.

Feeling grown-up, Doe jumped down on to the pavement.

"Careful," said Emily. "We want you to get there in one piece."

"I'm all right, Mam."

As the bus pulled away, Doreen could see a huge building on the other side of the road. Doe didn't know it yet, but this was Her Majesty's Prison Strangeways. It was where her dad was being held on remand.

"Come on, Doe. We need to cross. Keep hold of my hand, it's quite busy here."

Doreen did as she was told and followed Emily across the road towards the giant building. She noticed that there were people waiting outside. As they approached them, she could see that they were mainly women and children. There was lots of excited chatter going on and Doe could see that they had stopped at the end of a fairly lengthy queue.

"Why are we stood here, Mam?"

"We've to wait for them to let us in. Be patient. It won't be long."

The delay encouraged Doreen to take a closer look at the building that housed her dad. It was imposing; yet intimidating too. There was a massive archway with huge wooden doors; gigantic to a little girl like Doe. Built within the doors was a smaller one, which contained a window with a grille. Surrounding the wooden doors, the archway was made of light stone that had been splendidly carved, with three columns on either side. Above the arch were coats of arms and two large figures. Beyond the columns to both sides were imposing round towers topped by two tiled spires that projected forward from the huge roof. The building was made of red bricks covered with a wealth of ornamental stonework that wrapped around its numerous windows. The roof was topped by several huge, thin chimneys. Cobbles lined the approach to the huge doors, behind which Doreen sensed a sinister presence. Although desperate to see her dad, the little girl was now afraid of what she would find when she entered the building.

"Mam, why do we have to see Dad here? Can't we go somewhere else?"

"No. Don't worry, it's not so bad inside" replied Emily, smiling.

Reassured, Doreen began to settle down. Shortly after, she heard raised voices coming from the front of the queue.

"About time," remarked an old lady stood next to them. "They seem to take pleasure out of making us wait as long as possible."

Emily nodded but said nothing.

Suddenly, Doe could see a man in uniform walking along the side of the queue. Stopping in the middle, he looked up and down the line of people gathered there. He was elderly, with a small grey moustache. He looked imposing and his smart, peaked hat spoke to Doreen of his importance and authority. The way he addressed them, in a booming voice, made clear that he was used to having his instructions obeyed.

"Right, let's be getting you lot in," he barked. "Come on, quickly now and you kids had better make sure that you behave yourselves!"

The man walked back to the head of the queue which followed him through the small door and into a courtyard leading to another door. From here there was a wide passage which led them into a large room. Once inside, the man stopped them. Across the room there were lots of tables and chairs set out. Drawing himself up to his full height the man, with a stern look on his face, addressed them again.

"The men will be along shortly. Remember, we'll be watching to make sure that you don't pass on anything that you're not supposed to. Go and sit yourselves down."

Doreen and Emily picked a table and sat down. Almost immediately a door opened in the far corner of the room and men began to file in.

"Look, there's your dad," said Emily, pointing across the room.

Jim was looking round the tables and his eyes quickly alighted on his wife and daughter. He strode towards them and sat down. He looked so different. He was dressed in a type of navy-blue suit. He had a blue and white striped shirt on and a navy-blue tie. Yet he seemed cheerful and was clearly pleased to see them. Because he was on remand, Emily was allowed to see him regularly and except for money, could give him almost anything. Today, she had taken him cigarettes and chocolate. Doreen knew that Jim was a smoker, but was confused as he didn't like chocolate. Emily explained that her dad would be able to swap it for different items with the other prisoners.

"Are you being good for your mam, Doe?" asked Jim.

"Yes, Dad. When are you coming home?"

"Not yet I'm afraid, love."

"Why?"

"Because I've got to go to back to the court first for them to decide when I can."

"When will that be?"

Jim sighed. He was finding his daughter's questions difficult.

"Don't mither your dad," said Emily. "Let's just find out how he's getting on and I can talk to you about the court later."

Doreen nodded.

"How are things?" asked Emily, turning to her husband.

"Fine. The other prisoners are treating me well. Believe it or not, some think I'm a hero."

Jim smiled, seemingly pleased with himself.

"Jim, take care," warned Emily. "It won't go down well if the judge thinks you're not sorry for what you've done."

"Don't worry, Em. The lads will look out for you if things go wrong. You'll be fine."

"I'm not so sure," replied Emily. "You should be out here with us. It's not right that you're the only one locked up. You need to think about taking it all on yourself."

"I'm not a grass, Em. Leave it!"

Sensing the tension between her mam and dad, Doe wondered what they were talking about. Eager for harmony, she thought better of asking them.

Doreen had noticed how her parents kept watching the prison officers as they moved around the room. Suddenly, she saw Emily slip two £5 notes under her hand and move them across the table. The notes were in tiny squares that her mam had folded up on the bus. Her dad moved his hand towards her mam's, put it on top and as she withdrew her hand, placed his own over the money. Doreen glanced around the room, but none of the prison officers came over to speak to them.

"Thanks," said Jim. "The screws have got eyes in their backsides. You can't be too careful."

Jim withdrew his hands carefully under the table and after a short time, brought them back into sight. Doreen later found out that the prisoners were searched when they left the room. Her dad had put a slit in his leather belt in which to hide his money. He'd learned from the other prisoners that the screws never checked their belts.

"What are screws, Dad?"

"The prison officers, love. It's what we call them in here."

"Oh."

Just then, a bell rang and a voice shouted above the hum of the conversations that were going on around the room.

"Visiting time's over," it announced.

"You'll come back and see me again soon, won't you?" asked Jim, as he rose from the table.

"Of course," replied Emily.

"Make sure that you come too," said Jim, smiling at his daughter.

"I will."

The time had gone all too quickly and back outside, the little girl was subdued. She wanted her dad to come home but knew that it was impossible. The fact that he was in prison, meant that she had to grow up very quickly. The bus ride home was no longer exciting and she was relieved when she arrived back at Bright Avenue, got changed and was able to go out and play with her friends.

None of Doreen's close friends had mentioned anything about her dad and his predicament, but at school on the following Monday, she was confronted by older boys and girls, who shouted abuse and pushed her around the playground.

"Jailbird's daughter!"

"Scum!"

"Your dad's a dirty thief!"

Temporarily shaken, Doreen did the only thing she knew; fight. Being small, she had often been picked on and she had learned that if you didn't want to suffer, you had to hit back. Before class, during break and at dinner, Doreen had fights against several boys and girls. She ended up with a black eye and was called in to see Mr Roberts, the new headmaster at Ross Place. Roberts knew that Jim's case had recently been reported in the *Manchester Evening News*. The article had given his full name, age and address and declared that he would be on trial for robbery. Other pupils in the school had found out and as cruel as children can be, had decided that it was acceptable to taunt his daughter. Roberts was kind. He asked Doe if she was all right and said that he would make sure that no one said anything to her again. However, he told her, she mustn't be caught fighting, as that never solved anything. Doreen promised that she wouldn't but living in Ardwick, she already knew that sometimes you had to fight, if you didn't want to become a victim of the bullies.

When Doreen returned home at the end of school, Emily was shocked at the sight of her black eye and the scratches on her arms and face. She was pleased however, that her daughter had given as good as she'd got. She promised Doe that she would see Mr Roberts to make sure that there was no more trouble. Emily was true to her word, but kept Doreen off school for a week. In the meantime, Jimmy spent hours teaching his sister to fight properly; how to win. He told her that she always had to stick up for herself and not to rely on the teachers. After all, they wouldn't always be there. Doe was proud to tell him that she had and delighted when, on returning to school, she found out that she had given split lips and black eyes to three of her assailants, who were all older and bigger than herself. Jim too, was proud of his daughter, who had fought to defend his honour. Doreen didn't know it at the time, but she was far braver than her dad would ever be.

Whilst Jim was on remand, Emily and Doe saw him on several occasions. Doreen was now less intimidated by the formidable entrance to Strangeways. She had begun to accept that the limited contact she had there, was the only relationship she would be able to have with her dad. She knew that the trial was coming up soon and Emily had explained to her about the judge and the jury; that they would decide if her dad had carried out the robbery or not.

On the Saturday before the trial, Emily and Doreen had again gone to see Jim. When he walked into the room, both of them could see that he wasn't as happy to see them as he usually was. Sitting down he seemed anxious, as if he felt unable to tell them something.

"What's up, Jim?" asked Emily.

"Nothing."

"Come on, Jim. I can tell there is. What is it?"

"Well, I suppose you're going to find out soon enough," replied Jim. "I've got no chance of getting off. In fact, I've seen the solicitor and he says that I've no choice but to plead guilty."

"But why, Jim?" asked Emily, clearly shocked. "They've no evidence other than you having worked at the jewellers before it got robbed. They haven't found any of the items. They were all fenced long ago."

"They've got my fingerprints from the broken glass at the back entrance."

"But you all wore gloves."

Doreen could see that her dad looked uncomfortable. He wasn't about to appreciate having to tell his wife why things had gone wrong. Taking a deep breath, Jim continued.

"The reason the police came to the house so quickly, is because they lifted the fingerprints from the tape that I placed on the glass to stop it shattering on the floor and making a noise. I had to take my gloves off to unroll the tape and then forget all about removing the tape and glass afterwards."

"You stupid idiot!"

Jim looked down at the floor, clearly embarrassed.

"But why did they know it was you so quickly?" asked Emily.

"Because I went AWOL in the Army and had my fingerprints taken before they sent me to the glasshouse. They were told by the jewellers that I'd worked there before the robbery and so they ran a check of the police and army records and matched my fingerprints to those on the tape. If only I hadn't taken my gloves off, they wouldn't have had a thing on me."

"Typical, Jim. You have to be the one who takes the chances; none of the others. You worked there, cased the joint and took all the other risks too. Just what have any of the rest of them done? I told you no good would come of your grand schemes and you just wouldn't listen, would you?"

Doreen was spellbound, riveted to the unfolding drama. Her mam was furious and although she didn't understand everything her parents were talking about, it seemed clear to her that the situation wasn't looking good for her dad.

"Em, keep your voice down!" said Jim, urgently.

Emily, realising where she was, slowly calmed down. She took a couple of deep breaths and paused. It was important that none of the screws overheard their conversation. If they did, they were bound to pass the information on to the CID.

"Why didn't the coppers tell you this earlier?" asked Emily. "Why not until now, just before the trial?"

"Because they wanted to hurt me; take away any hope that I'd built up before the trial. They thought that once I knew that I'd go down, when I believed I might not, I may be prepared to give them the names of the other lads. But there's no chance of that. I've told them I did it all on my own."

"But they know that's not true, Jim. You couldn't have shifted all the stuff yourself and they know damn well that you haven't got a clue how to disarm the alarm or open the safe."

"Yes, they've told me that. They said I'll get hammered for protecting the others. The solicitor said he could get me a deal with the judge if I was prepared to help the cops. I told him no chance."

Emily was angry, but she knew that he was right. It was an unwritten code; you didn't grass. You were finished in Ardwick if you did. You'd have to get away and there would be no coming back. Ever.

"I've told you, Em. The lads will look after you."

Doreen remembered his final words. Whatever happened at the trial, her dad had told them that they would be looked after. It would be all right.

Two days later Jim appeared at Manchester Crown Court and pleaded guilty. The judge reacted just as he had been warned. As he was protecting other criminals, Jim would have to suffer for his silence. However, he was perhaps lucky that he was convicted to serve three, three-year terms to run concurrently. The judge had reasoned that it would have taken at least three men to carry out the robbery, hence Jim would receive all three sentences. When Emily had told Doreen the judgement, the little girl had cried, but felt a little better when Emily explained that being given the sentences concurrently, meant that all of them were served at the same time. Her dad would be in prison for three years and not nine. Emily also explained that Jim would probably be released early for good behaviour, as long as he did as he was told. But there was bad news too. As Jim had been found guilty, they wouldn't be able to see him as often as when he was on remand. When, later on, Jim was moved from Strangeways to an open prison, they would find it very difficult to get there to see him.

Inwardly, Doreen felt unhappy and vulnerable. There were no happy families for her anymore. She wanted her dad at home and worried about how they would carry on without him. Outwardly though, she acted tough. Doe wasn't going to let anyone push her around. When she went into school after the trial, although it had been fully reported in the *Evening News*, no one teased her. She had made her point. There were some children who admired Jim. Their parents understood why he had wanted to rob the jewellers. The gang hadn't hurt anyone; had entered the premises when there was no one there. They weren't stealing off their own kind, they were taking from those who had got more than enough. Yet Doreen kept well away from those children. They may have thought it was all right to steal, but she didn't. Doe only wished that Jim had felt the same way too.

Chapter 6

Doreen had known much happier times. She had been born in February 1949 in her grandmother's house in Greenheys and had spent all her young life at 17 Bright Avenue, Ardwick. Situated in the triangle bounded by Hyde Road, Stockport Road and Devonshire Street, the area was a warren of terraced housing. Doreen's home was rented for ten shillings a week and had a tiny 'garden' to the front with a rickety wooden fence. At the back was a yard which opened out on to a small croft, surrounded by the backs of the terraces of the nearby streets. There was an outside toilet in the yard and the typical layout for a 'two-up, two-down' inside.

Doreen's house didn't have electricity. Not that it wasn't available. The Electric Board had put supplies in for all the houses on the street, but some residents had chosen not to use it. Jim had said that it was too expensive to install the new circuitry for the lights and plugs in the house, as the landlord wouldn't pay for it. That was until Doreen was six and her brother's friend George, an electrician in the RAF, wired the property for them in return for her dad decorating his parents' house on Syndall Street. For Doreen, who had always been afraid of the dark, the results seemed magical. Unlike gas light, candles or paraffin lamps, electric lights were so bright that the night seemed transformed into day. At bed time, the little girl would leave the light switched on at the top of the stairs, so that it would shine through the open door and into the front bedroom she shared with her parents. The day came however when the gas lights and candles returned. Jim had almost been caught 'fiddling' the electric. The Electric Board had fuses for the supply to each house mounted in boxes at the end of the street. There wasn't a fuse present in the box for 17 Bright Avenue, so Jim took his ladder and put one in. As George had bypassed the electricity meter when wiring the house, it meant that there were no charges. Yet, like many of Jim's great schemes, it hadn't been thought through and with electric consumption up on Bright Avenue, the Electric Board suspected sharp practice and sent out an engineer to check the fuse boxes. Jim had been lucky enough to see him examining the boxes and told Emily not to open the door to anyone. Quickly, Jim got one of his friends, who was an electrician, to remove the evidence of the bypassing of the meter. When the engineer was finally let into the house, there was no sign that the circuitry was connected to the mains. The engineer assumed that his colleagues must have mistakenly put a fuse in the box for number 17. Thankfully, Jim had escaped prosecution, but for a time, there would be no more electric.

It wasn't long after, that the gas ran out too. Emily explained to Doreen that they hadn't been able to pay the bill and until they did, they would just have to use candles and paraffin lamps, instead of their gas lights. A few days later, the gas was back on. Doreen assumed that the bill had now been paid. Shortly after however, she found Jim in the gas meter cupboard with a spanner in his hand. The house reeked of gas and it made Doreen feel sick.

"Here love, take this," said Jim, to his daughter. "Shove it up your jumper, don't let anyone see it and go outside and hide it away from the house."

Doreen looked at a piece of rubber hose and did as she was told. Going out into the back yard she went across the croft and made her way over to Syndall Avenue, hiding the hose in some bushes that she knew were nearby. Doreen returned straight back home to find that the gas man had arrived. Jim was telling him how tough it was without gas, but noted that they were fortunate to have a coal fired stove to cook on and candles for lights. Jim had found out that the gas man had been checking properties whilst he was reading the meters. Once again, he had just avoided getting into trouble. Satisfied, the gas man left. Almost immediately, Jim sent his daughter back for the hose and on her return, reconnected the gas supply.

As a young girl, Doreen didn't understand the illegalities of her dad's actions and she always obeyed him when he told her not to mention any of his antics with the gas and electric. A self-employed painter and decorator, Jim evaded the system. He simply didn't exist at a time when records were incomplete and haphazardly kept. He never paid tax and insurance on any of his earnings. In an age of cash only and no receipts, there was no evidence of where he had worked and the wealthy people who employed him, were so pleased with his excellent work and cheap rates, that they wouldn't dream of passing on his details to the Inland Revenue. Yet there was a drawback to this way of operating. Decorating jobs fell off during the winter, especially outside due to the inclement weather. Often there was no work for long periods and so no money available. Furthermore, Jim was unable to apply for unemployment benefit, for if he did, he would have to face awkward questions about what he had been doing over the past few months.

During these periods, Emily found life particularly hard. To help with the household expenses she, like most working-class women, went out to work. Emily had a part-time job in the local cheese factory on Apsley Grove. Once, Doreen had gone there to see her. She remembered how much it stank of stale milk; just like horrible, sweaty feet. She wondered how anyone could possibly work there. Emily wasn't helped by the fact that her husband, like many an Ardwick man, was too fond of boozing and gambling. While she stayed home at night, looking after Doreen, Jim was almost always in the pub and forever gambling money that they couldn't afford on the dogs and horses. There were plenty of pubs to go to locally: the 'Clarence' and the 'George' at either end of Syndall Street; the 'Rutland' on the corner of Rutland Avenue and Jim's favourite, the 'Richmond', on the corner of Richmond Street.

Emily was an attractive woman. She had blonde hair, a tiny waist and caught the eye of all the men. During the war she had worked for a time as a conductress on the buses and had the regular attention of the American GIs, who always insisted that she "keep the change," when they gave her half-a-crown for the tuppenny fare into town. Having switched to working in munitions, Emily worked long, twelve-hour shifts and put in regular overtime, before returning home to her mother's house in Greenheys. The latter's help was invaluable in caring for little Jimmy, who had been born just a few months before the war had broken out in September, 1939.

Emily had been faithful to her husband whilst he had been away, following his conscription into the Army and was devastated by his betrayal of her just prior to D-Day. Having had no letters from him and receiving no money, she wrote to his commanding officer to find out what was going on. Most importantly, she was desperate to know if Jim was all right.

A few days later, Emily received a phone call at work. Her boss, who constantly asked her out, despite knowing that she was married, had allowed her to give Jim's commanding officer the factory's phone number. When Emily picked up the receiver, it was a man's voice at the end of the line.

"Hello, am I speaking to Mrs Brodie?"

"Yes, that's right," replied Emily.

"It's Captain Hughes here, Mrs Brodie. It's about your husband."

"Is everything all right?" asked Emily, who was starting to assume the worst.

"Well, yes. Your husband's fine, Mrs Brodie."

Emily relaxed and gave a sigh of relief.

"However," continued Hughes, "would it be possible for you to come down and see me? I know we're based in Dover, but there are things that I need to tell you and I'd rather not do that over the telephone. I can send a travel warrant and you can get a train from Manchester. You have to change in London, but I'm sure you'll manage. Will you be able to get time off work?"

Emily had been working all her shifts and overtime besides. She hadn't asked for any time off. Nevertheless, the factory didn't like women taking the breaks that they were entitled to. Requests to do so were met with a familiar response: "There's a war on you know!" and pressure to keep on working. Yet knowing that the boss was keen on her, Emily expected him to agree to her request and so responded positively to the captain's question.

"Yes, I should be able to."

"Good, I'll have a warrant made out for the end of next week. You'd best arrange to take three days off Mrs Brodie. I'll have you met by a driver when your train gets into Dover next Friday evening and I'll arrange accommodation for you."

Returning home from work, Emily explained to her mother that she had a chance to visit Jim and asked her if she could look after little Jimmy over the following weekend. Emily hadn't told her about not receiving any money. Her family hadn't approved of her marriage to Jim. Her mother thought that she could have done much better. To tell her that Jim hadn't contacted her and that it was his commanding officer who had mysteriously organised the trip, would have brought down a barrage of unwanted criticism upon her.

"I'd take him with me, but he's too young to go on such a long journey," explained Emily.

"It's all right, Em," replied her mother. "You just go and enjoy yourself."

It was a long journey south. Leaving at 7am from London Road station, Emily eventually arrived at Dover Priory to be met, as promised, by a driver who took her to a local guest house. He informed her that Captain Hughes would be over to pick her up at nine o'clock the following morning.

Emily looked delightful when Hughes arrived. She was wearing a smart, blue two-piece suit that she had bought before the war, a blouse and real nylons. The latter were a gift from one of her American admirers, from the time that she had worked on the buses. She had been saving them for a special occasion. Disarmed by her pretty face and striking blonde hair, the captain blushed like a teenager as he greeted her.

"Oh, hello Mrs Brodie. I'm Captain Hughes. I'm your husband's commanding officer."

Hughes made a pleasing impression. He had come alone and he was young, polite and quite handsome. Not at all what she had imagined him to be like after hearing his voice on the telephone. Holding the passenger door open for Emily, Hughes treated her with a politeness that she wasn't used to from most of the men she normally encountered. Sat beside her, Hughes turned to Emily and explained that he had made enquiries about Jim through one of his sergeants. He told her to brace herself for some bad news. The reason that Jim wasn't sending her any money he said, was because he was spending his time off camp with a woman in a local caravan park. It seemed that he'd been spending his pay on her, instead of sending it home.

"That's why I didn't want to tell you over the phone, Mrs Brodie. I wanted you to come and see him yourself, so that hopefully the two of you can sort things out. I do hope I haven't upset you too much, but I felt that it was for the best."

Hughes could see tears welling up in Emily's eyes. He wanted to take hold of her hand in order to reassure her. Yet the fact that she was pretty made him feel that it would be inappropriate. She may feel that he was simply trying to take advantage of her vulnerability. Hughes fears vanished however, as Emily reached out and grabbed his arm, squeezing it hard as she tried to stifle the sobs. Struggling to regain her composure, Emily finally pulled herself together.

"Where is he now? I want to see him," said Emily.

"He's with the woman, I assume," replied Hughes. "He has a pass to be off camp this weekend."

"Well, can you take me to him?"

"Are you sure that you want me to?"

"Oh, yes!"

Hughes admired her courage. She was a determined woman but he didn't want things to get out of hand. After all, his senior officers might feel that he was taking his responsibilities for the welfare of his men and their families, a little too far.

"I want to see her," continued Emily. "See why she's made him forget about his wife and son. She must know that he's married. How can she be so selfish?"

"What about your husband, Mrs Brodie?"

"Oh, he'll not say anything with you there."

"Well, as long as you're certain."

Emily reassured him that she was. Hughes started up the car and pulled away from the guest house. Around ten minutes later, the car turned off the main road. It travelled down a narrow lane and then through an entrance to a large house from which a driveway led to an enclosure containing several caravans. Hughes stopped the car and turned off the engine.

"It's the red caravan at the end," he said. "You don't have to go over you know."

"I have to see with my own eyes," replied Emily.

"Well, I'd best come with you. Make sure that everything is all right."

The pair got out of the car and walked across the grass. To their right was a grey and crumbling blockhouse that contained the communal washing and toilet facilities. It was a bleak location. Emily couldn't fathom why anyone would want to live there. Reaching the caravan, she stood on the temporary steps and banged on the door.

"Jim! Jim! Are you in there?"

There was no answer. Emily pounded on the door even harder.

"Jim. It's Emily. Open the door."

She heard movement from inside and hushed voices.

"Come on. Open up. I want to know if my husband's in there."

"There's no one here," replied a woman's voice. "Only me."

"I don't think so," insisted Emily.

Hughes was impressed. For all her delicate appearance, Emily was confident and assured. She was determined to hold her husband to account. Looking around, he noticed faces peering out through the windows of the nearby caravans. Some residents had actually ventured outside, eager to be entertained and hopeful that the fireworks would soon start to fly.

"She's lying darling," shouted one of the women spectators. "She's got a man in there. She's nothing but a trollop."

"Yes," said another. "A whole string of 'em have been through here in the last few months. We're about sick of it."

Hughes now thought it was time to intervene. He wanted to defuse what was becoming a potentially volatile situation. Stepping forward with purpose, he addressed Jim in a loud and clear voice; one charged with authority.

"Private Brodie. This is Captain Hughes. Get yourself out here, now!"

"Oh hell!" remarked Jim, from inside. "Hang on. Give me a minute."

There was the sound of someone rummaging around. It seemed as if Jim was struggling to get dressed; desperate to avoid being in a compromising situation when he finally faced his wife.

Emily had recognised his voice immediately. A part of her had hoped that he wouldn't be there; that somehow, the information Hughes had been given, was wrong. Up until that moment she'd envisaged herself giving the woman a 'battering' if it was true, but the shock of the revelation had numbed her. She was devastated. She no longer knew what to do.

Sensing Emily's change of mood, Hughes took his opportunity.

"Step back Mrs Brodie and let him out. Be strong. You're more civilised than them. Let's see what he's got to say for himself."

Hughes took her arm and led her a few steps back from the caravan. The door opened and Jim came out. It then shut quickly behind him and the lock was quickly applied to give added security to the unseen woman within.

"It's not what you think, Em. I only stayed overnight. The beer was off in the pub; it's always flat down here. I was ill and this nice lady took pity on me and gave me a place to stay. Nothing happened. Honest, love. I was just getting ready to set off back to camp."

Emily knew that he was a liar. She'd suspected him of 'carrying on' before, but never had any proof. He often worked in areas where no one knew him and so could cheat on her without any fear of discovery. Decorating wealthy homes where the wives didn't go to work, brought opportunities to comfort bored women who, all too often, felt deserted by their workaholic husbands.

"I don't believe you, Jim."

"It's true. Nothing happened," shouted the woman from inside the caravan.

"I'd shut up if I were you!" exclaimed Emily, responding to her rival. "That door won't save you!"

The woman fell silent and Emily turned her attention back towards her husband. Jim looked worried, but she didn't know whether it was because he was concerned that she might attack him, or that he wouldn't be able to talk his way out of his predicament.

"Why haven't you sent me and Jimmy any money?"

"I have. It must have got lost in the post."

"What, for the past couple of months? And I suppose all your other letters have gone missing too? Why don't you just admit that you're just not bothered about us."

Jim decided that a display of remorse could help regain his wife's sympathy.

"I'm sorry Em, you're right. I haven't written, but that's not because I don't love you. The training's so hard and we know what's coming across the Channel. It's got me thinking that I may never see you or our Jimmy again. My mind's all over the place. That's why I've not written."

Hughes knew that he couldn't intervene, but it was hard. Brodie, although sounding sincere, was a complete liar. He was totally untrustworthy, but it wasn't his place to expose Jim's dishonesty and so make the marriage even more difficult to maintain. Hughes thought Brodie a fool. Why cheat on such a pretty and devoted wife? Yet there would be no easy ride for Jim. Emily wasn't convinced.

"I don't believe you, Jim."

"Honest. It's true, Em."

"We can sort out the money quite easily Brodie," suggested Hughes, eager to take advantage of Jim's protestations of innocence. "From now on I'll arrange for your pay, barring a little for yourself, to be sent regularly to your wife. That way, you don't have to worry that you might forget."

Jim grimaced, realising he'd been outmanoeuvred. He had no choice but to agree if he were to have any chance of convincing Emily of his honourable behaviour. Hughes was a right bastard, thought Jim. A typical officer. He knew the score. A soldier away from home with no wife around, what was he supposed to be, a monk? He couldn't go without it for weeks and months on end. What did it matter? Most of the boys did it. What their wives didn't know about, couldn't hurt them. And besides, all the lads had heard stories about the Yanks coming over here with their fags, chocolate and nylon stockings, knocking off their women while their husbands were away from home.

"Look," continued Hughes, "let me take you both back to camp so that you can sort things out."

As Emily turned back to the car she looked around and noticed the people going back into their caravans. For them, the show was over.

Sitting with his wife in the back seat of the car, Jim grabbed Emily's hand. She had calmed down but was clearly troubled. He squeezed her fingers softly, but there was no response. Back at the camp, Hughes told Emily that a car would be ready in a couple of hours to take her back to the guest house. In the meantime, he suggested that she and Jim spend time in the canteen together and hoped that they could sort out their difficulties.

Alone with his wife. Jim worked hard to persuade her that it was all a misunderstanding. Honestly, he insisted, the woman had just been doing him a favour. No, he had no idea where Captain Hughes had got his information from. It was probably his sergeant. He had it in for him. He'd been at the pub last night and must have seen the woman help him and take him away after he'd been sick. He had probably asked the locals about her, found out where she lived and then told Hughes.

It never entered Jim's head that his story made no logical sense. Renowned for being happy-go-lucky, which was the quality that had first attracted Emily to him, he had a humorous personality. Jim turned everything into a joke and it was usually enough for him to sail effortlessly through life. No one took offence at him or believed that he would knowingly upset anyone. Now however, Emily had been with Jim long enough to know that it wasn't true. He would constantly forget what an intelligent woman she was. If not for being born to working-class parents, she could have achieved almost anything. But life had been tough. Her father had died when she was thirteen. The eldest of five children, Emily was soon working to help support the family. It seemed that she'd always been sacrificing herself for others.

"I know you don't get paid much Jim, but sending us some money every couple of weeks helps out. We've only got my mam's pension and my wages from the factory. I do all the overtime I can whilst Mam looks after our Jimmy. I know it's hard, coming away from home, but you must remember that you're married. You can't just forget that you've got a wife and son to look after."

"Em, I keep telling you. Nothing happened with that woman."

"Okay Jim, let's forget it," replied Emily, with an air of resignation. "I just hope the War's over soon and then we can get back to normal."

Emily spent the next hour telling her husband about Jimmy and work and listened to his protestations of love for her. When it was time for his wife to leave and she finally allowed him to hug and kiss her, Jim believed that all was forgiven. Yet Emily still felt a sense of betrayal. She was convinced that once she had gone home, her husband would go back to his old ways. But what could she do? She had little alternative but to carry on and hope that when Jim finally came home, they could rebuild some kind of life together.

Chapter 7

Escorted to the front entrance, Emily was surprised to see Captain Hughes standing beside the car that was to take her back to the guest house.

"I thought I'd run you back myself so that I can check that everything is all right."

Emily was pleased to see him. She appreciated what he had done and wished that Jim could show her such consideration.

"That's good of you," replied Emily, "but you don't need to be concerned."

"Yes, I do Mrs Brodie."

"Why don't you call me Emily. After all, we've been through quite a lot together. It seems so formal."

"Okay, Emily. My name's Bill."

"Nice to meet you, Bill."

Playfully, she offered her hand for him to shake. He grasped it and smiled.

"I'd prefer to sit in the front, if that's all right?" asked Emily.

"Of course," replied Bill. "If you like, I can take you a drive along the coast. Perhaps it will give you a chance to relax."

"Yes, I'd enjoy that. The air here is so different; so clean and fresh. It must be the sea. I seem to spend most of my time now in the factory and there's no chance of ever getting out of Manchester."

Bill started the car and they moved off. Emily was warming to him. He was quite handsome and it crossed her mind that perhaps she could be like Jim. She had needs too. Longing for a lover's touch, she had stayed resolutely faithful, despite the number of men who'd flirted with her in Jim's absence. Hurting from her husband's betrayal, Emily fleetingly entertained the thought of what it would be like to make love to Bill and steal some moments of happiness in her grey and depressing life.

"You're very quiet," remarked Bill. "Would you rather I took you back now?"

"No, I'm sorry. My mind was miles away. I'm all here now. Promise."

Seeing her smile, Bill's heart began to race. He could no longer ignore the fact that he found her very pretty. Besides, she was a woman who showed real mettle. Her behaviour at the caravan and the way she had dealt with her husband, had shown real dignity. Emily would make a wonderful wife for any man and being with her had certainly brightened up his day.

"I know a place in Folkestone. It's a hotel where we can have something to eat. You must be hungry."

As soon as the words had slipped out, Bill feared that Emily would misread his intentions. Quickly, he corrected himself.

"Of course, I'm not thinking. Perhaps it's getting on a bit. Maybe we should head back."

"No, Bill. It's fine. It sounds like a good idea."

Without thinking, Emily placed a reassuring hand on his knee. She smiled again and noticed that Bill's face was turning crimson. Silent, Emily left her hand for a little longer and then withdrew it. His reaction had initially pleased her. She was flattered that she had clearly aroused his feelings, but had no wish to encourage him. Emily turned away to observe the scenery as it flashed past the window, giving Bill a chance to regain his composure.

Arriving at the hotel, Emily was impressed. It was an imposing building and far grander than what she was used to. Getting out of the car, they went inside and sat down at a small table in the corner of the restaurant. It was a quiet spot and intentionally or not, created quite an intimate atmosphere.

"I'm afraid that it's not like before the War," said Bill. "The food here was very good then but with rationing, it's rather basic now."

"Don't worry," said Emily, neglecting to tell him that coming from her background, basic food was all that she had ever eaten. "I'm sure it'll be fine. Tell me about yourself, Bill. You know about me. What about you?"

"There's nothing much to tell. My father's a retired stockbroker and we live in Wimbledon. I went to Oxford and studied engineering. I worked two years as a civil engineer. I was fortunate to get taken on at a firm where one of my father's friends was a partner. Then this lot started."

Bill paused. Emily waited, but he didn't continue. If she wanted to know more about him, it would be up to her to keep the conversation going.

"I hope you don't mind me asking," said Emily, "but are you married?"

"No," replied Bill.

"Do you have a girlfriend, or fiancée?"

"I've had girlfriends Emily, but I haven't got one at the moment and I've never been engaged."

"Why?" asked Emily, surprised that such a handsome young man should be unattached.

"I've been fortunate to go out with some pretty girls," replied Bill, "yet I've not met anyone that I could feel seriously about. I'm a bit of a romantic I suppose. I want to share my life with someone I really love and who feels the same about me."

As he spoke, Bill was becoming more relaxed. A far more sensitive side to his nature had begun to penetrate his previously awkward demeanour. Bill felt increasingly comfortable in Emily's company. She had already made a positive impression on him and he couldn't ignore the fact that when she had touched him in the car, his body had tingled with anticipation. His confidence growing, Bill was eager to find out more about her life; about her feelings and expectations.

"Emily, you've asked me about my girlfriends, can I ask you something?"

"Of course."

"I shouldn't really say it, but why do you stay with him?" he asked. "You're far too good for him you know."

Bill paused and looked at Emily, but he received no response. For Bill, the silence was intense and it seemed to be lasting an age. He now regretted having broached such a private and personal subject.

"I'm sorry, Emily. I shouldn't have said that. Please forgive me."

Bill was embarrassed. He was angry with himself. He had been so fortunate to be able to spend time with this lovely woman, but through his carelessness and stupidity, he'd now ruined the whole day.

But he hadn't.

"What you say may be true Bill," replied Emily, "but my life and background is different to yours. What would I achieve by leaving Jim? I've got a son to consider. People where I live just don't tolerate divorce."

"But you're an intelligent and strong woman. Surely you can make a new life for yourself. I'd love to help you do so."

Although she appreciated Bill's concern and felt sure that his offer wasn't prompted by any ulterior motives, once again she dismissed his suggestion.

"No, Bill. As I've said. It would never work."

"But I meant what I said," continued Bill. "I can help you. I'd really like to."

"But Bill," replied Emily, softly. "We've only met today. You don't really know anything about me. It's kind of you to offer, but don't be daft."

Bill paused. He looked into Emily's eyes. She had gently rebuked him, but he wanted her to know that he was serious. He knew that the War, with its constant reminders about human mortality, had led many to seize a chance of happiness, temporary as it may well prove to be. So many couples had got married after whirlwind romances and sat there in silence, he asked himself whether he too had simply got carried away; infatuated with this pretty young woman. Yet he was sure that wasn't true. He was convinced that he was falling in love with her. Emily wasn't like anyone he had ever met before. She was real. Her tough upbringing had created a woman that was not only pretty, but strong and considerate in equal measure. Bill was becoming convinced that Emily could become his perfect partner.

"Emily, I know what I'm saying. If things don't work out with you and Jim, I would love to be there for you."

"No, Bill. You could never be. Your family and friends wouldn't understand. You need to find someone unmarried, without a child. Someone from your own background."

Emily reached out across the table and grabbed his hand.

"I really appreciate all you've done for me Bill. You're a lovely man, handsome and you've got lots to look forward to once the War is over. And don't worry, you'll get through it. Come on, let's go back now."

Arriving back in Manchester, Emily wondered whether she had done the right thing. Her head said yes; her heart told her no. She didn't tell her mother much about the visit. Putting on a show of emotion, Emily related how she'd spent a couple of wonderful days with Jim, who was fine and desperate to be back in Manchester. The latter was at least true. Alone with her thoughts, Emily wondered if there hadn't been a real chance of a different life for her and Jimmy. It would become a dark presence in her mind when later, Jim was convicted and sent to prison.

Chapter 8

One of Doreen's earliest memories involved her only brother, Jimmy. Ten years older than Doe, he idolised his little sister. He took her everywhere with him, to the obvious displeasure of his girlfriends who wanted Jimmy to themselves. But he didn't care and those that wouldn't accept Doe were quickly discarded. But one summer night, when Doreen was five, Jimmy wasn't in his usual humour. His mam and dad had made him stay at home and babysit, whilst they went to the 'Richmond'. Our Kid had just got a new girlfriend and was supposed to be meeting her that night. Sat on the sofa with his little sister, Jimmy was in a bad mood. Doreen knew that he wasn't pleased to be there.

"Why aren't you my friend, Our Kid?" asked Doe.

"I am!" snapped her brother.

"Can you read me a story please?"

Hoping to persuade him, Doe pushed the book she was looking at towards him.

"No!" replied Our Kid, fiercely.

The book was difficult for Doreen to read herself and rather than struggle through it, she decided to just look at the pictures. She was upset. Doe didn't understand why her brother was ignoring her. She kept looking at him but he refused to glance back towards her. He then got up, turned the wireless on and went and sat in the chair next to the fireplace. Not one to give up easily, Doreen tried again.

"Our Kid, please read me a story."

"No. I'm listening to the wireless. Read it yourself."

Doreen had never seen her brother like this, he was usually so loving towards her. She was upset that he wouldn't even look at her.

"But I can't."

"Well, just look at the pictures then."

Doreen gave up. She knew that there was no point saying anything else. Our Kid just wouldn't listen.

Shortly after, Jimmy got out of the chair and took hold of a knitting needle that Emily had left on the table. Doreen watched in fascination as he started to poke at the grout between the tiles on the fireplace. As it fell out, a powdery substance started to cover the bottom of the hearth. Suddenly, a tile fell off and smashed as it hit the solid base at the foot of the grate. Doreen was shocked. What would her mam and dad say? She knew that Jimmy was being naughty, but he seemed so engrossed in what he was doing. It was as if he hadn't realised the damage he was causing. Given how hostile her brother had been, Doe didn't feel able to say anything to stop him. And then, the needle became stuck between the tiles. Jimmy pulled this way and that, but it wouldn't come loose. Frustrated, he hammered down on the top of the needle with the palm of his hand. Doreen stared as blood came out of the wound. Both of them were stunned, before Jimmy cried out in pain.

"I can't get it out! It's too deep!"

The needle had come out of the tile, but it was stuck fast in his hand. Doreen felt sick. She couldn't look at it.

"I'll have to go and get Mam," said Our Kid, making his way towards the front door.

Jimmy was gone leaving Doreen alone. Shocked by the incident, Doe didn't realise that she had no one with her, but it was only a short time before her dad came into the front room.

"Where's Our Kid?" asked Doe.

"Gone to the hospital with your mam," replied Jim, who quickly noticed the smashed tile, blood and damage to the fireplace.

"What happened, Doe?" asked Jim.

"I don't know. Jimmy was poking at the tiles and his hand started bleeding."

"I knew it!" exclaimed Jim. "I knew he was taking the tiles off. I've told him before about picking at the grout. It was obvious that he had to be up to no good for it to get stuck in his hand."

Doreen was more worried now. She hadn't wanted to get Jimmy in trouble, but she was far too young to make up stories to get him out of it. Jim picked up the broken tile and threw it away. Having cleaned up the blood and dust, he sat down on the couch with Doreen to read her a story. Before long, she was fast asleep. Her dad lay her down, put a cushion under her head and covered her with a coat. Sometime later, Doreen was woken by the sound of Jim shouting in the kitchen.

"You little sod!"

"Not now Jim, he's just been through hell. They couldn't get it out and they've had to stitch it."

Emily's calming words soothed her husband's temper. She wasn't going to allow her son to become any more upset, regardless of his bad behaviour.

"Go into our Doreen, Jimmy. Let her know that you're all right," said Emily. "She's bound to be worried about you."

Jimmy, relieved that he could avoid his dad, moved gratefully into the front room. He sat down by his sister, pulled her towards him and gave her a cuddle.

"I'm sorry I was horrible to you before, Doe. It's just that I was supposed to be meeting Monica Wheatley tonight. I've been trying to go out with her for ages and she finally agreed, then mam and dad told me I had to babysit you."

"I'm sorry, Our Kid," said Doe.

"It doesn't matter now," replied Jimmy.

"Are you better?"

"Yes. Do you know that I've got nine stitches?" asked Jimmy, proudly showing her his injured hand.

Meanwhile, the siblings could hear the sound of Jim ranting furiously in the kitchen.

"It's all because he had to babysit Doe and couldn't go out larking around," said Jim. "He did it on purpose to stop us enjoying ourselves for once. How often do you manage to get out? Once in a blue moon, that's when! The selfish little sod!"

Eventually, Emily calmed him down and then came into the front room with two mugs of sugary Horlicks for Jimmy and Doe.

"Drink those and then get off to bed," said Emily.

As far as she was concerned, Jimmy had suffered enough. The incident was closed.

Chapter 9

Emily was an expert dressmaker and the need to maintain a tight family budget had given her every incentive to make her own daughter's clothes. Already earning money from her part-time job at the cheese factory, Emily realised that she could supplement the family's income by making clothes for other children in the neighbourhood. It was logical for Doe to become her model; a perfect way to advertise her skills.

Emily had owned a large Singer treadle sewing machine for years and used it to make Doreen's dresses, blouses and skirts. As Doe's gran knitted her cardigans, the only articles of clothing bought from the shops were her underwear and socks. Once Doreen started at school, Emily spotted her opportunity. Going into town to search out new patterns for dresses, she would return with the smartest fabrics and make up the designs for her daughter to wear at school. Other mothers soon took notice of the smartly dressed young girl and would stop her on her way home to ask about her dress. In particular, they wanted to know where she had got it from. Primed by Emily, Doe was always ready with the answer.

"My mam made it. She makes all my clothes."

The women would then usually ask for Doreen's address and would later call round to see if Emily could make their daughter something similar.

Doe was so proud of her mam, especially the day when she was six and went to school wearing a red and white summer dress with thin straps, an elasticated bodice and a flared skirt. She had never been stopped by so many women before, all of them wanting to know where her mam had bought the pretty dress.

"Oh no," the little girl had replied. "My mam made it. She can make any kind of clothes for anyone. However, they might want them."

It wasn't long before everyone knew Emily as the local dressmaker. The extra money she earned came in very handy, but provided her with even more work to add to that of looking after her house and family, as well as her part-time job.

Nineteen fifty-five saw a lot of orders for Emily, especially in the summer holidays when the kids were hit by Davy Crockett mania. All of them had been to see 'Davy Crockett, King of the Wild Frontier' at the ABC and now they all wanted to be him. Jimmy had taken Doreen to see the film and like all the other kids, she was fascinated by Davy Crockett's coonskin cap. Arriving home, she had rushed through the kitchen door in excitement.

"Mam, Mam, are you there?"

Emily was upstairs cleaning the bedrooms.

"I'm up here love," she shouted.

Doreen charged up the stairs. Her face was beaming and Emily could see that she was excited.

"Mam, can you make me a Davy Crockett hat?"

"What's that?"

"It's what Davy Crockett wears."

"And who's Davy Crockett?" asked Emily, who had been far too busy to take much notice of what her daughter was going to see at the pictures.

"He fights wild animals and bad men on the frontier and he's got a song about him."

Doe was getting quite giddy. Emily could see that Davy Crockett, whoever he was, had made quite an impression on her. Hoping to calm her down, Emily took Doreen downstairs. Jimmy was in the kitchen.

"What's she on about Jimmy?"

"Tell her about Davy Crockett's hat, Our Kid."

"It's a fur hat ..."

"Don't forget the tail!"

"It's supposed to be made out of raccoon skins," continued Jimmy. "It's furry and still has the animal's tail attached to it. There's a poster up outside the ABC showing Davy Crockett wearing it, Mam."

"You'll be able to make one, Mam. You can make anything," insisted Doreen, praising Emily in the hope that she would.

"Well, I'll have to see. I'm really busy at the moment. I've got quite a few orders for dresses you know."

"Oh, pleeeese Mam."

"I'll try Doe, but I'm not promising."

"Thanks Mam," said Doe, throwing her arms around Emily's waist, pressing her face into her side and squeezing her tightly. She felt certain that her mam would soon be getting on to the job.

Emily didn't disappoint. She nipped out later to look at the poster at the ABC and when she next went to buy materials for her dress orders, obtained some synthetic fur and after her daughter had gone to bed, made up a perfect replica of the coonskin cap. When Doreen came down to breakfast the next morning, Emily had a surprise for her.

"There's something for you on the front room table, Doe. Go and see."

Doreen wondered what it could be.

"What is it?" she asked, hesitating.

"Go and see," insisted Emily.

Doreen went into the front room and squealed with delight. She picked up the hat, put it on and raced back into the kitchen.

"It's brilliant Mam and the tail's just like Davy Crockett's!"

Emily smiled. She was delighted to see Doreen so excited. It was the reason why she had made the cap whilst her daughter had been asleep. Emily had wanted it to be a complete surprise, knowing that she would get a reaction like this. It made all her hard work worthwhile.

Doreen couldn't wait to finish breakfast and go out to call for her friends. She felt certain that with her new hat, she would be the centre of attention. Doe was right. Even children she didn't know very well came over to ask her where she had got the hat. Everyone wanted one. It wasn't long before Emily was approached by a whole host of mothers who wanted her to make them Davy Crockett hats. Their kids too wanted to share in the craze for the 'King of the Wild Frontier'.

The summer holidays saw the little girl's outlook on life begin to change. She became aware that the world she inhabited wasn't necessarily a simple place and that she relied on her mam and dad, as well as Our Kid, to keep her safe and secure.

It was a Monday morning when Doreen went with her friend Jane Harris to see Miss Brown who lived in Parker Street. Doe knew that Jane was told by her mother to go there once a week in order to fetch Miss Brown her shopping. This week Jane had asked Doreen to go with her. Walking down Bright Avenue and along the uneven pavement, the two girls turned right into Syndall Street, walked past the Richmond Inn and on to Parker Street. The latter was still cobbled like Bright Avenue and had different styles of houses along its length. At its start the properties had bay windows and small front gardens with solid brick walls. Yet as the road veered right towards Devonshire Place, the houses fronted straight onto the pavement. Just like in Bright Avenue, the doorways were recessed into the walls of the houses, with two steps leading up to them. Stopping before a house with a green front door, Jane indicated that they had reached their destination.

"We're here, Doe."

Doreen looked at the door. It hadn't been painted in quite a while. She noticed that the paint was flaking and as a decorator's daughter, she could see that the front window frame was in a bad state of repair, the putty having fallen out in lots of places around the glass. The house stood out on the street due to its decrepit appearance.

Jane knocked but there was no answer. She knocked again. Finally, a voice emerged from behind the door.

"You should have come to the back. Go round."

Jane and Doreen retraced their steps back to Syndall Street and the Richmond Inn. Behind the pub, they accessed the alley that ran the length of the backs of the houses on the side of Parker Street on which Miss Brown lived. Reaching her house, the two girls went into her back yard and knocked on the door. The door opened slightly. Doreen could see a head pushed into the gap. She was struck by the wild, unkempt hair, which looked like it had never been brushed and the wide, staring eyes.

The door opened fully and Doe could see a woman who was very tall and thin. Although it was summer, she was wearing an old-fashioned, long black dress and a thick, heavy cardigan. She seemed dirty and Doreen thought that she looked like a witch. In reality, Miss Brown wasn't that old. Given her appearance however, she seemed it to the two young girls.

"Come in," said Miss Brown.

Jane went through the door and Doe started to follow.

"Not you. Stay there!" snapped the woman.

Doreen was pleased as she didn't really want to go into the house. She would have felt worried for Jane, but her friend seemed unconcerned. Doe realised that Jane had been there many times before, so assumed that there wasn't anything to be anxious about.

Quickly, Jane re-emerged with the shopping basket and list. The two girls set off to Stockport Road to visit the butchers, bakers and greengrocers, before returning up Syndall Street to get the rest of the items from Fenton's, the corner shop that acted as a general store. Arriving back at Miss Brown's, Doreen was again told to wait outside, whilst Jane took the shopping in. Jane was soon back out however and the girls returned up the alley to Jane's house in Richmond Street. Jane's Mam, May, greeted them.

"Have you finished getting Miss Brown's shopping?" asked May.

"Yes," replied Jane.

"Why is she so strange, Mrs Harris?" asked Doe.

"She's not very well, Doreen. I hope you girls didn't make fun of her."

"We wouldn't have dared," said Jane. "She tells you off if you don't do things as she wants."

"She doesn't mean anything by it," said May. "She'd never hurt anyone. I wouldn't let you do her shopping otherwise."

"Does she live on her own?" asked Doreen.

"No," replied May. "Her two older brothers live with her. Anyway, no more questions, go out and play."

Later, Doreen asked Emily about Miss Brown. She found out that she never went out of the house because she was afraid to. She never washed and was still a young woman in her mid-twenties. Doe thought that it must be awful to live like that, but Emily had told her not to worry as she was in her own house and her brothers and Mrs Harris kept an eye on her. Emily pointed out that there were many others like Miss Brown, who were simply deserted and ended up in an institution. Doreen was unaware of what an institution was, but the negative way in which her mam had referred to it, made her hope that she was never sent to one. It made Doe realise just how lucky she was that she had a family and was able to play out with her friends. The following week, Doreen told Jane that she couldn't go with her to Parker Street. It wasn't true, but she felt uncomfortable at the thought of seeing Miss Brown again.

A few days later, Doreen was in the alley at the back of Bright Avenue. It was accessed between two houses on Syndall Street. About four yards wide, it opened out into a square with paving stones around the edge of a large grassed area. The houses on Bright Avenue and Richmond Street backed on to the grass and it became a natural playground. Doe loved all the games they played: whip and top; two or three a ball against the walls; skipping salt-and-pepper; hopscotch; school and dolls and prams. These were the games for the girls but Doreen liked to play with the boys too. Often, she would kick a football with them, play hide and seek, 'ticky it' and jacks. Like the boys, Doe had her own peashooter, given to her by Jimmy. Emily had told her that she shouldn't use it, but her dad had laughed and told her to keep it. On really hot days mothers would take their tin baths on to the grass and fill them with cold water. The kids would play in them with their toys and buckets, splashing water and filling up and firing their water pistols at one another.

That day was particularly hot, so lots of children were playing in the water. As teatime approached, one by one they were being called in. When Doreen's friend Beverley was called, she jumped out of the bath and ran towards her house. Suddenly, she slipped and fell. The other kids started to laugh and Doreen, who noticed that Beverley hadn't hurt herself and seemed all right, joined in too. Beverley began to cry and went in.

The remaining kids returned to splashing about in their tin baths. Suddenly, Doreen felt a sharp pain across her back. She turned round to see Beverley's mam with her arm raised. She glared at Doe before walking back to her house. Shocked, Doreen didn't understand why she had been hit. She didn't cry, but the blow had hurt her. She ran to her back door and into the kitchen. Emily was at the range preparing the tea.

"Mam, Beverley's mam just hit me."

"What?" asked Emily.

"She hit me. Beverley slipped over and we were all laughing. Then she hit me."

"Where?"
"On my back."
Doe wasn't crying and she seemed surprised, rather than hurt. Walking over to her daughter, Emily turned her around and lifted up her top. She was shocked to see that there was a big red mark on the top of Doreen's back. She was furious.
"We'll see about this!"
Emily went flying outside, followed by her daughter, straight into Beverley's back yard. Emily tried the back door but it was locked. Beverley's mam had taken precautions. She must have had second thoughts about what she had done and realised that she'd overstepped the mark. If she had a grievance against Doreen, she should have seen Emily, who would have punished her if necessary. Doe had never seen her mam so animated and watched on fascinated as she pounded on the door.
"Get out here! Nobody hits my kid!" shouted Emily.
Looking around her, Doreen could see that quite a crowd had gathered. The kids who were still out playing in the baths had all rushed over to see the spectacle and hearing Emily shouting, quite a few adults had come out of their homes to take a look too. But it was clear that nothing was going to happen. The fortress that was Beverley's house, wasn't to be breached.
"You coward!" shrieked Emily. "You can hit a kid, but you can't come out to face me! Well don't you worry," she continued, with menace. "You'll have to come out sooner or later and then I'll get you."
Doe knew that you had to stand up for yourself, even if you were a girl. Still young though, she hadn't realised that it was the same for adults. Emily was giving the whole neighbourhood a warning; touch my kid and you'll regret it. Any problems, you see me first.
Doreen was pleased with her mam. Emily had been there for her; she knew she could always rely on her to care. Her friends were impressed too.
"Your mam would have battered her if she had got into the house," said Jane.
"Yes, she would," replied Doe, with obvious pride.
Later that night, Beverley's dad came to see Emily and Jim to apologise. He explained that his wife had been stupid and had

overreacted. He begged Emily to forgive her, saying that his wife was scared to come out of the house and that Beverley was having nightmares. He said that his wife wanted to come and apologise herself, but was afraid to. Jim persuaded Emily that she had made her point; that Doe hadn't really been hurt and that she should forgive her. Reluctantly, Emily agreed.

Chapter 10

After attending Sunday school, Doreen and her parents usually made their way over to Greenheys to see her gran and Uncle Bill. Doe was always excited. Disregarding the ordeal of eating Sunday dinner, when her gran wouldn't let her leave the table until she had eaten all her greens, Doreen couldn't wait to meet up with her cousins Mark, Richard and Louise. The children loved to play in the large back garden. Contained within it was an Anderson shelter, dug into the ground and covered with turf. To the side, along the garden wall, was the mound of excavated soil, that had long since grassed over. It was an ideal spot for the children to sit and look down on the top of the shelter.

Doreen's gran, Edna, was strict, but kind. She made her own ginger beer which she stored in the cool of the shelter. She would allow her grandchildren to go in and get a couple of bottles to share between them. Her first husband had been badly wounded in the Great War. He returned home the mere shell of a man; psychologically broken. Unable to work, he received a small pension, but the family's hardship meant that Emily, as the eldest daughter, had played a huge role in raising her younger siblings: Debbie, Frank, Joe and Albert. When her husband died, Edna had shown no interest in finding a new companion, until after the second war when she had met Bill. He was fifteen years younger than Edna, but the two of them were inseparable and eventually got married.

Edna loved Doreen, but always chided her when she felt that she wasn't behaving as a young lady. She frequently told Emily how clever her little granddaughter was and to make sure that she was given every opportunity to shine. Edna was critical of Emily and Jim, saying that they indulged their little girl too much and that she needed more discipline. Overhearing such conversations, Doe was pleased that she didn't have to stay with her gran on her own. Uncle Bill however, was just like her dad. He was 'soft as a brush' and would always play with the children when they came to visit. Doreen remembered how he had arrived one Christmas Day, having pushed a child's toy pram all the way from Greenheys. She had heard a knock on the back door and Emily had told her to open it. When she had, Uncle Bill was stood there smiling.

"Hello Doe. Father Christmas left this at our house. It's for you and I've had to push it all the way here."

Doreen was over the moon. It was the best present she'd ever had. A twin Silver Cross maroon dolls pram. She gave him a huge hug and he brought it into the house. Doe picked up two of the new dolls that her parents had bought her and placed them in the pram. It was a lovely memory and one she would never forget.

On her sixth birthday, Doreen received another memorable present; a pair of roller skates from her parents. They had red leather fittings to cover her feet and a screw and nut to adjust them. Most streets were cobbled and impossible to skate on, but Tiverton Street had been concreted over, with strips of tarmac joining the sections together. Children would head there after tea, when the adults were home from work, as there were few cars and it was relatively quiet. At any given time, twenty to thirty of them would be racing on the concrete, one street against another, until it went dark and their parents called them in.

One night in the summer of 1955, Doreen and her friends Sandra, Carol, Jane and Joyce had been roller skating on Tiverton Street. They had taken their skates home and then returned to play 'two a ball' on the wall outside the 'Richmond'. The Richmond Inn was Jim's favourite pub and he could be found there most nights whilst Emily stayed at home. The front of the 'Richmond' ran along Syndall Street, with three large windows and a small entrance that led into the lounge. Around the corner into Richmond Street was the main entrance to the vault; the men's domain. The vault had just one main window. The rest of this side of the building having a section of brick wall, against which the girls were taking turns to throw and catch their balls. Suddenly the pub window exploded, showering shards of glass into the street. The girls were shocked, especially Doe, whose turn it had been. She thought for a moment that she had broken the window, but soon realised that this couldn't be true as she still had the balls in her hands.

The girls then heard shouting and saw bodies pouring out of the vault. Two men then came tumbling out of the door, grabbing at each other and throwing punches. The girls jumped back but stayed within the cordon of customers who had come out to watch the fight. Doreen could see her dad watching too. Looking at the combatants she recognised one of them. It was her dad's friend Bobby, but she didn't know the other man. It wasn't going well for Bobby. He wasn't as strong as his taller, powerfully built opponent, who had knocked him to the floor and was proceeding to kick him. Clearly hurt, Bobby was trying to cover up as best he could, especially his face and head which his opponent was attempting to use as a football.

Jim and a couple of men jumped in and pulled the man off. They told him to leave it; that Bobby had had enough. More men then moved in to help restrain him and pulled him away. Bobby was badly hurt and several women were crowded around him trying to help. It wasn't long before the police and an ambulance arrived. Bobby was put on a stretcher and taken to hospital, whilst his opponent was arrested by the police. When Doreen asked Jim what had happened, he told her that the other man had insulted Bobby's wife in the lounge. Bobby had followed him into the vault and thrown his pint pot at him, only to miss. It was this that had shattered the window. The man had then punched Bobby and the fight had broken out.

Doreen wasn't a stranger to violence and shortly afterwards, became a victim of it herself. Bright Avenue didn't have an inside toilet or a bathroom. The tin bath that Doe played in during the summer, was kept hung up on the wall out in the back yard. Once a week every member of the household had a bath in it, whilst every day they would have what her mam called, a 'stripped wash'. Doreen loved the tin bath. Her mam would boil buckets of water on the range and pour them into the bath, which was put in front of the fireplace; a fire burning in winter making it lovely and warm. Unhappy with the poor standard of facilities in most homes in Ardwick, the Corporation provided regular showers to children whose houses lacked a bathroom. Once a week, mobile showers were brought into the local schools.

Doreen attended Ross Place School. It housed both Juniors and Infants and Doreen had to cross Devonshire Street with her friends to get to it. The little girl didn't like the showers. She wasn't keen on the smell of the carbolic soap and she hated the water going directly into her face. Consequently, Doe spent most of her time trying to keep out of the way of the jets of water.

On one occasion after the showers had finished, the staff, as usual, had told them to hurry to their lessons. As the children made their way back into school and up the stairs they were chatting. Suddenly, Doreen felt a sharp pain across her right calf. She froze.

"Shut up, you lot! What do you think this is, a cattle market?" boomed a man's voice.

Doreen looked round and saw Mr Gale. He had a ruler in his hand and she assumed that he had hit out with it through the rails supporting the banister, as the children were climbing the stairs. Being at the back of the group, she had been unfortunate to have been caught with it. As the other children carried on up the stairs in silence, Doe found herself stood there alone. Her leg was stinging and when she looked down, she could see that the ruler had drawn blood.

"Get yourself to class young lady," ordered Gale.

"No," said Doreen, the anger rising inside her. "I'm going to get my dad!"

Making sure that Gale couldn't catch her, she turned quickly and ran down the steps to the ground floor and out through the school entrance. Running down Ardwick Terrace to Stockport Road, across Devonshire Street and on to Syndall Street, Doreen made her way to Hyde Road, where she knew that Jim was working on one of the big houses. Finding her dad painting the outside of a front window frame, Doreen stopped. She was breathless, not realising in her excited state, just how far she had run.

"What are you doing here?" asked Jim.

Doreen, fighting for breath, had to take several gulps of air before finally being able to tell him what had happened.

"It's school," she said. "I got hit. For nothing!"

Doe showed Jim her leg. A trickle of blood from the cut had run on to her white ankle sock and there was a nasty red welt where the ruler had landed.

"What bastard's done that?" growled Jim, his anger making him forget to moderate his language in front of his daughter.

"Mr Gale."

"He's not your teacher, is he?"

"No, he shouted at us and hit me with a ruler when we were coming in after having our showers."

"Did he now?"

"Yes, Dad. He's horrible."

"Right, come on," said Jim. "We'll go and have a word with this Gale."

Jim took his daughter by the hand and set off at a brisk pace towards the school. Doreen found it hard to keep up, having to run a couple of steps, walk and then run again. It was a struggle, but it was no good telling her dad. He was oblivious to everything. Reaching the school, Jim pushed through the iron gate leading into the playground. He quickly found the entrance into the school building and headed to the headmaster's office, Doreen leading the way. Stopping, Jim had a thought.

"Where's Gale's classroom, Doe?"

"It's at that the other end of the building. Down here and up the stairs."

The school premises were large and contained three sections and two floors, housing both infants and juniors. Gale taught a junior class and Doreen had only come across him when he was on playground duty. None of the children liked him. Strong on discipline, he scared them. Effectively, he was nothing but a bully.

In the quiet of the school corridors, the office staff heard Jim and Doreen talking. Realising that they had an irate father on their hands and hearing Gale's name mentioned, one of the secretaries had gone quickly to his room. Quietly, she advised him to make his way downstairs. The secretary stayed to watch the children, as Gale crept quickly down the corridor in the opposite direction to Jim and Doe. When the latter arrived, they found that 'the bird had flown'. Jim glanced over to the secretary. Not wanting to upset the children, he kept himself firmly in check.

"Where's Mr Gale?" asked Jim.

"Oh. He's had to leave. There's an emergency, so I'm watching the children."

The secretary attempted to smile, but her voice was shaking. Although Jim appeared calm, she was scared. Worried that he might explode at any moment.

"Yes, I'm sure there's an emergency," replied Jim, his voice laced with sarcasm. "Come on Doe, let's go."

Jim strode towards the classroom door and out into the corridor, his daughter hurrying behind him in order to keep up.

"Where's Mr Thorpe's office, Doe? Take me there," said Jim.

Thorpe was the headmaster. He was popular among the pupils. He could be strict, but he was always fair. Nothing at all like Gale.

As they approached the office, another of the school secretaries walked towards them. Recognising Doreen, she tried to engage Jim in conversation, hoping to calm him down.

"Mr Brodie. What's the matter? Can I help you?"

"Look at this," said Jim, pointing down towards his daughter's leg. "Show them, Doe."

Doreen moved closer and turned her right leg towards the woman. She could see the red welt and the blood on her sock.

"That's what Gale did," said Jim, angrily. "I want Mr Thorpe to see this and when I get hold of Gale, I'm going to take it out of his face!"

"No, I'm afraid you can't see him. He's busy at the moment. He's got someone in there," insisted the secretary.

"I don't care."

As Jim moved towards the office door, the woman attempted to bar his way.

"Get out of my way, please. I don't want to have to move you, but I will."

"But he's got someone in there, Mr Brodie."

"Who?" asked Jim.

"Oh, just someone."

The penny suddenly dropped.

"It's Gale, isn't it?" snapped Jim.

The woman blushed. Jim knew he was right. The teacher had taken refuge in the headmaster's office.

As the secretary stepped aside, Jim approached the office door. He tried the handle but the door was clearly locked. A solid, old Victorian building, the doors in the school had been built to last.

"Get him out here, now!" shouted Jim. "I don't want you, Thorpe. I want him!"

Doreen heard Mr Thorpe's voice coming back through the door.

"Mr Brodie, you know I can't open the door. Please calm down or I'll have no alternative but to call the police. I've got a phone in my office. I can assure you that I will deal with your complaint, but violence isn't the answer."

"Tell that to Gale. I'll get through this door and then we'll see how he deals with a man, not a kid. He's nothing but a coward."

Jim started kicking the door and banged furiously on it with his fists.

Watching on, Doreen felt a sense of satisfaction. She was positive that Gale would be quaking in his boots. The bully was now getting some of his own medicine. She just wished that her dad could break down the door and give him what for, but it wasn't looking likely.

Meanwhile, alerted by the disturbance, a couple of teachers had appeared out of the doors of the nearby classrooms. Taking one look at the wild and furious figure that was Jim, they thought it best to beat a hasty retreat. They weren't paid to deal with dangerous situations like this and in any case, they felt that Gale should have the guts to come out and face his accuser. In fact, most of the staff disliked him. In an age where corporal punishment was the norm, Gale was considered to be particularly nasty. He regularly overstepped the mark when dishing out beatings to his pupils. If Gale ended up getting hurt, many of his colleagues believed that he deserved it.

Yet an impasse had been reached. The irresistible force that was Jim, denied by the immovable object; the headmaster's office door. Determined on retribution for his daughter's injury, Jim had no intention of leaving and continued periodically, to hammer on the door. Mr Thorpe was as good as his word however and after a short time, a sergeant and a constable arrived.

Doreen saw them first.

"Dad," she said. "You need to stop."

Doe was worried. She was afraid that the policemen would take Jim away.

Turning to her, Jim saw the officers and understood her request.

"What's going on here, then?" asked the sergeant.

"Show him Doreen," said Jim.

The officers looked at the little girl as she turned her right leg towards them.

"Oh dear. That's not nice, is it love?" remarked the constable.

Doreen looked at him and shook her head. He was tall and younger than the sergeant. He seemed quite nice.

"That's what Gale, her teacher, did. Whacked her with a ruler. He's locked himself in there," noted Jim, pointing towards the office door. "He can't come out and face me like a man."

"Let me have a closer look," said the sergeant.

Crouching down, he examined the wound. Getting back to his feet, he started to question the little girl.

"Tell me what happened, love."

Doreen gradually felt more at ease. The sergeant seemed quite old; older than her dad. He was a portly figure and had a kind disposition. Doe recounted what had happened and the sergeant listened carefully. His years of experience was paying dividends. Jim was calming down and that pleased him. He understood why Jim was angry. He had a daughter too and if it had happened to her, he would have reacted in the same way. As such, he had no desire to arrest Jim, especially in front of his little girl.

"What's your name, sir?" asked the sergeant.

"Jim. Jim Brodie."

"Well, Mr Brodie. I'm sure you know that you can't be pounding on the headmaster's door and shouting in a school full of young children. You're going to frighten them you know."

"Yes," said Jim, "but this Gale needs to be taught a lesson."

"I'm sure he will be Mr Brodie, but you can't take the law into your own hands. We'll be talking to him and I'm sure the headmaster will too. Action will be taken. Look, I don't want to have to arrest you. Take Doreen home and give her the rest of the day off. We'll come round to see you once we've spoken to the pair of them."

Reluctantly, Jim accepted that events had run their course. However, he also knew that every teacher in the school was aware that Doreen Brodie was now off-limits. None of them would dare lay a finger on her again. So at least his daughter would be safe. Even more importantly, young though she was, Doe knew it too. Later that afternoon the sergeant was as good as his word and came to the house. He warned Jim that he mustn't go to the school again. If he did, he would be arrested and charged with threatening behaviour. Yet he also told Jim that it was unlikely that Gale would be back at Ross Place. Mr Thorpe had been appalled by his behaviour towards Doreen and the police were also considering charges. Much depended on whether he stayed at the school or not. Gale had been told, 'off the record', that it would not go well for him if he tried to stay in his job.

When Doreen went back to school, Gale was nowhere to be seen. He would never return to Ross Place School.

Chapter 11

Whit Week had arrived. It was a time when mothers bought new clothes for their children. If they didn't have them, then they didn't go out. Doreen and her friends knew that it was a special time. Second only to Christmas.

The Whit Walks had been a tradition in Manchester for around 150 years. Originally taking place on Fridays, they were then celebrated on Whit Monday, before switching to the second Monday May bank holiday. They involved children walking in procession, together with adults, from their church, chapel or Sunday school, to demonstrate their Christian faith. The children followed behind the banner of their church or chapel in their best clothes, many of them carrying flowers. Each group had a 'Rose Queen', one of the older girls of the congregation, who was accompanied by her 'attendants', selected from the younger girls of the church. Starting before the Great War, all the different churches had headed into the centre of Manchester, where huge crowds of tens of thousands of people had lined the streets to watch and cheer, listening to the brass bands that were interspersed with the different congregations.

Doreen's parents had taken her into Manchester to watch the Walks. It had been exciting. There were street vendors selling ice cream, sandwiches, sweets, shakers and little union flags. Doe had excitedly held on to her shakers, tasselled hand-held pompoms, waving them as the procession passed by.

Now she was six, it was decided that Doe could take part in the parade herself. For weeks before, Emily had been preparing her dress for the occasion. It was long and pink with lots of lacy layers on top. It had pink ribbon around the bottom, neck and sleeves. Doreen lost count of the number of fittings that her mam made her go through, making constant adjustments to ensure that the dress looked just right. Given Emily's popularity as a dressmaker, many of Doe's friends came to number seventeen; girls for their dresses and boys for their little suits. It was a point of honour for all mothers that their children would be dressed as smartly as possible for the Whit Walks. They, as much as their children, were on show. None of them wanted to be left embarrassed in front of their friends and neighbours and risk being 'called' by the other women for failing in their maternal responsibilities.

Doreen's Sunday school was based at St Matthews Church on the corner of Devonshire Street and Hyde Road. Doe was chosen to be one of the four attendants, along with her friend Linda Johnson, to the Rose Queen, Joyce Brown. Both Linda and Joyce wore outfits made by Emily. Joyce, a long, silky white dress and Linda, a long, pink dress, with lots of lacy layers. All the girls had headbands covered with flowers. The night before the parade Emily had put 'rags' in her daughter's hair. In the morning, when the rags were removed, it produced a stunning collection of ringlets; the fashionable style of the day.

Reaching the town centre, the group from St Matthews were full of enthusiasm for the day ahead. Taking their place in the procession, Doreen and Linda found themselves right out in front, leading the way for the Rose Queen. Joyce was at the centre of the formation that saw two older girls holding the St Matthews banner behind her. The four attendants were positioned to the front and rear of Joyce, each of them holding a long ribbon attached to the apex of the banner. St Matthews banner, like all those on show, was decorated with flowers. Its message boldly proclaimed that 'Jesus Loves'. Every girl was carrying a bunch of flowers.

Doreen had never been so excited as she walked past the packed pavements of cheering people. The brass bands were playing, the flags waving. She concentrated hard to make sure that she didn't fall out of step with the others, or let go of her ribbon. She felt so special. Emily and Jim proudly watched their daughter. She looked lovely; so pretty in her pink dress. The church had arranged for a photographer to take pictures of their group and shortly, pride of place on the front room sideboard at 17 Bright Avenue, were two photographs: one of Doreen resplendent in her dress, the second of her and the other girls marching together with the St Matthews banner.

Not long after the Whit walks, it was time for the adults to have their fun too. Most Manchester pubs organised day trips to Blackpool for their patrons. The visits were organised separately by gender and the women would be the first to go. Doreen and her friends looked forward to these days as it had become a tradition that before the 'chara' set off, they would gather outside the 'Richmond' and pick up the coins that would be thrown out of the windows to them. Afterwards they would compare their takings, working out who had collected the most. The children always looked with greater expectancy towards the women, who tended to be more generous than their husbands. The latter were thinking more about holding on to their beer money. To make sure that no one was left out, the women always brought lots of halfpennies and pennies to throw on to the street. Occasionally, some lucky child would find a threepenny bit, sixpence, shilling or even half-a-crown.

Doreen wondered what it was like in Blackpool. Some of her friends had been and had told her stories about the Golden Mile, the Piers and the Tower. She knew that you could ride donkeys on the beach, then play on the sands and go in the sea. There were lots of shops selling sweets and rock and a massive fun fair filled with rides and amusements. She knew that her mam and dad always returned from the seaside in great spirits, telling her that they'd had a fantastic day out.

One Saturday in June, Doe was playing school out in the front garden. She had a blackboard, desk and chair and was being the teacher for her friends. Doreen's prized possession was a blackboard rubber which her brother Jimmy had taken from his own school before he'd left. It meant that she was able to write lots of different lessons on the board. It was mid-afternoon and Doe saw her dad walk into the garden and through the front door with his friend, Bill Charles. Bill was a decorator like Jim, but more successful and had a couple of other men working for him. The friends had come back from the 'Richmond' and they were carrying a crate of beer. Doreen could see that they were intending to carry on drinking in the house.

After playing some more, the children got bored of school and so Doreen brought her board, chair and desk back into the house. In the front room her dad and Bill were talking and laughing.

They were drinking beer and eating the sandwiches that Emily had made for them.

"Are you all right, love?" asked Jim, looking up from his seat on the sofa.

"Yes, Dad. I've just been playing school."

Doreen could tell that her dad was merry and seemed well on the way to getting drunk. It was a sign that he would be in a generous mood.

"Can I have some money for sweets please, Dad?"

"Of course, you can."

Reaching into his pocket he pulled out half-a-crown. It was a lot of money to give to his daughter, but he regularly spoiled her. She was the apple of his eye and could do no wrong. Doe had been aware of this for a while and knew that she could use it to her advantage, especially when getting out of trouble with her mam. At times Doreen, though not realising it, had been quite cheeky to her, but when Emily had mentioned it to Jim, he would dismiss her concerns, insisting that Doe was only a child and that she would grow out of it. This only encouraged Doreen to challenge her mam's authority further and on one fateful occasion she had actually sworn at her. The resulting 'crack' that her mam had administered, had shocked the young girl and she wouldn't speak to Emily for the rest of the day. When Jim returned home from work Doreen told him what her mam had done. She immediately wished that she hadn't. Jim was furious. He grabbed hold of Emily and started to shake her.

"Don't you dare hit my daughter. I've told you. She's just a kid."

"Dad! Stop!"

Screaming at Jim, Doe was terrified for her mam's safety. She hadn't imagined that he would react so furiously.

Jim let go.

"I'm sorry Mam," said Doreen, flinging her arms around Emily's waist. "I won't be bad again. I promise."

Emily put her hand on her daughter's head and softly stroked her hair.

"It's all right, Doe. I'm fine. Don't get upset."

Doreen looked up at her mam and could see tears in her eyes. She didn't know if it was due to Jim's aggression, or her own protestations of affection. Never wanting to see her mam threatened again, Doe never told her dad when Emily reprimanded her. The incident had proved traumatic. The little girl was frightened by the darker side to Jim's nature and worried that her mam may not love her as much as she had previously done.

Although Doreen was happy to take money off her dad, she usually shared it with others; particularly her brother. Jim was nowhere near as generous with his son and therefore Doreen would always give Jimmy at least half of what she received. Her kindness extended to others too and it wasn't surprising that having taken Jim's money to buy sweets from Horseman's newsagents, she then shared them with her friends, whilst she played jacks with them in the street.

When Emily called Doe in for tea, Bill was still there. Looking at his daughter, Jim asked her a question.

"How would you like to go to Blackpool tomorrow?"

Doreen could hardly contain her enthusiasm.

"Oh yes! Can we? Can we?"

"Yes," Jim replied. "Bill has asked us to go with him and his family."

Doe looked at Bill. He smiled back at her.

"Yes, Doe. Your Dad says that you've never been to Blackpool, so I thought it would be nice for us to take you, your mam and dad in our van tomorrow."

Suddenly, Bill was transformed. A tall, lanky and balding man, with little to distinguish him, Doreen now regarded him with awe. He owned a van. No one on Bright Avenue did and there were precious few vehicles in any of the roads around Syndall Street.

"Mind you," said Jim, "you're going to have to get up really early."

"I'll go to sleep early," replied Doe, eagerly.

The little girl's enthusiasm was clear to see. Doreen hated to go to bed early and indulged by her parents, would usually be allowed to stay downstairs until they too went to bed, after Jim came home from the pub.

"Are you sure?" asked her dad. "If you don't, you'll be too tired to get up."

"Yes, I am. I promise," insisted Doe, with all the conviction that she could muster.

Excited as she was, Doreen found that she just couldn't get to sleep that night and was still awake when her parents came to bed. She pretended to be asleep, not wanting them to call off the trip because they thought that she would be too tired. The next morning it was five-thirty when Doreen was awoken. She felt exhausted but when her mam reminded her that they were going to Blackpool, she soon found the energy to get out of bed and prepare for the day.

Bill and his family arrived just after six. Bill's wife, Mary, had auburn hair. She was taller than Emily and plump. She had a pleasant face and greeted them warmly.

"We'll sit in the back of the van and let the men sit together in the front," said Mary. "Don't worry, it's nice and comfy with the cushions."

Mary opened the doors to the back of the van and Doreen could see that there were some cushions scattered on the floor. Sat on them were Mary's three children. David was a couple of years older than Doe whilst his sister Pat, was the same age. Their younger sibling was a toddler called Anne. All three of them had bright, red hair and were covered in freckles.

Before getting in, Doreen looked closely at their transport. It was a Bedford CA van. It was bright red and had side doors at the front with shiny handles to pull them open. Both sides of the van had Bill's name written on them, with the words 'painter and decorator' prominent beneath. The front of the van seemed squashed in. There were two round headlamps, but the bonnet was shallow before the twin windscreens rose up to the roof; a wiper lying flat against each one. The van had metal bumpers and black plates with silver letters and numbers. To Doreen, it looked magnificent and she found it hard to believe that she was about to ride in it.

Getting into the back, Doe settled down with her mam on the cushions. After the initial excitement at setting off, the ride became quite boring. With no windows in the sides or back of the van, there was nothing to see. Feeling tired, the little girl drifted off to sleep, catching up on the missed hours from the night before.

Sometime later, Doreen awoke. The van had stopped and there was no noise coming from the engine. The back doors of the van opened and standing there was Bill.

"Everybody out," he ordered.

"Are we there?" asked Doe, her eyes widening.

"Not yet," replied Bill. "We need everybody's help. You're all going to have to take a pee."

Doreen wondered what he meant. As they got out of the van, she could see that they had stopped in a lay-by at the side of the road. There were no buildings nearby, just fields and hedges. There certainly weren't any toilets. It was all very confusing. Walking to the front of the van, she noticed that the bonnet had been lifted up and the engine was steaming like a kettle. Bill explained.

"We've run out of water in the radiator. There's none around here so you're all going to have to pee in a bottle, so that I can fill it up again. If you don't, we'll end up stuck here."

Bill handed a milk bottle to Emily and with Doreen following, she walked through the hedge, behind a tree and the two of them filled up the bottle. Meanwhile, everyone else contributed to the other containers that Bill had handed out. The eagerness to get to Blackpool meant that no one seemed embarrassed as they handed their containers over to Bill, who then proceeded to pour them into the radiator. Back in the van, Bill restarted the engine and they were off again. After about ten minutes, Doreen noticed an awful smell. At first, she thought that it had come into the van from outside, but it didn't disappear. It seemed unlikely that the smell could be everywhere on the road to Blackpool.

"Mam, what's that smell?" asked Doreen.

Mrs Charles began to laugh, followed by her mam. Hearing them, Jim turned round in his seat and asked why Emily and Mary were laughing.

"It's Doe. She asked us what the smell was."

Hearing the answer, Jim and Bill burst out laughing too.

It wasn't until later that Doreen found out that it was the smell of pee. The radiator had a leak and so the odours created by its simmering contents, were wafting back into the vehicle.

Reaching Blackpool, Bill parked the van behind the seafront. They had been lucky with the weather. The sun was up and it was a beautiful day. As Bill had taken them, Jim and Emily insisted that they should pay for the entertainment. Everyone headed to the beach which was full of holidaymakers. The children got to ride on the donkeys, whilst the men went for a pint. After their return, it was time for some fish and chips and then everyone boarded a tram to the Pleasure Beach where the children had candy floss and ice cream and went on the gentler rides. Having listened to Jim's poor attempts to sing George Formby's 'Little Stick of Blackpool Rock', it was finally time to go home.

The kids were tired and relieved to settle down on the cushions in the back of the van. Doreen soon fell asleep with the drone of the engine and the swaying motion of the vehicle as it headed back to Manchester. She could hardly remember arriving home; climbing out of the back of the van and through bleary eyes looking at Bill, thanking him for taking them out and then waving him off. Emily led her daughter into the house and Doreen dropped down on the sofa, quickly falling asleep. Half-awake, she felt her dad lift her up and carry her upstairs to bed. Under the covers, she felt safe and satisfied. It had been one of the best days ever.

Chapter 12

The happy memories of Blackpool had provided Doreen with a real belief in the advantages of motor transport. She wished that her dad owned a car or van like Bill, so they too could go anywhere for days out. Disappointed that it was unlikely to happen, the summer of 1955 would at least provide Doe with the fascination of Jimmy's motorbike.

With Jim's help, Our Kid had been obtaining spare parts, purchased from his wages, to renovate an old motorbike that one of the neighbours, George Laine, had sold to him. The bike was kept out in the front garden. Most nights Jimmy could be found working on it, surrounded by groups of girls. A handsome lad, Jimmy was never short of admirers and the motorbike was sparking even more interest in him than usual. Doe often felt annoyed with his girlfriends. Few of them seemed to want her around and she was usually pleased when he finished with them.

Jimmy was making good progress on the bike. Both George and his dad were prepared to help him on the most difficult, technical tasks and so it wasn't long before the day came when the bike was ready to go and it certainly looked spectacular. Jimmy had cleaned and polished it thoroughly and he had painted bright red and orange flames on the sides of the petrol tank. It looked brand new. Still too young to legally ride himself, the bike was taken out for a trial run by his dad. The engine had roared into life and Jim had ridden the bike out of Bright Avenue, over the cobbles and on to Syndall Street and then down Stockport Road. Doe and Our Kid waited eagerly for his return, hoping that the machine wouldn't experience any mechanical problems. As time ticked by, Our Kid was becoming increasingly nervous. Finally, however, the siblings heard the noise of the bike approaching and then saw Jim turning back into Bright Avenue. The bike sounded fine. Jim came to a halt and turned off the engine.

"You've got a little belter here," proclaimed Jim, eminently satisfied with his ride. "Remember though," he continued, "you're still too young to take it out yourself."

"I know, Dad."

The following Friday night, Emily and Jim having gone to the 'Richmond', Our Kid had stayed in to babysit his sister. He had arranged for a potential new girlfriend to come and see his bike, but she had arrived with several friends, who were chatting loudly outside the front door. Inside, Doe and Jimmy heard the commotion. Taking a quick look from behind the front room curtains, Jimmy quietly swore. The little girl was shocked. Her brother rarely used bad language in front of her. She knew that he wasn't happy.

"What's the matter, Our Kid?"

"There's a group of girls outside but I only want to see one of them. Come here, but be careful."

Jimmy motioned her over to the window.

"Look through the curtains, Doe. Do you see the girl with the blue skirt and the brown hair?"

"Yes."

"Well, she's the girl I want to go out with, but I won't be able to talk to her with all her friends there. Can you do something for me, Doe?"

"What?"

"Go out the back and around to the front and tell the girls that I'm not in. But get the girl I pointed out to come into the house. She's got two dogs, so ask her to come in to see our Rex."

"All right."

Doreen duly did as she was asked. She told the group of girls that Jimmy wasn't there, but took the girl with the blue skirt by the hand.

"I want you to come and see our Rex. He's a lovely dog."

The girl, called Dorothy, thinking that she could please Jimmy if he found out that she'd been friendly to his little sister, followed Doreen around the back of the house to be surprised by the presence of Jimmy in the kitchen. It turned out that Jimmy had impressed her by talking about his motorbike and had promised her a ride on it. This was the perfect time to do it with his mam and dad out at the 'Richmond'. There was a problem, however. Two of Dorothy's friends were still in the front garden, making it impossible for Jimmy to get out to the bike. Once again, he called for Doe's help. With Dorothy playing with Rex in the kitchen, he took his sister on one side.

"I want to take Dorothy out on the bike, but I need you to get rid of the girls in the front garden."

Doreen was concerned.

"Dad told you not to go out on the bike."

"It'll be all right, Doe. I know how to ride it. Dad doesn't want me to take it out because I'm still too young. But as long as I don't have an accident, there'll be no problem."

"Are you sure, Our Kid?"

"Yes. Go on, Doe. Please."

"All right, Our Kid," said Doreen, who didn't want to disappoint him. "What do you want me to say to the girls?"

"Tell them that Dad's in and he's fed up of them hanging around the front. Tell them he'll throw water on them if they don't shift."

Doreen went out, relaying what Jimmy had said. Reluctantly, the girls departed. After a few minutes, Jimmy took Dorothy out to the front, uncovered his bike, started it up and invited Dorothy on to the back. Wearing a skirt, she found some difficulty placing her legs astride the pillion. Having done so, she then put her arms around Jimmy's midriff, Our Kid clearly enjoying their close and intimate contact. Quickly, he roared across the cobbles and then turned left down Syndall Street, in order to avoid going past the 'Richmond'. Ten minutes later he was back, with Dorothy suitably excited and impressed. Doe now spotted an opportunity. She knew that Jimmy was grateful for her silence. Perhaps, she suggested, he could give her a ride too. Just around the block.

Jimmy was in good spirits and therefore agreed. Whilst Dorothy waited, Doreen was whisked around the streets. At first, she hung on tightly, burying her face into Jimmy's back and scared to glance around her. The cobbles of Bright Avenue were bumpy, but once on Syndall Street, with its concrete and tarmac, the ride felt smoother and safer. With the shops and houses rushing past her and the wind flowing through her hair, Doe's fear turned to exhilaration. Arriving back home, Dorothy was still there, playing with Rex. Our Kid had a new girlfriend, but one who didn't seem jealous of the attention he gave to his sister.

Jimmy's attachment to Doreen had been the bane of many of his girlfriends' lives. Only sixteen, all Our Kid wanted was to have a good time. He had no desire to commit himself to any one girl, but they rarely felt the same about their relationship with him. Most found it irritating when Jimmy insisted on taking Doe with them to the pictures, or the ballroom at the Ritz. Often, he would dance with his sister, rather than his girlfriend. The two of them had even won a jiving competition; the judges impressed by the bizarre combination of siblings whose ages were ten years apart.

Although Doreen didn't notice at the time, Jimmy would often take her with him when he felt his current girlfriend was getting too serious. He knew that they saw the lively, confident and to them, demanding little girl, as getting in the way. This encouraged them to finish with him; a relief to a carefree young man who didn't really have the resolution to end the relationship himself.

Jimmy's girlfriends couldn't understand why he was so devoted to little Doe. That was because they hadn't been there to see her continual love and kindness towards him. From being a toddler, she had shared everything with Our Kid. As Doreen had grown up, she would often ask her dad for money when he came home 'merry' from the pub. Jim would give her all the change out of his pockets and afterwards, she would give it to Jimmy. Until her brother had left school at fifteen and got a job, it was the only way he could afford to go out to the pictures, or to the Ritz. It meant that Jimmy was close to his little sister. He loved her to bits.

Doreen was confused by her dad's cold attitude towards his son. She didn't understand why he was so loving with her, yet so strict towards Jimmy. It was almost as if he didn't want to accept Jimmy as his son. With Doe, Jim was always affectionate. He would carry her to bed when she fell asleep on the sofa and would sit talking to her for ages. He would take her to work on jobs in the holidays and proudly talk about how clever she was to his customers. One night when some of his friends were at the house playing cards, Doreen had been allowed to stay in the front room. Slightly drunk, Jim had asked Doe to show him her hands.

"There," said Jim to his friends. "Just like mine. The fingers are just the same. No one could ever say that Doe isn't my kid, could they?"

Doreen noticed Emily, who'd just brought in a tray of drinks, glance sharply at her dad. Recollecting the incident some years later, Doe understood that her dad had implied that he had doubts over whether Jimmy was actually his son. It was a ridiculous statement; one probably rooted in his own infidelities. Suggesting that Emily had betrayed him, like he had her, seemed to be a perverse way of trying to feel better about his own shortcomings. There was no doubt however, that Jim's statement did indicate that he had a far closer bond with his daughter, than he did his son.

Near the end of the summer holidays, Doreen became aware of just how poor the relationship between her dad and Jimmy had become. When Our Kid had left school, he was taken on by Dewhurst as an apprentice butcher. He was enjoying his work. He had been placed in one of their shops on Stockport Road. He was close to home and enjoyed serving behind the counter. In particular, he was able to meet a range of girls coming in to pick up the shopping for their mothers, grans and neighbours. The 'gift of the gab' was part of the butcher's trade, so his boss had no problem with Jimmy chatting to the teenage girls coming into the shop, especially as he was an outgoing lad and equally polite and talkative to the old ladies. Jimmy loved meeting the customers, was learning a trade and getting lots of new girlfriends. He finally had money of his own. His life seemed to be heading in a very positive direction.

One Saturday morning though, Doreen awoke to hear her dad shouting at Jimmy in the kitchen, before her brother went to work. He was demanding that Our Kid give up his job at the butchers. Jim told him that it wasn't a real trade; that he was nothing but a shop assistant. It was a job for a woman. Jimmy had tried to stand his ground, arguing that butchers were tradesmen and that he had real prospects. His boss had told him that once he was a qualified butcher, he would be given the management of a shop himself, for Dewhurst were a big company and they were always opening new branches. Yet Jim wouldn't have it. He wanted Jimmy to be a painter and decorator like himself; in fact, he wanted his son to work for him. He insisted that Our Kid would never earn enough to support a wife and family on the money he'd earn as a butcher. Once he'd worked for him, said Jim, he could set up his own decorating company. He would be far better off. When Jimmy tried to tell him that his boss had a house and family, his dad simply ignored him.

Jimmy had gone to work and during the following days continued to set off for Dewhurst on Stockport Road. On Friday however, he was still in the house when Doreen came down to breakfast. Surprised, she asked him why he hadn't gone to work. Silent, Our Kid was clearly in no mood to answer. Shortly after, Jim came in from outside.

"Here you are," he said, tossing something over towards Jimmy. "They'll keep you covered up all right."

As Jimmy opened them out, Doreen could see that it was a pair of overalls.

"Come on then, I need you to push the cart," said Jim.

Jimmy, in silence, followed his dad out of the door.

"What's going on Mam?" asked Doreen. "Why isn't Our Kid at Dewhurst?"

"He's working with your dad now, Doe. He's given up his job at the butchers."

"But why? He liked it there."

"Well, he's decided that he wants to work as a painter and decorator. Anyway, you need to have a quick wash before you go out to play. Come on."

Doreen knew that there was no point continuing with her questions. Her mam had quickly changed the subject, so indicating that the matter was closed.

The following Monday, Doe found out just how unhappy Jimmy was working for his dad. Up early, she went out into the back yard to see Jimmy taking the hand cart into the alley to push out into Tiverton Street. Jim's handcart was a long wooden platform with sides. It had two wheels and two long handles to manoeuvre it. The hand cart carried all her dad's ladders, paints, dust sheets and equipment.

"Where are you going, Our Kid."

"Down to Stockport. Dad's got a job on there."

Doreen looked at her brother. He looked desolate; almost as if he was going to cry. She hated to see him like this and felt the need to comfort him.

"What's the matter, Our Kid?"

"It's this handcart."

Doe didn't understand. She couldn't see how it could have caused her brother to be so upset. She had often sat on the ladders on top of the handcart being pushed along the road by her dad. Doreen loved it, yet she was thinking as a child.

"Why?" she asked.

"You see Doe, it's like this," replied Jimmy. "Today all the decorators have vans. Pushing a handcart around the streets, tells everyone that you're poor. When I have to do it around here, the girls laugh and they don't respect me."

"Don't worry, Our Kid. I can push the handcart. The girls will see me doing it and not you."

Doreen had clearly not thought about how she would have the strength to do it. She wouldn't be able to move it out of the alley, never mind all the way to Stockport. But her little heart went out to her brother. If she could do anything for him, she would. Jimmy was touched. Kindness was something that he had come to expect from his little sister.

"It's nice of you to offer Doe, but there wouldn't be any point. I'll have to walk with you to show you the way and the girls will see me anyway. But if you still want to come, you can get on top of the ladders and we'll go together."

"Oh yes! Let me go and tell Mam."

Emily was pleased. She knew that her son was upset and perhaps Doe could cheer him up. She had argued constantly with Jim, telling him to leave the boy alone. She had explained that he liked his job and it wouldn't be easy for him having to work for his dad. But this was 1955 and wives and children did as they were told. Jim made it clear that she should mind her own business, for he knew what was best for his son. Emily feared that Jimmy would be used as cheap labour; overworked and underpaid. After all, Jim never had anyone working for him, as he couldn't afford to pay them. Now he had grand schemes. He could take on bigger jobs he claimed, especially outside. Jim suffered from vertigo and was unable to go too high up a ladder. Jimmy would come in very useful. The only obstacle to Jim's plans had been that his son was happy at Dewhurst. As a result, Jim had gone to see his son's boss and insisted that he shouldn't be working there. All the Brodies had been painters and decorators and Jimmy should be the same. Finding Jim difficult to deal with, the manager suggested to his young trainee that he should reconsider going to work for his dad. Deprived of his boss's support and only just sixteen, Jimmy had finally given in. Like virtually all boys his age, he would have to do what his father said.

Chapter 13

Doreen loved 'our Rex'. He was only small; a black and tan mongrel dog with a bit of white fur under his chin. Doe had grown up with him. He was her pal.

One day, after she had received her pram from her uncle Bill, she had a brilliant idea. She took the pram out and called to Rex in the back yard. He came running towards her, his tail wagging. As 'soft as a brush', Rex allowed the little girl to do anything to him. Telling him to sit, Doreen proceeded to put one of her doll's hats on his head. She picked him up, lay him in the pram and covered him with a blanket.

"Stay Rex. There's a good boy," said Doreen, as she proceeded to wheel him down the alley and out on to Syndall Street. Her friends were amazed at how still and quiet Rex was as he lay in the pram. All the girls wished that they had a dog like Rex. It was just like having a baby.

Like most dogs at the time, Rex was given the freedom to roam the streets. No one thought this unusual. When the children were at school, the dogs seemed to know that they would be alone for the day. Rex, ever faithful to his little mistress, was always waiting at the end of the back alley to watch for Doe coming home. He would arrive there ten minutes before she was due back and would lie on the cobbles, his head resting on his front paws, one ear cocked, listening out for her voice. It amazed Doreen that he always seemed to know the time, but it never failed to make her smile as he charged towards her as she emerged around the corner of Bright Avenue. He had missed her and she, him.

A couple of weeks after Doreen had returned to school following the summer break, she arrived home to be greeted by Rex as usual. Doe had her tea and then set out to visit her friend Sandra on Richmond Street. As usual Rex followed her. As Doreen was going to play inside Sandra's house, she had to tell Rex to go home. The two girls then went upstairs and began to play dominoes. After half an hour Sandra's mam shouted up to

Doe and asked her to come down. Descending the stairs and entering the kitchen, she saw her dad stood at the door with Rex in his arms. One of Rex's front paws was bleeding and he was clearly in distress.

"I'm sorry Doe," said Jim, "but Rex has been run over by a police car. He's badly hurt."

Doreen gasped; her eyes began to fill with tears.

"Doe," said Jim, firmly. "Rex needs you to be brave. Don't let him see you upset."

The little girl tried hard to hold back the tears. She tried to soothe Rex, touching him gently on his head where she felt she wouldn't hurt him further. Rex, his head motionless, moved his eyes up towards her. He looked so sad and hurt.

"It'll be all right Rex," whispered Doreen, putting her face right up to him and kissing him on his soft, wet nose.

"It will, won't it, Dad? Don't let Rex die. I love him."

"I know. Come on Doe, let's go home. The vet's coming to the house. Your mam's gone to fetch him."

Jim and Doreen walked back to Bright Avenue and found the vet waiting for them. Taking one look at Rex, the vet asked Jim to carry him to his van. Jim got into the front and with Rex held firmly on his knees, the two men drove off to the surgery.

Doreen was inconsolable. She was sure that she would never see Rex again. She sat on the sofa and wouldn't move. Refusing food and drink, she fixed her eyes on the clock, hoping and praying that her dad would come home with good news. There was nothing Emily could do to lift her spirits. Much later, Jim returned, but there was no sign of Rex. It seemed clear to the little girl that her prayers had not been answered and she began to cry.

"No, love. Calm down. Rex is still with us."

"Why isn't he here then?" asked Doreen,

"Because he's still very poorly and so he has to stay with the vet for a few days," replied Jim. "You do want him to get better, don't you?"

"Yes," said Doreen, nodding.

"Well, we can't make him better, can we? Only the vet can do that and they'll need to take special care of him until he's all right."

"Is that what the vet has told you, Jim?" asked Emily.

Knowing that Jim didn't want to see his daughter upset, she was concerned that he might be providing Doe with a false sense of hope. It was best, thought Emily, that Doe was given any bad news, sooner rather than later.

"Yes," said Jim, quietly. "The vet had to amputate his front paw, but he said that Rex is a fighter and so he should be able to survive the operation. Most dogs that get through it, usually recover."

"What does amputate mean?" asked Doreen.

"It means that Rex's Paw was so crushed by the police car, that the vet had to take it off."

"But how will Rex walk?"

"It won't be a problem," insisted Jim. "I asked the vet the same thing and he said that he's known lots of dogs that can run with only three paws. Rex is going to be able to do everything that he could when he had the use of all four of his legs."

Doreen didn't understand how this could be the case but relieved, she was prepared to accept any good news about her pal. She thought that she had lost him and now she hadn't.

"When can I see him, Dad?"

"The vet said to leave him for a couple of days. Rex needs to be sedated and given a long sleep to help him get stronger after the operation. Don't panic, I'll check with the vet tomorrow that he's all right."

Going to bed, Doreen made sure that she said her prayers for Rex. The next day she couldn't stop thinking about him and before tea waited eagerly for her dad to come home from work, so that she could check that he had contacted the vet. When he arrived back, Jim confirmed that he had. Rex was doing well, he told her and he would be able to take her to the RSPCA tomorrow to see him.

The following day, after school, Doreen and Jim made their way to the RSPCA. They were shown into a room in the back of the building. Doe could see that Rex was lying on a blanket at the bottom of a large cage. The veterinary nurse said she would leave them for a few minutes on their own, whilst she attended to some other visitors. She warned them before she left, that Rex needed rest and so they couldn't stay too long. Hearing voices, Rex lifted his head off the floor. Seeing Doreen, he tried to stand up, but fell over. Doe began to cry and put her hand on the catch on the front of the cage.

"You shouldn't open the cage love," said Jim.

Doe ignored him, desperate to console her pal. Opening the cage door, she knelt down on the floor, before crawling forward into the cage. Raising his head, Rex nuzzled her face and licked her salty tears. Doe smiled; everything would be all right. She kissed him on his nose and head, as Rex faintly wagged his tail.

"Best get out of the cage now, Doe. We don't want to upset the nurse, do we? We want them to give Rex the best care they can."

Satisfied, Doreen did as she was asked. For the next five days Emily and Jim took turns to take her to the RSPCA. With every passing day she could see that Rex was getting stronger. Effectively, he now only had three legs; one at the front, two at the back. Yet he could stand up. When it was time for him to come home, Doreen was overjoyed. Her Dad carried him back to the house. To the little girl, it seemed like her family was complete. At first Rex found it difficult to walk on three legs and he wouldn't venture any further than the back yard. After a few days though, he had gained his balance and Doe was amazed at how easily he was following her around. After two weeks, Rex had learned to run again. All the kids were amazed. Rex was a local celebrity. For a short time, he was also a source of great amusement. Like all dogs, Rex was desperate to mark his territory and around Bright Avenue, this meant regular attention to the lamp posts. Unfortunately for Rex, every time he tried, he fell over. Doreen and her friends couldn't help laughing. Finally, Rex adapted, cocking his back leg on the side that he still had his full front leg. In that way, he retained his balance and dignity.

Prior to Rex's accident, Doe had become very good friends with Sandra and had spent lots of time playing at her house. Her mam was always kind to Doreen but very strict with her daughter. Mrs Cooper was a small, plump woman with her hair in a bun and she always seemed to be wearing an apron. By contrast, Sandra's dad was a very tall, thin man. He rarely spoke to the girls and when he had come home from work, would usually retire to the front room to read the *Manchester Evening News*, which Sandra and Doreen would often fetch for him from

Horseman's newsagents. With Mr Cooper would be the family's lodger, his wife's brother; Sandra's Uncle Roy. Doreen had first got to know Sandra through Our Kid, who was friends with Johnny, Sandra's brother. Like Jimmy, he was also ten years older than his sister. Sandra and Johnny had another brother called Barry, who was a couple of years younger than Johnny.

A few weeks after Rex's accident, Doreen and Our Kid were at the Cooper's house in Richmond Street. Jimmy had then gone out with Johnny, whilst Doe stayed to play with Sandra in the kitchen. Around half an hour later, Barry came in and Mrs Cooper immediately started shouting at him. The girls were stunned; unable to work out why she was so angry. Barry, head bowed, backed up near the kitchen sink. Still shouting, Mrs Cooper moved towards the cellar door and opened it. Hanging on a hook on the back of the door, was a long rubber pipe. Mrs Cooper snatched hold of it, advanced towards Barry and hit him repeatedly. Cowering away, Barry raised his arms in an effort to deflect the blows. He howled in anguish as the hose slammed into his arms and around his back. Mrs Cooper seemed to have lost control. She was raging. Doreen could see that Barry was in pain. She was desperate to help him but, terrified of his mother, felt powerless to do so.

"If I didn't care about what happens to you, I wouldn't be hitting you!" shouted Mrs Cooper. "But I do care and you will behave yourself. You'll do what's right and proper!"

Whilst she paused to catch her breath, Barry seized his chance. He charged towards the back door, banging into the kitchen table and almost falling over. Before his mam could react, he had made it outside in to the back yard and had raced off down the alley. The girls were stunned. Mrs Cooper quickly composed herself and put the hosepipe back on the hook behind the cellar door.

"That boy will be the death of me!" she exclaimed.

The girls waited, expecting an explanation, but Mrs Cooper was silent. Doreen wondered if she had actually registered the fact that they had both witnessed her actions.

"I think I'd better go home now, Sandra."

Without saying goodbye to Mrs Cooper, Doe slipped quietly out of the kitchen door and back down the alley.

Doreen was confused and shocked by what she had seen. Mrs Cooper's words had made a deep impression on her. She had told Barry that he was being punished with the hose, because she loved him. How could that be?

When Doe arrived home, Emily was sat at the kitchen table reading the *Evening News*. Her mam was surprised to see her.

"You're back early, aren't you?"

Doreen, unusually subdued, quietly nodded her head. Emily could see that something was bothering her.

"Is everything all right, Doe?"

Sitting at the table with her mam, Doreen told her about what had happened.

"Well, I suppose Barry must've done something very bad," observed Emily.

"Mam," said Doe, "I know I don't want to get hit and that my dad doesn't want me hit, but what Mrs Cooper said, does it mean that your parents don't really love you if they don't beat you, like she did Barry?"

"Don't be daft!" said Emily, sharply. "Mrs Cooper's talking rubbish!"

The conversation may have come to an end, but the episode had left a deep impression on the young girl and several years later, the words that Mrs Cooper had used, would continually come back to haunt her.

The incident meant that Doe would now only play with Sandra in her own house or outside. Doreen was concerned that Mrs Cooper may get the hosepipe out again and it frightened her. One day however, she finally ventured back into the Cooper household. It all came about when Sandra came round to Bright Avenue after tea. She was excited but out of breath from racing over from her home in Richmond Street.

"Doe, Doe!" she gasped, excitedly. "You've got to come to the house. I've got to show you something brilliant!"

"What is it?"

"No, it's a surprise. You've got to come and see!"

Doreen was unsure, she still hadn't been in Sandra's since Barry had been walloped by his mam.

"Oh, come on Doe," pleaded Sandra. "It's okay. My mam's in a good mood. She likes you. She only laid into our Barry because he'd been really bad. You've got to come and look."

Slightly reassured and now really intrigued by Sandra's air of mystery, she agreed to go.

As the girls approached the Cooper's back door, Sandra was getting ever more excited.

"It's through here," said Sandra, as her friend followed her through the kitchen, past the bottom of the stairs and into the front room.

Doreen could hear music. It was Elvis Presley singing 'Heartbreak Hotel', one of her brother's favourite songs. Looking past Sandra, she could see Barry and Johnny stood near the window. Elvis had now stopped singing, but he was quickly followed by Pat Boone and 'I'll Be Home'. Doe was confused, as the radio didn't normally play the songs that her brother and his friends liked at this time of day. Standing to one side, Johnny motioned Doreen towards him. She could now see a long wooden cabinet on four legs, with a hinged lid that had been lifted up. Inside it were a number of knobs, a radio tuning display and a round raised platform with a metal spindle. Resting on the spindle and held down by a thin metal arm, were a number of small, black shiny discs, pressed tightly together. Spinning around on the turntable was a record being played by the arm containing the needle resting upon it. Doreen had never seen anything like this. It was fantastic; far larger and more impressive than an ordinary gramophone. It was a radio and record player combined. It had two loudspeakers that could be heard all the way down the street and it was a beautiful piece of furniture. Sandra told her that it was called a radiogram.

The girls were mesmerised as they watched the records revolve, the needle arm lift up and retract, then another record fall down to the turntable after the previous one had ended. Sandra proudly told her that the radiogram could play seven singles, one after another. Doreen was astounded. She was amazed that it was possible for this new and strange kind of gramophone to play the records all by itself.

Having listened to the music, Doe returned home. Her dad was getting ready to go to the 'Richmond'. Doreen eagerly told him about the wonderful new radiogram that the Cooper family had just bought. Jim knew what was coming next.

"Can we have one, Dad?"

"I'm sorry, Doe. They're a lot of money. We can't afford one."

"Why?"

"They've got three wages going into that house and Sandra's Uncle Roy has no wife and kids, so he's got plenty of spare cash to throw around."

"Oh," said Doreen, clearly disappointed.

"Anyway," continued Jim, "there wouldn't be any point in getting one, because you need electricity to run it and we don't have any. It needs a lot more power to make it work. You can't just use a battery like we do for the radio."

It was another indication to Doe that her family were relatively poor and it followed hard upon the fact that their neighbour at number nineteen, Doris Palmer, had a television set and of course, the electricity supply to use it. When she had first got it her son Glenn, two years older than Doreen, had called to take her in to see it. There was only a test card shown until four o'clock, but she still found the grainy black and white picture amazing. After going home for tea, Glenn came back and took her in to watch 'Sooty'. Doreen was desperate to look inside the back of the set, but was told that she couldn't. Doris was kind and would often allow Doe in to watch the children's programmes if it was too wet to play outside.

Chapter 14

As Doreen became older, she was more prepared to play with the boys. One boy in particular, Peter Laine, became one of her closest friends. Peter's Mam and Dad, Mary and George, owned the house at the bottom of Bright Avenue. They had three sons: Peter, who was in Doe's class at school and twins George and Joey, who were two years younger.

One Saturday, Doreen and Peter were playing rounders with their friends in Bright Avenue. They were on opposite sides. Peter had hit the ball down the road and started to race around the bases. Believing that the fielder wouldn't get the ball back quickly, he decided to run past second and on to third base where Doe was standing. To his surprise the ball came whizzing into Doreen, who caught it and stumped him out. Peter wouldn't accept it and argued fiercely that he had reached the base just before she had stumped him. Doe, who never backed down if she felt she was right, insisted that he was out. Peter continued to argue, but so did Doreen. Their friends watched on, no one wanting to intervene in what was becoming a very heated argument.

Peter, becoming irate, suddenly pushed Doe and tried to snatch the ball from her hands in order to continue the game.

"No, get off!" shouted Doreen.

Hanging on firmly to the ball, she was getting angry. Doe was determined that she wouldn't give in to a boy who thought that because he was bigger and stronger, he could bully her into giving way.

Bang! Peter suddenly lashed out.

That was it. Doe immediately laid into Peter, punching him, kicking him and pulling his hair. Taken aback, Peter took time to react before setting about Doreen with his fists. The other kids scattered. Some went running to Doreen's house, others to Peter's.

The next thing Doe remembered was being picked up off the ground by her mam. Doreen then noticed Peter's mam holding on to him. Emily shouted at Doe for fighting and marched her back to the house, whilst Peter was taken in the opposite direction by his mam. After being kept in for a couple of hours, Doreen was allowed back out and was playing whip and top on the pavement with her friend Linda. After a while, Peter came walking down the road, but crossed over before he reached them. Doreen looked at him but neither of them spoke. Peter went into Horseman's on the corner, then returned with a newspaper. Doe called across to him, but he ignored her, looking straight ahead as he walked down the opposite side of the road. Doreen noticed that he had big scratches on his cheek. She knew that she must have done it to him. It served him right she thought. He shouldn't have attacked her.

A little later Peter's brothers, George and Joey, came out. They told Doreen and Linda that their dad had given Peter a good hiding for fighting with a girl. Doe began to feel guilty and wished that the fight hadn't happened. She liked Peter and was concerned that he may not want to be her friend. For weeks afterwards, Peter kept it up. He ignored Doreen, refused the sweets she offered him and wouldn't go to the park or play football with the other children if Doe was involved. Doreen couldn't understand why he couldn't put the fight behind him. She talked to her dad, asking him what she could do to get Peter to play with her again. Jim explained that it would take time. It wasn't because his dad had leathered him for hitting her said Jim, but that she had fought him to a standstill. He was a boy and she had humiliated him. He would have to get over that before he would play with her again. Eventually Peter did talk to her, but never again would they be close friends.

Doreen's gran had a saying: "trouble always comes in threes" and it seemed that she was right, as in the weeks prior to her dad's involvement in the burglary of the jewellers on Stockport Road, two devastating blows lay in wait for the unsuspecting little girl.

The first involved 'Our Rex'. Rex had quickly adapted to life on three legs and had little difficulty racing around the streets. He'd picked up his familiar routine of waiting at the end of the alley, his eyes fixed on the corner of Bright Avenue, watching and listening for Doreen to come round the corner on her return from school. But the accident had scared him. A lovely dog with no hint of malice, after he had been run over by the police car, he became afraid of any type of vehicle. It was fine when he shied away from cars, but he was much braver when, barking uncontrollably, he chased after anyone who rode by on a bicycle. More seriously, Rex started to react badly to anyone in uniform. Jim believed that it was because after the accident, when the policemen had got out of the car to attend to Rex, he could see that they were wearing uniforms.

Jim became aware that there could be a problem when Rex bit the postman. The 'postie' had seen the back door open and had mounted the steps to shout through to Doreen's mam. Rex, inside the kitchen, had darted towards him, biting him on the bottom of his leg. Fortunately, the postie was understanding. Emily had grabbed Rex, smacked him and had closed the kitchen door behind him. The postie had checked his leg, which was only slightly grazed and told her it was all right; that it was his fault for going up the steps and Rex was simply protecting his home.

When Emily told Jim and said that she was worried about Rex, he agreed with the postie. Rex was just defending the house; they should all make sure they closed the door when he was inside. Yet Rex soon began to bark at the policemen he saw walking the beat. When one policeman approached Rex on Syndall Street and tried to calm him down, Rex bit him and ran off. It happened just outside Horseman's and two of Doreen's friends had just come out of the shop. The policeman looked at them and asked if they knew who owned the dog. They told him that Rex belonged to Doreen Brodie and that she lived at seventeen, Bright Avenue. They pointed to the house that was just around the corner and the policeman put the details in his notebook. Arriving back at the station, he recorded the incident and another officer was sent to visit Doe's parents to tell them to keep their dog under control. When the constable knocked on the door, Doreen opened it. Rex, who was inside, darted past her and bit the policeman before running out and away down the alley. The policeman, nursing his leg, was furious. Jim tried to placate him, but to no avail. He was told firmly that they must never let Rex out again without a lead, for he was too dangerous.

Ominously, the policeman said that he had no alternative but to bring the matter to the attention of the magistrates.

Shortly after, Jim received notice to attend at court. On his return he was forced to give his daughter the bad news. The magistrates had decided that Rex had to be put to sleep; that Jim would have to take him to the vets the following morning.

Doreen was devastated. She couldn't believe it and wasn't able to understand why her dad couldn't do anything to stop it happening.

"You don't have to take him, Dad."

"I have to, Doe. The court has ordered it."

"But Rex is our dog. They can't make you."

"Yes, they can. If I don't take him, they'll just come and fetch him."

"But we can hide him, Dad. They won't know where he is."

"Then they'll arrest me and put me in prison. They'll find Rex eventually. You can't stop him going out."

Doreen was too young to understand. Her only thought was that she was going to lose Rex and it was her dad's decision whether or not to take him to the vets the following morning. Not prepared to let the matter drop, she continued to put pressure on Jim. After all, he almost always gave in to her. She would make him do so now. So instead of spending time with her beloved Rex before he had to go, she decided to make a stand by protesting on the outside toilet roof. Some time ago, Doe had learned to climb on to the toilet roof and would go up there when she was sulking; usually because her mam wouldn't let her have her own way. She was convinced that if she stayed out there long enough, her dad would give in to her demands. The little girl was determined that he wouldn't take Rex.

Before tea, Doreen took her place on the toilet roof. When her mam called her in for something to eat, she wouldn't budge. Jim came out and told her to come down. She refused.

"Doreen. Come down. You've got to have something to eat."

"No."

"You being up there isn't going to make any difference," said Jim. "I've told you that I'll go to prison if I don't do as the court says. Rex has bitten two policeman and they don't even know about the postman. The court has ordered him to be put to sleep. There's nothing I can do about it. I wish I could."

"You can," insisted Doreen.

"Look, love. Come back into the house. Rex needs you. You have to spend as much time as you can with him before he has to go. He wants to see you."

Jim had no need to make his daughter feel guilty at leaving Rex, she was all too aware that she may be losing the opportunity to spend some final moments with him. But she was a strong and resolute young girl. She knew that this was Rex's only chance. She had to sacrifice time with him in order to force her dad to change his mind. She was determined to stick it out.

As the hours passed by, Doreen wouldn't budge and Jim didn't have the heart to try and force her down. He kept coming out, pleading with her to come in. He told her how much Rex wanted to see her and how she would regret not spending time with him. But it was all to no avail, Doreen was sure that Jim would give in. He always did, eventually. But it got darker and very late and still her dad's response hadn't changed. She still couldn't understand how the magistrates had so much power to ruin her and Rex's life. She just had to stick it out and not give in. And she did, staying on the toilet roof until midnight and beyond. Jim, worried that his daughter may run-off, couldn't go to bed. He stayed up in the kitchen, looking out of the window and went out every fifteen minutes or so, to try and coax her down. He was sure that she would give up eventually. He knew that Doreen was afraid of the dark and hated 'creepies'; her fears would surely bring her back indoors. But they didn't. Doreen stayed resolutely on the roof, but as dawn began to break, she realised that Jim wasn't going to change his mind. It was a new day and time had run out. She knew beyond a doubt that her dad was telling her the truth. He would go to prison if he didn't take Rex. The next time Jim came out to see her, she pleaded with him one final time.

"Dad, please don't take Rex."

"Doe, I have to. I don't have a choice. Look, please come and spend a couple of hours with Rex before I take him. You'll never forgive yourself if you don't say goodbye to him."

Finally, the long hours, the lack of sleep, the determination of the struggle, the realisation that Rex was lost, broke the little girl. She burst into uncontrollable tears.

"Oh, Dad. Why does he have to go?"

Doreen dropped off the edge of the toilet roof and reaching the ground, flung out her arms towards her dad. He cuddled her and kissed the top of her head.

"Come on, love. Let's go to Rex."

Doe went into the kitchen where Rex was lying on the floor. She was sobbing and the little dog became agitated and upset. He got up and moved towards her. Doreen dropped to her knees, wrapped her arms around his neck and squeezed him gently. She tried hard to stop crying, not wanting to upset Rex further, but she knew that her time with him was coming to an end and she couldn't hold back the tears. The last hour before Rex had to go was awful. Doreen kept closing her eyes as she watched the hands of the clock inexorably moving around to the appointed hour. She prayed to God to help them. Begged for something to happen; something to save Rex. She wanted the court to change its mind; the vet to refuse to put Rex to sleep. But she knew that it was no good.

All the little girl could do was cry, but she knew at nine o'clock that she had to be brave for Rex's sake. She held him close, nuzzled his face, kissed his soft, wet nose and let him go. Jim, struggling to keep his composure and hating the magistrates for putting his daughter through such an ordeal, attached Rex's lead and took him outside. He dreaded that Doreen would race after him, plead with him as he walked through the streets. But his daughter was a spent force. She sat at the kitchen table and cried and cried, Emily trying to console her the best she could. Doe knew that she would never see Rex again. Her best pal was gone forever.

Having barely recovered from the loss of Rex, Doreen suffered a further setback when her brother decided to leave home.

For some time, the relationship between Jim and Our Kid had been deteriorating. As Emily had predicted, Jimmy didn't find it easy working for his dad. He had proved a quick learner and was soon as skilled a painter and paper hanger as Jim. Wherever he was sent, customers were impressed with the quality of his work, his politeness and application. Yet his father was slow to appreciate this. Jimmy's biggest grievance however, was the poor wage he received. Jim had criticised Dewhurst for not paying him enough; for giving him no real prospects of supporting a family. Yet Our Kid had earned significantly more working at the butchers. Understandably, this made him angry, especially when Jim had talked about them building a thriving business together; the two of them as partners. It seemed clear to the young man that his father had lied and was simply intent on exploiting him.

Over time, Jimmy had become friendly with several of his dad's competitors and in particular, Frank Furniss. Furniss owned a large company. He had secured sub-contract work from the Corporation and was regularly employed by the large stores and businesses in central Manchester. He had kept an eye on Jimmy and was impressed with the quality of his work. Our Kid had made it clear that he was unhappy working for his dad. Frank said that if he wanted a change, he would offer him a job immediately.

Seventeen, Jimmy was prepared to have it out with his father. He now had a steady girlfriend called Valerie and was often at her parents' house. Jimmy had made a good impression on them and as they had a spare bedroom, allowed him to stay over when he and Valerie had been for a night out in town.

Late one evening Doreen, asleep in bed, was woken by the sound of her dad's voice. He was angry and shouting loudly. She then heard her brother's voice raised in reply. It startled her, for it was the first time that she had ever heard him answer his father back. Concerned that Jim may set about him, she pulled back the covers and sprang out of bed. Before reaching the bottom of the stairs, she heard the back door bang. Rushing into the kitchen, there was no sign of Our Kid. Emily was crying and Jim was bellowing at her to shut up.

"Where's Our Kid?"

The sound of Doreen's voice had a calming effect on her dad. He didn't want to see her upset.

"It's all right," said Jim. "He's gone to Valerie's."

Doreen was confused.

"But it's late. He should be here."

Her dad didn't reply. Emily, who had stopped crying, looked at her daughter.

"Come on, Doe. You should be in bed. It's time I came too."

Emily guided Doreen towards the bottom of the stairs and they made their way up to the front bedroom, leaving Jim in the kitchen.

The next morning, when Doreen came down to breakfast, there was no sign of Jimmy. Concerned, she asked Emily why her dad and Our Kid had been arguing.

"Jimmy told your dad that he didn't want to work for him anymore and that he was going to get a job with someone else."

Doe now understood why Jim had been so angry. She knew that he expected Jimmy to do as he was told.

"But why were you crying?" asked Doreen.

"I wasn't," replied Emily.

"You were. I saw you."

"Well, Jimmy told your dad that he was leaving. He's gone to live with Valerie and her parents."

Doreen was shocked.

"What, forever?" she asked, quietly.

"Yes, I think so."

"But why? He lives with us. Why does he want to live with her?"

Doe was already concerned that Jimmy was becoming too attached to his latest girlfriend. They had been going out together for some time now; a situation that confused her. His girlfriends never seemed to last long, but with Valerie still around, Doreen began to fear that she wanted to take Our Kid away from them.

"Don't worry love," said Emily. "Jimmy isn't disappearing. He'll be coming back to see us. He'll still take you jiving."

Yet Doe was unconvinced. She had seen her mam cry and now she understood why. It was clear that Emily hadn't wanted Jimmy to go. Yet he had and both mother and daughter were unsure of what the future would bring. To Doreen, who had only recently lost Rex, it seemed as if everything close to her was being taken away.

"He'll explain to you this afternoon," continued Emily. "He needs to collect a few things from his bedroom. Come on now, hurry up or you'll be late for school."

Doreen found it hard to concentrate in class. She was concerned about Jimmy and worried that he may not turn up to see her. When school was over however and she raced back home, he was stood in the kitchen talking to Emily.

"Our Kid!" shouted Doreen, charging into him and almost bowling him over.

"Steady," said Jimmy, laughing at the bundle of enthusiasm in front of him.

Never had he felt so loved. His sister idolised him and it was obvious just how much she needed him around.

Straightaway, in her usual fashion of getting down to the business of securing what she wanted, the young girl went on the offensive.

"When are you coming home, Our Kid?"

Doreen was determined to have her brother back as soon as possible.

"I can't. I've got a new home now. I'm staying at Valerie's. Her parents have put themselves out for me. I can't let them down now, can I? It wouldn't be fair."

Doreen knew that her brother wasn't being entirely honest.

"It's Dad, isn't it? This is all because he was shouting at you."

"No," said Jimmy.

His answer sounded unconvincing.

"Dad's going to be all right. He'll forget about it. Things will be better, you'll see. I'll talk to him," said Doreen, reassuringly.

Jimmy was touched at the thought of his little sister having a man-to-man conversation about him with their dad. He smiled, but he was well aware that she would. It was at times like this that he felt so proud to be her brother. She was so brave, so determined, so ready to fight for what she thought was right. She showed such kindness and consideration to others and at such a tender age. Jimmy wondered why adults couldn't have the same qualities. How different little Doe was to his dad.

"But it's not that simple," said Jimmy.

"Why?"

"Because I've told Dad that I won't work for him anymore and he's not happy. He won't forgive me for a long time."

"He will," said Doreen. "I'll make him."

"No, it's better like this. I'm older now, it's time I moved out on my own."

Whilst Jimmy was talking, Doreen noticed that there was a box on the kitchen table with shoes, ties, pictures and other items in it. By the table leg there was a large bag and she could see a shirt popping out of the top of it. Jimmy was serious. He was taking his things; he was definitely moving out.

"It hasn't worked out, being a decorator for Dad. I'm going to find another job. It doesn't make any difference to you, me or Mam. I'll still come round to see you and take you dancing and to the pictures."

Doe was encouraged by his words.

"Anyway, I'm going to have to get off. I'll come back and see you tomorrow."

With that he bent down and kissed her on the cheek, hugged Emily, picked up his box and bag and set off.

True to his word, Jimmy came back every day at four o'clock for the next two weeks, but not at the weekend. Doreen realised that he wouldn't come when her dad was likely to be at home. Jimmy then told Doe that he couldn't see her straight after school anymore, as he had a new job to start on the following Monday. Frank Furniss had told Jimmy that he would wait a couple of weeks before taking him on. Frank was concerned that Jim may cause trouble if he suspected that he had poached his son. When Jim seemed to have accepted Jimmy's departure, Frank asked if it would be all right to offer him a job. Not wanting his friends to think that he was being too hard on his son, Jim had no option but to say that it would.

Our Kid, now on a proper wage, was more than able to keep his promise to Doe and soon, like all his previous girlfriends, Valerie had no choice but to get used to visits to the ABC and the Ritz with Doreen in tow.

Chapter 15

The day after Jim's conviction at court, Emily had taken Doe to see Terry O'Hara. Doreen knew that he was one of the men she had seen on the two nights when the robbery was being planned and the takings had been brought to their home. Terry's house was a bus ride away along Hyde Road. Doe recognised the area. The house, much larger than the one they rented in Bright Avenue, was in Gorton. It wasn't too far away from where her Auntie Mary and Uncle Joe lived. On the bus, Emily told Doreen not to mention anything about seeing Terry on the night of the robbery; that it was important for her dad. Realising that her mam was serious, Doe promised that she wouldn't. The young girl was gradually learning that at certain times she had to avoid being her usual forthright self. Sometimes she needed to be 'seen and not heard', a phrase that her gran was so fond of using. Doreen was still unaware of exactly who was involved in the robbery and it wouldn't be until years later that she would find out that her mam had visited Terry to discuss the arrangements to help them, now that her dad was in jail. Jim's silence meant that his accomplices were still at liberty. The unwritten rule was that he should, in no circumstances, 'grass' on them. In return, the other members of the gang would see his family 'all right'; they would keep an eye on them and save Jim's share of the take for when he left prison.

Terry and his wife greeted Emily warmly at the door and she and Doreen were quickly invited inside. Doe was given a drink of orange and some biscuits. Terry had two children. Jane was almost eight, like Doreen, whilst Paul was six. Paul was in a wheelchair. He couldn't walk and seemed unable to answer her when she spoke to him. Doe soon realised that he was very ill and Jane told her that Paul had been hurt when he had been delivered at birth.

Doreen and Jane were told to go outside, so that the adults could talk privately. The girls took Paul out with them and walked around the streets. Doe again tried to talk to Paul but finally gave up, realising that he wasn't able to answer. The girls took turns to push him, but it was heavy work and tiring.

Jane had a striking appearance. She had short, jet-black hair and wore glasses. As none of Doreen's friends did, she couldn't stop herself from staring at her. It wasn't long however, before she decided that she didn't like Jane very much. Her companion talked continually about her family's car, their television set and radiogram and about their week-long holidays at places she had never heard of. Doe thought that Jane was showing off and didn't like it. Nevertheless, not wanting Jane to know that it bothered her, she insisted that her own family still preferred to listen to the radio and go on days out to Blackpool. Of course, it wasn't true. Doreen was envious; even more so because Jane's dad was still at home, unlike Jim.

After an hour and thoroughly fed up, Doe suggested that they should go back to the house. Jane quickly agreed. She too had had enough of pushing her brother around and didn't really want to make friends with Doreen. Yet, on their return, the pair were greeted by Mrs O'Hara. She told them that they needed to stay out for another half an hour, as the adults hadn't finished talking. Reluctantly, the two girls set off again. It seemed an age before the thirty minutes were finally up and the girls returned to the house. This time, Emily met them at the front door, along with Terry. Saying goodbye, Emily and Doe set off home. Sat on the bus, Emily was very quiet. Doreen asked her if they would be going to the O'Hara's again.

"No, not to the house, Doe. I've managed to sort everything out."

The matter was closed; Emily wouldn't be answering any more questions about their visit. Doreen was learning that she would have to accept her mam's authority. Jim wasn't around to spoil her anymore and she wouldn't get her own way as much as she was used to.

A couple of months later, Emily took Doreen into a new ironmonger's store on Hyde Road. Doe was surprised to see Terry behind the counter. He was busy serving a customer. Once the shop was empty, Emily told Doreen to go and wait outside. Having done so, Doe was looking at the objects in the shop window when she noticed a gap in the display boards. Through it she was able to see her mam and Terry at the counter. Terry handed a small envelope to Emily and Doreen watched her as she opened it, took out some money and tucked it into the purse which she had taken from her bag.

Every few weeks, Emily and Doreen returned. Each time Emily would wait until the shop was empty before sending her daughter outside. The display boards had been repaired and Doe was frustrated, as she could no longer see what Terry and her mam were doing. Over the next few months, Doreen noticed how the window display continued to grow. There were lots of different tools and equipment on display and the prices of the items became increasingly expensive; a fact that Doe remarked upon to her mam.

"Yes, Doe. It's certainly a thriving business. Terry's done well for himself, hasn't he? That shop's a little gold mine," said Emily.

After Jim had been released from prison, he also took Doe with him to the store and made her wait outside so that he and Terry could talk privately. Many years later, Doreen learned that Terry had set up the business with his share of the proceeds from the robbery.

Chapter 16

After Jim had started his sentence at Strangeways, Doreen and Emily's life settled into a routine. Emily continued to work part-time in the cheese factory, kept up her activities as a dressmaker and was helped out by the money that she collected periodically from Terry O'Hara. Emily was always there when Doe arrived home from school. The neighbours didn't treat them any differently; they were people who Emily had known for years. Doreen still kept the same friends and their parents had no concerns over her playing in their houses. Only at school, where some of the children and their parents didn't know her, had Doe experienced any difficulties and those she had dealt with herself. Doreen wasn't able to see her dad as often as when he was on remand, but she still had contact with him. Emily would still manage to slip him money to put in his belt, although the screws were far more vigilant now. Jim would always put on a cheerful face for his daughter and tell her to be a good girl and do as her mam told her.

Jimmy still came to see his sister and would often take her out. Doreen always looked forward to seeing Our Kid, but had never taken to his girlfriend, Valerie. She couldn't explain why she felt as she did. Valerie was always nice to her and wasn't at all irritated when Jimmy took Doe out with them. She would encourage Jimmy to jive with his sister and told the little girl that she was a far better dancer than herself. Doreen knew that her brother found Valerie attractive. She had heard Johnny Cooper tell Jimmy how lucky he was to have such a gorgeous girl to go out with. Valerie had long brown hair, brown eyes, a cute, slightly upturned nose and soft lips. She had a lovely figure and when she walked into the Ritz, there was no shortage of admiring glances. A trainee librarian, Valerie seemed to talk with a 'posh' accent, which made the young girl feel uncomfortable. Perhaps what concerned Doe the most, was the fear that Jimmy would marry Valerie, start his own family and then forget about her. As illogical as this might seem, Doreen was scared and vulnerable. She was terrified of losing her brother, just like her dad. Valerie therefore became the focus of her dark, imagined fears.

Just before Christmas 1957, Doreen was in for a surprise. Jimmy had called to take her to the pictures but instead of seeing Valerie, Our Kid had another girl with him.

"Where's Valerie?" asked Doe.

"She's here." replied Jimmy.

"No, she's not!" said Doreen, assuming that Jimmy was teasing her.

"Yes," said the girl. "I'm Valerie."

"No, you're not!" insisted Doreen, who was now beginning to get annoyed.

"I am," said the girl, smiling. "I'm called Valerie too, but everyone calls me Val. You're Doreen, aren't you? It's nice to meet you."

Doreen looked closely at Val. She had long, blonde hair and was wearing lots of makeup. She had a nice figure. She was pretty, as were all the girls Our Kid went out with.

"Come on Doe. Hurry up, or we'll miss the start of the film," said Jimmy.

Val had a bubbly personality. She was very different to Valerie. She chatted away to Doreen as they walked off down Syndall Street, on to Apsley Grove and down to the ABC. Doreen was quite taken by her. Val seemed friendly and gave her lots of attention, buying Doe some sweets when they went into the pictures.

After returning home and Jimmy had left, both Doreen and her mam wondered what was going on. Jimmy had said nothing about Valerie, but clearly something was wrong. The answer came the following day. After tea, Jimmy arrived at the house. He had a couple of large bags with him and asked Emily if it was okay for him to sleep in the back bedroom for a few days. He explained that he was moving out of Valerie's, as the two of them had broken up. Valerie had wanted them to get engaged, but he didn't feel the time was right. It had left him with no choice but to move out of her parents' house.

Doreen was excited to have her brother back and hoped that he would stay much longer. The next evening however, brought new developments. Val called to the house to see Jimmy. It was now clear that she was his new girlfriend. Emily felt sorry for Valerie, especially as she suspected that Jimmy had been going out with Val before he'd finished with her. Or so Emily thought, because that evening it became apparent that Valerie didn't actually know that her relationship with Jimmy was over. Whilst Our Kid was in the front room with Val, there was a knock on the kitchen door.

"Doe, can you answer that?" asked her mam, who was busy at the sink.

Sat reading her comic, Doreen put it down and went to the door. Opening it, she was surprised to see Valerie.

"Hello, Doreen. Is Jimmy in?"

Hearing Valerie's voice, Emily rushed over, but she wasn't quick enough to stop her daughter's reply.

"He's in the front room with Val. I'll go and tell him you're here."

Eight years old, her innocence was plain to see. Without any awareness of the potential minefield that she had just created, Doreen went into the front room.

"Valerie's here, Our Kid. She wants to talk to you."

"Oh, no. That's great!"

Jimmy shook his head, sighed and turned to Val, who was sat beside him on the sofa.

"You stay here. I'll go and see what she wants."

Following his sister back into the kitchen, Jim approached Valerie at the door and suggested that they stay out in the back yard, where they could talk privately. Valerie nodded and walked away from the back steps, followed by Jimmy who shut the door behind him. Doreen went to the kitchen window and peeked out from behind the net curtains to try and see what was going on.

"Doe, get away from the window," said Emily, sharply.

"Why? I want to see what's happening."

"Because it's rude, that's why," insisted Emily. "The two of them need to be left alone."

Reluctantly, Doreen moved away from the window, disappointed that she couldn't satisfy her curiosity.

As the time ticked by, Val began to get impatient and walked through to the kitchen. She expected Jimmy to have got rid of

Valerie by now. She was becoming frustrated and Doreen's comment, didn't help.

"He's still out there."

"Yes, I know," replied Val.

"Best leave them to it," advised Emily. "You don't want things to become unpleasant."

"Oh, I'm not bothered about her. She doesn't worry me," said Val, dismissively.

"She isn't like that," said Emily. "Valerie couldn't hurt a fly. Let Jimmy sort it out. The girl's clearly upset and she needs to be dealt with calmly."

Val sat down at the kitchen table with Doreen. Tapping her fingers, she looked continually at the kitchen clock, beginning to doubt whether Jimmy was ever going to reappear. Doe could see that Val was becoming agitated and it was no surprise when she got up, walked over to the kitchen door, opened it and went outside. Concerned that the situation might get out of hand, Emily went after her, closely followed by Doreen.

Valerie and Jimmy were stood together in the yard and as Val emerged from the kitchen, she saw Jimmy jump back. Convinced that he had been consoling her, Val was angry. She was determined that Jimmy would rid himself of her rival, once and for all.

"You need to tell her, Jimmy. Don't spare the details," insisted Val. "You've finished with her and you're going out with me. Tell her to stay out of our lives."

Doe was shocked. Until now, Val had appeared pleasant and friendly, but it was clear that she had a much darker side to her nature.

Valerie looked at Jimmy. Doreen could see that she had been crying. Her eyes were red and swollen and there were tears down her cheeks. Proudly, she tried to wipe them away. She loved Jimmy and didn't want to lose him, but she had no wish to be humiliated.

Jimmy, said nothing. He was just like his father, thought Emily. Always wanting to be the good guy. He wouldn't tell Valerie the truth, because he didn't want her to dislike him. The fact that his silence would hurt her even more, never entered his head.

Emily decided that she had to intervene. Valerie was a lovely, young woman and she felt sorry for her. It was only right that she knew the truth. Emily was convinced that once she got over Jimmy's rejection, Valerie would be far better off without him.

"Jimmy, you owe Valerie an explanation," insisted Emily. "You have to let her know where she stands."

Still, Jimmy said nothing. The four females continued to look at him expectantly.

It was Valerie who finally broke the silence.

"I thought you'd come home to think things over, Jimmy. To decide whether we should get engaged. That's what you told me and I've come to see you and then I find you with this other girl. You know that I love you and I'd like you to come back to our house. Please."

Listening to her heartfelt words, Emily thought that Valerie was a fool, but then recognised that she'd been there herself many times with Jim. It seemed to be a woman's lot; devoting themselves to an unworthy man. Although Jimmy was her son, Emily felt nothing but sympathy for Valerie. Although she loved him, Emily couldn't help but feel ashamed of Jimmy's behaviour.

Val now took matters into her own hands. She turned towards Valerie.

"Look love, Jimmy's been going out with me for the past month. There's nothing left for you. He's mine now. Get off home."

There was a menacing tone to Val's voice. She was quite prepared to back up her words with deeds; give Valerie a battering if necessary. Yet to Val's surprise, her words provoked no reaction from her rival; it seemed clear that this posh girl had no intention of fighting for her man.

With the situation in the balance, Jimmy finally broke his silence. Yet he still proved incapable of acting decisively. In a vain attempt to abdicate responsibility for Valerie's fate, he turned towards his sister.

"Doe."

"Yes, Our Kid."

"Who do you think I should go out with? Valerie or Val?"

The two young women both looked at Doreen. She had been a fascinated bystander in the events so far; a mere observer. Now she was being asked to be the judge and jury; make the decision on who would be left happy and whose life would be temporarily devastated. It was a despicable act. Jimmy was certain that Doe would choose Val and so do his dirty work for him.

As Doreen looked at the two of them, vying for her brother's affection, she felt uneasy. She could see that Valerie was upset and it made her feel uncomfortable. Yet Doe had never really liked her. She wasn't fun like Val. She was too serious and Doreen still worried that she would change her brother's personality and ultimately stop him from seeing her. Val was different and she seemed to pose no threat. As her brother had suspected, she was the one that Doreen favoured.

"I think you should go out with Val."

Jimmy looked at Valerie and spoke to her quietly.

"Yes, Valerie. I think it's best that we finish. I'm going out with Val."

Turning away, Valerie walked slowly out of the yard and into the alley. Concerned, Emily followed after her, whilst Jimmy, Val and Doreen went back into the house.

"You stay here, Doe and wait for Mam to come back. Val and I have to nip out."

Emily returned shortly after.

"Where's Jimmy?" she asked.

"He had to go out with Val," replied Doreen.

"More like he can't face me."

"Why?"

"Never mind," said Emily. "Let's go in the front room and listen to the radio."

That night, Emily didn't go to bed at the usual time. Doreen wanted to stay up with her, but Emily refused. Her daughter suspected that she was intent on waiting up for Jimmy. It was clear that she wasn't happy about what had happened. Still in a state of nervous excitement, Doe found it hard to get to sleep. Her natural curiosity contributed to her insomnia, as she was eager to hear what her mam would say to Jimmy when he returned. Eventually, Doreen heard voices coming from downstairs. Quietly, she got out of bed and crept halfway down the stairs, just far enough to hear what was being said. Emily never ranted and raved like her dad. She spoke quietly and calmly to her brother. As a result, her words seemed to have far more impact.

"You shouldn't have used our Doreen like that, Jimmy. It wasn't fair to her, or to Valerie. Doe may feel guilty now for upsetting her and you should have had the guts to be honest with Valerie. You owed her that."

"I know, but it was all getting a bit too much. I'm sorry."

Jimmy wanted to go to bed and hoped that the apology would be enough to satisfy his mam. But it wasn't.

"I'm only going to tell you the once and it's up to you whether you listen to my advice, or not," said Emily.

Jimmy didn't want to hear it. He had come home late on purpose, hoping his mam would be in bed and that in the morning the day's events would have been forgotten. Yet he was back home, because he needed a place to stay and so he knew that he had little choice but to listen to his mam and prepare himself for her inevitable criticism.

"You're daft finishing with Valerie. She's a good-looking girl. She's got decent parents and a good job. She idolises you and is prepared to forgive you. You should go back to see her tomorrow and make it up with her."

"I know, Mam. She is pretty, but she's boring. She's too serious. I prefer Val. She's far more fun."

"Val's bad news. I know you don't want to hear it, but it's true. Her family have got a right reputation. Everyone's heard of the Holdens. The father, uncles, brothers; almost all of them have been in 'the Nick'."

"Well, my dad's in there now. So, what's different about Val's family?"

"That's why I'm telling you. One jailbird in the family is enough. If you get mixed up with the Holdens, you'll end up joining your dad. I don't want that for you, Jimmy. Promise me you'll think about it."

"All right, Mam."

Jimmy had no wish to argue with his mam, but neither was he about to reconsider his decision. He went over to Emily and gave her a kiss.

"I need to get to bed, Mam. Thanks for letting me stay."

"Why wouldn't I? This is your home too."

Doreen quickly climbed back up the stairs and slipped into the bedroom, her mam and brother unaware that she had heard their conversation. When Emily got into bed, Doe pretended to be asleep, not responding to her mam's good night kiss.

Jimmy only stayed a few more days. Unwilling to heed Emily's advice, he moved into his new girlfriend's home. Doreen quickly came to regret her support for Val. For the next few weeks, she rarely saw her brother and when he did turn up, on his own, he told her that he could only stay for a short time. The trips to the ABC and the Ritz had ended. Doe realised that Valerie hadn't been so bad after all. It was ironic that the young girl's fears about Valerie taking her brother away from her, had now been fulfilled by Val. Worst of all, she felt that it was her own fault. As Emily had predicted, Doreen began to feel guilty about telling Jimmy to choose Val. She realised that she had been horrible to Valerie, who hadn't deserved it. She had been selfish and now she was being paid back. Doe believed it with a passion. She had learned in Sunday School that there were consequences to carrying out evil acts and this convinced her that you would always be punished for the things that you did wrong. Doreen felt that her brother, just like her dad, would be lost to her. She accepted it as the inevitable consequence of her actions.

Chapter 17

By the Autumn of 1958, Jim had been transferred from Strangeways to Sudbury Open Prison. It was in Derbyshire, miles away from Manchester and exceptionally difficult to get to by bus and train. Emily had visited him once on her own, whilst Doe had stayed at her friend Jean's house. Doreen had been disappointed not to go, but was pleased to receive a letter that Emily had brought home from her dad. In it, he told her not to worry about not being able to see him. The journey was too difficult and the reason he had been moved there, was to prepare him for his release. If everything went well, he would come home next March, just after her tenth birthday. Doreen was overjoyed. It wouldn't be too long before her dad was back home again.

After the turn of the New Year, on the first Saturday in January 1959, Doreen and her mam had gone to bed quite late. Emily was sat up, reading the *Evening News*, whilst her daughter lay beside her. It was ten-thirty and Doe was tired, but she was looking forward to seeing her cousins the following day at her gran's house in Greenheys. Emily's family hadn't reacted well to the news of Jim's imprisonment. Edna was thankful that it wasn't her family name that had been revealed in the newspapers. The family had decided however, that Emily and Doe wouldn't be cut off; after all, they weren't the ones responsible for the crime. It did of course mean that Edna had even more ammunition to fire at Emily, concerning her poor choice of husband. Thankfully, for Doreen's benefit, nothing was ever said in her presence. It meant that the visits to Greenheys remained an enjoyable experience for the young girl.

Finally, having read her newspaper, Emily turned out the paraffin lamp and lay down to sleep. Outside, the gas lights had been turned off and it was pitch black inside the bedroom. Doreen finally drifted off to sleep. Sometime later, she awoke with a start. A voice was eerily calling her name.

"*Dorrreeeen. Dorrreeeen.*"

Doe sat up in bed. The voice called out again.

"*Dorrreeeen. Dorrreeeen.*"

A long, drawn-out moan, the sound was frightening. Who, or what could it be? Rubbing her eyes, Doe tried hard to see through the gloom.

"*Dorrreeeen. Dorrreeeen.*"

The voice seemed to be getting nearer. It had moved from the window, over to the fireplace and finally, to the other side of the bed. Doreen looked over and saw a strange green and white glow surrounding a bearded, old man with long, white hair. Staring directly at her, he seemed to scowl.

"Doreen!" he snapped, impatiently.

He began to glow ever brighter, so much so, that it began to hurt Doe's eyes. Startled amazement had turned to fear. Doreen was desperate for him to go away; she was unable to move and she couldn't take her eyes off him. She wanted to scream, but she could barely raise her voice.

"Go away," she whispered.

But the old man remained, the light around him becoming even more intense. Summoning all the energy she could muster, Doe slipped under the covers, disappearing from view to escape his terrifying stare. Yet it didn't help. She lay trembling, well aware that at any moment he could fling back the covers and grab her. Closing her eyes tightly and clenching her fists, Doreen pushed herself into the mattress as far as she could, hoping and praying that she would become invisible to him. Then she realised; she had her mam. She would save her. Still under the covers, Doe reached out and grabbed at Emily. Pulling hard on her shoulder, she wondered why, with the old man's moaning, her mam was still asleep.

"Mam, Mam! Wake up!"

Startled, Emily sat up in bed, removing the covers off her daughter in the process. Unable to hide, Doreen kept her eyes tightly shut, hoping that if she couldn't see the old man, he wouldn't be able to do anything to her.

"What's the matter?" asked her mam.

"It's the old man. Tell him to go away!"

"What man? There's nobody there," replied Emily, confused.

Doreen didn't believe it.

"There is, he must have moved. He was by the window, then the fireplace and then round your side of the bed."

"Well, he's not here now. Calm down, Doe. I'll get out of bed and light the lamp."

Doreen heard her mam's footsteps on the floor of the bedroom. She heard her strike a match and tend to the lamp. Slowly, Doe opened her eyes. Her mam was right. The old man was no longer there.

"You've had a bad dream, Doe. There's nothing to worry about. Settle down and go to sleep. I'll leave the lamp on for a bit."

Doreen was relieved, but still scared. The old man had seemed so real and she found it hard to accept that what she had experienced, was nothing more than a dream. She was sure that the old man had wanted to tell her something.

The next morning, Doreen felt better. Perhaps, after all, her mam was right. Emily often told her daughter that she had too vivid an imagination. It was this that led her to have such lifelike dreams. By the time the two of them set off to her gran's, she had almost put the incident out of her mind. Yet whilst Doe was playing out in the garden with her cousins, Emily had recounted the night's events to her siblings and their partners. Just like Emily, they too had put the incident down to a bad dream. Edna however, saw the matter differently and went outside to fetch Doreen into the kitchen, where she could speak to her alone.

"Doe, the old man wanted to tell you something. That's why he called to you three times and then showed himself," said Edna. "If he comes again, you have to be brave and ask him what he wants and why he's there. Perhaps he came to give you and your mam a warning."

Doreen nodded, but she wasn't reassured. Her gran's words had simply reawakened her fears. The thought that the old man may return, was terrifying. She had always felt nervous in the dark and especially when she was sleeping alone. What Edna had told her would make it even worse. She had no intention of talking to the old man and hoped that she would never ever see him again. Quietly, she went back out into the garden to play with Mark, Richard and Louise. Her cousins wanted to know why their gran had called her into the house. Having no desire to talk about the old man, Doe told them that Edna had simply wanted to know how she was getting on.

On their return home, Doreen felt that she had to tell her mam about her conversation with Edna. Emily wasn't pleased. She didn't want her daughter upset any further.

"Doe, your gran's being silly. She takes too much interest in dreams, ghosts and spirits. She even wastes time and money going to spiritualist meetings. It's all nonsense. You mustn't take any notice. It was just a bad dream. You won't have it again."

Doreen didn't know what spiritualist meetings were, but it was clear that Emily was in no mood to explain. In fact, her mam was right; the old man didn't reappear. Later however, when her life was plunged into despair, Doe would often wonder if the old man had visited her that night, in order to warn her of the dangers that she was soon about to face.

Chapter 18

As the end of January approached, Doreen was feeling optimistic about the future. She knew that she would only have to wait a few more weeks before Jim would be released from prison. On the last Wednesday of the month, Emily had been busy trying to complete some dress orders. Unable to cook the tea, she had given her daughter a sandwich on her return from school and told her that she would send her to the 'chippy', once she had finished working. Doe was pleased. She loved steak and kidney pudding with chips and gravy from Chiappe's, her favourite chippy. Chiappe's was located on the other side of Stockport Road, opposite the end of Syndall Street. When Doreen was younger, she hadn't been allowed to go there on her own. Stockport Road was a busy thoroughfare and dangerous to cross, so her parents had sent her to Andrews instead. Located just around the corner on Syndall Street, Andrews was a far safer location for the little girl to walk to.

The food at Andrews was very good and her family were more than happy with it, but Doe didn't like going there. It had started the first time she had been sent there on her own, when she was seven, to get herself 'six penn'orth' of chips. With a slight speech impediment, Doreen always added a couple of 'ths' to the words six and chips. The chippy had been full and when she asked for her order, Mr Andrews had asked her to repeat herself.

"Sorry, love. What was it that you wanted?"

"Sixth penn'orth of chipths please."

"Say it again, love. I didn't hear you."

"Sixth penn'orth of chipths please."

Doe realised that the other customers were laughing. They were laughing at her.

"Pack it in!"

Mrs Andrews, who was working behind the counter with her husband, was clearly angry with him.

"It's all right love," she said, turning to Doreen, "take no notice. I'll get you your chips."

Mrs Andrews had given her a few extra and some scratchings too. She took the shiny sixpence that Doe had been tightly clutching in her hand and said thank you.

As the young girl left, the sound of laughter followed her out. Although unsure as to why people were reacting in such a way, it didn't alter the fact that she was unhappy that it was directed at her.

When Doreen next went to Andrews, she finally realised why people were laughing. Once again, the chippy was full and she took her place in the slowly moving queue of customers. When she finally reached the counter, Doreen didn't get the chance to speak before Mr Andrews smiled and asked a question.

"Is it sixth penn'orth of chipths that you want Doreen?"

"Yes please."

"Sixth penn'orth of chipths coming up."

The people in the queue started laughing. Doreen realised that Mr Andrews was making fun of the way she spoke. She didn't like it and this time Mrs Andrews wasn't there to shut him up. Doe didn't want to go in after that if Mrs Andrews wasn't there, but it meant not having anything to eat if her mam hadn't had time to cook the tea. Doreen just had to put up with it. She did try not asking for "six penn'orth of chips", telling Mr Andrews that he knew what she wanted, but it didn't stop him from imitating her and demanding that she asked for her order before he would serve her. Unhappy and upset, Doreen finally told her mam and dad why she was reluctant to return there, but they assured her that Mr Andrews was only having fun and didn't mean her any harm.

Tonight though, Doreen would definitely be going to Chiappe's and when she returned, her mam had the plates and bread and butter ready for them on the kitchen table. Having finished their tea, Emily and Doreen cleared the pots and settled down to read before listening to the radio in the front room. When Doe fell asleep on the sofa, Emily covered her with a coat and went into the kitchen to work on some dresses. Just before eleven, Emily returned to the front room. As she was waking her daughter, a loud knock came to the front door. Immediately,

Emily thought the worst; a visit so late could only mean bad news. Doreen was afraid too and stayed close to her mam as she walked over towards the door.

"Who's that?" called out Emily.

A man's voice, in a strange accent, replied.

"I have a letter from Jim."

Emily hesitated, then placed the chain on the front door and opened it slightly. A hand inserted some folded papers through the gap and then withdrew as Emily took them. Emily started to read the letter. She had left the door ajar but was blocking most of the view to the outside. Doreen manoeuvred so that she could look through to see who was there. She was struck by the sight of a man with fair hair and what seemed like piercing, bulging eyes. Having finished reading the letter, Emily went to remove the chain from the front door.

"No, Mam. Don't let him in."

"It's all right, Doe. Your dad's sent him. He's asked us to give him a place to stay for a few days."

Doreen felt uneasy. The man hadn't created a good impression. His eyes frightened her. She didn't want him to be allowed into the house.

"I don't care what Dad says. I don't want you to let him in. Please, Mam."

"Don't be silly, Doe. There's nothing to worry about. Your dad would never send anyone, if he thought they would cause any trouble."

Emily removed the chain and opened the door wide.

"Come in, you'll have to forgive my daughter. It's late and she can get a little nervous, especially as Jim hasn't been at home for such a long time now."

The man stepped into the front room. Emily told him to sit down while she went into the kitchen and made a brew.

"You must be tired. I'm sure you could do with a hot drink after your long journey."

"Yes, I am. Thank you very much. It's very kind of you."

Doreen sat down on the sofa, the man opposite her on the chair. He was carrying a large bag and he placed it on the floor between his feet. Doe watched him closely as he kept playing unconsciously with the handles. Trying to break the somewhat awkward silence, the man tried asking Doreen questions about herself, but she refused to be drawn into conversation, uttering monosyllabic answers or simply saying that she didn't know. The man's strange voice, the lateness of the hour and his unusual appearance, meant that she continued to feel uneasy about him being there.

When Emily came in with the tray of drinks, she sat down next to Doe on the sofa and the two adults engaged in conversation. Doreen now began to learn more about their visitor. His name was Sam McLaughlin. He'd been born and raised in Belfast, before coming to England as a young man. It was the reason why his accent sounded unfamiliar to the young Mancunian. Doreen had come across Irishmen before, but they were always from the South and their accents were different to that of the Ulsterman. Sam had just been released from Sudbury, where he had become good friends with Jim. Sam had thought of heading for Manchester to look for work. He was a plasterer and so Jim had told him that he would write a letter of introduction to Emily, who would provide him with somewhere to stay until he'd found a job and was back on his feet.

Doreen couldn't take her eyes off Sam. She had noticed how tall and thin he seemed when he had entered the house and she could smell beer on him. He had obviously been at the pub before he had turned up late at the house. But it was his blonde hair and his staring eyes, that made the most impression on her. Sam told Emily about his growing friendship with Jim and how much her husband was looking forward to his release. As the conversation continued, Doe found it hard to stay awake and Emily told her to lie down. Soon, she was asleep. Woken by her mam, Doreen looked over to the clock on the mantel piece and saw that it was ten to four. The two adults had been talking for ages. Emily told Sam that he could sleep on the sofa and she fetched some sheets and blankets for him. Emily and Doe then went to bed. It seemed no time at all before it was seven o'clock and Doreen was being told to get up by her mam.

"Doe, I know that you're still tired, but I want you to come downstairs. I don't want to have to talk to your dad's friend on my own."

Doreen didn't complain and followed her mam downstairs. They were surprised to see that Sam was already up and was filling the kettle at the kitchen sink.

"I was just going to make some tea, if that's all right. Can I make some for you and Doreen?"

"No, it's all right Sam. I'll make it," replied Emily.

As eight o'clock approached, Doreen was concerned. Her mam would soon be going to work and as she didn't leave for school for another half an hour, feared being left on her own in the house with Sam. Aware that her daughter was feeling anxious, Emily took her round to Mrs Cooper, who was happy for Doe to stay until she and Sandra set off to Ross Place.

Emily finished work at three o'clock in the afternoon, so that she would always be at home when her daughter arrived back from school. Today however, when Doreen pushed on the back door, it was locked. She knocked loudly and shouted to her mam, but there was no answer. Confused, Doe went next door to ask Mrs Pickford if she knew where Emily was. She didn't. Doreen was worried and sat waiting on the back door step. About twenty minutes later, her mam arrived with Sam.

"I'm sorry, Doe. I got delayed. I was out trying to help Sam."

"How?"

"Oh, just seeing if there was a job for him. Come on now, let's get in and I'll get the tea on."

Emily unlocked the door and they all went inside.

Except for that one day, just before Jim was taken away by the police, Doreen had never arrived home from school without her mam being there to greet her. She was upset, but determined that she wouldn't show it in front of Sam. For the first time she felt that Emily had let her down, putting the interests of Sam before herself. Doe was now convinced that her bad 'dream' about the old man and her gran's words of warning to her, were a portent of danger. It had foretold the arrival of Sam, a stranger who made her feel distinctly uncomfortable. The young girl was becoming extremely anxious, convinced that something terrible was going to happen. If only her dad was home, she thought. Then, everything would be all right.

Chapter 19

That evening after tea, Emily asked Doreen to help her clean the back bedroom. It was the room that Jimmy had slept in and it still had boxes of his old comics and other old toys in there. Emily changed the bed clothes and cleared out all Jimmy's odds and ends. She checked that the chest of drawers and wardrobe were empty.

"Why are we doing this and why are we shifting all Jimmy's things?" asked Doreen.

"We're making room for Sam. We don't want him having to sleep in the front room. We need to be able to get in there."

"But I don't want Sam to stay. I don't like him. What happens if Our Kid comes back? This is his room. Where will he stay?"

"Jimmy isn't coming back, love. He lives with Val."

"Well, I still don't want Sam here. Tell him that he's got to go somewhere else."

Emily could have no doubts that her daughter didn't like Sam and was unhappy at this new situation.

"Doe, your dad wants us to help Sam. He wants me to find him a job and somewhere to live. He can't get somewhere to live until he earns enough money to be able to start paying the rent. That's why your dad has told him he can stay with us for a while. Your dad likes him. He says that Sam's been a good friend. You want me to do what your dad says, don't you?"

"No, Mam. I don't like him."

"You're being daft. Why don't you talk to Sam, you'll soon get to like him."

"No, I won't! I want him to go!"

But it was no good. It was the second time when appealing to one of her parents, that she felt totally helpless. Just as she had been unable to save Rex, she now couldn't get Sam out of their lives. It was a situation that seemed to be rapidly deteriorating. The following evening Emily told her that Joyce Brown, now a teenager, would be coming to sit with her, as she had to go out with Sam to help find him a job. The day after, the two went out again, Joyce turning up to stay with Doreen. This time Emily told her that she and Sam were going to the 'George' on the corner of Syndall Street and Stockport Road. Doe was confused, but her mam explained that one of the builders, who might be able to give Sam a job, drank in there. Doreen accepted the explanation but over the following days Emily, dressed up in her best clothes, went out with Sam on a regular basis.

Doe was concerned. She didn't like Sam and she couldn't understand why her mam was doing so much to help him. He was settled in Jimmy's bedroom, intent on becoming a permanent fixture. Emily was always out with him, leaving her with Joyce Brown. Doreen could only count the days, desperate for her dad to come back home. When that happened, then surely Sam would be gone and her family would be back together again.

It was extremely difficult for Doreen to cope. Her mam didn't seem to listen to her anymore; she wouldn't hear a word against Sam. Emily had been with her every night since Jim had gone to prison, yet now it seemed as if she didn't want to be. What had she done? Why had her mam started to dislike her? The young girl's sense of abandonment was confirmed a couple of weeks later. Emily and Sam wanted to go out, but Joyce was unable to sit with her.

"Don't worry Doe," said her mam. "Sam and I will only be in the 'Clarence' or the 'George'. You can come and get us if there's a problem. You'll be quite safe."

Doreen said nothing. She knew it was pointless. Her mam wouldn't listen. She had changed and Doe instinctively knew that something wasn't right. When her dad had taken Emily out, it was always to the 'Richmond' or the 'Rutland'. Why wasn't her mam going there? That was where all her parents' friends would go. Her dad rarely went into the 'Clarence' or the 'George'.

Left alone in the house, the slightest noise brought the terrible promise of terrifying consequences. Doreen was tormented by her fears. Someone may have got into the house, ready to grab her, whilst others outside waited for a chance to get in. There seemed just one way to stay safe. Going to the front door, Doe removed the chain and opened it. She stood with the edge of the door wedged between her legs. Listening intently, she could run out if there was a noise from inside and shut the door quickly, if she heard anything outside. Having taken up her position at seven o'clock, when her mam and Sam returned at eleven, Doreen was frantic with worry.

"You're not going to leave me on my own again Mam, are you?"

Emily seemed distracted and offered no reply.

"It's horrible Mam," continued Doreen. "Please don't leave me on my own again."

"Don't be daft," said Emily, finally acknowledging her daughter. "You're all right. You had no reason to worry."

"You never left me on my own when my dad was here."

"You were a lot younger then, Doe. You're more grown up now. Come on, stop being silly. It's time for bed."

Emily had simply dismissed her concerns. The conversation was at an end.

Regardless of Doreen's obvious discomfort, over the following week she was left alone on another couple of evenings when Joyce wasn't available. From just being fearful of Sam, Doe was now starting to hate him. She wanted a return to the life she had shared with her mam and that seemed impossible as long as Sam was staying in the house.

Shortly after, Doe arrived home from school to find the door locked. She knocked and shouted for her mam, but there was no answer. Neither of the neighbours knew where she was, so Doreen settled down on the back doorstep and waited. Half an hour later Sandra called and asked if she wanted to play. Doe, bored of waiting, agreed. As she walked off towards the back gate, she heard her mam calling her. Looking back, she saw Emily stood at the back door. Doreen suspected that her mam had been in all the time, but for some reason hadn't wanted to let her in.

"I'm sorry Doe," said Emily, "I've only just got back."

Doreen wasn't convinced and decided to challenge her.

"But you always use the back door."

"Well, the lock's been playing up. I've asked Sam to have a look at it. I had to take the front door key instead."

Although her mam sounded convincing, Doreen didn't know what to believe.

That night Doe and Emily went to bed at ten o'clock. Her mam hadn't gone out with Sam and Doreen was pleased to have some time alone with her. They had spent time listening to the radio; Doe reading comics and Emily, the *Evening News*. The young girl was content; it was just like before Sam had arrived. Doreen had more reason to be happy when Emily told her that Sam had found work, for she assumed that it meant that he would soon be leaving them. It was nearly the end of February and her dad was close to returning home. In bed, Doe felt relaxed and soon fell asleep. In the middle of the night however, she awoke. She turned over in the bed and reached over to her mam. She wasn't there. Panicking, Doreen got out of bed and crept over to the mantelpiece. Fumbling around, she found the matches and lit a candle. Bravely, she walked over to the bedroom door and opened it.

"Mam!" she shouted.

Her mam called back to her but Doreen couldn't see her. Suddenly, she heard the turning of a handle. Lifting the candle higher in front of her, she saw Emily coming out of the back bedroom. She had been in there with Sam.

"It's all right, Doe. Don't worry. Let's go back to bed."

Doreen withdrew into the front bedroom and her mam followed, closing the door behind her. Young and innocent, Doe was unable to understand the implications of what she had seen.

Chapter 20

It hadn't escaped the notice of the neighbours on Bright Avenue that Emily and her new lodger seemed to be getting along famously. Although the pair had avoided the 'Richmond' and the 'Rutland', plenty of people had seen them going out together and into the 'George' and the 'Clarence'. Many were expecting fireworks when Jim returned.

Doreen had inadvertently fuelled the gossip. When Mrs Horseman at the newsagents had asked what her mam was up to, she had innocently replied that "she was in bed with the lodger." The shop had been full of customers and the news had spread like wildfire. Emily's antics became the main topic of conversation in the neighbourhood. It was almost inevitable that Jim would find out about his wife's infidelity. In the days before his return, Emily had distanced herself from Sam and Doe began to realise that she must be careful about what she said. Some of her older friends had expressed surprise that her mam had been in Sam's bedroom and Dorothy Cooper made it clear that if Doreen didn't want to upset her dad, then she mustn't let him know.

On the day that Jim returned, his daughter was overjoyed. She hugged and kissed him and wouldn't leave his side. Emily also seemed delighted to see him. Jim was pleased to be home and promised Doreen that she would have a big party once he resumed work and was earning money. Jim, Emily and Sam went out to the pub to celebrate. This time, Doe didn't mind. Joyce Brown came round to watch her and Doreen was content in the knowledge that everything would soon get back to normal.

Yet as the days passed, Sam remained at the house. Doreen had assumed that Jim's return would see him moving out, but it didn't happen. Jim was pleased to see Sam and the two men spent the following nights out at the pub, returning home to talk about their time in prison together. And then it changed. Sam was still staying with them and Jim seemed happy about the situation. Yet, away from Sam and Emily, he began to ask his daughter questions: What had Sam and Emily done in the evenings? How often did they go out to the pub together? Did her mam always come up to bed with her? Doreen answered yes to the last question and mentioned nothing about Emily being in Sam's room. The young girl began to feel uneasy and wished that her dad would stop asking questions. She wanted to forget all about the days following Sam's arrival. But what could she do? If she asked her dad to get rid of Sam, it would only make him ask more questions and it may put Emily in a difficult position. Not wanting to hurt either her mam or dad, Doreen felt awful. She was worried and scared. She was convinced that something terrible was going to happen.

After Jim had been home for a couple of weeks, he had gone out with Emily and Sam to the 'Richmond'. It was Friday night. When they returned, they all seemed in good spirits, especially Jim. Joyce went home and Jim said that he and Doe would go to bed, whilst Emily made a drink for Sam. Leaving Sam and Emily in the front room, Jim and Doreen made their way upstairs and into the front bedroom. Doe expected that she would be going straight to sleep, but Jim was agitated and sat down on the edge of her bed. She knew that something wasn't right.

"After we came back from the 'Richmond'," said Jim, "I fetched the ladder and put it outside our bedroom window."

"Why?" asked Doe.

"In a few minutes I'm going to climb down it and look through the fanlight into the front room."

The fanlight was a small glass window located over the front door.

Jim told his daughter to be quiet and continued to sit waiting on the bed. Doreen was uncomfortable; her stomach knotted up, her breathing laboured and she was becoming increasingly nervous. Finally, Jim spoke.

"Right, keep quiet. I'm going out of the window now."

Jim opened the bedroom window and carefully eased himself out over the windowsill, on to the top of the ladder and disappeared down it. Doreen quietly moved over to the window. She looked out and saw her dad reach the bottom of the ladder. Carefully he picked it up and gently moved it across and over the front door. He then climbed up a few of the lower rungs so that he could see through the fanlight. Quickly, he was back on the floor. Quietly he moved the ladder back to its original position and climbed back up through the bedroom window. Doe was bemused; she wasn't sure what was going on. Jim was silent. He put his finger to his lips, gesturing to Doreen that she mustn't make a sound. With that he crept over to the bedroom door and went silently down the stairs.

The next moment all hell broke loose. Doreen could hear her dad shouting and her mam sobbing. Sam said nothing. Frightened, Doe ran down the stairs and into the front room. Emily was stood by the fireplace; Sam over near the window. Jim was in a rage turning from one to the other. Doreen could see that Sam was inching towards the front door. When Jim turned again to vent his fury on Emily, Sam saw his chance. He darted for the door, quickly opened it and ran out into the night. Jim, determined that he wouldn't get away, went after him, closely followed by his wife and daughter. Before he reached the end of the road, Sam stumbled and fell. It was Jim's opportunity. Before Sam could get up Jim had launched his attack, kicking his opponent viciously as he struggled to get to his feet. Not satisfied, Jim threw a barrage of punches, Sam putting up his arms to defend himself the best that he could. By now the neighbours, hearing the commotion, had come out into the street to see what was going on. Doreen was still in shock, not fully realising why her dad and Sam were fighting. Emily was distraught, screaming at Jim to stop. Yet her husband was like a man possessed, determined to inflict as much damage on his rival as he possibly could.

Emily pleaded with her neighbours to stop the fight but no one would intervene, especially as Jim had the upper hand. They knew of her affair with Sam and believed that he was getting what he deserved. Yet Jim's attack, though vicious, was too frenzied. His punches were wild and most missed their mark, or were blocked by Sam's long arms. Bending low, Sam finally evaded a couple of Jim's swinging hooks and drove up hard into his body. Caught off balance, Jim was knocked to the floor. Desperate to escape, Sam ran out on to Syndall Street and down towards Hyde Road. Back on his feet, Jim raced after him. Doreen and Emily, trying hard to keep up, caught a glimpse of

Jim as he disappeared into Richmond Street. Stopping at the corner, there was no sign of either man.

"Mam! Mam! What's happening? Why is Dad so angry? Where is he? Is he going to be all right?"

Finally, Emily realised that the three adults weren't the only ones involved in this debacle. She paused, wondering how she would be able to explain what was going on. Choosing to ignore her daughter's questions, Emily tried to appear as calm as possible.

"Doe, I think it's best for us to go home and wait for your dad."

"No," insisted Doreen. "He might need our help. We have to find him."

Reluctantly, her mam agreed.

"All right. We'll walk towards Hyde Road. Perhaps he headed down there."

As they were about to set off, Doe noticed Jim emerging from the gloom of the alley that ran behind the 'Richmond'. Concerned, she ran towards him.

"Are you all right, Dad?"

Jim was bleeding from the mouth and he had blood all over the front of his shirt. Yet there seemed far too much for it to have come from his mouth alone and he didn't seem to be cut anywhere else. Doreen assumed that it could only have come from Sam.

"Yes, I'm fine," confirmed Jim. "Come on love, we're going home."

Emily had waited on the corner when Doe had run over to her dad. Now she was unable to hold back the tears as Jim, holding his daughter's hand, walked past her without a word or a backward glance. Arriving at 17 Bright Avenue, the front door was still wide open. Entering the front room, Jim shut it behind them. About half an hour later, there was a knock on the front door. Doreen, sat on the sofa next to her dad, looked at him expectantly, but he ignored it. Now washed and changed, he continued to dab at the cut on his mouth with the end of a damp cloth. After a short pause, there was a further, tentative tap on the door and the sound of Emily's voice penetrating the silence from outside.

"Jim, let me in."

"Go to hell!"

"Jim, please. We need to talk."

"There's nothing to talk about. Piss off with your fancy man!"

There was silence. Finally, Emily spoke once more, her voice sounding a deep note of resignation.

"I need my things, Jim."

"Then come back tomorrow."

The minutes passed and Doreen knew that her mam had gone away. It wasn't what she had wanted. She wished that her dad had opened the door and had let Emily back into the house, but now realised that the prospect of them becoming a happy family once more, was becoming increasingly unlikely.

Sat beside her, Jim began to cry. The young girl was shocked. She thought that men never cried. She was confused and upset. Alternating between angry curses directed against Emily and Sam and uncontrolled sobbing that convulsed his body in pain and agony, Jim was in an awful state. As Doreen desperately tried to comfort him, Jim finally realised how shocked and afraid she must be. Having regained some semblance of composure, he turned to his daughter.

"You need to go up to bed now, Doe. It's very late."

"What about you?"

"I'll be up later."

"I'm not leaving you on your own. You're upset. I'm staying here with you," insisted Doreen.

Touched by her concern, Jim began to feel guilty. He realised that he should have dealt with matters differently. Fully aware that his wife had cheated on him, there was no need to take Doe upstairs to bed as an excuse to catch Emily out. By asking for her silence, he had secured his daughter's complicity in the night's events. It was wrong to have put a child through that experience, forcing Doreen to witness the distressing scenes between her parents.

"Okay Doe, but you need to lie down on the sofa and try to get some sleep."

Doreen laid down and Jim put a cover over her. She closed her eyes and heard him moving about. Finally, he went into the kitchen where she heard him break out into uncontrollable sobbing. Exhausted, Doe finally fell asleep.

She was woken by the sound of voices coming from the kitchen. They were speaking quietly, so she was unable to make out what was being said. Sitting up, Doreen looked over to the clock and could see that it was ten to nine. All thoughts of going out to play with her friends, were abandoned. The young girl wanted answers. What was happening between her mam and dad? Walking through to the kitchen she saw Jim talking to their neighbour, George Pickford.

"Hello Doe," said George.

Jim turned round. Doreen could see that his lip was still swollen and furthermore, although it hadn't been apparent the night before, one of his eyes was almost closed and black and blue.

"Do you want some milk, love?" he asked.

"Yes, please."

Jim turned back to George.

"I'll come round to you and Mary when I've seen to Doe. I won't be long."

Nodding, George left.

"Where's Mam?"

"She's okay. She's next door."

Doreen was pleased. She had gone to sleep worrying that her mam was all alone and outside in the dark.

"Can I go next door to see her?"

"Yes, but only after you've had a wash and something to eat."

His words were encouraging, for Doe could see that he had no desire to stop her from seeing her mam. She began to hope that everything would be all right. Her mam and dad were going to be friends once more. Pleased, Doreen went to kiss her dad, but he pulled away.

"Sorry, love. I'm still a bit sore."

It wasn't long before Jim told her that she could go to see Emily. Knocking at the Pickfords, the door was opened by her mam. Doe flung her arms around her and gave her a squeeze, before they walked down the steps and into the back yard. Emily's eyes were red and swollen. She had been crying.

"When are you coming home, Mam?"

Emily hesitated, then answered slowly and deliberately.

"Me and your dad are going to sit down and sort things out. You mustn't get upset, everything's going to be fine."

Doreen tried to remain hopeful, especially as there was no sign of Sam. She hated him more than ever. Life had been fine before he turned up. It was his fault that her mam and dad had fallen out.

"Can I stay with you?"

The question reflected Doe's belief that her presence would help to ensure that her parents stayed together.

"No, Doe. It's not a matter for children. We have to deal with it on our own. You go and play with your friends and I'll see you later."

Doreen was disappointed. She would have no opportunity to influence her parents' decision and began to have the unpleasant feeling that her family was falling apart. Back home, it wasn't long before Jim went to fetch her mam. Alone, Doe closed her eyes and prayed for a reconciliation between her parents. When they returned, Jim told Doe that she had to go out to play. Just like Emily, he insisted that they needed to be alone. Doe was to return at dinner time, in order to see her mam.

Collecting her balls and jacks, Doreen went to call for Sandra. She had little interest in play however and as the time dragged by, it seemed like dinner time would never arrive. When it finally did, Doe rushed back home. Entering the kitchen, Jim was on his own.

"Where's Mam?"

"You know where she is; next door."

Doreen's heart sank. It wasn't the news that she had wanted to hear.

"Go round and see her," continued Jim. "She's expecting you."

Emily had been looking out for her daughter's return and was waiting at the door for her.

"Why aren't you at home?" asked Doreen.

"There's still a few things to sort out, so I'll be staying away for a bit longer," replied Emily.

"But who's going to be here to meet me after school?"

After Sam's arrival, she was used to no one being there for her, but Doe hoped that the observation would put pressure on her mam. It seemed reasonable to make Emily feel guilty, if it resulted in her coming home. Yet it was a simple tactic and one that reflected the naivety of a young girl, who lacked understanding of the complexities of the situation that Emily found herself in. It wasn't going to be that easy to get her family back together.

"Your dad will be around until his decorating work starts up again and I'll be seeing you too. I promise," said Emily.

"But you won't be with me and dad at home. It's like I've lost you. I never see Jimmy anymore and now I won't see you."

"You will. I've told you before, Doe. You're growing up. You're not a baby anymore. I'm sure that you can manage on your own for a short time after school, if necessary."

The conversation was proving awkward but Emily was rescued by the sound of Jim's voice calling over to his daughter. Relieved, she sought to bring matters to a close.

"Go on, Doe. You'd best go back to your dad. I'll see you soon."

"But aren't you staying here, at the Pickfords?"

"No, I can't. They haven't got room for me. Last night they were doing me a favour. Don't worry, I've got somewhere else to go. I'll see you soon."

Emily bent down and kissed her daughter goodbye. With a heavy heart, Doreen went back to her dad.

Chapter 21

It was three weeks before Doreen saw Emily again. She had been playing at Sandra's after coming home from school and Glenn Pickford had turned up to tell her that her dad wanted her to come home. Glenn explained that her mam was waiting to see her.

Doreen rushed back home with Glenn. She was excited and hopeful that her mam had dad were now getting back together. Running down Bright Avenue and approaching her front door, the young girl was in for a shock. There, stood with Emily, was Sam. It was the last thing that she had expected.

Emily smiled at her and held her arms out to her daughter. Doe hesitated. She could see the large suitcase that was at Sam's feet. It was clear that her mam hadn't come home; she had collected her clothes and was leaving.

Emily took the initiative and moved forward. She attempted to embrace her daughter, but Doreen pulled away and stood alone; angry and upset.

"Why are you leaving with him?" she asked, pointing at Sam.

"Doe, when you get older, you'll understand."

"Why can't you send him away and come back to me and Dad? This is your home. It's not with him."

Doreen started to cry. Moving towards her, Emily crouched down and wiped away her daughter's tears.

"Doe, I have to go, but you can come too. Do you want to come and live with me and Sam?"

Doreen stopped crying. She stood erect and proud.

"No! I don't like him! I'm going to stay with my dad!"

Shocked by her daughter's response, it was now Emily's turn to cry. For a moment, Doreen was pleased. She wanted her mam to feel upset too.

"Go with him. I don't care."

She wished that she hadn't said it. Doe did care and she desperately wanted her mam to stay. Yet she knew that Emily wouldn't give Sam up. Still crying, her mam got to her feet and started to walk away. Stubborn as ever, Doreen didn't say goodbye. But inside she hurt so much. She wanted to run after her mam and beg her to stay, but Emily had upset her. Doe felt betrayed. Since Sam had arrived, her mam had put him first. If she truly loved her daughter, then she wouldn't have left her to go out with him and torn their family apart. Doreen despised Sam. He had always frightened her. His staring eyes; his shifty behaviour. Why couldn't her mam see it? Why had she deserted them for him?

It was four months before Doe saw Emily again. She had left her job at the cheese factory and no one knew where she had gone. Doreen still didn't understand why her parents couldn't be back together. Many years later, when she had learned of Jim's infidelity in the War, she thought that he was a hypocrite. Yet perhaps he had been prepared to forgive Emily and it was her mam, wanting to be with Sam, who was to blame. Doreen never knew the exact details of the situation and her parents never discussed it with her. She just had to learn to get on with it.

Jim and Doreen certainly did. Just like her mam and Sam, Jim went to the pub almost every night. Doreen though was adamant that she wouldn't be left on her own and Jim made sure that she wasn't. He paid Joyce Brown to sit with her and if Joyce wasn't available and he couldn't find anyone else, he wouldn't go out. Joyce would stay until ten o'clock, at which time she would walk with Doe to the 'Richmond'. Doreen would pop her head into the vault, her dad would see her and then he and Doe would return home. Jim's friends said that they could set their watches by the time of Doreen's arrival and they were often amused by the sight of her cheery face poking around the door. Much merriment was caused on the night that Jim still had a full pint on the table.

"No, Dad. Finish your beer," Doe had said. "You've paid good money for that, so get it drunk!"

Jim duly did as he was told.

Doreen loved to walk home with her dad from the 'Richmond', especially when he was a little drunk. Jim was always merry. Doe had never seen him turn nasty in drink. Often, he would put her on his shoulders and walk back to Bright Avenue singing:

♪When the thunder crashed and the lightning flashed, where can I be. Oh, my lonely soul, set me free♪

The neighbours weren't as appreciative of Jim's efforts. They would open their bedroom windows and shout at him to shut up. This only made him sing louder. Doe thought it was hilarious and would laugh continuously until they got back to the house. Yet the period without her mam proved difficult. Doreen was having to grow up before her time. No longer sheltered from the harsh realities of the world, she was coming to realise what an unforgiving place it could be.

Doreen had lost Rex but she hadn't been touched by a death in her own family or those of her friends. This changed when Jane Harris's grandmother died shortly after Emily had left. Doe knew Jane's gran well. She lived on Richmond Street, a few doors down from her family. May, Jane's mam, kept an eye on her, but she was proudly independent. She seemed huge to Doreen and had a gruff voice and 'whiskers' on her face. When she had first seen her, Doe was convinced that she was a man. Frequently ill and with her heavy frame, Jane's gran slept in the front room, her bed placed under the window. Often, when she was confined to bed, Doreen and Jane would go and sit with her and play dominoes or cards. They would gamble for pennies until May turned up at nine-thirty to prepare her mother for bed and then the girls would be taken home. In the winter, the house was dark and cold. There was a big black range in the front room, but it only ever contained a tiny fire. Doreen remembered the old lady telling her off for putting too many pieces of coal from the scuttle on to the fire. Never happy to receive a reprimand and hating the cold and the dark, Doe rarely enjoyed her time there. Nevertheless, Jane was her friend and Doreen knew that she didn't like going on her own.

The two girls had been present on the evening that Jane's gran had passed away. They had been playing cards with her but she had seemed unable to focus on the game. Finally, the cards had slipped out of her hands, her head had rolled sideways against the pillow and they could hear strange, gurgling noises coming from her throat. Worried, Jane asked Doreen to stay, whilst she ran to get May. Doreen followed her to the front door and held it open, watching as Jane made her way down Richmond Street. She was scared to be inside, so edged a little way beyond the door. Jane was soon running back with her mam who, realising the seriousness of the situation, told the girls to run to the doctor. The girls quickly reached his house and brought him back. May then told the girls to go home.

The next day Jim confirmed that Jane's gran had died and asked Doreen not to go to the house, as her family needed time to mourn. Doe respected his wishes but whilst her dad was out, Jane arrived and asked Doreen to accompany her whilst she paid her respects to her gran. When Jane explained what this involved, Doe wasn't at all keen on the idea. Yet it was clear that Jane's mam was insistent that her daughter should go. Realising that Jane was afraid to go alone, generous as ever, Doreen agreed to go with her.

Half an hour later, the girls returned to Richmond Street. Accessing the alley at the side of the 'Richmond', Jane took Doreen down to the back entrance of her gran's house. There were several people already in the kitchen. Jane's older sister, Elizabeth, was there, as well as May and some of Jane's aunts and uncles.

May said hello to Doreen and took the girls through to the front room. The bed had now gone from in front of the window. In its place was a coffin, raised off the ground on a table that was hidden by a large sheet extending to the floor. At either end of the coffin were placed two candles on large candlesticks. They were alight; their flames flickering. Doreen had never seen a dead body before and hesitated as Jane and May moved towards the coffin. Taking a deep breath, she stepped forward to join them. Doreen was shocked. The coffin seemed so thin. The body seemed so too. How could that be? How had they been able to make Jane's gran so small, when she had always been so big? And when Doreen looked at the old lady's features, she seemed unrecognisable; her face so pale and full of anguish. Closing her eyes and lowering her head, Doreen's bearing appeared reverential, yet in reality reflected her desperation to get outside. When May finally told them that it was time to return to the kitchen, Doe felt relieved. Not waiting for Jane, she turned and walked quickly out of the room.

It had been a truly traumatic experience. Doreen hoped that she would never see a dead body again. It wasn't something that she would easily forget and it was to bring her nightmares for weeks to come.

Chapter 22

Not only had Doreen lost contact with her mam, but since he had gone to live with Val, she had also seen very little of Our Kid. With only Jim at home, Doe felt that the situation was unlikely to change. Jimmy still didn't get on with his dad and so she expected that he would stay away. The situation was made more difficult when she heard that Val's family had moved to Denton. This meant that there was no opportunity for Doreen to visit Jimmy herself.

Doe had remembered Emily's conversation with Our Kid, where she had warned him that the Holdens were notorious petty criminals. She had advised him to go back to Valerie and not fall under the influence of Val's family. Jimmy hadn't listened and it now seemed that he was ignoring his sister too.

Shortly after the death of Jane's gran, Doreen found out that there would be no chance of Jimmy coming to see her. She had learned the news from her dad. Jim wasn't a great reader of the local newspapers, confining himself to the sport on the back pages. He was therefore surprised when he and Doe had gone to Terry O'Hara's Ironmongers, his daughter waiting outside as usual and Terry had asked him how Jimmy was coping. Jim looked bemused.

"Strangeways. How's he getting on?" continued Terry.

"I don't know what you mean," replied Jim.

It was now Terry's turn to look confused.

"It was in the *Evening News* a couple of nights ago. He got two years for breaking and entering. So did two of the Holdens. He was going out with one of the daughters, wasn't he?"

"Yes," said Jim, "but we've not seen him for a long time. I didn't know."

When Jim came out of the shop, he didn't tell Doreen straight away. He knew that she would be upset. Arriving home, he asked her if she wanted a brew. Doe was surprised. During the day, she dealt with the food and drinks, her dad only making them a brew in the morning before she went to school. When Doreen told him that she would do it, he declined her offer.

"No, Doe. I can manage. Sit down."

Doreen sensed that something was wrong. She had noticed that Jim seemed distracted on the way back from seeing Terry. Nevertheless, she sat quietly at the table whilst Jim got on with making the drinks. Having finished, he brought over the mugs, placed them on the table and sat on the chair beside her.

"It's Our Kid, love. He's in Strangeways."

Doreen was silent. Jim paused, allowing the news time to sink in before continuing.

"He's been done for burglary along with two of Val's family."

"Mam told him that the Holdens were no good. He didn't listen to her, did he?"

"No, love. Obviously, he didn't."

Jim had no intention of criticising his son. He had no right to do so and Doe wouldn't have let him get away with it. Furthermore, he knew that his daughter was upset and so attempted to offer her some semblance of reassurance.

"It's not so bad in there. I managed all right. You shouldn't worry about him. He won't be in prison as long as I was."

"But I'm never going to see him," replied Doreen, with a sigh of resignation. "Val doesn't want him to come round and now he's locked away."

"No, he'll be out before too long and then he'll come to see you."

Doe was unconvinced. The news had come as a real shock and the realisation that she wouldn't be able to see Our Kid, was proving too much. Yet another disaster had befallen her and she was feeling overwhelmed. Getting out of her chair, Doreen threw her arms around Jim and started to cry.

"You won't leave me, will you Dad? Everybody's leaving me. I don't want to be on my own."

Jim had a lump in his throat. He felt her little body struggling to breathe, as she gulped in mouthfuls of air between her heartfelt sobs. He squeezed her softly.

"We're all right, Doe. You and me. We're getting along just fine. Don't get upset now."

Gradually, comforted by Jim's reassuring presence, Doreen began to calm down.

"Come on love, drink this tea I've made. Don't waste it."

Doe slowly removed her arms from around him and sat back down. She wiped her eyes and took a sip from the tea. It was awful.

"Dad!" she said, with a hint of a rebuke. "What have you done with this tea?"

As she allowed herself a slight chuckle, Jim felt relieved. The worst now seemed to be over.

"I think we'll have steak and kidney pudding and chips from Chiappe's for tea. What do you think, Doe?"

Knowing it was Doe's favourite, Jim hoped that his suggestion would cheer her up further. He wasn't disappointed.

"Yes, please Dad," replied Doreen, eagerly.

The young girl was becoming resilient. Although she was upset about Jimmy, she accepted that she would have to wait until she saw him again. At least she still had her dad and as he had said, the two of them were getting along just fine. Doe hoped and prayed that it was a situation that would continue.

Chapter 23

One Saturday morning in the middle of June, Jim asked Doreen to fetch some paraffin for the Tilley lamps. The shop was in Longsight, about a mile from their home. Doe had the can in her hand and was swinging it merrily as she made her way down Stockport Road. She knew that once filled, the can would be far heavier on the way back and her desire to delay that situation, encouraged her to dilly-dally along the way. Doreen took time to look in the shop windows and was nipping down the side streets in order to see what lay behind.

Progressing slowly towards her destination, Doe discovered a large house and gardens. It was surrounded by a high meshed fence, in front of which were iron railings. As she walked alongside the fence, Doreen looked over and saw a head peeping out from the middle of some bushes. Believing that it was safe to come out, a boy emerged into the open. Doe could see that he was of a similar age to herself. He had brown hair and was wearing short trousers and a grey pullover. His hands and face were dirty, obviously as a result of him scrambling around in the bushes. Doreen stopped and the boy moved towards her.

"Hello, I'm Robert. I'm ten."

"So am I," replied Doreen. "Do you live here?"

"Yes."

"You must be rich to live in a big house like this."

"No. I'm an orphan. This is a children's home."

Doreen shuddered. She'd heard so many stories about how the children were mistreated in such places; beaten and made to scrub floors all day long. Many of her friends had told her that their parents had threatened to send them there if they misbehaved.

"Do you have to scrub floors?" asked Doreen.

"Yes," replied the boy.

"Oh," said Doe, hesitating. "Do they beat you?"

"Yes, if I'm bad."

"And how are you bad?"

"Sometimes, I don't do as I'm told."

"Why do you do that?"

"Because they pick on you. They blame you for things you haven't done."

"I've been told that if you're bad in a children's home, then you don't get anything to eat."

"That's right," confirmed Robert.

"Are you hungry?" asked Doe.

"Yes."

Doreen was full of questions. It was almost like an interrogation, but she was fascinated to learn more about life in a children's home. She wanted to find out if it really was as bad as she had been led to believe.

"Why are you outside, when no one else is?"

"Because I'm going to run away," explained Robert.

"Where to?"

"I don't know. I'm going to get over the fence and then I'm going to run off."

It seemed to Doreen that Robert didn't have much of a plan.

"How are you going to climb the fence? It's too high."

"I've been collecting some bricks and rocks and putting them in the bushes when we've been allowed out. I'll make them into a pile big enough to help me climb over."

"Oh."

Doreen now realised why she had seen him emerging from the bushes.

"I'm waiting until it's dark," he continued. "There are too many windows for people to look out of. They'll see me if I try to do it in the day."

Touched by Robert's plight, Doe felt the need to help him get away.

"You can come to my house," she offered. "My dad will let you come and stay with us."

"What about your mam?" asked Robert.

"She doesn't live with us anymore."

"Oh. Where do you live?"

"Just off Syndall Street, at 17 Bright Avenue."

"Which way is that?"

Doreen pointed.

"It's about a mile. You follow Stockport Road to just before the ABC and Syndall Street is on your right."

"I'll see you soon then," said Robert. "I'll come tonight."

Doreen said goodbye and went back to Stockport Road and on to the paraffin shop. The man on the counter was friendly and having seen her before, chatted away as he pumped out the paraffin into her can. Doe however, wasn't responding. She was thinking about Robert. The man stopped to ask her if everything was all right. In the past, she had always been so cheerful and now it seemed as if something was bothering her.

"You're not listening to me, are you?"

"I'm sorry," replied Doreen. "I was thinking."

"What about?"

"The children's home down the road."

"Why?"

"I spoke to a boy. He was really unhappy. He told me that they don't give him any food, make him scrub the floors and beat him. I'm going to speak to my dad to see if we can help him."

"You don't need to worry your head about that love," said the man. "They get well looked after in there nowadays. Not like when I was growing up. It's a lot easier now."

"What do you mean, easier?" asked Doreen, who was clearly not convinced.

"Well, they get three meals a day and a roof over their head. Clothes on their back and they get some pocket money."

Doe nodded, took the paraffin, paid for it and walked towards the door. As she left, the man called out to her.

"Remember, kids in children's homes are well looked after. Get straight back home. Your dad will be wondering where you are."

The man needn't have worried for Doreen was expecting Robert to arrive that night and was hurrying back in order to tell her dad. She knew that the man had been trying to reassure her; stop her from worrying about Robert. She didn't believe him though. How could the children be well looked after, if they were beaten and forced to scrub floors? It explained why Robert was so unhappy. Why would he have lied to her, if he was being treated so well?

When Doreen got back, her dad wasn't there. He had gone to price a wallpapering job on Hyde Road. Glenn Pickford was playing in the back yard and told her that Jim had asked his mam to keep an eye on her when she returned. Doe stored the paraffin and went in to see Mrs Pickford and asked her what she thought about children's homes. Doreen told her what both Robert and the shopkeeper had said, but didn't mention that she had offered Robert a refuge. Mary told her not to worry and that she could be sure that Robert was being well looked after. Doreen went out to play jacks with Glenn and shortly after her dad returned, nipping in to see Mary to thank her for keeping an eye on Doe.

Back in the house, Doreen began to tell Jim about Robert. It seemed however, that Mary had already told him about her concerns. Her dad was therefore quick to reassure her about Robert's situation.

"Doe, a lot of kids in children's homes are in there because they're bad. They're always in trouble with the police and because their parents can't control them, they have to be put in a home for their own good."

If Jim thought this would end the conversation, he was wrong. Doreen wasn't convinced.

"But that's not true for Robert. His mam and dad are both dead. That's why he's in there."

"Well, he must be unusual," replied Jim.

"He's going to try to escape, Dad. He's going to climb over the fence tonight."

"He won't be able to, Doe. They check on them all the time. The staff take registers like at school, so as to make sure that they're all in there. Once he's gone to bed, he's got no chance of getting out of the building."

Jim hoped that the idea of the impossibility of escape would result in Doe being resigned to accepting that Robert would have to stay there. But this was his daughter and when there was a cause to fight for, as there had been with Rex, she was like a dog with a bone. She would not let go. Doreen was convinced that Robert would escape and her job was to get Jim to agree that he could live with them. At ten years old, the legal and practical realities of the situation meant nothing to her. Robert needed their help, so they had to give it.

"If he does get away, can he live with us?"

"We'll see," said Jim, convinced that there was no chance that the lad would be arriving any time soon.

"You won't make him go back, will you?" asked Doreen, looking straight into his eyes.

Jim was finding it hard. His daughter was putting him on the spot and he hated to disappoint or upset her.

"I don't know. I'd have to meet him. See what he's like."

"Please, Dad. He's nice. Let him stay with us."

Jim tried to make Doreen realise that even if Robert did get away and find them, it wasn't a decision that he alone could make.

"You don't understand, Doe. It's the law. The court says that he has to live in the children's home. I don't think that they would allow him to stay here. We'd get in trouble with the police and you know that I have to be careful now. Because he has no parents or any other family to look after him, the children's home is there to care for him. It's their job and they know what they're doing."

"But they've put him in with all those kids you said were naughty. It's not fair. Why should he be punished as well? Why does he have to be beaten and clean floors like them, when he hasn't done anything wrong?"

Jim knew that he couldn't provide a convincing answer. She was as sharp as a tack. He was proud to have such a clever daughter. He joked to his friends that in the brains department she certainly didn't take after him. But at times like these, he was thoroughly frustrated. Aware that he couldn't placate her, he also knew that she was right.

"I'm sorry, love. We'll just have to wait and see what happens. Why don't you go out and play."

Doreen was satisfied. Her dad hadn't said no and she still believed that she could convince him to allow Robert to live with them. All that now remained, was for her new friend to make good his escape and get himself to Bright Avenue.

That evening, Jim hadn't gone to the 'Richmond'. After nine o'clock he suggested that Doe should go to bed. She refused, convinced that Robert would be knocking on the door at any moment and determined to be there when her dad answered it.

Yet the knock didn't come and as the hands on the clock moved around to ten, Doreen was starting to get sleepy. She had laid down on the sofa in the front room and was listening to the radio. Her eyes were beginning to close.

"Come on, Doe. You need to go to bed," said Jim.

"Not yet, Dad."

"Why not? You're tired."

"I'm waiting for Robert."

"He's not coming, love. He would've been here by now. It's late at night. They'll have missed him and gone out looking for him. He'll have been found and taken back. No doubt he'll be sound asleep in bed by now and that's where you should be."

Tired out, the young girl went reluctantly up to bed. She dreamed of Robert living at her house and going to school with him. But no knock had come to the door and the next morning at breakfast, she realised that he wasn't coming. Two days later Jim showed her a story in the *Evening News*. He had got the newspaper from Mary Pickford. A small headline said 'Child returned safely to Children's Home'. The article stated that the boy had gone missing but was found on Stockport Road and had been returned to the home. It didn't mention Robert by name but Mary, Jim and Doe, all assumed that it was him.

Unknown to her dad, Doreen went with Jane Harris to the home on several occasions over the next few weeks, but Robert was never there. On the first Monday of the summer holidays, Jim having arranged for May Harris to keep an eye on Doe, they tried again. This time Robert was there, but so were many other children who were also playing outside in the grounds. Robert was quite a distance from the railings and so Doreen had to shout over to him. It took several attempts to grab his attention but finally he noticed her. As he walked towards them however, Doe and Jane were approached by a woman. Reaching the fence, she looked sternly at the girls and told them to go away and stop annoying the children. Doreen said nothing and she and Jane began to walk away along the pavement. Satisfied, the woman turned back towards the house, not realising that the girls were making their way around to the rear of the property. Doe hoped that Robert would realise where they were going. He did and shortly after they'd reached their destination, Robert turned up at

the back fence. Doreen introduced him to Jane and then asked him about the story in the newspaper.
"Were you the one they picked up on Stockport Road, Robert?"
"Yes."
"You're never going to get out of here, are you?"
"I'll keep trying. I'm not giving up," insisted Robert.
"Good," replied Doreen, clearly impressed by his defiance.
"Do you buy comics?" asked Robert, changing the subject.
"Yes."
"Can you bring me some when you've read them, please? We don't get any."
"Of course."
Robert told her that the children came out into the grounds every afternoon between five and half-past. If she came with the comics, he would keep an eye out for her and they could then meet at the back, out of sight of the staff. Doreen said that they would see him the next day.

As promised, the girls returned but Robert wasn't there. It was the same on Wednesday. Unable to go on Thursday, the girls decided to try again on Friday. Finally, Robert was there. He saw the girls and made his way round to the back. Doreen and Jane gave him old copies of the *Beano* and *Dandy*. He put them inside a jacket he was wearing, safely into a deep pocket.

For the next four months, almost up to Christmas, the girls managed to see him at five o'clock on most Wednesday afternoons. They would take him their old comics and Doreen would use some of the money that her dad had given her, to buy chocolates and sweets for him. Then suddenly, he was no longer there. The girls shouted over to the children near the front fence asking them if they had seen Robert. Strangely, none of them seemed to know him, even after they had described what he looked like. The girls went back for the next three weeks, but Robert never reappeared. Jane became fed up of going there but Doe, now feeling confident enough to go alone, still made occasional visits to give comics and sweets to some of the other children. In her own way, Doreen was trying to make their lives a little better. It was a way in which she could avoid dwelling on how difficult her own family situation had become, with her separation from Emily and Our Kid. Eventually, the staff at the home were on the lookout for her. It seemed that they were unhappy at her generosity towards the children. On Doe's final visit, a woman seized comics from two of the children she had given them to and ripped them up in front of her, whilst another member of staff threatened to call the police. The young girl was shocked; unable to understand how anyone could be so horrible. Doreen was grateful that she wasn't living in a children's home. For all her difficulties, she still had her dad and her freedom.

Chapter 24

On the last Monday of November, the fourth-year pupils at Ross Place School were called to a special morning assembly with the headmaster, Mr Roberts. He told them that it was a very important week as they would all be doing their eleven plus exams. Sandra Cooper turned to Doreen.

"What's the eleven plus?" she asked.

"Shush," answered Doe. "I'll tell you later."

Knowing that they weren't allowed to talk in assembly, Doreen didn't want either of them to get into trouble. Mr Roberts led the prayers and the children were told to file out of the hall. As they were returning to their classroom, Doe explained to Sandra that her gran had told her all about the exams, just before her mam had left with Sam. Their purpose was to determine where children would be sent next year and if they passed, they would be going to the grammar school.

"Oh," said Sandra, "but why haven't we been told anything about it?"

"I don't know."

Back in the classroom, the children were told that they had to go to Mr Barclay's room. Arriving there they found papers on all the desks. Mr Barclay explained that it was an English test and it would be timed. He told them that they had one hour to read through the passages and questions on the paper and then write their answers. It was all rather daunting. Mr Barclay was known to be very strict and he made it clear that there was to be no talking, no looking at anyone else's answers and no copying. Anyone caught cheating wouldn't be allowed to finish the test and their exam paper wouldn't be marked. The children had never experienced anything like this before and Doe felt nervous.

She needn't have been. As the exam started, she found the tasks easy and finished quite early. Working at the back of the room, Doreen could see that three other children were also sat up and had put their pens down. Mr Barclay told them that they should check their answers for any mistakes and then sit quietly until everyone else had finished.

Having found the first exam a positive experience, Doe was confidently looking forward to the following tests in maths, mental arithmetic and spelling. Her friends however, were eager for the exams to be over. As yet, none of them seemed to realise the full implications the tests would have in terms of their future education.

Having gone back to their normal lessons, the pupils were called out individually to return to Mr Barclay's room, where an elderly woman was sat waiting for them. Telling them to sit down, she then proceeded to ask them to spell certain words. Doreen found it strange. If asked to spell the word by writing it down, she felt confident, but she was told that she wasn't allowed to do that and would have to recite the spelling. As the first few words were easy, Doe became more relaxed and had little difficulty. The woman then asked her to spell scissors. Doreen did so, but felt that her answer was wrong and asked if she could have another go. The woman smiled and told her not to worry; that she had already done splendidly and everything was fine.

Two days later, the class had to sit their maths exam. Once again, they went to Mr Barclay's room. They now knew all about the rules of the exams and settled down quickly. Maths was Doe's favourite subject and she finished well before anyone else. Checking through her answers, she was confident that she had done well. The afternoon saw the final exam, the students being called into Mr Barclay's room individually to be tested on their ability in mental arithmetic. Met by the same woman as before, Doreen immediately felt at ease. She breezed through the test and was soon sent back to her class.

With the exams over Doe and her friends quickly forgot about them, especially as they were told that they wouldn't get their results for some considerable time. Recently, life had been getting better for Doreen. At the end of October, she had finally seen Emily again. She had turned up alone to visit her daughter on a Wednesday evening. Jim invited her in but said that he would go to the 'Richmond' and leave them to talk. He told Doe to come and fetch him when Emily had gone.

Jim's departure was a clear indication to his daughter that there was little chance of a reconciliation between her parents. Doreen was pleased to see her mam but found it hard to welcome her back with open arms. Emily had hurt her; she had put her 'fancy man' before her family. Doe was filled with anger and frustration. She found herself wanting to make Emily feel guilty and see some evidence that her mam regretted her behaviour. Sat together at the kitchen table, it was Emily who made the first move.

"Are you okay, Doe? Are you and your dad getting along all right?"

"Why ask? You're not bothered anyway."

"Don't be like that, Doe."

"Why not, it's true. You've not been to see me for ages. You promised that you would."

"I know love, but there's been a lot going on. It's difficult."

"Like what?"

"You wouldn't understand. Adult things."

"Oh. Important enough for you to forget about having a daughter then!"

The quick and acerbic comment made Emily realise just how much Doreen had grown up since she had left. Yet what could she say to give her any satisfaction? Emily knew that her daughter, even though she would never admit it, was hurting deep inside because of what she, her mam, had done.

"Come on, Doe. I can't change what's happened, but I'm here to try and make it up to you. I'm going to see you regularly from now on. I'll come round in the week before school and I'll try and help your dad out with your clothes and some spending money."

"Me and Dad are okay. We don't need your help. Give it to your 'fancy man'."

Doreen couldn't contain her anger. Just like at their previous meeting, she had rejected Emily's olive branch. Momentarily, she panicked. Had she gone too far? Would her mam simply walk away? When Emily had left with Sam, Doreen had told her to go; had said that she didn't care. Until now, she hadn't seen her mam for months. Doe realised that she was desperate for it not to happen again. Fortunately, Emily was determined to win her over.

"You've every right to be angry, Doe and I'm here to say I'm sorry. Please give me the chance to make it up to you."

Relieved at her mam's response and wanting to believe that it was true, Doreen got out of her chair and moved around the table. She hugged Emily and kissed her on the cheek. Both of them began to cry.

True to her word, Emily came every day before school and when Doreen told her about the eleven plus exams, she was pleased that her daughter felt that she had done well. It was Saturday morning, weeks later, when Doe had almost forgotten about the exams, that the letter containing her results arrived. Her dad, opening the post at the kitchen table, hesitated as he rechecked the words on the page. Doreen, drinking her milk, watched him curiously.

"You've done it!" he exclaimed. "You're going to the grammar school!"

Jim was proud and delighted. He hugged his daughter and ran out of the house. Doreen could hear him as he excitedly and noisily went around the neighbours, letter in hand, to show them that his daughter had passed the eleven plus. His generation had never been given the opportunity. There was no chance of sitting exams or gaining qualifications and Jim knew that he wouldn't have passed them anyway. He was amazed that he could have a daughter who was so clever. When Emily arrived on Monday morning, she was just as pleased. Yet by then, Doe had serious misgivings about her success.

After hearing the news, Doreen had waited to read through the letter herself. It contained details of the schools that she could apply to go to. Armed with the list, Doe went to see her friends. None of them had passed. Their list of schools was completely different. Doreen realised that she would be alone and facing an uncertain future. Dismissing her fears, Jim insisted that she would make new friends, but as the summer of 1960 approached, Doe began to regret passing the eleven plus. Whilst her friends became excited about going to their new school together, she felt a sense of isolation. Emily, more understanding than her dad, constantly reassured her. She told Doreen that she would definitely make new friends, as many girls were in the same situation and wouldn't know anyone else. Emily reminded her that she always had lots of friends. She was generous and warm-hearted and other girls would see that and like her. And of course, she would still see her current friends after school, at weekends and in the holidays. She must cheer up. Everything would turn out fine.

Yet For Doreen, the last eighteen months hadn't been fine. Resigned to the fact that in September she would have to go to Manchester Girls Grammar, she hoped that her mam was right.

Chapter 25

In late July, just before the summer holidays began, Jim had some startling news for his daughter. It was early in the evening and he and Doreen were sat in the front room. Doe was in a good mood as she had just bought a copy of the new 'Fans Star Library' magazine. It was a special edition dedicated to Cliff Richard. Doreen idolised Cliff and was sure that she was in love with him. Jim was waiting for Joyce Brown to come and sit with Doe before going to the 'Richmond'. Engrossed in her magazine, Doreen hadn't noticed him shifting uneasily on the sofa. Finally, he broke his silence.

"Doe. I want to tell you something."

Engrossed in her magazine, Doreen continued to read.

"Doe," said Jim, a little louder.

"Yes?" she replied, still looking at a picture of Cliff.

"Just leave your magazine for a minute, love. It's important."

Doreen put it down and turned towards him.

"We're moving, love."

"What do you mean?"

"We're going to live somewhere else."

Doreen was shocked.

"Why? I don't want to. Where are we going?"

"You remember meeting Betty, don't you? Well, we're going to live with her."

"But why?"

Doe was confused. She didn't know Betty. She had only seen her on a couple of occasions and then just to say hello. In fact, it was the first time that her dad had ever mentioned her.

"Well," explained Jim, "Betty owns a big house and it has room enough for all of us. It's going to work out much cheaper, as we won't have to pay rent on this one anymore."

Doreen sensed that there was more to their proposed move than her dad was prepared to admit. Feeling apprehensive, she tried hard to persuade him to remain in Bright Avenue.

"I don't want to move. I'm near to all my friends. I've got to go to a school where I don't know anybody and now, you're taking me away from the friends I do have."

"No, love. Betty lives on Hyde Road. On the corner with Tiverton Place, next to the church. It's not far. You'll still be near all your friends."

"But I like this house. We're all right as we are; just the two of us. I don't want to live with anyone else. We won't have our own home anymore. Why do we need to move? Why do you want to share a house with someone else?"

Doreen was pressing hard for a proper explanation and Jim knew that she would persist until he had given her one. His relationship with Betty had become more serious, but aware of Doe's lingering desire for a reconciliation between her parents, he had avoided the difficult task of telling her. Unable to face her disappointment, he had prevaricated and misled his daughter. Jim had hoped that they would have already moved in with Betty, before Doreen found out about the true nature of their relationship. It was dishonest and cowardly behaviour; indicative of his desire to avoid any semblance of personal criticism.

Slowly and reluctantly, Jim tried to explain.

"I've known Betty for quite some time now. We've come to love one another and that's why I want us to go and live with her."

"But what about mam? She'll expect me to be here."

"Don't worry, Doe. You'll still see her."

"I'm not moving," insisted Doreen. "I'm staying here. I can look after myself. I do the washing, clean the house and cook for us. You can keep paying the rent and go and live at Betty's on your own."

Doe knew that it was impossible. She was too young for her father to agree and even if he could have, she would have been terrified to have been left in the house on her own. Nevertheless, she had to make a stand and impress upon her dad just how unhappy his news had made her. Doe had to hope that she could persuade him to forget the idea.

"You can still see Betty if we stay here. It won't make any difference."

It was a clever attempt to turn the tables on her dad, but he was having none of it.

"Don't be silly, Doe. I love Betty. I want to live with her. It's no different to your mam leaving here to go and live with Sam."

Hoping that his observation would impress upon Doreen that his proposal was reasonable, Jim was disappointed. His reference to Emily only convinced his daughter that he had set out to get himself a 'fancy woman', in order to get even with her. Doe's main concern was the fear that her dad would become just like Emily. She had put Sam before the interests of her daughter and Jim, by wanting them to move from Bright Avenue, was putting Betty's wishes before her own. Doreen knew that she was fighting a losing battle, but she still made one, last effort, to change Jim's mind.

"But I really, really, really don't want to move Dad," she pleaded.

"You'll understand when you're older, love. Everything will be fine, you'll see. Betty is really nice. You'll like her."

It was a cursory and somewhat dispassionate response and Jim's way of making clear to her that their discussion was at an end. Doreen felt an ominous sense of déjà vu. "You'll understand when you're older." Wasn't that what her mam had consistently told her after she had left with Sam? The fact was, that she didn't understand and felt that she never would. Why did her mam and dad seem so intent on destroying their family? Her brother had been driven out and ended up in prison and both her parents seemed intent on ignoring her, in order to give their affections to someone else. She had continued to hope that Emily and Jim would finally get back together. But now the home they had shared, to which her mam could return, had been abandoned. Furthermore, her dad had now taken up with someone else. The loss of Bright Avenue would prove symbolic. A line had been drawn in the sand and neither Emily or Jim had any desire to rebuild their relationship. Doreen finally had to face the reality that had been apparent since her mam had disappeared with Sam; but one she hadn't been prepared to accept. Her family was finished. Her old, happy life, would never return. Doe had no choice but to accept Jim's decision. She was only eleven years old. There was no alternative. She wasn't going to ask to live with her mam. Although Emily came to the house, Doe had no idea where she lived and Sam, with his staring eyes, scared her. Perhaps she would get on with Betty and surely her dad would make certain that everything was all right.

Chapter 26

Betty's house seemed huge. It was a large Victorian end of terrace that fronted on to Hyde Road and projected back along Tiverton Place. At first, Doreen thought that it was two houses, as it seemed to have two front doors. In Tiverton Place, the side of the house had a small wall along its length, with a gap leading to three steps that rose towards a solid looking door. At the front was a larger wall with five steps leading to the actual front door, which contained two glass panels. The front of the house was much taller than Bright Avenue. It had two huge brick bay windows on the ground and first floors, with a large dormer projecting from the roof, showing that the property had a large attic. Having lived in a two-up, two-down on Bright Avenue, Doe was struck by how much space the house contained. It had a small, separate kitchen and a room that was accessed directly by the outside door on Tiverton Place. This room was used by Betty as her bedroom and Doreen was amazed to see that it contained a gas fire. Downstairs there was also a living room and at the front of the house, a huge parlour which was only used for special occasions. The rooms on both floors had high ceilings with carved coving around the tops of the walls and ornate ceiling roses. Doe, with her limited experience, thought that in the past, it must have been a home for someone wealthy.

Doreen and Jim moved in at the end of July. Initially, Betty took little notice of her, saying a brief hello and then turning her attention towards her dad. She was taller and of more ample proportions than Emily and she had long, black hair. Jim was obviously attracted to her, telling Doe that his friends thought Betty had more than a passing resemblance to Elizabeth Taylor, a fact that pleased him immensely. Doreen was surprised when two boys arrived for tea; they were Betty's sons. Jim hadn't told her that Betty had children and it made her feel uncomfortable. Trevor, the older boy, was actually a young man. He was seventeen and Doe thought that he was quite handsome, although perhaps his nose was a little too big. Kevin was thirteen. He had red hair and freckles. Although they were both polite, neither seemed inclined to talk to her. Doreen felt alone; an increasing sense that she didn't belong there.

Over the following days, Doe began to talk to the children who lived nearby and was soon making new friends. Nevertheless, it didn't remove her desire to return to Bright Avenue, where every morning her mam had come to visit her. During the two weeks they had been living at Betty's, Emily hadn't been to see her at all. Doreen was missing her and asked Jim where she could be.

"Where's my mam? Why hasn't she come to see me."
"She won't come to Betty's," replied Jim.
"Well, we can go and see her."
"We can't. I don't know where she lives, love."

Doreen didn't understand. After all, her dad had insisted before they moved, that she would still be seeing her mam. Almost immediately, Jim was facing a barrage of questions. Why didn't he know? Why hadn't her mam told him? Why couldn't he find out? Why wouldn't she come to Betty's? Unable to produce any convincing explanations, Jim fell back on an all too familiar response.

"You'll understand when you're an adult, Doe. Things aren't as simple as you think. Don't worry, everything will be all right."

The following week, Doreen finally knew that it wouldn't be 'all right'. Since she had moved in, Betty had asked her to help Kevin clean the house. Doe thought nothing of it, given that she had carried out all the domestic tasks at Bright Avenue for her and Jim. Furthermore, after arriving at Betty's, she had continued to wash all their clothes. She did notice that Betty seemed obsessive about being clean and tidy and she had lost count of the times that Betty had remarked that 'cleanliness is next to godliness'. Doreen was sure that it was her favourite saying. She was particularly insistent that they take all the rugs out of the house on a regular basis and beat them over the washing line in the back yard. She had noticed too, that Betty liked to be the 'gaffer'. She was eager to give out the orders, but not so keen to do any of the work herself. Yet Doreen had accepted this and to a degree, it provided her with a sense of reassurance. The young girl felt that by carrying out this work, she was looking after herself and Jim and making her own contribution to the running of the household. Effectively, Betty couldn't claim that she and Jim owed her anything. However, when she was taken for her new school uniform, it was clear that Doe's willingness to accept the demands that Betty placed upon her, counted for nothing. In fact, the young girl's world was about to come crashing down around her.

Betty had told her on Monday morning that before going to work, her dad had left some money, as it was time that they went to get everything that she needed for her new school. Initially pleased, Doreen was stunned as Betty took her around a succession of second-hand clothes shops, searching for items of uniform. Doe protested. She asked Betty why she wasn't being taken to the official uniform shop. Her mam and dad had never bought her second-hand clothes. She was adamant that she wouldn't put on garments that other people had worn and she noted that many of the ones in the shops they visited, hadn't even been washed. Yet when she had complained, Betty wouldn't listen and proceeded to buy a succession of items, regardless of the fact that many didn't meet the uniform requirements of her new school. Arriving back at Betty's house, Doe went upstairs to her bedroom, shut the door and cried uncontrollably into the pillow, not wanting to let Betty know how much she had upset her. Doreen's parents had often been poor, but she had never had to suffer the ignominy of having to wear second-hand clothes. If Emily was around, she would have insisted that her daughter was bought the correct uniform, from the official suppliers. Yet Doe didn't know where she was and had no way of contacting her. All she could hope was that once her dad came home, he would make things right.

When Jim arrived back from work, Doreen told him about the shopping trip.

"Betty bought me all second-hand clothes. They smell. I don't want someone's old uniform. I want a proper one."

"Oh," said Jim, surprised. "Go upstairs and I'll be along in a few minutes to look at them."

As the time ticked by, Doreen began to feel uneasy. When Jim finally came into her room, his response was disappointing.

"I've spoken to Betty and she's explained everything. She's right, Doe. It's a good idea. Why pay a fortune for a new uniform when there are lots of perfectly good clothes in the second-hand shops? Once they've been washed, they'll be just like brand new. They're your clothes now and no one's going to know any different."

"But they will, Dad. They don't look new and they're not the items that the school expect me to have. We're supposed to buy them from 'Henry Barry' in St. Anne's Square. I'll get in trouble with the school if I'm not wearing the proper uniform."

"I know, Betty told me about that. But like she said, we can't afford the proper uniform and there's bound to be other families like us; having to do the best they can, with the little money they've got. The school will just have to accept it. We'll send them a letter if they won't."

Doreen was shocked, for her dad had never denied her anything in the past; money had never been an issue. It seemed that Jim had fallen completely under Betty's sway and was unlikely to change his mind. Nevertheless, his daughter was intent on fighting her corner.

"But you were the one that wanted me to go to grammar school, dad. You knew that the uniform was going to be expensive. When I was worried that I'd have no friends there, you said that I was being silly and that I would. Now, if you force me to go to school in the wrong uniform and the other girls can see that I'm wearing someone's old clothes, everyone will laugh at me and I'll never have any friends."

"Of course, you will. You're being daft, Doe."

"No, dad. I'm not. Most of the girls who go there aren't from around here. Their parents have more money and they'll always have the correct uniform. They'll look down on me and I won't want to be there."

She paused, waiting for Jim to respond, but he was silent; his eyes averted.

"If Mam was here, she'd understand. Mam would make sure that I had a proper uniform."

As soon as she'd said it, Doreen realised her mistake. Now devoted to Betty, her dad had become increasingly hostile towards his wife.

"Well, she's not here, is she? If she cared so much about you, she wouldn't have run off with her fancy man."

It was a cruel comment and so unlike him. For a moment, Doe expected him to apologise; change his mind and reassure her that he still loved her. But he didn't. Turning away in silence, Jim went out of the room and back down the stairs. The matter was closed. Doreen felt betrayed. For all his promises, he was no better than Emily. Both had put personal pleasure before responsibility to their daughter. Jim had always indulged her. He'd not allowed Emily to chastise her, yet now he didn't care that Betty's actions would lead to her humiliation when she arrived at her new school.

The close bond between Doe and Jim would never be the same again. She still loved him dearly, but now began to see his obvious faults. Jim and Betty went to the pub every night and when he wasn't working, at dinner time too. Doreen became convinced that she had been bought second-hand clothes so that Jim and Betty would have more money for the pub, or gambling on 'the dogs' at Belle Vue. Doe knew that they were desperate for money when her bicycle mysteriously disappeared. Jim had bought it for her shortly before they moved to Betty's. He had taught Doreen how to ride it, running along behind her, holding on to the saddle until she could get her balance. Doe loved it and would ride around the streets with her friends, exploring the back alleys. The day the bike disappeared, Jim and Betty had gone to the dogs. The day before, Doreen had heard them complaining about having no money. It seemed that Jim had sold her bike in order to pay for their night out. Doe began to despise Betty, yet sensible of her predicament, realised that she must avoid upsetting her. Although it hurt her deeply, the young girl agreed to her dad's request to start calling Betty, Mam. Slowly, but surely, Doreen was learning the art of survival and as time progressed, she realised that she would need all her wits and ingenuity to get by.

With Jim no longer providing her with regular pocket money, Doe ran errands and carried out jobs for the neighbours. With her earnings, she could buy food, personal items such as underwear and socks and if she had anything left, a comic or magazine. Her most lucrative task was brown stoning front door steps, but she also cleaned windows, fetched shopping and got occasional jobs from shopkeepers, who wanted her to tidy up their displays or store rooms.

The money certainly came in handy because under Betty's influence, Jim began to take little interest in his daughter's welfare, trusting his new partner to take care of her. Doreen realised that it was pointless to complain, for he was unlikely to listen and it would only cause trouble with Betty. Doe wasn't alone in her misery however, as Kevin was treated similarly by his mother. Every teatime the table would be set for Jim, Betty and Trevor. As Trevor was working and giving part of his wages in 'keep' to his mother, he got a meal every evening and sandwiches every morning. If money was tight and needed for the pub, Kevin and Doreen would get nothing; not even sixpence for a bag of chips to share between them. Betty would always tell Jim that she would leave them something to eat for later. Yet Doe and Kevin would often go days without eating and neither of them were allowed to take anything from the larder. Caught in there by Betty, Kevin was locked in the attic room as a punishment. Doreen had occasionally asked her friends if they could get a couple of slices of bread for her, but when Joyce Miller did so, her mother had accused her of stealing and had hit her with the belt. Doe couldn't believe it. Mrs Miller must have counted the slices in the packet. It seemed that she was just as bad as Betty. The incident had made Doreen feel terrible. Not wanting to put any of her other friends in trouble, she never asked anyone for food again.

Doreen and Kevin learned that it was best for them to be out at teatime. Having to watch Jim, Betty and Trevor eating, made them feel even more hungry. Rarely did they get to share in Betty's favourite meal of tinned steak and dumplings with mashed potato and gravy. Doe soon realised that the money she earned couldn't be spent on anything but food and clothes. When she and Kevin were desperate to eat, Doreen had to be sure that she still had enough to buy them both a bag of chips. It was just enough to ensure that the two of them would continue to survive.

Chapter 27

Towards the end of the school holidays, Doreen found out that there was a dark secret in Betty's family. She had made friends with a girl called Janet who lived in Devonshire Place and she had gone to call for her early on a Saturday morning. Doe had woken up at six o'clock. Since leaving Bright Avenue, she regularly rose at that time. That morning, in order to please Betty, Doe had cleaned the living room, kitchen and bathroom. She had beaten the rag rugs and runners over the clothes line in the back yard and had polished the sideboard, table and chairs. She had finished at nine and slipped out of the house with her dad, Betty, Kevin and Trevor still asleep in bed.

After knocking on Janet's door, it was opened by her mam. Doreen was told that Janet wasn't ready to come out yet and the door was quickly closed. Doe thought it strange. The parents of her friends around Bright Avenue had always asked her to come in and wait, but for some reason Janet's mam seemed hostile. Doreen moved a few doors down the street and sat on the kerb playing with her jacks, whilst she waited for her friend to come out. About twenty minutes later, with Doe about to leave, Janet finally emerged. Doreen picked up her jacks and the girls headed off across the road and down Parker Street. When they came to the corner with Syndall Street, they stopped. They had arrived outside 'Graham's', the corner shop. Graham's had display windows running along both the Syndall and Parker Street sides of the property and there were huge signs advertising 'Tizer' and 'Woodbines'. All around the shop was a wall about eighteen inches high. On the Syndall street side, the wall was backed by flat concrete that stretched back to the shop at the height of the wall. It was perfect for playing marbles or jacks on. The kids could sit lazily on the wall, level with the playing area. More importantly, as long as they weren't a nuisance, the shop wouldn't tell them to clear off.

After they had been playing for a while, Janet asked Doreen a question.

"You and your dad have lived at Betty's for quite some time, haven't you?"

"Yes," replied Doe.

"My mam doesn't like me playing with you."

"Oh?" asked Doreen, surprised.

"Yes. It's because of Ted Burton."

"Who's he?"

"Don't you know?" asked Janet.

"No."

"He's Betty's husband."

"But she's not called Burton," replied Doreen. "Her name's Craig."

"That's not her real name. Your dad must know that."

"Well, he's never told me. If this Ted Burton's her husband, then why isn't he living with her?"

"Because he's in prison."

"Why?"

"Because he murdered Betty's mam and he assaulted Kevin."

Doe was shocked but eager to find out more.

"How did he kill Betty's mam? Did he stab her?"

"No," replied Janet. "He pushed her down the stairs and the fall killed her."

"When he assaulted Kevin, what did he do?"

"I'm not sure. All I know is that I heard my mam say that he sexually assaulted him; whatever that means."

"Oh," replied Doreen, who didn't know what it meant either.

Doe now understood why Janet's mam didn't like her coming to the house. It was because her dad was living with the wife of a murderer, but at least Janet had made it clear that she wanted to remain friends. Returning to Betty's, Doe waited until her dad was alone and then began to ask him questions about what she had been told.

"What does sexually assaulted mean?"

"Why do you want to know?" asked Jim, surprised.

"Well," replied Doreen, "I heard that Kevin's dad, Ted Burton, had sexually assaulted him and murdered Betty's mam by pushing her down the stairs. I was told that he was put in prison for a very long time."

"Yes, that's true, Doe."

"But what does sexually assaulted mean, Dad?"

"It's something that you needn't worry about. I'm not telling you until you're older."

As inquisitive as ever, Doreen was determined to find out and a few days later one of her older friends explained it to her. Doe was shocked and wished that she'd listened to her dad and forgotten all about it. Now she didn't know what to think. For a couple of weeks, she found it very difficult to even look at Kevin. She wasn't sure that she could talk to him and so kept trying to avoid him. Eventually however, Doe began to feel guilty. She lived in the same house with Kevin and suffered the same hardships that he did. Doreen couldn't understand how Betty could be so cruel to her son, when his father's treatment of him must have been so terrifying. Ashamed at how she had ignored Kevin, Doe resolved that once more, she would treat him with kindness and compassion. Never asking Kevin about his father, she eventually managed to erase any thoughts about the incident from her mind.

Chapter 28

Life with Betty became increasingly difficult. From the moment he had dismissed Doreen's concerns about her school uniform, Jim had effectively handed over the responsibility for his daughter's care to his new partner. Doe knew that she would have to tread warily, but it wouldn't be enough to protect her from the vagaries of Betty's temper.

Betty didn't like the precocious young girl. She thought that Doreen was too 'forward' and that she 'should be seen and not heard'. In her opinion it was clear that Jim had given her little or no discipline. It was something that she was determined to put right. She had, she believed, been given the green light to take charge of the 'young madam'. Jim was now content for her to make the decisions. It was her house and Doreen would do as she was told. She had Jim, like other men before him, in the palm of her hand. This irritating little girl wasn't going to ruin that.

Just how cruel Betty could be, became apparent after Doreen had started school. One afternoon, having arrived back after lessons, Doe had washed her blouse and knickers ready for the next day. The knickers, navy blue ones with elasticated legs, were for PE. They were heavy cotton and adequately preserved her dignity when her short gym skirt would fly up during netball lessons. Doreen put her washed items on the clothes line and as the Sun went down, brought them back in. The blouse, made out of a thinner material, was almost dry but the knickers were wet through. As a result, Doe put them over the open door of the oven, which was located near the fire, before she went to bed. When she awoke the next morning, the kitchen fire had gone out and her knickers were still wet. Fortunately, Jim had lit a fire in the living room before setting off to work. Doreen took the knickers and held them out in front of the fire. They were steaming, but were getting dry. Suddenly, Doe was disturbed. It was Betty.

"What are you doing?"

"I'm drying my knickers."

Betty moved towards her.

"Give them to me."

Doe handed them over.

"They're soaking wet. You can't wear these."

"It's PE today, I need them. I haven't got any others that I can wear. It won't take me much longer to dry them."

Maliciously, Betty flung the knickers on to the fire.

"You stupid girl! Go and get some others."

Satisfied at having admonished her young charge, Betty marched out of the room.

Doreen was distraught. She did have other knickers, ones her mam had bought her just before they had moved to Betty's. But they were flimsy, loose fitting around the legs and they were white. Doe knew that they could be seen through and they wouldn't cover her adequately. At school, the PE teacher proved unsympathetic to her plight and insisted that she must take part in the lesson. Doreen thus avoided the ball and kept her arms by her sides, in an effort to hold down her skirt. She was terrified that the other girls would make fun of her predicament and hoped that none of the male caretakers would come near the courts. She felt as if she were almost naked and desperately poor. No one else had to wash items of uniform every night to wear again the next day. Doe vowed that it would never happen again. She determined that the next money she earned would be used to buy a couple of pairs of Navy knickers, so that she would never be without any for PE. The incident also hardened her attitude towards school. It was clear to her that most teachers had no sense of fair play. For the young girl, life had become a matter of survival and her education seemed unimportant. Doe would never be humiliated in PE again. If in future she lacked the necessary clothing, she would simply 'wag' school.

Inadvertently though, Doreen was to gain revenge on Betty a couple of weeks later, but it would come at a heavy price. Her dad had been working at a dress shop and as part of their refurbishment, the owners were throwing out some old mannequins. Jim thought that Doe might like one to play with; she would enjoy being able to dress it up. He therefore brought one home at the end of the week and put it in the living room to show Doreen. Betty had followed him in. Jim placed it in the centre of the room and Doe could see that the head was covered by a blonde wig.

"Huh. With that hair, it looks just like the bitch," observed Betty.

'The bitch' was the term Betty used to refer to Emily. She clearly didn't care if it upset Doreen, especially as Jim never asked her to desist.

Later, after the adults had gone to the 'Richmond', Doe decided that she would try to please Betty by painting the mannequin's hair black. Going down into the cellar and ignoring the 'creepies' that were attracted to the damp, she found a tin of black gloss paint. Back in the living room, Doreen put a dust sheet on the floor, placed the mannequin on top and proceeded to turn its blonde hair black. Having finished, she carefully picked up the mannequin and sat it back on the rocking chair near the window, in order to dry its hair. Doe made sure that the mannequin's head was well above the back of the chair and away from the curtains.

Doreen now waited for her dad and Betty to return, which they did just after eleven.

"Look what I've done, Mam. Now, she looks just like you."

Looking for approval, the young girl tried to draw Betty's attention towards the mannequin.

"That's nice love," said Jim, appreciatively.

Indifferent to Doreen's efforts, Betty grunted and moved towards the rocking chair. As usual she leaned on it to reach over to draw the living room curtains, which were still open. The result was a disaster. The chair lurched forward and the mannequin fell against her. The hair was still wet. Betty had only recently bought a new outfit. It was a white shirt waister dress and it was very fashionable. That evening was the first time that she had worn it. Looking down, she could see that it was covered in black paint. Betty was hysterical.

"Take it off. Calm down. I'll get the turps," said Jim.

Betty and Jim both shouted at Doreen, but only briefly as Jim raced off to the cellar to get the turps. Meanwhile, Betty was taking off the dress, unbuttoning it with meticulous care to try and ensure that she didn't spread the paint any further. Jim soon arrived back and taking the dress, gently dabbed at the paint with a clean turps cloth. It seemed to be working; the black paint slowly transferring to the cloth. Doreen quietly breathed a sigh of relief. Perhaps she would get away with it. But fate decided otherwise. Looking at the dress, Doe noticed that although the black paint was gone, the turps had left a yellow stain on the material that couldn't be removed. Effectively, the dress was ruined. Doreen knew that she'd had it. Betty was out for retribution.

"You've ruined it. You can't do anything right. You did it on purpose, didn't you?" ranted Betty.

There was no point in telling Betty that it was her own clumsiness that had caused the accident; that she was the one who had stood on the rocking chair when the mannequin was squarely in front of her. It wasn't long before Betty decided that Doreen would get the same punishment that Kevin regularly received. She was to be locked in the attic until Betty decided to let her out. Looking at her dad, Doe noted his lack of concern; there was no chance that he would intervene on her behalf.

The attic consisted of two rooms at the top of a narrow staircase. Neither of them had lighting or electricity and their doors had been removed. The smaller room had a skylight and an old mattress on the floor, covered by a blanket. The larger room contained a dormer window. Much lighter during the day, it was completely empty. On the small landing between the rooms was propped an old door and a plank of wood. Doreen was told to go into the small room. It was dark. She asked Betty for a candle, but was refused. Betty then moved the old door against the open doorframe. Taller and wider, it blocked out any glimmer of light from downstairs. She then took the plank of wood and jammed it between the opposite skirting board and the centre of the door. Trapped without food, light or heating and aware that there had been rats in the attic, the young girl was terrified. Alone in the dark, she squirmed and sobbed. She couldn't believe that her dad was allowing this to happen.

Doreen was sat against the wall and wrapped in the blanket, as the dawn began to filter through the skylight. She was alone until dinner time when Kevin came up to speak to her. Jim and Betty had gone to the pub, so it was safe for him to do so. Doe didn't want him to open the door, in case Betty realised that the plank had been moved. Kevin's concern helped sustain her through the hours of isolation following Jim and Betty's return. Doreen's spirits also lifted when she thought about the ruined dress. With hindsight, the whole episode was hilarious and Doe felt that Betty had been paid back for calling Emily the 'bitch'. Significantly, prior to the incident, Doreen had set out to try and please Betty, but after being locked in the attic, the young girl knew that she could never win her approval. Doe vowed to herself that never again would she attempt to gain favour with Betty, no matter what her dad might say.

It was seven o'clock at night before Jim finally came to let her out. There was little sympathy in his voice and his words clearly indicated that he believed that his daughter was in the wrong.

"I've managed to get Betty to agree to let you out. Just make sure you don't annoy her again."

Although angry at his comments, Doreen was tired and hungry and so decided to ignore them.

"I've had no food for two days, Dad. Can I have sixpence to go and buy some chips?"

"You've got to promise me, Doe. You're not to upset your mam, Betty, again."

This time, Jim's response was too much.

"She's not my mam! I won't call her it, Dad,"

Proud and resolute, Doreen was her own worst enemy. She needed to be out of the attic, but not at the cost of meekly accepting her dad's demands. Jim had allowed Betty to treat her unfairly and all because he was prepared to pander to his partner's every whim.

Eager to avoid a confrontation, Jim decided that he wouldn't push her to accept his demands. Reaching into his pocket, he brought out half a crown and gave it to his daughter. Saying nothing, he walked back down the stairs and went off with Betty to the 'Richmond'.

Chapter 29

As Doreen had feared, life at the grammar school did not go well. She only knew one girl from Ross Place that attended and the two had never been friends. Arriving on the first day, Doe was conscious of the fact that she was wearing second-hand uniform and the other girls, their clothes looking smart and pristine, had noticed too. As she was small and therefore seemed an easy target, it wasn't long before several girls had made some wounding comments. References to her looking like a tramp had brought the inevitable reaction. Doreen dealt with it in the only way she knew how; the way she had learned at Ross Place where other pupils had ridiculed her 'jailbird' father and referred to her as 'scum'. She wasn't going to take it and lashed out with real venom in order to shut them up. It wasn't only girls in her own year; older ones had also taunted her in the playground. They learned to their cost however, that the little first year was a tough nut to crack and wouldn't be a victim of the bullies. Caught fighting with a third-year girl, older and bigger than herself, Doreen received no sympathy. Unlike at Ross Place, there was no Mr Roberts to show her compassion and understanding. She was forced, with the older girl, to put on boxing gloves and entertain the other pupils in a boxing match organised by the very PE teacher who would later force Doe to play netball without her proper underwear. With no attempt by the school to silence the bullies, Doreen therefore continued to sort out her own problems. Eventually, the message began to get through and the bullies moved on to easier targets.

In her lessons though Doreen was excelling, especially in maths and physics, but she hated being at Manchester Girls Grammar. At home when she went out to play with her friends, who were at Ardwick Secondary, she was struck by the positive way that they spoke about their experiences. Telling them of her problems, they suggested that she should ask to be transferred to their school. It seemed the answer, but what would her dad say? Doreen remembered how excited he had been when she had passed the eleven plus, but that was before he had met Betty. Would he still be so eager for her to stay at the grammar school? The answer quickly became apparent. He no longer cared. The only problem was that if Doreen were to transfer schools, he would have to make an official application to the Education Committee. As this would involve him going to a meeting with officials at the education offices, Jim was unsupportive. He had thought that it would be a simple matter to change schools. Meetings though, took him out of his comfort zone. He lacked confidence in his ability to deal with any type of officialdom and had no wish to appear inadequate. Yet his eleven years old daughter had no such concerns. Fortunately for her, she found an unlikely ally in Betty who, almost inevitably, saw a transfer as beneficial to herself.

Although she would never have admitted it, Betty was somewhat jealous of the obvious intelligence of Jim's daughter and to a degree was slightly intimidated by it. Unlike her own sons, Doreen could always provide logical reasons why Betty's demands and punishments were unfair. Doreen's attendance at the grammar school was a constant reminder to Betty, who'd struggled to learn at school, that Jim's daughter was far more able than her. Although Jim didn't know it, buying Doreen a second-hand uniform was Betty's vindictive way of denying her legitimacy at the school. It was a subconscious suggestion that she didn't really belong there; wasn't real grammar school material. Betty hated to see her wearing the uniform, as it was a constant reminder that Doe had done better than herself. A transfer of schools would be perfect as far as Betty was concerned; the little madam would no longer be 'superior' to her. When Doreen pressured her dad over contacting the Education Committee, Betty quickly took her side.

"Going to that school is nothing but a waste of the girl's time, Jim. All that nonsense about her having to do homework. What for? It stops her from concentrating on her jobs here. All Doreen needs to know is how to clean up, cook and look after a family for when she's grown up and gets married. She doesn't need any of the rubbish that she's learning there."

With such a powerful ally on her side, Doe finally got Jim to agree to go with her to the education offices during the half-term holidays at the end of October.

There was one teacher however, who did care about Doreen. The young physics teacher, Mr Owen. As one of only a handful of men teaching in the school and young too, Owen had become something of a favourite with the girls and Doe had always thought of him as being very kind. He had learned that Doreen was looking to transfer and at the end of a morning lesson, he had asked her to wait whilst the rest of the class were dismissed. Doe wondered why he wanted her to stay behind, as she always completed her work to a high standard. It wasn't long before she found out.

"Doreen, I wanted to talk to you about you wanting to transfer to the secondary school. I know you aren't happy here, but it's not the right thing to do."

"Why not?"

"You're a clever girl. If you stick it out here, you get the chance to get qualifications that will open up so many jobs and opportunities for you. I know it seems a long way off, but you've got real ability. It would be such a shame for you to give up on it."

Doe appreciated what Mr Owen was saying. It made her feel good to know that he had so much confidence in her. However, she would be sixteen before she took her O-levels. It was just too far away. She found it difficult to cope with the thought of getting through the next day; another five years was just too much to comprehend. Doe knew that there was no way that she could get through it.

"It's not easy," replied Doreen. "Every day I have to put up with nasty comments and it never stops. If I try to deal with it and stand up for myself, I get in trouble and told that I'm not behaving like a young lady. I'm just not happy here; this school's not for me. It isn't for girls who come from my background."

Owen was impressed. Doreen was only eleven, but she was articulate and mature. He had entered teaching hoping that he could make a difference and here he had found a pupil who definitely deserved his help.

"You're wrong, Doreen. This school is just for girls like you. It's here to provide you with new opportunities. You don't have to accept a life without prospects, like your parents had to when they were growing up."

"But they're part of the problem. My parents aren't together and they don't really care about me. That's why I don't have the proper uniform and it means that many of the other girls try to make fun of me."

"Well, just ignore them."

Owen paused, realising that his advice was ridiculous. How could she just ignore the hurtful comments aimed in her direction? Yet, as difficult as his task was, he had to try to convince Doreen to stay.

"Treat them like the idiots they are," he continued. "You do understand that they're jealous, don't you? They know that you're smarter than them. They might have new uniforms and equipment, but half of them haven't got any brains."

A faint smile flickered across Doe's face.

"You'll regret it Doreen, if you leave. Yes, you're bright and I'm sure that there'll be lots of jobs that you'll be able to do, but the sixth form and perhaps university, won't be possible. Just stick it out. I'm always prepared to talk to you and I'll try to help if things get difficult. Promise me that you'll talk to me again before you finally decide on what you want to do."

"I will."

Getting up from her stool, she left the classroom.

Doreen never did speak to him again. Shortly after it was half-term and she went to the education offices with her dad. The officials were loath to agree to the request, but Doe was adamant. She was so unhappy at Manchester Grammar, she told them, that she didn't want to go to school at all. Jim finally roused himself and declared that all her friends went to the secondary school and it was most important to him that his daughter was settled. Yes, exams were important, he agreed, but she probably wouldn't do well anyway, if she was so unhappy. Doreen was amazed that he was suddenly expressing his concern for her happiness; he hadn't cared about it at all since they'd left Bright Avenue. Yet she knew it was to impress upon the officials that he was a concerned parent. As usual, he didn't want to look bad to other people.

Nevertheless, Doreen was pleased with his intervention, as the officials reluctantly agreed to the transfer. After half-term Doreen moved to Ardwick Girls Secondary, where she was allocated a place in the GCE class. Reunited with her old school friends, at least one part of her life had become more bearable.

Chapter 30

Towards the end of October, Doreen and her friends were out after school and at weekends, searching for wood. It was getting near to bonfire night; for children, one of the most exciting times of the year. It was like a military operation. Some of them would go out in large groups to bring back anything combustible that they could find, whilst others would be knocking on doors and asking whether the householders had any 'bonny wood'. They never came back empty-handed. 'Bogies' were used to carry back lots of the smaller items, whilst the larger ones would be carried along by a collection of bodies straining together under the heavy weight. Most adults were pleased to 'donate' items; especially the bulky ones that would have been awkward to dispense with themselves. As such the 'foragers' would return with all sorts: wooden beds; mattresses; three-piece suites; cupboards; chests of drawers; old doors; tables; chairs; wardrobes; sideboards; old wooden fences and just about anything that would burn.

As bonfire night got closer, the search would spread even wider and during half-term, with all day to go at, the children would walk for miles. It was a point of honour to build the biggest fire possible; for it to be more impressive than those produced by other gangs. It now became crucial to organise sentries to keep an eye on the wood. Most gangs would have no hesitation in raiding other bonfires in order to make their own bigger. The wood was stacked very carefully; just like a huge tepee. This was to make it as high as possible, so as to produce a towering inferno once it had been set alight. Only the chairs were held back, kept at the side of the fire for seating and only thrown on at the point when almost everyone had gone home. It was possible for Doreen and her friends to pile the wood so high, as there was a 'croft' on Tiverton Place which gave them plenty of room for their fire to burn safely.

Bonfire night was so special for several reasons. It was a night when, whatever day November 5th fell on, the older children were allowed to stay up until the following morning to watch the fire gradually burning down. Before the event, youngsters had the chance to make some extra money with which to buy fireworks. They would sit with their 'Guy Fawkes' outside the shops on Hyde and Stockport Roads, asking passers-by to give them a 'penny for the guy'. The more enterprising among them would go to the university, where the students could be relied upon to be particularly generous. All the children loved fireworks and found it great fun to set off 'rip- raps' and 'bangers' in order to scare their friends. They also loved the baked potatoes and roast chestnuts placed in the embers on the edge of the fire. They would cook slowly and everyone would feel hungry as they waited eagerly for them to be ready. All ages would come to the bonfire: grandmas and grandads; mums and dads; teenagers and toddlers. Everyone was invited from the surrounding streets and almost everybody contributed something to the night. Even Jim and Betty bought some fireworks.

For this bonfire night, there would be a new dimension; music. Trevor, who was working, had saved enough money to buy a record player. It was grey with white plastic squares on the front and four long, thin legs. The legs were detachable, so it was possible to put an extension cable outside and place the record player on the wall at the side of Betty's house. As Jim and Betty were going to the pub, Trevor was allowed to play his own records and those provided by some of his teenage friends. For Doreen, the night also gave her the chance to spend time with Freddie Newton. Freddie was Doreen's age and he was her first 'crush'. She was looking forward to dancing with him.

As soon as it went dark, people began to arrive at the croft and Trevor started to play the music. The kids cheered as a couple of the adults lit the bonfire and then proceeded to set off the fireworks. In the meantime, everyone except Doe and Kevin, were putting their potatoes and chestnuts into the embers. It was a communal feed however; friends and neighbours willing to share what they had. And there was plenty available. Freddie Newton's mam was a greengrocer on Hyde Road and she had brought along a large bag of horse chestnuts and a sack of potatoes; just two of the many generous contributions that people had made to the festivities. Aware that they would be able to share in the feast, Doreen and Kevin had bought a pack of 'Echo' margarine to put on their potatoes. Once the main fireworks had finished, there was dancing in the street; jiving and twisting. Everyone was happy, with a smile on their face. Doreen jived with Freddie, Trevor danced with Joan and Kevin with a blonde-haired girl they had never seen before. Occasionally, 'rip-raps' would be set off among some unwitting teenagers and 'bangers' would be thrown. Youngsters would laugh uncontrollably at the panic that ensued in the vicinity of the victims. But it wasn't malicious, no one considering the potential dangers of their actions. For Doe, 'rip-raps' were the best, jumping all over the floor after they were lit. She loved having to get out of the way of them, jostling with those around her, everyone screaming and laughing.

At ten o'clock the music stopped, as many of the adults and younger children went home. The kids remaining settled down around the fire, chatting away as it radiated its warm glow on to their faces. Just after eleven, Jim and Betty came back from the pub. As Doreen watched their approach down Tiverton Street, she could see that they had someone with them. At first, she took little notice and turned back towards the fire. Then suddenly, the realisation began to dawn. She looked again and recognised the figure walking towards her with a familiar, steady gait. It was Our Kid. Jimmy had come back. Racing towards him, she flung out her arms. Taken by surprise, her brother was almost knocked off his feet.

"Our Kid! Our Kid!" shouted Doreen. They were the only words that would come out of her mouth.

Doe began to laugh and then to cry tears of joy. Jimmy hugged her tightly, surprised by the power of his sister's emotions. It was so long since he'd seen her. Finally, Jimmy pulled himself away.

"Come on, Doe. Show me the fire. Are there any baked potatoes? I'm hungry. That's where Dad and Betty have gone."

As they walked towards the fire, Jimmy was aware that his sister would have lots of questions for him.

"I suppose you heard that I was in prison, Doe?"

"Yes."

"Well, I got out at the end of August and since then I've had to sort a few things out."

"Oh. Is that why you've not been to see me?"

"Yes. I had to deal with Val, get a new job and find somewhere to live."

"Did you find it difficult to find me?" asked Doreen.

"Not really. I went round to Bright Avenue and I was shocked when you weren't there, but I always knew that I could find Dad in the 'Richmond' and that's where I went tonight."

"Will I see more of you now, Our Kid?"

"I hope so."

By the warmth and enthusiasm of her welcome, Jimmy understood just how much she had missed him.

"Anyway, Doe. How are you?"

"I'm all right."

Jimmy sensed, from her brief and quiet response, that perhaps things weren't going too well.

"What's Betty like?" he asked. "She seems okay."

Doreen hesitated.

"Do you like her?" continued Jimmy.

"No, Our Kid. She's horrible. I hate living with her, but I don't know where Mam is. Anyway, I would never live with Sam. I don't really have much choice. I have to stay here."

"Oh."

Jimmy didn't know what to say. He wanted to help her, but knew that he was incapable of doing so. He hadn't seen his sister for so long, had been to prison and his marriage was in ruins. Our Kid could never guarantee that he could provide the stable home that she so badly needed. Yet Doreen wasn't bothered. She had given up on hopes of a brighter future. It was enough that Jimmy was back in her life.

"Come on, Our Kid, let's go and get you a potato and see if there's any chestnuts left."

Doe led Jimmy to the fire. She wanted it to be a perfect night. Reflecting on her miserable situation would spoil it. Just before midnight, Betty, Jim and Our Kid made their way back to the house. Jimmy would be staying the night.

When daylight broke the next morning, Doreen, Kevin and their friends were still sat beside the fire talking. As the gloom lifted, they were reminded of how long they'd been awake and tiredness finally began to take its toll. Picking up their chairs, they took turns to throw them into the remains of the fire. It meant that the flames once again leapt into life, but it was nothing compared to the fierce intensity of the night before. It had been a great bonfire night, one of the happiest that Doreen had known. For a short time, she had been able to forget her difficulties and most of all, Jimmy had returned. Perhaps, her life might get better after all.

Chapter 31

It was Saturday night, a couple of weeks after the bonfire. Jim and Betty were on their way out to the 'Richmond'. The house was freezing; the coal for the fires having run out. Betty's bedroom however, containing the only gas fire in the house, was nice and warm. The fire had been on whilst Betty had been getting herself ready. After she and Jim had left, Doreen decided to go in there. She could switch on the radio, stay warm and leave before Jim and Betty returned. If she were careful not to disturb anything, Betty would never know that she had been in there. Yet as she lay on the bed listening to the radio, Doe began to feel tired. She had been up since six o'clock, cleaning and beating the rugs in the morning and out with her friends all afternoon. As the room gradually became colder, she decided to get under the eiderdown. She remembered thinking that perhaps she shouldn't. What would happen if she fell asleep and Betty came back and found her? A spell in the attic would no doubt await her; an unwelcome prospect at this time of year. Nevertheless, Doreen told herself not to worry; she would be able to stay awake and get back to her own bedroom, well before Betty returned.

Sometime later, Doe awoke with a start. Sitting up, she could hear a loud banging on the door and saw her dad moving towards her. Half-awake, she rubbed her eyes and felt Jim shaking her.

"Doe, Doe! Come on! Get up!"

Jim shook her again and then grabbed hold of her arm, pulling her towards him.

"Quickly!"

His words carried a sense of urgency that bordered on panic.

The banging continued. It was getting louder and several men's voices added to the cacophony of sound. Gradually, Doreen recovered her senses. She realised that the banging was coming from the door in Betty's bedroom that led outside on to Tiverton Place. The door wasn't used for access anymore and Betty had placed a chest of drawers at an angle in front of it.

Suddenly, there was an almighty crash as the door splintered. An axe head had made its way through one of the wooden panels. It jiggled around as the invisible assailant tried to withdraw it back through the door to strike again. It wasn't proving an easy task. The head was stuck and Doreen heard a man's voice swearing and cursing. Then another man spoke.

"Get out of the way! I'll do it!" said the voice, impatiently.

After a short pause, the axe head was pulled back through the door and another blow immediately followed, widening the split in the panel.

"Get out here, you bastard!" shouted a voice.

"Come and take your medicine!" said another.

"Doe! We've got to get out of the room."

Jim grabbed his daughter and pulled her out into the hallway. He then shut the door quickly and locked it.

"What's going on, Dad?" asked Doreen, shocked by what was happening.

"There are some men looking for Our Kid," said Jim.

"But he's not here."

"He is, love. He's upstairs."

"But why are they so angry?"

"It's because of that girl he met the other day. The one he brought back from the pub."

Just then, an almighty crash came from inside Betty's bedroom. Finally, the door had been smashed in and the chest of drawers kicked over.

"Oh my God, they're in!" gasped Jim.

Within seconds the men were hammering at the hallway door. There was no chance of them being denied. Inevitably the door gave way and men, shouting and swearing, rushed through. It was a terrifying scene. Six huge men, armed with axes and hammers. Jim acted quickly, pushing Doe into the parlour and telling her not to come out. As he stood aside, a couple of men came in to have a look. Glancing at Doreen, they went back out without speaking. Suddenly, there was a shout from upstairs.

"He's up here!"

Doe heard a flurry of footsteps thundering up the stairs and then the sound of her brother crying out in pain. Ignoring her dad, she ran out into the hallway. She could see two men dragging her brother down the stairs, the others were trying to kick and punch him as they did so. Doreen was terrified, but this was her brother and she had to do something. She looked expectantly towards her dad. He hadn't reacted. Why didn't he try to do something? One of the men came over and pushed her back into the parlour.

"Keep out of the way, love. We're not here to hurt you."

He blocked the doorway but Doe could see Jimmy being dragged towards the front door and out into the street. The man then moved off to join the others. Doreen knew that they were going to beat Jimmy senseless and using their hammers and axes, would probably end up killing him.

Doe realised that she needed a weapon of her own if she were to challenge them. She quickly gathered her thoughts. The adrenaline was kicking in. Her fear of the men was gone; she knew that she was the only one who could save her brother. She flew to the cellar steps, turned on the light and went down. Here were Jim's tools. She grabbed a hammer and raced back up the steps, down the hallway and almost knocked over her dad as she raced outside. The scene that greeted her was shocking. The men had Jimmy spread-eagled on the ground in the middle of the street. They were taking turns to kick him. In the head, the ribs, the back, the groin, the legs; everywhere possible. Doreen knew that he couldn't withstand much more.

In a rage she flew towards the first man and hit him on his back with the hammer. He turned round and she carried on to the next, flailing away and screaming at them to get off her brother. Wary of being attacked from behind, the men holding Jimmy loosened their grip. The discovery that their adversary was a small, young girl, made them hesitate. Jimmy, who fortunately still had enough strength to get off the floor, grasped the lifeline and ran off for all he was worth.

Doreen knew that she had to keep the men occupied in order to give her brother time to escape. She continued to flail away with the hammer. From behind, a man's arms reached around her waist. Doe felt herself being lifted off the ground, as two men approached her from the front trying to grab her weapon. Yet her arms were still free and the men were forced to back off. Finally, she felt her hair being pulled from behind. Distracted, her arms were pinned to her body and the hammer wrested from her grasp.

Once they had it, she was put back on the floor. The men took a step back.

"By God. This kid's got guts!" said one, in admiration.

The others nodded or grunted in agreement.

"We best get off," said another. "There'll be coppers here any minute."

Quickly, the men ran off down Hyde Road. Doe found herself alone in the middle of the street. She looked around her. Whilst fighting the men, she had been oblivious to everything else. Now she could see that her actions had been witnessed by a large crowd of neighbours, who were standing in their dressing gowns at their front doors; spectators to the night's events. Most significant to Doreen however, was the sight of her dad and Betty stood on the corner of Tiverton Place. She was shocked. Why hadn't he tried to help her when she was fighting the men? In fact, no one had tried to help; not her dad, Betty, nor any of the neighbours. All of them had just looked on and allowed the men to do what they wanted.

For now, Doreen's only concern was Jimmy. As he had run off, she thought that he had slipped down the alley by the side of St Matthews. She headed straight there. He must be badly injured she thought; she had to find him and get help. Doe shouted out his name and told him that the men had gone; that he could come out now, it was safe.

Walking down the alley, she heard a weak cry from behind the gate of one of the yards at the back of the houses on Tiverton Place. The gate was locked, so Doreen climbed over and made out the shadowy figure of her brother slumped on the floor against the dustbins. He was in a bad way but recognised his sister, who kneeled beside him and gently cuddled him. She knew that she mustn't cry, even though she wanted to, for it was important to make him feel that everything would be all right. Yet Doe was finding it difficult to fight back the tears.

"Don't worry, Our Kid. I'll go and get help. You need an ambulance. I won't be long."

Unbolting the gate, Doreen ran back to her dad, so that he could call for an ambulance, before returning to help Jimmy. As she sat quietly, holding her brother's hand, she began to think about her dad. Doreen recognised how her feelings towards him had changed since they had moved in with Betty. She no longer had any illusions about him; tonight's events had destroyed them all. She knew that he had done nothing at all to help her brother and that he hadn't intervened to help her. She realised that she had been lucky that the men recognised that she was a young girl and had respected her bravery and so had tried hard not to hurt her. Yet it could have turned out so differently. Her dad didn't know that she wouldn't get hurt. Nevertheless, he had continued to watch on from the corner. Everyone, all the neighbours, had witnessed his failure to help his children. Doreen had to face the fact that her dad was a coward.

The ambulance arrived quickly and took Jimmy to the Royal Infirmary. He had multiple injuries and would end up being in hospital for three months. Doe visited him on her own the following day. Her dad and Betty didn't go. Whether Jim was ashamed of his inaction and couldn't face his son, or simply didn't care, Doreen never knew. At least her brother was awake and lucid. He smiled weakly at her as she entered the ward at visiting time. He told her that she was very brave, that she had saved his life and that he loved her. His words triggered the release of the emotions that had built up since the previous night and Doreen broke out into uncontrollable sobbing. Finally, her tears at an end, Doe rested her head on the pillow next to Our Kid and the pair of them took solace in the peace of the hospital ward, so far removed from the horrors of the previous night.

Sitting back on her chair, Doreen asked her brother about the men. Why had they come for him? Jimmy explained that it involved the girl that she had seen him with a few days ago.

"It turns out Doreen, that she wasn't eighteen, but only fifteen. I met her in the 'Clarence' and she was with a group of friends. She'd told me that she was eighteen and her friends hadn't corrected her. She certainly looked eighteen."

Doreen had met the girl herself, as Jimmy had brought her back to Betty's one Sunday afternoon, when he had stayed for a few nights after the bonfire. She was very tall and so Doe had also assumed that she was much older. However, Doreen had been told by the girl that she wasn't eighteen, when the two had been alone talking in the parlour. The girl had asked her not to say anything to her brother. Doe had kept her confidence, not understanding the significance of what she was saying.

"Our Kid," said Doreen. "I'm sorry, but I think that I've done something wrong."

"What do you mean?"

"Well, when you brought her to see us that Sunday, she mentioned that she wasn't eighteen and asked me not to tell you. I didn't, because I just thought that she wanted you to think she was older, so that you would still want to go out with her. I'm really sorry. It's all my fault."

"No. Don't be daft Doe," said Jimmy, reassuringly. "You've not done anything wrong."

"But why is her age so important?" asked Doreen.

"Never mind, Doe. You'll understand when you're older."

Normally, his comment would have proved irritating. Far too often she had been denied explanations on the basis of her tender years. Our Kid's condition however, meant that she quickly forgave him. Yet Doe still felt that she deserved to be told why the girl's age had prompted such a vicious attack. Doreen therefore decided to push the matter further.

"Our Kid, please tell me. I want to know why all this happened."

Jimmy paused and then tried to explain the best that he could.

"Well Doe, if you want to be really close to your girlfriend, then they have to be at least sixteen. Because she wasn't, when the girl's father found out that we were going out together, he got really angry, because he thought I was taking advantage of her. He was wrong, because I didn't know how young she was. The landlord of the 'Clarence' believed that she was eighteen and she's been served in all the pubs around Ardwick. So, you can see that it isn't your fault. You should just be pleased that you saved my life. I'll certainly never forget it."

Doreen felt reassured. Jimmy had told her that it wasn't her fault and he never mentioned the matter of the girl's age again. It was some time however, before she understood what being 'really close to your girlfriend' meant and that intimacy, under the age of sixteen, was against the law.

Chapter 32

Jim was conscious of the fact that he had lost credibility with his daughter. He had stood by and allowed his son to be brutally assaulted without attempting to help him. Furthermore, he hadn't gone to his daughter's aid when she confronted his brother's attackers. Doreen had shamed him in front of the neighbours and the daughter who had once treated him as a hero, had grown very cold towards him. Christmas had now come and gone and as Doe's twelfth birthday approached, Jim saw an opportunity to rebuild their relationship. He had been fortunate to land a big decorating job in Didsbury. It was a huge house and the owner was so pleased with Jim's work, that he'd given him a considerable bonus. Flush with money, he decided to lay on a party for Doreen on the Saturday before her birthday.

Doe was pleased when she was given the news. Although there was no mention of a present, Jim said that Betty would make some cakes and jelly and that she could invite a few friends. Doreen couldn't believe it. She hadn't had a birthday party since she was seven years old; before her dad had been sent to prison. The party promised to be a bright spot in what was a terrible winter. The snow was on the ground and it had been bitterly cold for weeks. There was just one fire in the living room and bedtimes meant leaving outside clothes on under the covers in order to keep warm.

Doe had been allowed to invite eight of her friends to the party. They included Freddie Newton who Doreen had danced with on bonfire night. The two youngsters liked one another but were too embarrassed to admit it and Doreen had asked Kevin to invite him to the party for her.

For about an hour, everything had gone well. The children enjoyed the sandwiches, cakes and jelly and chatted away. Jim was pleased. He was hopeful that Doe would be grateful and that it would bring the two of them together. It was then that Betty decided that they should all play a game; a version of 'spin the plate'. The rules were that if the person called wasn't able to pick up the spinning plate, before it dropped to the floor, they would be forced to sing. Doreen felt uncomfortable. She couldn't sing. She sounded awful. Every one of her music teachers had dismissed her as being 'tone deaf'. She dreaded having to sing in front of Freddie and was sure, if she did, that he would laugh at her. When Doe tried to suggest that they play something different, Betty was dismissive and Jim agreed. All Doreen could hope was that she wouldn't, if her name was called out, drop the plate. All went well at first, but as the game continued with no end in sight, the inevitable happened. The plate was spun too weakly, Doe's name was called and she didn't have the time to grab it before it fell clattering to the floor.

"Come on Doreen," said Betty. "It's your turn for a song."

"Can't I recite a poem instead?"

"No. You have to sing."

Doe looked across at her dad. He made no move to support her. Doe was on her own. She would have to try and persuade Betty herself.

"But I'm terrible at singing. I'd much rather say a poem, please."

Doreen was pleading and the realisation made her feel angry with herself. She didn't like it that Betty could see her weakness. The rest of the children were starting to feel uneasy. They knew just how cruel Betty could be. The jolly atmosphere was starting to disappear.

"If you don't sing, then your dad and I will have to tickle you," replied Betty.

It was her attempt to break the impasse. Determined that she wouldn't be defied in front of Doreen's friends, Betty would make sure that Jim's daughter would do as she was told.

Doe hesitated. She hated to be tickled and Betty knew it. She would lose her self-control and it would hurt her. But it had now become a battle of wills played out before an invited audience. Doreen didn't understand it. Why was Betty intent on spoiling the happy atmosphere? After all, it was her party. Why, just for once, couldn't Betty show her some understanding and see things from her point of view. All thoughts of being embarrassed in front of Freddie, disappeared from her mind. It was more important than that now. Doe wasn't going to give way. With the children wondering what was going to happen next, Doreen broke her silence.

"I don't care. I'm not going to sing."

Betty and Jim now came across the room, forced Doe to the floor and started to tickle her. Doreen was laughing and then crying as Betty dug her fingers hard into her ribs, eagerly using the opportunity to inflict pain on her young adversary. Doe begged to be left alone, but they refused. She felt that she was being smothered; unable to breathe and gasping as she tried to push them off her. The more she struggled, the worse it got. Her friends were concerned. Betty and Jim had gone too far. It was now time to stop. Kevin could sense Doreen's distress, but he was too afraid to help. He knew that if he asked them to leave her alone, he would be locked in the attic after their visitors had gone. Then Betty got up and moved away, as Jim continued to tickle his daughter. It seemed that the incident was over; but it wasn't. Going to the table, Betty picked up a bottle of vinegar, walked back across to Doreen, lifted up her skirt and in full view of the boys, pulled down her knickers and shook the vinegar all over her.

Doe was hysterical. The vinegar burnt her tender skin. She screamed and kicked out so forcefully that Betty and Jim were forced to back off. As quickly as she could, she pulled up her knickers. She was distraught. All of her friends and especially Freddie, had seen her exposed. She felt dirty and ashamed; so embarrassed. She was enraged. All she could now think of was just how much she hated Betty. Doreen exploded.

"You bitch! You evil cow!"

Running out of the room, she went upstairs to her bedroom. Shutting the door behind her, Doe flung herself on the bed, sobbing.

Yet there would be no respite. Almost immediately, the door was flung open. Doreen turned to look. It was her dad. He was staring like a man possessed. Without a word, he pulled Doe off the bed and began to strike her. She tried to get away, but couldn't escape the punches that rained down upon her. She cowered in the corner, putting her arms above her head as she tried to ward off the blows. A couple of her friends had followed Jim up the stairs and were pleading with him to leave her alone; but he wouldn't. Doreen rolled up into a ball, covering her head, with no alternative but to wait until he stopped. Finally, with her friends' continual pleas, Jim gave up. Without a word, he walked from the room, slamming the bedroom door behind him.

Bruised and battered, Doreen was reluctant to move, but reassured by her friends, she finally got back to her feet. She ached all over; especially her sides, arms and legs, which had taken the full force of the blows. She thanked her friends and told them that they had best go home. Alone, she sat on the bed in a state of shock. It was the first time that Jim had ever hit her. She now understood that it wasn't a sign of love. What Mrs Cooper had said to Barry, when she had hit him with the hosepipe, was nonsense. You couldn't love someone by beating them.

About an hour later, Betty came to Doreen's room. She was to be locked in the attic for the rest of the weekend. It was freezing and Doe was forced to go immediately; not allowed to take up a coat or extra jumper. Finally, when Betty and Jim had gone out, Kevin came up to see her. He carefully removed the plank that was jamming the door. He handed Doreen a book, an old candle and some matches and brought a coat to help keep her warm. Kevin talked to her for a time and then carefully replaced the door and wooden jam. Horrified by Doe's treatment, Kevin was prepared to be punished himself in order to help her. The next evening, with Jim and Betty in the 'Richmond', he returned to the attic. Betty hadn't noticed that the door had been moved, so he now felt more confident. He had thus saved some sandwiches for Doreen and brought her a drink of water. Difficult as her isolation was, his compassion helped Doe through her ordeal. Kevin warned her to hide her coat and the candle under the mattress as soon as she heard anyone outside. Otherwise, they would both be punished again.

Kevin needn't have worried. It was Jim who removed the plank and door the following morning, when he got up for work. Betty wouldn't be emerging from her bed for at least a couple of hours. Doreen looked at him, but he said little.

"You shouldn't have spoken to Betty like that. Don't ever do it again."

And that was it. There was no apology or any sense of remorse for what he'd done. The incident was never mentioned again.

Just twelve years old, there seemed little that Doreen could do about her situation. Her brother had only just come out of hospital and she didn't know where he lived. Her mam hadn't seen her since Jim had moved in with Betty and in any case, she had no wish to live with Sam. Doe hadn't seen her gran since her mam had left Bright Avenue and at no time had Edna tried to contact her. She felt alone in the world, with no option but to stay where she was. After all, she was convinced that even Betty's house was better than the children's home.

There was a growing affinity between Doreen and Kevin; a result of Betty's cruelty and Jim's indifference. With Kevin's successful removal of the plank and door, the youngsters realised that they could help one another should either of them be locked in the attic. Yet it couldn't alter the fact that they remained victims of physical and mental abuse. Doreen understood the meaning of evil. Once, it had been a simple word; one confined to the scripture lessons at Sunday school. Betty had now provided evil with substance; a form and a face. And Doreen realised that evil was strong. For all she prayed for God to help them, there seemed no escaping the misery that Betty was determined to inflict upon her charges.

Chapter 33

For the next couple of months Doreen tried hard to avoid any further incidents with Betty. She did her regular chores and even extra cleaning in order to try and ensure that things ran as smoothly as possible. She wasn't happy, but was making the best of her situation.

Towards the middle of May, Jim had news for her. Emily had been to see Betty whilst Doreen had been at school and had asked if she could come to see her. Betty had invited her to Sunday dinner. Doe was shocked. She hadn't seen her mam for nearly a year and had almost given up hope that she would ever see her again. Doreen was confused, experiencing a mixture of emotions. She was angry that Emily had ignored her, but felt a sense of anticipation at the thought of seeing her again. Yet Doe wasn't sure how she would react when the two finally met, but hoped that she would remain calm and not provide Emily with an excuse to neglect her in future.

Doreen was initially surprised that Betty was prepared to allow 'the bitch' into her house. However, the reason soon became apparent. It was a competition. Emily would see that Jim was far better off now than he had ever been with her. Betty knew that her own house was much bigger than Bright Avenue. It wasn't just a simple two-up, two-down and she owned it; it wasn't rented. Betty had decided that Emily would be entertained in the parlour. As a result, in the days leading up to the visit, Doe was forbidden to go out with her friends. Instead, she had to work on making the parlour look 'spick and span' for her mam's visit. The curtains were washed and ironed, the skirtings bleached down, the rugs beaten on the line, the furniture and ornaments dusted and polished. As usual, Betty proved to be a great foreman; Doreen an industrious worker. Out of the sideboard came the special crockery. Betty's mother's Royal Albert dinner service was to be used for the occasion.

Sunday arrived and Doreen waited anxiously. Would her mam actually turn up? She looked at the clock. It was already noon, the time for her arrival, but she wasn't there. Doe had tried hard to control her expectations, for she knew that her mam may let her down. After all, that's what her parents usually did. That way she couldn't be hurt and disappointed. But she wanted to see her mam and inevitably her heart sank as the clock ticked on beyond quarter past twelve. Betty had told Doreen to wait in the parlour, insisting that she had to behave herself. She wasn't going to be allowed to wait outside and race off to meet Emily like some unruly urchin.

At half past, there was a knock on the door. Betty went to open it and welcomed Emily into the house. Speaking in her best, 'posh' voice, Betty's words were so obviously lacking in sincerity, that Emily couldn't fail to notice.

"Hello, Emily. It's so nice to see you. We're so glad you could come. Would you like to follow me into the parlour, where Doreen's waiting?"

"Yes. Thank you," replied Emily.

Doreen looked at her mam as she entered the room. She appeared just as her daughter had remembered. Looking smart in a blue, two-piece suit, Emily smiled.

"Hello, Doe. Are you alright?"

"Yes, Mam."

Doreen hesitated. She wasn't sure how to react.

"Well, aren't you going to give me a kiss?"

Overcome by emotion, Doe threw her arms around her mam and squeezed her tight. All thoughts of her abandonment were forgotten.

"Doreen, why don't you go out and play with your friends for half an hour," suggested Betty. "You need some fresh air and your mam and I want to talk."

Doe did as she was asked and headed down the hallway towards the front door. Passing the living room, she saw Jim sat reading the Sunday newspaper. It was clear that he wouldn't be participating in the conversation about his daughter.

Returning after half an hour, Doreen was ushered back into the parlour by Betty. Kevin was there too. Jim was shouted in and they were all told to take their places at the table. Betty had put a joint of beef in the oven that morning and it was now ready. The vegetables, prepared by Kevin and Doreen, had been cooked and Betty, with Emily in attendance, was demonstrating her culinary skills.

It was a fine meal. Roast beef and Yorkshire pudding, accompanied by roast potatoes, vegetables and gravy. Kevin and Doe couldn't believe it. It was heaven. For once, they had enough to eat and the food was lovely. Afterwards, there was an egg custard and cake. The youngsters wished that they could have visitors every week.

The meal was interspersed with polite, but meaningless conversation. The significant talking had clearly gone on whilst Doe had been playing out. Observing Betty, the young girl had to admit that she really was like Elizabeth Taylor, the actress who she claimed to resemble. What an accomplished performer, thought Doreen, perfectly playing the ideal mother and partner. Occasionally, she and Kevin exchanged knowing glances across the table, making sure that they weren't observed by Betty.

At the end of the meal, Doreen went to collect the remaining dinner pots to take them to the kitchen to start the washing up.

"Leave those, love. Kevin can help me," said Betty. "You need to talk to your mam."

"Yes, come on, Doe. Let's go out for some fresh air," said Emily.

"All right, Mam."

Doreen didn't need a second invitation, although she fully expected that the pots would be waiting for her in the sink when she got back.

Leaving the house, mother and daughter headed off down Hyde Road towards the ABC.

"Can we go and sit in Ardwick Green Park?" asked Doreen.

"Yes, that'll be nice."

Doe grabbed Emily's hand and proceeded to answer questions about what she had been doing since her mam had last seen her. The walk to Ardwick Green seemed to be over in no time. Finding a bench, the two of them sat down.

"She's not usually that nice," said Doreen.

"Yes, I know. I've already been told quite a bit about her."

"What did she talk to you about?"

"Oh, nothing much," replied Emily.

"She must have done. I was gone for half an hour."

"We only talked for a few minutes. Most of the time I was helping her with the dinner."

Doe didn't believe her. Emily clearly didn't want her to know what they were talking about. She decided to change tack.

"Why haven't you been to see me, Mam?"

"It's not easy, Doe. Your dad and Betty don't like me coming and I can't bring Sam."

"But I'm not bothered about seeing Sam. I only want to see you."

"I know, but it isn't pleasant for me with your dad and Betty, when I'm on my own."

Doreen was determined to remain calm, for she feared pushing her mam away. Nevertheless, she could see that Emily was just like her dad; concentrating on herself and keeping her new partner happy. Both of them had forgotten about their responsibilities to their daughter.

"That shouldn't bother you," continued Doe. "You're coming to see me, not them."

"If you remember, I did ask you to come and live with me, but you chose your dad."

"That was because I'd have to live with Sam and you know that he frightens me."

"Don't be silly, Doe."

"I'm not. I don't like him. Why can't just you and I live together. Our Kid could come and live with us too."

"I've not seen Jimmy for ages," said Emily, taking the opportunity to change the subject. "I don't think he's bothered about me anymore."

"You do know that Jimmy was beaten up and put in hospital for three months, don't you?"

The look of surprise told her that she didn't. Her mam's reaction wasn't unexpected. Why would Emily be concerned about her adult son, when she'd ignored her young daughter for the past twelve months? Yet Doreen passed no comment. She knew that it was pointless.

"Is there anything I can get you?" asked Emily, breaking the silence.

"Yes. A bra. Betty won't buy me one and my dad rarely gives me any money without checking with her first. I need one. I'm growing and it's getting embarrassing."

"All right, Doe. I'll come again next Saturday and bring you a couple. Come on, we'd better get back. It's getting late and I need to get home."

The two returned to the house where Betty remained as polite as ever. As Emily said farewell, Doreen gave her a hug. She was still her mam and wanted Betty to know it. Yet Doe wasn't sure if Emily would return, for she no longer had faith in the promises of adults.

True to her word, Emily came back the following Saturday, bringing her daughter two new sets of underwear. Doreen thought that they were beautiful. They were white and covered with coloured flowers; one set was pink and one blue. Doe wore the blue set on the following Monday. Having washed it at night, she went to her chest of drawers to find the pink set. To her surprise, it had disappeared.

A couple of weeks later, Doreen was told to clean Betty's bedroom. She was to make sure that she attended to every nook and cranny; it had to be spotless. When Betty and Jim had gone out, Doreen set about the task. Surveying the room, she could see that there were dirty clothes piled behind the chest of drawers in the corner. The clothes must have been there for quite a time. For all that Betty preached that 'cleanliness was next to godliness', she certainly didn't practice it herself. As Doe reluctantly pulled the clothes forward, she saw her missing pink underwear, dirty and rolled up, among the pile of items. It was clear that Betty had simply taken them, even though she knew that they were too small for her. They had been ruined. Doreen was angry, but as usual, there was nothing she could do. There was no one to complain to.

One thing was for certain, she couldn't tell her mam. On her return, Emily had only stayed a short time, claiming that she had to put a bet on for Sam and then meet him at a job he'd picked up as a 'foreigner' in town. Doe had asked her where she was living, but her mam had told her that they were on the verge of moving and she would let her know the new address as soon as she had it. She told Doreen that she would see her soon and at first, given that Emily had kept her promise to return, Doe dared to believe that her mam was serious. But as the weeks passed and she didn't show up, Doreen knew that Emily had deserted her. In fact, she wouldn't see her for another twelve months.

So much of Doreen's life had left her with unexplained questions. Now there were others. Just why had Emily turned up at Betty's after not seeing her for almost a year? What had she and Betty talked about and why would neither of them tell her? Why did her mam come back the following week and then simply disappear? Doe had gone through times in the past when she had blamed herself for her parents losing interest in her. Perhaps she had been too cheeky. Was it because she had been spoiled by her dad and this had made her into a 'difficult' child? Was it therefore her fault that neither of her parents wanted her anymore? Yet Doreen knew that she had tried hard to please Betty and where had it got her? It began to make her realise that it couldn't be all her fault. Doe didn't want to be a child anymore. She longed to be grown-up and have her own home and family which she could love and cherish. Yet for now, that lay well in the future and Doreen was destined to face a long and difficult road ahead.

Chapter 34

Hope came for Doreen from an unexpected quarter. She had transferred to Ardwick Girls Secondary School and had been placed in form 1E. This was part of the school's GCE stream. These girls were encouraged to remain at school until they were sixteen, rather than seek employment at the statutory leaving age of fifteen. The girls would then take their O-levels, just like the students at the grammar school. Doe knew lots of the other pupils and therefore didn't suffer any taunts over her uniform. In fact, girls outside the GCE stream weren't expected to wear one and for those who were in it, the teachers were far more sympathetic. Unlike at Manchester Grammar, they understood that many families were poor and the expense of uniform was often beyond them.

After the summer holidays, when Doe moved into the second year, she found that she had a new maths teacher called Mrs Morgan. It wasn't long before the latter was impressed by her genuine talent and enthusiasm for the subject. Aware that Doreen had transferred from the grammar school, Mrs Morgan believed that her new pupil had given up a huge opportunity. The young girl was a likeable and lively character and clearly had great potential. Mrs Morgan was a socialist. Her husband, deputy-head at the boys' school, was a Labour councillor and had ambitions to become an MP. Mrs Morgan believed that it was her mission to help her working-class students escape from the limitations of their parents' expectations. This could be achieved by giving them the confidence and qualifications necessary to escape the rigid social order that still prevailed in post-war Britain.

After a few lessons, Mrs Morgan had impressed 2E as being fair and approachable. The girls all loved her. She didn't just sit at her desk, as so many other teachers did; demanding silence for the entire lesson and setting boring tasks from the text book. Mr Norris, the geography teacher, was the worst. He would make them copy from the board or a book in silence, whilst he sat reading the 'Angling Times' and on Thursdays, filled out his pools coupon. If anyone disturbed his concentration, the inevitable detention would follow. Mrs Morgan was different. She circulated around the pupils, helped them when the tasks were difficult and let them talk to each other as long as they were working. Mrs Morgan would ask them how they were and all the girls knew that she was someone in whom they could confide.

Doreen Brodie caused Mrs Morgan concern. She had overheard the young girl talking to her friends and learned about Betty's cruelty. She noticed too that Doreen continually wore the same clothes; the Navy-blue cardigan that was well past repair and the frayed skirt. Yet they were always clean and her young pupil paid real attention to her personal hygiene. It showed that Doreen had pride in herself and given the chance, she could achieve great things.

Mrs Morgan spoke to her husband. She told him of her conviction that with a secure family background, the young girl would thrive. It wasn't long before the couple decided that they could help. Their own children had grown up. They had been to university and had left home. The Morgans now had the time and resources to nurture someone else. Mr Morgan told his wife to approach the situation carefully; find out more about Doreen's homelife and whether she would actually like to be given a fresh start. If she did and her father was agreeable, they could offer to foster her.

Aware that Doreen often had little to eat, Mrs Morgan started to bring in sandwiches to put in her pupil's desk before the start of school. Sometimes, Doe would sit with Mrs Morgan in her classroom at dinner. The two would talk whilst she ate her sandwiches. Doreen told Mrs Morgan about her parents' breakup, Sam and Betty and how difficult life had been since leaving Bright Avenue. The young girl loved these moments alone with her teacher. Mrs Morgan was the first adult that she had felt able to trust since her parents had separated.

At the end of October, just before half-term, Mrs Morgan felt that her relationship with Doreen had developed to a point where she could talk to her about the future. Broaching the subject, she spoke tactfully and with respect to her young charge.

"I hope you don't mind me saying Doreen, but Mr Morgan and I have been talking about you quite a lot recently and we're worried."

"There's no need to be. Things aren't as bad as you think. I just have to get on with it."

"Yes, you have been doing and I respect you for that, but it's not unreasonable for you to expect life to be a little easier. You should have regular meals and new clothes, like your friends all do. I can appreciate why you want to help around the house, but with so many chores, you can't always complete your homework."

"I always do in maths," insisted Doe.

"Yes, you do and always to the highest standards, but you need to do it in all your subjects. That's important if you're going to pass your exams and get a good job in the future."

Mrs Morgan paused and took a deep breath before continuing.

"I want to ask you something, Doreen. You don't have to answer me if you don't want to and if that's the case, then I'll say no more about it."

"All right."

"Are you happy living with your dad and Betty?"

Doreen was surprised. It wasn't a question she had expected to hear.

"What I'm asking, is whether you would rather live somewhere else," continued Mrs Morgan. "Somewhere that you don't have to worry about food and clothes, or whether you'll be punished or not."

Doe started to panic.

"I don't want to go in a children's home, if that's what you mean. The kids in there are treated even worse than me. I know it for a fact. I'm far happier where I am."

Hearing the fear in her voice, Mrs Morgan was quick to reassure her.

"No, Doreen. It's not what I meant at all. Far from it. The fact is that if you and your parents agree, Mr Morgan and I would like to offer you a home with us. You're a clever girl, but at the moment, it's very difficult for you to concentrate on your school work. There's a danger that opportunities are going to pass you by. We can help to make sure that doesn't happen. We want to give you the same chance that our own children had."

"But what would your children say?" asked Doreen. "They might not like me, or want to live with me."

"They've all left home now. They've been to university and have jobs. We've talked to them about fostering a child and they think it's a good idea."

Doe nodded and took in a deep breath. Mrs Morgan's offer had come as something of a shock, but it had pleased her. It was so long since anyone had shown an interest in her future. Doreen wanted to hug Mrs Morgan, but knew that she couldn't.

"If you did want to live with us," continued Mrs Morgan, "I can contact your dad and explain to him about how we'd like to help you. We can then see if he agrees. Don't worry. If you were to come to live with us, you would still be able to see your parents."

"I don't see my mam now, anyway."

"Well, you'll be able to see your dad any time you want. We don't want to replace him; we just want to help you. If you think that you'd be interested, you can take a couple of days to think about it and then decide."

Doreen sat quietly. It was an offer that would resolve all her problems. She trusted Mrs Morgan and her friends, who attended the local boys' school, had spoken positively about her husband. Doe had no doubts about them caring for her. There would be no uniform issues, no being beaten and locked in the attic and food on the table. She knew that they would expect her to work hard, but that would be on her schoolwork. No longer would she be expected to get up at six in the morning in the depths of winter and beat the rugs on the outside washing line. It was an offer she couldn't refuse.

"I don't need any more time to think about it. I'd like you to talk to my dad."

Mrs Morgan was delighted. She had been unsure whether she was doing the right thing, given her position as Doreen's teacher. The fact was however, that this was going to be her last year in the job. Next summer, she intended to take early retirement in order to help her husband in his council work and support him in his ambition to enter Parliament. They had decided that she would resign her post early, if the school had any concerns about her 'fostering' Doreen, whilst she was still working there.

"I'm pleased," said Mrs Morgan, trying hard to contain her emotions, "but I still want you to take a couple of days to think about it. If, at the end of the week, you're still keen on the idea, I'll give you a letter to take home to your dad. Don't say anything to him yet. Wait for me to ask him first."

"I will."

At the end of the week, Doe confirmed her acceptance of Mrs Morgan's offer and was given a sealed envelope addressed to her dad.

"In the letter, I've asked your dad if I can come to see him," explained Mrs Morgan. "I've said that I want to discuss your progress. I've made it clear that you're doing well, so that he won't think you've done anything wrong."

"He won't care," observed Doreen.

"I'll ask him about you coming to stay with us, when I meet him."

Doe said goodbye and went home. Jim was already back from work, which meant that he and Betty would soon be going out. Doreen handed him the letter in the front room. He opened it and started to read. Just as he was about to put it down, Betty came into the room.

"What's that, Jim?"

"It's from Doe's teacher. She wants to come and see me."

"What's she done now!"

There was more than a hint of menace in Betty's voice. She glared at Doreen, who was stood near her dad.

"No. She says Doe's doing well. She wants to see me about helping her to make more progress."

"She doesn't need to waste any more time on school," insisted Betty. "I've told you before, all she needs to learn is how to keep a house clean and look after a husband and family. These teachers, with their highfalutin ideas, are spoiling kids by filling their heads with nonsense. It's no wonder that she doesn't do as she's told."

"Well, she says that she wants to meet me," said Jim.

"Don't worry," replied Betty. "You leave it to me. I'll see her. Doreen can take her a note to tell her that she can come next Tuesday after school."

Doreen's heart sank. If Betty met Mrs Morgan, she feared the worst. Desperate, she appealed to Jim.

"But she said that she wants to see you, Dad."

"What have you been told, Doreen. Kids should be seen and not heard!" snapped Betty. "This is adult business. Go and make sure that bedroom of yours is spotless. No dust in the corners. I mean, spotless!"

"Go on love," said Jim. "Leave this to me and Betty."

Doreen knew that there was no point arguing, but she dreaded the fact that Betty had now taken over the direction of the meeting with Mrs Morgan. Once again, her dad had been spineless. He just drifted into the background where Betty was concerned; allowing her to take charge of his daughter's fate.

On Monday morning, Doreen took a letter from her dad, dictated by Betty, to school. It asked Mrs Morgan to come to the house on Tuesday at half past four. Doe explained to Mrs Morgan that Betty would be present at the meeting too. She warned her teacher that Betty would try her hardest to stop Jim accepting the Morgans' offer.

The following morning, Doreen knew that her chance of a better life hung in the balance. When she arrived home from school, her sense of foreboding increased. Jim hadn't returned from work. When Doe asked why he wasn't there to see Mrs Morgan, Betty was dismissive.

"He hasn't the time to sit around, chatting and wasting time. He's got money to earn. How do you think he feeds and clothes you, young lady. I'll deal with her. If you haven't forgotten, you live with me. I'm your mother now."

Doe gritted her teeth and clenched her fists. She suspected that Betty was trying to provoke her before her teacher arrived.

"But Mrs Morgan needed to speak to him."

"Well, that's just too bad, isn't it? She'll have to speak to me instead. Now get into the parlour and make sure everything's as tidy as it should be. I've got the best china out and I'll be offering her something to eat. I've already got cake and sandwiches in the kitchen and when she arrives, you're to bring them in and then you can brew us some tea."

Doreen went into the parlour. Just like she had with Emily, Betty was intent on impressing her visitor with her Royal Albert dinner service. Doe suspected that Betty would be putting on her 'airs and graces' and pretending that she cared about her 'daughter'. Doreen hated lies and despised Betty even more. She felt trapped. But as usual, she was helpless. What could she possibly do to help make her new life happen? Even if her dad was there, she knew that he wouldn't ask his daughter's opinion; find out what she actually wanted. Jim would do exactly as Betty told him.

At four-thirty, Mrs Morgan duly arrived. Betty was at the front door to let her in.

"Hello. It's nice to see you. Come in."

Betty smiled graciously at her visitor.

"Doreen, I'll take Mrs Morgan into the parlour and you can go and make some tea and fetch the sandwiches and cakes."

Betty watched Doreen go into the kitchen and then turned her attention back to Mrs Morgan.

"You must be ready for a drink and something to eat," she continued. "It must be wearing looking after all those unruly children. I'd rather you than me."

Betty laughed and led her guest into the parlour. It was a false laugh and Mrs Morgan knew it.

After a few minutes, Doe brought in a tray with the cake, sandwiches, teapot, milk and sugar. She placed it down on the table around which Betty and Mrs Morgan were sat. The two were still engaged in idle chatter, discussing the weather and Betty's Royal Albert tea set. It was soon clear, as Doreen expected, that she wasn't going to be a party to the conversation about her future.

"Thank you, Doreen. That's very good of you," said Betty, smiling. "Now off you go, so that Mrs Morgan and I can talk privately. You can go outside and play with your friends."

Doe looked at Mrs Morgan who gave her a reassuring smile.

"Remember, out you go, young lady. No listening at the door."

Doreen left the room and closed the door behind her. She knew better than to try and defy Betty and besides, she had no wish to appear rude in front of her teacher.

Looking at Mrs Morgan, Betty sighed.

"I don't know. Kids!"

With Doreen out of the way, Betty quickly got down to business.

"I'm sorry, but Doreen's dad can't be here. He's had to stay on at work to finish off a job. It's not important though. As he told you in the letter, I'm Doreen's mother now and he's happy for me to deal with anything."

Mrs Morgan knew that she would have to be diplomatic. She wasn't naïve and could see that Betty was being disingenuous. Like Doreen's father, Betty didn't care at all about the young girl's wellbeing. All the evidence told her so: the frayed clothes; the pieces of lino that covered the holes in the soles of her shoes and the spectre of hunger too. Yet Mrs Morgan knew that she would have to tread carefully, for Betty wouldn't tolerate any implied criticism of Doreen's situation. Persuading Betty to allow the Morgans' responsibility for Doreen's care, would prove a difficult task.

"Doreen's a very bright girl. She should really be at the grammar school. She could achieve so much and I've come to see you and her father to offer Doreen the help of my husband and I."

"Oh?" said Betty, sounding surprised.

In reality, she was disappointed. Although Mrs Morgan's letter had been positive about Jim's daughter, she had suspected that information about her misbehaving was being withheld until their meeting. Betty had thus been looking forward to an opportunity to punish the 'little brat'.

"Yes," continued Mrs Morgan. "My husband and I know how hard you and Mr Brodie work for Doreen, but how difficult it must be for you to afford to give her the chance to take full advantage of her talents. Mr Morgan and I would like to help you."

"And how would that be?" asked Betty, a hint of suspicion in her voice.

"We'd like to offer Doreen the chance to come and live with us and we would take full responsibility for all the costs of bringing her up. We're not intent on taking her away from her father. We would expect her to see him regularly and of course, you would both be welcome to come and visit her at any time."

"I see," said Betty.

"Doreen has real ability and we want to ensure that she achieves everything that she possibly can. I'm sure you both want the same. My husband and I would love the chance to make a difference and we're lucky enough to have the means to help her. Our children are grown up now and we would like to give Doreen the opportunities that they had. You and Mr Brodie are working hard for Doreen. Please let us help both you and her."

Betty's initial thoughts were ones of anger. How dare this woman suggest that she and her husband could do better by Doreen? Betty felt slighted, even though she realised it was true. As she considered the proposal however, she had to admit that it did have merit. After all, it would be wonderful if she could finally get rid of that spoilt 'little madam'; to not have to pay out any more money for her keep. But then, jealousy raised its ugly head. Why should the 'little bitch' get all those advantages? She and Jim had never got them and neither had her boys. Besides, Betty couldn't help being vindictive and so was unwilling to see Doreen get the chance of a better life than she had now.

Mrs Morgan, waiting for Betty's response, watched as the expression on her host's face began to change. The side of Betty that Doe and her friends had so often spoken about, was coming to the fore.

"How dare you! You're accusing me and Jim of not looking after Doreen properly."

"No, nothing can be further from the truth," replied Mrs Morgan. "We're offering to support you in helping Doreen. I'm not criticising you at all."

Mrs Morgan could see that her efforts to reassure Betty were failing badly, but how else could she have broached the subject? She was desperate to try and salvage something from the meeting.

"Perhaps I should come back again when Mr Brodie is here," she suggested.

"That won't do any good. I can assure you that he's totally behind me and I'm telling you that he's no intention of letting his daughter come to live with you. He'll say exactly the same as me."

"But I'd still like to see him," insisted Mrs Morgan.

"That isn't going to happen."

If Mrs Morgan still had any doubts about how selfish and nasty Betty could be, they were soon dispelled as her host went on the attack.

"Your husband is a councillor, isn't he?" asked Betty, quietly.

"Yes," replied Mrs Morgan.

"Well, let's put it this way. You're a teacher and he's a councillor and both of you are trying to steal our child. If I contact the *Evening News* about this, you'll have no job and neither will he. This conversation's finished. Jim and I don't want to hear anything more. If we do, then I've told you what's going to happen. And I don't want you filling Doreen's head with any of this nonsense about exams and university. She'll be leaving school before then and earning a wage. It was good enough for me and her dad and it's good enough for her!"

Betty motioned towards the door. Mrs Morgan got up and followed her out into the hallway and was shown out through the front door. Doreen, outside by the front wall with a couple of her friends, looked up. She saw the disappointment on Mrs Morgan's face and knew, as she had expected, that it hadn't gone well. She moved towards her teacher, but Betty stopped her in her tracks.

"Doreen, in!"

"Best do as she said" said Mrs Morgan, quietly.

Doe went up the steps and through the front door.

"What did she just say?" asked Betty.

"Nothing, just goodbye," replied Doreen.

"Get those pots cleaned up and straighten the parlour."

Doe did as she was told. Thankfully the incident was over. Betty said no more. The conversation with Mrs Morgan would remain her secret.

When her dad arrived home half an hour later, Doreen was desperate to get him on his own. She had to try to talk to him. Doe knew that Betty had turned Mrs Morgan down. It was obvious from her hostility at the door when she had left. Yet

Betty insisted that she and Jim went straight to the pub after he'd eaten his tea. There was now little chance of changing Betty's decision.

The next day at school, Mrs Morgan asked Doreen to remain behind at break. Without going into details, she told her that she was sorry; that Betty wouldn't agree and had made it clear that her dad wouldn't either.

"Doreen," she had continued. "Do remember that if you need help, I'm always here and if things get really bad, I'll do all I can to make it easier for you."

But how could she? Doreen's only hope was to have gone to live with Mrs Morgan. The only other possible alternative was the children's home and that certainly wasn't an option. No, Doe would just have to get on with life as she always had. Mrs Morgan still brought her the sandwiches and she was grateful. A few days later, Doreen finally managed to talk to her dad alone. Betty had told him that Mr and Mrs Morgan were trying to steal her away from him. Betty felt that it wasn't right and that he should report Mrs Morgan to the Education Committee. She should lose her job, said Betty. Doreen was horrified and begged him not to. She lied and told him that she wouldn't have wanted to live with them anyway. Mrs Morgan just meant well; there was no harm in her. Jim, lazy and lacking in confidence, was highly unlikely to make a formal complaint. Yet Doe wasn't to know that for certain. In order to protect Mrs Morgan, she therefore told her that it was best for them both if she didn't bring the sandwiches anymore and that she didn't spend any time talking to her outside lessons.

It was a wonderful gesture on the young girl's part and Mrs Morgan was deeply moved. It was the very reason that she had wanted to help. Doreen was such a selfless, thoughtful and kind child, regardless of all the horrors that life had thrown at her. Concerned for others and not herself. When she went home that night, Mrs Morgan was inconsolable; crying for the poor young girl and the awful predicament that she lived in. It was such a waste and it was wrong. She felt impotent, knowing that she could do nothing to stop Doreen's situation from deteriorating further. Like her pupil, she was becoming fatalistic. Mrs Morgan had tried hard, but she just couldn't make a difference. It was a brutal world and everyone was at its mercy.

Chapter 35

Ever since getting the Cliff Richard fan book, Doe had been 'in love' with the young singer. Her older friends, like Jane, had told her that it was nothing but a schoolgirl crush. Doreen though, was having none of it. She had kept the book in pristine condition and it was her prized possession. It was also a reminder of happier times back at Bright Avenue, before she and Jim had moved in with Betty. Doe wondered what it would be like to be sixteen and Cliff's girlfriend; to be married to him and have a completely new life. She imagined that it would be a much different world; full of friendly people and wonderful places. And it didn't matter if she suspected that her dreams of Cliff were mere fantasy, for the book remained a symbol of hope that sustained the young girl in the face of adversity.

As Christmas 1961 approached, Cliff was big news. His latest film, 'The Young Ones', had been released and it was coming to the ABC. The kids were excited. The girls wanted to love Cliff, whilst the boys wanted to be him; or at the very least, a member of the Shadows. To the boys, rock 'n' roll seemed a route to fame and fortune and in particular, the way to get the girls. Doreen had lost count of the number of boys in Ardwick, who'd somehow managed to scrape the money together to buy a guitar. The shame was, that so few of the lads seemed able to play them.

Sammy Lewis, who lived on Parker Street, was a year older than Doe and lots of the girls liked him. He played the trumpet, but Cliff's popularity had encouraged him to persuade his mam to get him a guitar. Doreen irritated Sammy. She was the only girl in the gang that hung around Tiverton Place, that ignored him. He had 'been out', as far as young, teenage boys could 'go out', with all her friends, but she totally ignored him. It was the same with his new guitar. He had learnt 'Living Doll' and thought that he sang it really well; just like Cliff. His fawning, female fan club, told him so. But not Doe. She had been dismissive; told him that he was out of tune and sounded awful.

She left him open-mouthed as she walked off laughing with her friends.

Sammy didn't understand it. All the girls asked him out. He quickly got bored of them and moved on to someone else; usually one of their friends. None of them ever complained. They were too broken-hearted; or so his doting mother would have him believe. Doreen however, was driving him to distraction. His ego was becoming bruised and battered. Yet he never knew what Doe had told her girlfriends. She actually thought that Sammy was handsome, but he was big-headed and she couldn't stomach that. She had suffered so much at the hands of Betty and her parents, all of whom were self-centred and cared little for anyone else. Doreen saw arrogance as a sign of selfishness and Sammy was the kind of boy that she could well do without.

Sammy wasn't part of the group who, along with Doreen, decided that they would sneak into the ABC to see 'The Young Ones' for free. The ABC was a huge cinema that also doubled as a concert hall. The building had side doors, which acted as fire exits, that could only be opened from the inside. Often though, people would come out of them whilst the film was running. Kids would be waiting outside and if they were quick enough, they could stop the door from swinging shut and then nip unnoticed into the dark auditorium. The cinema staff were aware that they would do this, but normally they turned a blind-eye to it. This was because they didn't have enough staff to continually guard the exits and as the kids usually didn't get to see the whole film, many of them would pay to get in anyway. However, on occasions the manager would launch a crackdown and would have staff nearby ready to nab the miscreants. Doe and her friends had been caught several times, but the worst that ever happened to them was a stern telling off. It wasn't enough of a deterrent and so kids continued to sneak in and if they weren't caught, got to watch the film for free.

Tonight's experience was to be different however. Doreen and five of her friends were desperate to see the film, but as not all of them could get the entrance money, they decided that they would sneak in together. If a couple of them couldn't afford to watch the film, then they decided that none of them would. It was a camaraderie born out of the hard times they had all gone through. Their tough upbringing, encouraging them to pull together. In the coming months, Doe had cause to be very grateful for her friends. They were the only ones who would show genuine concern for her welfare.

The group of friends had timed their arrival at the ABC for just before the early showing of the film had ended. It meant that they could nip in after people had come out through the exit doors, hide in the toilets, wait for the lights to go down and then sneak into the seats in the stalls, as the supporting film was under way. It all seemed to be going fine. Doe, Sandra and Jane all getting into the ladies unnoticed. There they waited, their excitement growing in anticipation of seeing the film. Once they heard the music for the supporting feature, they came out of the door, only to be stopped by a strange man and two usherettes who grabbed hold of Sandra and Jane.

"Just as I suspected," said the man. "There's no end to these bloody kids!"

The girls were shocked. They weren't used to being sworn at. So were the usherettes, who considered the language a bit strong. Taken aback, they released their grip on Doreen's friends. The girls were now free and Doe told them to run for it. Sandra and Jane didn't need a second invitation and charged towards the stalls, from where they could access the foyer and get outside. As Doreen attempted to follow, she felt a fierce blow to the side of her head and then there was nothing.

It must have been about ten minutes later when Doe found herself slowly coming round. As she looked up, she could see a high ceiling above her and realised that she was lying down on a long seat. A woman's face came slowly into view.

"Can you sit up, love?"

Doreen's head was buzzing and she felt dizzy. Nevertheless, she slowly raised herself up on the seat. As her head and vision cleared, Doe could see a desk and some filing cabinets in front of her. She heard a man's voice.

"Are you all right, love?"

Turning to look at him, Doreen recognised the man that had caught her.

"Where are my friends?" she asked, concerned.

"They're long gone. They ran off. They'll be home by now," the man replied.

"Oh."

Doe looked closely at the room around her. To her right she could see an open door. It had been wedged open; probably so that they could carry her in. On the door it had a sign that said 'Manager'. She now knew who the man was. It was clear that he had just been appointed and it explained his eagerness to catch them. Yet the manager was concerned. He had hit Doreen and had been afraid that he had seriously injured her. He was feeling guilty and regretted his stupidity.

"I'm sorry, love. I don't know what got into me. I shouldn't have hit you. Do you feel all right?"

Doreen sensed that he was genuinely sorry, but she couldn't forgive him for hitting her. Her dad and Betty had done so and she had never forgiven them either. Yet her main concern was that he might call the police. Having seen that the door was open, Doe was eager to be gone.

"It's all right. I just need to walk around a little. I feel a bit dizzy, that's all."

The usherette moved towards Doreen to hold her arm.

"I'll keep you steady, love. We don't want you to fall over."

"No, I'm fine," said Doreen. "Just let me try a few steps on my own. I'm starting to feel better now."

The woman moved back, as did the manager and Doe walked gingerly towards the door. Suddenly, she bolted out into the foyer and through the entrance doors into Stockport Road. Not daring to look behind her, she had no idea whether they were following her or not. Turning left down Apsley Grove, she kept on running and then ducked down a back alley after she'd got past Brampton Street. She stopped and listened carefully. Nothing. She crept up the alley and looked back down Apsley Grove. The coast was clear. Breathing a sigh of relief, Doreen made her way back to Betty's, where Sandra and Jane were waiting outside. Relieved to see her, they were starting to worry that the manager had called the police and that Doe was being questioned by them.

Doreen was left with a large bruise on her temple but she never told anyone, other than her friends, what had happened. Looking back, it was all very exciting and she had done it in order to see Cliff. The three girls were hugely disappointed not to see the film and decided, a couple of days later, that they would try to sneak into the ABC again. This time they were successful. In all, they ended up seeing the film five times. Doe wondered if the manager's conscience had overtaken him. It was so easy for them to get in. Perhaps he'd decided that it didn't really matter if a few lively, mischievous kids, got in for free.

Chapter 36

In rejecting Mrs Morgan's offer, Betty had been adamant that she and Jim cared about his daughter and could provide her with the opportunities that the teacher had spoken about. Yet, as expected, Doreen's life carried on as usual. Trying to remain objective, the young girl was thankful that she had a roof over her head and some independence to go out with her friends. Meeting Robert had shown her that the latter wouldn't be permitted if she were to end up in a children's home. Given that neither of her parents cared about her anymore, Doe was worried that such a situation was a real possibility. Living with Betty, for all its disadvantages, was preferable to that.

Doreen soldiered on. She found that accepting her lot was the best way forward. 'Why worry about things you can't change', was her favoured response, when asked how she coped with living at Betty's. Doreen's circumstances were about to change however. Unfortunately, it wouldn't be for the better.

It was February half-term, a couple of weeks before Doreen's thirteenth birthday. On Tuesday morning, having finished her chores, Doe was preparing to go out with her friends. Before she could do so, Betty told her that she must take out all the rugs and beat them on the line, after which she was to thoroughly clean the downstairs rooms.

"Not a speck of dust, Doreen. Get cleaned under the cupboards and the skirtings better be spotless when I get back."

It was ten o'clock and Doe was surprised. Her dad had gone to work at seven-thirty and Betty usually stayed in bed until much later. Now she was ready to go out. Doreen wondered where she was going, but knew better than to ask.

At eleven, Jane and Sandra called to the house. Doreen explained that she couldn't go out until after tea, as she had far too much cleaning to do. When her friends expressed their sympathy, Doe insisted that as she was so busy, the time would pass relatively quickly. Neither Jane nor Sandra was convinced, feeling that their friend was simply putting on a brave face. Yet

Doreen was a worker and the time did seem to go quicker when she was industrious. Furthermore, she never shirked difficult tasks. Unlike her friends, she was prepared to brownstone steps for sixpence a time. It was a job which they would never have considered, as they weren't as desperate for money as their friend was. For each sixpence Doe earned, could buy her a bag of chips from Chiappe's.

Doe had almost completed her work and was just finishing off the front room, when she heard the front door opening and the sound of voices and footsteps entering the hall. She looked at the clock. It was three-thirty. Betty walked into the front room, accompanied by two men who Doreen didn't know. They were 'merry' and had obviously been in the pub. All three of them dropped down onto the settee. Betty sat between the men, who were both carrying bottles. Doe knew that it wasn't beer, but she presumed that it was alcohol. Betty seemed in an unusually good mood.

"Doreen, still working I see. Sit down and have a rest."

Initially, Doe assumed that the drink had made her more reasonable. Given the presence of the men however, she wondered whether Betty was just pretending to be nice in order to create a good impression.

Doe looked at the men. They were wearing suits, shirts and ties and seemed old. The man on the left was smaller. He had a receding hairline and his black hair had started to go grey. He had a large nose and squinty eyes. Doreen didn't like the look of him. The other man had light brown hair and a friendlier face. He was holding one of the bottles out towards Betty. He looked at Doe and then back at Betty.

"We should offer this young lady a drink," he said. "What's your name, love?"

"Doreen."

"Would you like a drink?"

"I'm not sure. It's alcohol, isn't it?"

"No. It's just something nice. You'll enjoy it," replied the man.

Doe saw him wink at Betty.

"Why don't you go and get us some glasses, Betty."

"Doreen, fetch us some glasses. The smaller ones will do."

Typical, thought Doe, 'why have a dog and bark yourself'?' Going to the kitchen, she returned with four glasses.

"Hold out your glass, Doreen. Let's pour you a bit of this. Honestly, you'll like it," said the man, as he held out the bottle towards her.

Doe looked uncertainly at Betty.

"Go on, Doreen. It's all right. You can let him pour you some."

Although she felt uneasy, Doe felt that it was best not to refuse the drink. She didn't want to be accused of insulting their visitors, which would give Betty an excuse to punish her. Remembering her twelfth birthday party, Doreen had no desire to see a repeat of the events of that day. Tentatively, she held out her glass and the man poured the red liquid into it, only stopping when it had almost reached the top.

"Go on, drink it," said the man.

Doreen drank it down. It was slightly sweet and tasted nice. Having finished it, she went and sat down on the pouffe next to the fireplace.

"Give her another," said Betty.

"Give us your glass, love."

Doreen got up and walked over to him. He filled her glass and she returned to sit on the pouffe. When she had drunk it, the man offered her a third glass and she readily accepted.

Sat opposite the settee, Doe had been observing the three adults. She wondered who the men were and why they were there. Betty looked relaxed and was happily chatting away to them. It seemed clear that she knew them. At first, Doreen had tried to follow the conversation. It had been about the house, her dad's job and the local pubs. After the third drink however, she began to feel light-headed and it became difficult to concentrate. Gradually, the voices began to fade and Doe felt her eyes beginning to close.

Awake with a start, Doreen looked out through bleary eyes across to the settee. Shaking her head, she tried hard to focus. Suddenly, she realised that one of the men was kissing Betty. Doe was confused; unsure if it was really happening. She told herself to wake up, but it wasn't a dream. The second man began to kiss Betty too and then placed his hand on her knee, before moving it slowly under her skirt. Emboldened by his actions, his friend knelt in front of Betty. Reaching over, he lifted up her jumper and started to kiss the top of her breasts.

The young girl was shocked and confused. She had no idea what was going on. Betty was her dad's girlfriend, so why was she allowing them to do it? They had plied her with drink, thinking that she would stay asleep, but now she had caught them out. Doreen felt angry. They were making a fool of her dad and she had to let him know.

Making her move, Doe ran out of the living room and into the entrance hall. Betty, in a state of undress, was slow to react and although she struggled with the front door catch, the young girl was able to get outside. Once 'decent', Betty stood on the front doorsteps, shouting at her to stop. Doreen, turned and shouted back.

"No. I'm going to tell my dad! You're nothing but a prostitute!"

It wasn't a term she was fully conversant with, but she'd heard many of her older friends using it to describe women who weren't loyal to their husbands.

Doe knew that her dad was working at the 'Church Inn' at the back of Ardwick Green and raced off down the pavement. Betty had no chance of catching her, but she wasn't concerned. Everything would be in order when Jim returned. Betty was confident that he wouldn't believe his daughter anyway. After all, she was drunk.

Frantic in her desperation to get away from Betty and still feeling the effects of the alcohol, Doreen's judgement was impaired. Instead of stopping to look out for the traffic, she ran straight out into the middle of Hyde Road. There was an almighty screech; a bus driver slamming on his brakes as Doe shot across his path. Luckily, she was quick enough to get clear and her good fortune continued as there were no cars coming on the opposite side of the road. As she ran towards Darley Street, she heard the voices of concerned passers-by, as they shouted at her to stop. Reaching the corner, a couple of pedestrians tried to block her path, but she was too small and quick for them to grab hold of. Running down Darley Street, left at Dolphin Street and then Doreen was at Ardwick Green. She found the 'Church Inn' and saw Jim's bicycle outside. Her dad was painting one of the window frames at the front.

Looking up, Jim was surprised to see his daughter. Breathing hard, her face was flushed and she looked in distress.

"What's the matter, love?"

"It's Betty. She's nothing but a prostitute! She's disgusting, Dad!"

Jim was shocked. What could possibly have happened? He felt an uncomfortable sensation in the pit of his stomach. Once again, there was a problem between Doreen and Betty. All Jim wanted was a quiet life, where everything ran smoothly. Now he seemed to be facing a serious problem and he was going to have to deal with it.

Looking at his daughter, Jim was surprised by her appearance. Her face was flushed, her eyes had glazed over and her speech seemed a little slurred.

"Come here, Doe. You don't look well."

As Doreen moved closer, Jim thought he could smell something familiar.

"Have you been drinking alcohol?"

"I think so. Betty and her friends forced me to have some strange red liquid. It made me feel dizzy."

Clearly able to smell the alcohol on his daughter's breath, Jim was angry. He had never known Doreen to lie, but he could see no reason why Betty would have given her a drink.

"Calm down Doe and tell me everything."

Doreen recounted the events of the afternoon. Jim grimaced as she told him about the antics on the settee and she watched as he clenched his fists, a clear sign that he was angry. For a moment, Doe felt pleased. She dared to hope that Betty would be out of their lives forever. Yet it wasn't long before she realised that Jim had still to be convinced.

"Are you positive, Doe? You have been drinking. Are you sure that you didn't imagine it?"

"Yes, I am. I was really dizzy but I know what I saw and Betty chased after me to try and stop me from telling you. I nearly got run over getting away from her."

When Doreen had raced off to tell her dad about Betty's antics, she had assumed that he would believe her. After all, she had never lied to him. Yet now she could see that Jim was wavering and he was quickly calming down. It soon dawned on the young girl that it was going to be a case of her word against Betty's and her early confidence that her dad would simply accept her version of events, was evaporating fast. Having expected that Jim would drop everything to return to the house, Doreen was disappointed to see him pick up his brush from the paint.

"I just need to finish off the bottom of the frame Doe and then we'll go."

"But Dad, those men are still at the house with Betty. You need to get there now."

Doreen was desperate. The longer they delayed, the more chance that the men would be gone when they got back. Jim however, was insistent.

"I'll only be a few minutes and besides, I can't afford to annoy the landlord. He'll have more work if he's pleased with me. Betty isn't going anywhere. I can sort it out whenever I get back."

"But you'll miss the men. You need to see them for yourself."

Doreen was pleading, but Jim wouldn't budge. He carefully finished painting the frame and then wrapped his paintbrush in newspaper, to clean it out with turps when he got home. He then went inside the pub to say farewell to the landlord and finally, he was ready to push his bike home.

"Can't you leave that here, Dad? We're losing time!" said Doreen, in frustration.

"There's nowhere safe to leave it," replied Jim. "If Betty's done wrong, it makes no difference how long we take to get back, does it?"

"If." It was such a small word, but powerful enough to shatter all Doe's illusions. Her fears had been realised. Her dad was questioning her honesty. His initial anger had disappeared and Doreen suspected that Betty was going to win. The men wouldn't be there when they got back. She knew Betty. She could 'charm the birds from the trees' where her dad was concerned. Doe had seen her do it so many times and she was convinced that Jim would believe whatever she told him. As the two of them walked back to Hyde Road, there was silence. Doreen knew that if Jim didn't support her, Betty would insist on exacting her revenge. Doe now regretted standing up for her dad. By doing so she was facing an uncertain future. Once again, she felt alone and betrayed.

Reaching the house, Jim and Doreen went to the side entrance on Tiverton Place where they could get into the back yard to store the bike. Opening the back door, they walked through the kitchen and found Betty sat in the front room.

"There you are, you little madam!"

Betty jumped to her feet, ready to confront Jim's daughter.

"You had me worried sick, running off down the road like that. What have you got to say for yourself?"

Doreen didn't know what to say. She looked defiantly at Betty.

"Well?"

Doreen continued to stare straight at her.

"You had a couple of men in here," said Jim, breaking the silence. "Who were they?"

"It was John and Eric who go in the 'Richmond'," replied Betty. "They were coming to the house to see you. I bumped into them walking back from the bus stop after I'd been into town."

"Oh," said Jim.

"Yes, they wanted a quote off you for some work they might want doing. They're thinking of buying a big house in Denton and it needs a lot of work. It's rundown but going cheap. They're not going to buy it though, if the renovations are going to cost too much."

"Why did you bring them back when I wasn't in?" asked Jim.

"They said it was urgent and I know you can't throw away the chance of good money. You've not had much work lately, have you? I didn't want to risk putting them off and I thought you'd be back soon."

Doreen could see her dad falling for every dishonest line that Betty gave him. He was just like putty in her hands.

"But what about the drink?" asked Jim. "Doe was drunk when she came to the 'Church'. Who gave her that?"

"It was Eric. He brought a couple of bottles with him to give you for giving him a quote. He said that we should open one and have a drink. It was a sweet red wine. Doreen asked him if she could have some. I said no, but he went and gave her some anyway. You know what she's like for pestering. Then, when I took them into the hallway to show them where the toilet was, she took a load more, didn't she. Guzzled it down like pop. When we came back there was hardly any left. She'd almost had it all."

Angry at Betty's lies, Doe could no longer stay silent.

"You liar! Don't believe her dad. She's nothing but a liar. They gave it me and told me to drink it. I didn't want to argue with her and get locked in the attic again. Ask her about what they were doing on the settee, undressing her and being rude."

"Why, you little bitch!"

Betty exploded in rage, or pretended to.

"How dare you!"

Jim stepped quickly between them.

"What has she said to you?" demanded Betty.

Jim recounted what Doreen had told him.

"She's nothing but a liar, Jim. She was drunk, but even then, she knows it's not true. Ever since you met me, I've done my very best by that girl and this is the way that she repays me. I've tried hard to be a mother to her and all she does is cheek and insult me. This is my house. Where's her own mother? Doesn't give a damn about her! I gave her a roof over her head and what thanks do I get? She's lied on purpose because she hates it that I love you. She's jealous. It's not normal. That girl needs a bloody good hiding and she needs help. She's got problems. I had a drink with your friends to get you a job. To get you money and I'm disgusted with you, Jim. How the hell can you possibly believe that little bitch? Go on, the pair of you, get out! I don't want you in my house any more. Is that what you want, you evil little cow?"

Betty paused to look at Doreen and then turned back to Jim.

"Is that what you want, Jim?" she asked. "Well, let the little madam ruin your life for you. Selfish little bitch. Everything has to revolve around her, doesn't it? I've told you that you spoil her and now this is the result. Make your mind up, Jim. I'm not living like this anymore. She's not staying here and taking me for a fool. She's out and if you don't like it, you know where the door is. This is my house and I will be respected."

Jim looked down at the floor. It confirmed to Doreen that she had lost. She had told the truth but, as she had so frequently learned in life, that meant nothing. Whoever came up with the phrase 'cheats never prosper', one that she had heard continually since being an infant at Ross Place, was an idiot. In Doreen's experience, they almost always did. Yet Doe felt that she would give it one last chance. After all, she was now finished at Betty's.

"I'm not telling lies, Dad. She knows it. I wasn't that drunk that I couldn't see those men undressing her and touching and kissing her bust."

"That's enough, Doreen. Shut up and go outside. I need to talk to Betty," snapped Jim.

"Yes, get her out of my sight. I don't want her in this house ever again."

Doreen walked out of the front room as Betty, sighing and muttering, sat down on the settee. After getting her outdoor coat, Jim accompanied her to the front door.

"I'll talk to you later. I need to calm Betty down now."

Opening the door, Jim pushed her outside and shut it behind her without another word.

Chapter 37

Doreen waited outside. She knew that her dad was trying to smooth things over with Betty. Yet she wasn't naïve. He wasn't doing it for her sake, but for his own. She waited, sitting on the front wall, for about half an hour, but he didn't come out to see her. Realising that he and Betty would soon be going to the pub, Doe thought that she'd better make herself scarce. She knew that Betty would be angry if she saw her, which would only create further problems. She thus decided to come back when they had returned home and Betty might be in a better mood. As Doreen started to walk away, she heard the front door open and her dad calling over to her.

"Doe."

She stopped, turned and walked back towards him.

"Well?"

"Betty doesn't want you living here anymore. You shouldn't have said those things about her. They weren't nice."

"But they were true."

Jim was silent.

"Well, that's all right," continued Doreen. "We can move out and live like we used to in Bright Avenue."

Jim seemed anxious. He was finding it hard to look his daughter in the eyes.

"Dad?"

"It's not that simple. I've told you before. I love Betty."

"So, you're staying with her, then?"

Jim tried to change the subject.

"Doe, just for tonight, see if any of your friends' parents will let you stay. Tomorrow I'll find someone to take you in. It'll be fine. You'll see. Anyway, I'm going to have to get off now."

"Yes, you and Betty need to get to the pub, don't you? You'd better run along. You don't want to upset your girlfriend. She obviously means the world to you."

It was a scathing observation; an attempt to provoke some semblance of guilt. Yet Doreen had very little expectation that it would. Jim hated feeling inadequate and she knew that he would be unwilling to acknowledge that he had failed her. In fact, he was now eager to get away.

"Look, stay with one of your friends tonight and I promise that tomorrow, I'll find you somewhere to live."

Satisfied that the situation was resolved, Jim disappeared back into the house.

By now, Doreen was starting to feel hungry. She hadn't eaten since breakfast, but she had no money to go to Chiappe's and her most urgent concern, was finding somewhere to stay. Calling for her friends, Doe was able to tell them about her situation. Each of them asked their parents if she could stay the night, but they all refused. At ten o'clock, Doreen went to wait outside Betty's for her dad to return from the 'Richmond'. She was loathe to do it, knowing the satisfaction that Betty would take from seeing her predicament, but she had no alternative. It was almost eleven when he and Betty appeared. They were laughing and joking. It was clear that Jim had forgotten all about her. When Betty noticed Doreen sat on the wall, she exploded.

"What's she doing here? I thought I told you she had to go!"

Shaken by the ferocity of Betty's outburst and eager to avoid a confrontation, Jim sought to mollify her.

"Don't worry. I'll sort it out. You go in."

Glaring at Doreen, Betty stormed up the steps and into the house.

"Why are you here?" asked Jim.

"I've asked all of my friends and none of their parents will let me stay. I've nowhere to go."

"Well, you can't stay here. You've heard Betty. She won't allow you in."

"What am I supposed to do then, Dad?"

Before Jim could reply, the front door opened. It was Betty.

"Hurry up, if you're coming in," she snapped. "I'm locking up. Tell her to get to her mother's. Let 'the bitch' look after her. She's her kid after all."

Betty slammed the door shut behind her. Doreen could see that Jim was getting concerned.

"How am I supposed to stay with Mam, when we don't know where she is?"

"Wait here. I'll have another word with Betty."

Jim went back inside. Doe sat on the wall and waited. About an hour later, the front door opened and Jim popped his head out and then walked down the steps towards her. Doreen noticed that he seemed surprised to see her and she couldn't help thinking that he'd delayed coming out in the hope that she would go away.

"She won't let you in," said Jim. "It's no good, love. I've tried, but she won't change her mind."

"Why? I only spoke the truth. You know I did."

Jim was silent. Doe could see that he was too weak to stand up to Betty and too selfish to recognise the awful situation she was in. Nevertheless, she was prepared to make a final appeal for his love and support.

"Why can't we find somewhere to stay for tonight, Dad. We can get our own house tomorrow and then you won't have to do as Betty says. We didn't have any problems when the two of us lived in Bright Avenue. Did we?"

"There's nowhere we can go now, love. Anyway, I've got to go to work tomorrow. I need to get to bed."

"Surely there's a bed-and-breakfast we can stay at."

They both knew that there were lots of them along Hyde Road.

"I haven't got any money, Doe. I can't afford it."

"Oh, yes," replied Doreen, angrily. "You've spent it all in the pub on you and her, haven't you?"

"Yes, I know," replied Jim, meekly.

"Well, what am I supposed to do, Dad? Where am I going to sleep?"

"I've got the address of a friend, Doe. If you wait, I'll write you a letter to give to him. I'm sure that he'll let you stay."

"Oh, yes. I suppose he's a friend just like Sam, isn't he? Well forget it. Just get back to your prostitute. I'll look after myself!"

Doreen had rejected the offer out of hand. Intensely proud, she wouldn't beg anyone for help, even though she had absolutely no idea of just how she would keep herself safe overnight. It was a matter of principle; a way in which she would show her dad and Betty that she didn't need them. But it was an ill-considered move and it was just the excuse that Jim had been looking for, in order to draw a line under the whole unsavoury business.

Doe stormed off down Hyde Road and towards the ABC. Jim didn't try to stop her, or even call after her. He wasn't concerned that it was the middle of the night, with all its attendant dangers. When Doreen looked back, ready to cross Devonshire Place, Jim was no longer there. He'd gone straight back inside. The young girl felt a deep sense of injustice. Walking the streets, she feared being spotted by a policeman on the beat, who would take her to a children's home. Tired and desperate for a place to sleep, Doe arrived at Ardwick Green Park. Climbing over the fence, she headed for the park shelter. As she approached, she could make out the shapes of four men lying on the benches. They were snoring and there were bottles beside them. Doreen suspected that they were some of the 'down and outs' who would normally be found sleeping around the railway arches.

Afraid, Doe knew that she couldn't sleep there. Quietly, she crept around the shelter, desperate not to disturb them. Perhaps they'd murder her; she certainly wasn't waiting to find out. Once clear, Doreen made her way towards a large metal storage 'bin'. It was where the 'Parky' kept all his sacks, which he used to clear away the rubbish, cuttings and leaves. If she could get in there, Doe would be sheltered and hidden away from anyone who may be wandering around the park. There was a problem, however. The latch holding down the lid had been secured with a padlock and Doreen couldn't get it to budge. Searching around in the gloom, she found a large stone. Although she risked waking the men on the benches, Doe smashed the stone down hard on the padlock. It broke apart. She stopped and waited. Silence. Luckily for her, the men hadn't stirred. Lifting the lid, she climbed into the bin. It was stuffy and a little smelly, but the cloth sacks provided a warm, comfortable bed. Exhausted, Doe covered herself and snuggled in. Almost immediately, she fell asleep.

Doreen awoke with a start. She could hear a man swearing and fiddling with the latch to the 'bin'. Suddenly, the lid came up and she was confronted with the face of the 'Parky'. He was livid.

"What the bloody hell are you doing in my sack bin? Get out!"

Struggling to come to her senses, Doe was unable to get to her feet. Grabbing her under the arms, the 'Parky' yanked her out of the bin. She was terrified. The kids never misbehaved when the 'Parky' was around. Incurring his displeasure, they would almost certainly receive a 'crack'. Doreen knew that she'd had it.

Whack! The 'Parky' cuffed Doe across the head and then started to shake her.

"You're coming with me, you little brat. Smashing my lock and bin. I'm calling the Police."

Adjusting his hold, Doreen was momentarily free from his grasp. She needed no second invitation and raced off down the path to the nearby gate. She kept running, not daring to look behind her, ducked out of the gates, which fortunately, the 'Parky' had opened and headed across Higher Ardwick and down past the warehouses on Dolphin Street. Passers-by on their way to work, were amazed at the sight of the young girl racing down the road. She seemed oblivious to everything around her. Reaching the corner of Darley Street, Doreen paused for breath. She craned her head around the corner, looking back in the direction from which she'd come. The 'Parky' was nowhere in sight. She had got away. A wave of relief swept over her. It had been a close call.

Back at Betty's, Doe knew better than to knock on the door, so sat on the wall waiting for Jim to emerge for work. She hated having to come back, but she was cold and hungry. She had no money and until she could try to earn some, needed help from her dad. It seemed ages before he appeared from around the side of the house, pushing his bike. When he did, he expressed his surprise at seeing her. Doreen was sure that her dad had forgotten that she had nowhere to live.

"What are you doing here?" asked Jim.

"What do you mean, Dad? I've got nowhere to live, remember?"

"Oh," replied Jim. "What about your friends?"

"You already know. None of their parents would let me stay."

"Oh," repeated Jim. "I'm sorry Doe, but I've got to get to work. I'm late."

"I've got no money and I've had nothing to eat. Can you give me something, please?"

Doreen was trying to remain calm. She needed Jim's help and she had learned that if she lost her temper, he was likely to ignore her.

"I've got two bob you can have," replied Jim, putting his hand in his pocket.

Doe knew that he had more, but he was working at a pub and would want a drink at dinner. He wasn't going to leave himself short.

"Thanks. What arrangements are you going to make for me, Dad?"

"About what?"

Doreen looked at him in dismay. Was he really giving up on his responsibilities towards her? It seemed that every time she believed that his attitude couldn't get any worse, it invariably did.

"About where I'm going to live."

"Yes, of course, love. You come and see me after work and I'll get something sorted out. I've got to get off now. I'll see you then."

Jim got on his bike and rode off to work. It was still early and so although she was hungry, Doe had no option but to wait outside Newton's Greengrocers on Hyde Road, until they opened at eight o'clock. When the young girl entered the shop, Mrs Newton realised that something wasn't right. Doreen looked tired and dishevelled; she wasn't her usual bright and cheerful self.

"What do you want, Doreen?" she asked, smiling.

"How much is it for a tin opener and a small tin of baked beans, please?"

"One and six."

"Oh."

Doreen sounded disappointed; it was more than she was prepared to pay. She needed to keep as much money as possible, in case she wanted a bag of chips. Doe thought carefully about the situation and asked Mrs Newton a question.

"How much is the tin opener?"

"It's a shilling," replied Mrs Newton.

"If I forget about the tin opener, would you be able to open the tin of beans for me, please?"

Mrs Newton looked bemused.

"Can't you open them, Doreen? Surely Betty's got a tin opener?"

"Betty won't let me in the house anymore and I'm hungry."

Mrs Newton said no more. She picked up a small tin of baked beans, took it over to the tin openers and used one of them to open the lid. She then handed the beans to Doreen, who gave her the two shillings and received one and six in change.

"You can pay for the beans later, if you like."

"Thank you, but I'd prefer to pay for them now."

"Are you sure that you're all right, Doreen?"

"Yes, I'm fine."

Doe said goodbye and left the shop with the door ringing behind her. She appreciated Mrs Newton's concern, but proud and determined, she wanted to work and pay for her food, herself. Needing a spoon to eat her beans, Doreen headed to Janet's house. Her friend promptly produced one and the young girl enjoyed one of the best meals she had ever tasted. When Doe told Janet about what had happened to her in the night, her friend suggested that she should keep the spoon.

"If you have to buy baked beans again, you're going to need something to eat them with," observed Janet. "You needn't worry, my mam doesn't count the spoons. It's only an old one, anyway."

The two girls decided that they would take Janet's bike to the park. Not Ardwick Green though. Doreen was sure that the 'Parky' would be on the lookout for her, so it was best to keep away. Instead, they headed off to Bunny Park, which was near the railway arches and where the gypsies stayed. As young children, they had been told to keep away from them. Ignorant of the ways of the community, older friends and siblings told frightening stories which claimed that the gypsies kidnapped children and forced them to make pegs. Doe didn't believe it and last night, whilst she had been wandering the streets, had even thought of approaching them and offering to work in return for food and shelter.

Reaching the park, they played for a couple of hours and spent time chatting to some of the local children. Both girls were now at an age where they were becoming interested in boys, but

Doreen was choosy and spurned the attentions of a couple of lads who had latched on to them.

"I know," said Doe, "let's go to the arches and see the gypsies. It'll get us away from these boys as well."

Janet was shocked.

"No way! I'm not going there."

"Come on. Don't be a 'scaredy cat'"

But there was no shifting Janet. She simply wouldn't go. The girls therefore stayed in the park.

As dinner time approached, Janet had to go home for something to eat and Doreen waited outside until she had finished. The rest of the afternoon passed quickly. The girls went to call for some of their friends and together, they spent time playing in the streets. For a time, Doe could almost forget her troubles, but it was soon five o'clock and time for tea. Arriving back at Janet's house, her mother was waiting at the door. She had heard about Doreen's predicament and invited her in for a cheese sandwich and a drink of Vimto. Grateful for her concern, Doe thanked her. Having finished her meal, it was time to see her dad. Making her way to Betty's, she wondered if he had done anything to find her a place to live. How lucky Janet was. She had parents who clearly loved her. It was exactly as it should be.

Chapter 38

As she turned into Tiverton Place, Doreen wondered what lay in store for her. She knew that there was no chance that Betty would allow her to return and she suspected that Jim had all but given up on his responsibility for her. Doe suspected that it would be another night of walking the streets, searching for somewhere safe to sleep. She certainly couldn't go back to Ardwick Green Park. She was sure that the police would be waiting to catch her and as she had damaged park property, the courts would order that she be taken into care.

It was with a sense of trepidation, that Doreen mounted the steps to Betty's front door. Tentatively, she knocked; half-expecting Betty to fly out at her in a rage. But there was no answer. Jim and Betty hadn't set out for the pub yet, so perhaps they were ignoring her. Part of her was relieved; told her that she should walk away. At least it would avoid a confrontation. Yet her practical side reasserted itself. She had to try and resolve her difficulties and she was determined to make her dad find her somewhere to stay. She thus hammered loudly on the door. Again, there was no answer, but Doe persisted. Jim would have to leave for the 'Richmond' at some point and his daughter would wait until he did so. Eventually, the front door opened. It was her dad.

"Sorry, love. I was in the middle of getting washed. Betty wouldn't come to the door. You know that you've upset her."

"Oh, yes. Poor Betty."

Jim ignored her withering sarcasm.

"I'm glad that you're here love, because I've found you somewhere nice to stay."

"Oh, where?"

"Next door at Alan and Rosa's," replied Jim. "I've told them that you'd be willing to help Rosa with the kids and the cleaning. After all, you looked after the house at Bright Avenue after your mam left, didn't you? And you've helped Betty too. I'll be giving them money for your keep, of course. They're good people, Doe. You'll be well looked after."

Doreen was surprised. It wasn't what she had expected. Rosa was Italian. Alan, her husband, was a Mancunian. They had two young children; Gina, a baby and her brother Tony, who was two. Doreen knew the family to 'nod to', but other than that, she knew very little about them. She was slightly concerned when Jim mentioned the cleaning, but she had always liked to be helpful and was confident that Rosa wouldn't turn out to be as demanding as Betty.

"Well, what do you think?" asked Jim.

"How come they're offering to take me in?"

Doreen needed to satisfy herself that everything was aboveboard.

"Well," replied Jim, "they heard the commotion yesterday and asked Betty what had happened. She told them that she'd had enough of you and mentioned that I was trying to find somewhere for you to live. When I came home from work, Betty said they wanted me to go and see them. When I did, they offered to take you in. Alan asked if you'd be prepared to give Rosa a little help with the house and kids. I said that I was sure you would."

"All right," said Doreen. "When can I go to see them?"

"Now," replied Jim. "I'll come with you."

When Jim knocked on the front door, it was quickly opened by Rosa. Smiling, she greeted them warmly and ushered them inside. It was a positive start, which continued as they were led into the front room.

"Here they are; my little angels."

Rosa pointed proudly to Gina, who was asleep in her pram and Tony, sat in his playpen. Doreen was beginning to feel more comfortable. Rosa had certainly made a good impression. With her lovely, long black hair and beaming face, she seemed decent and friendly.

"Aw, he's lovely."

Doe walked over to the playpen and crouched down to say hello to Tony.

"Your dad says that you like babies and you'll give me a hand looking after Tony and Gina," said Rosa. "Alan's very busy, so I'd appreciate any help."

"Oh, Doe's very good at cleaning and helping around the house," said Jim, reassuringly.

Doreen noticed that he hadn't given her the opportunity to answer, but she didn't see it as significant. Rosa seemed friendly enough, although she had yet to meet Alan, who had gone to work. Aware that her only alternative was walking the streets, Doe knew that she would have to give it a chance and hopefully, everything would be all right.

"You'll be sleeping in the attic room," continued Rosa.

Doreen froze. The word attic conjured up an image of being locked in the bare, dark and freezing room at Betty's.

"Come and have a look," said Rosa.

"It's all right. I'm sure it'll be fine," said Jim.

It was obvious that he was now eager to get off to the 'Richmond', but Rosa insisted that they climb the stairs up to the attic. When they arrived, Doe was pleasantly surprised. There was a proper bed, curtains over the window, a rug on the floor and a chest of drawers. Crucially, there was a working electric light. It seemed as if she would feel comfortable sleeping there.

"This is nice," said Doreen, appreciatively.

"So, you want to stay here then?" asked Rosa.

"Yes, please."

"Well, that's settled then," said Jim.

"I'll need to get my clothes and things from Betty's," said Doreen.

"Okay love, come on then," said Jim. "She'll be back in a bit, Rosa."

Jim said farewell and they returned to Betty's. When they reached the front door however, Doe was told that she wouldn't be allowed in.

"You'll have to wait, love. Kevin will let you get your things after Betty and I have gone to the 'Richmond'."

"Dad, you're sure that you're paying Alan and Rosa for me to stay there, aren't you?"

"Yes, love."

"How much?"

"Two pounds a week. Why do you ask?"

"Well, I don't mind helping Rosa, but I need to know that I'm paying my way. That I'm not having to work for my keep."

"Oh no, I wouldn't have that," replied Jim. "Anyway, give it half an hour and then come back, love. I don't want Betty to see you hanging about when we go out."

"Yes, like you said Dad, we mustn't upset poor Betty, must we?"

As she expected, Jim ignored her. She knew that it was unlikely that her stinging rebukes would ever force him to examine the consequences of his actions, but she continued to deliver them in the vain hope that perhaps one day, they would.

After returning to get her clothes, of which she had very few, together with her pens and pencils, school exercise books and her Cliff Richard fan book, Doreen went back to Rosa's. Tony and Gina were now in bed and Rosa suggested that her new lodger should get an early night. Doe readily agreed. Having slept little over the last couple of days, she was feeling quite tired. Upstairs in the attic, she put her clothes and belongings away and then fell asleep as soon as her head hit the pillow.

Next morning, Doe felt a hand shaking her shoulder. Slowly, she began to open her eyes. It was Rosa.

"Time to get up, Doreen."

The electric light had been switched on. It was harsh and bright, forcing Doe to shield her eyes.

"Come on, rise and shine," said Rosa

Doreen blinked her eyes repeatedly and slowly they adjusted to the light. Sitting up in bed, she looked across at the clock on top of the chest of drawers and saw that it was only five-thirty. Her immediate thought was that the clock must be wrong. But it wasn't.

"I need your help with the washing. Get dressed and come down to the kitchen."

Feeling a little confused, Doe dragged herself out of bed and got ready. Going downstairs, she was called into the kitchen. There, on the draining board, were two buckets full of dirty nappies. Rosa immediately delivered her instructions.

"These nappies have been soaking, Doreen. You need to take them to the bathroom, rinse them off and then wash them in the sink with soap. Then, rinse them again and hang them up on the washing line in the back yard. It shouldn't take you long, so when you've finished, go back into the bathroom and stick the dirty clothes from the wash basket in the bath. Fill it with water and then take the scrubbing board and soap and get them clean, rinsed and on the line."

Doreen was shocked, but nevertheless, she did as she was asked, even though rinsing the dirty nappies made her feel sick. Rosa meanwhile, stayed in the kitchen where, on a large wooden table, she made her own spaghetti and pasta and then hung it up to dry before it was cooked for the evening meal. Doe was amazed by the sight of the peppers and garlic; items that she had never seen before. The food that Rosa would be cooking was strange, but Doreen was sure that she would get used to it. Importantly, there was plenty of it, suggesting that she wouldn't go hungry.

Wanting to create a good impression, Doe got on quickly with the tasks she had been given. As she worked, she tried to remain positive about her situation. This morning must be unusual, she thought. Surely, there couldn't be this amount of washing to do every day and perhaps she wouldn't always be woken up so early.

As she was finishing off the clothes in the bath, Doreen heard Tony crying and shouting for his mam. Shortly after, Rosa went to fetch him and was giving Tony his food at the kitchen table, as Doe walked through with the last of the washing. Hanging it out on the line, Doreen returned to the kitchen, expecting that it would now be time for her to have some breakfast. She was soon to be disappointed.

"Well done, Doreen," said Rosa, who was now cradling Gina in her arms.

"Before you have some breakfast," she continued, "I'd like you to sweep the front and back rooms, make the kids beds and then beat the runner carpets outside."

Doe was staggered. She was used to having to clean the house at Betty's before she went out. She had to do the sweeping, the beating and the polishing, but she hadn't been forced to wash her own and Jim's clothes, until she had returned from school.

Finishing the tasks and feeling tired, Doreen was finally able to sit down and have some toast and cereals. Once again, as she contemplated her situation, she tried to remain positive. It was clear that she would be given enough to eat and she had a comfortable bed to sleep in. Furthermore, as it was still the school holidays, Doe assumed that Rosa would demand less of her on a school day. As it was now Friday, all she had to do was to get through the weekend and when school started again on Monday, everything would change.

Having completed her work, Doreen was eager to go out with her friends. Rosa told her to be back by teatime. Alan, who'd been working away, would be arriving home and they were having a get-together for some of their friends and family. Doe felt pleased, assuming that she would be joining in the festivities. She had worked hard, but it seemed that Rosa and Alan were already accepting her as part of the family.

Nothing could have been further from the truth. Arriving home for tea, Doreen was told to make some sandwiches for Tony and herself and then watch the toddler whilst Rosa got everything ready for the evening. Shortly after, Alan arrived. He seemed pleasant enough with his blond hair and cheerful face, asking Doe if she had settled in all right. Doreen nodded affirmatively and he quickly disappeared to get ready for the evening.

At seven-thirty, Tony was put to bed and Doe was told to wait in the front room. It wasn't long before the guests arrived and began to join her. Around a large table, were placed eight chairs. On the large cloth, protecting the surface, were numerous bottles of wine. At the sides of the room, plates of sandwiches, cakes and biscuits were laid on top of the sideboards. As the guests began to arrive, Doreen was surprised to see that all of them were men. She'd assumed that it would be a gathering for women and children too, but the crates of beer stood by the window, suggested that it wouldn't be. The situation reminded her of the times her dad invited his mates into the front room at Bright Avenue. So, if that was the case, why was she there?

Everything became apparent when Alan came into the room holding two packs of playing cards.

"Right boys, let's get to it."

The men, muttering in agreement, sat down on the chairs. Alan got out his wallet and put a pile of notes and coins in front of him. The others followed suit and Alan began to deal out the cards. Rosa came over to Doreen, who was standing against one of the sideboards.

"Who are these men?" asked Doe. "I thought your family were coming over."

"Some of them have. They're my brothers."

Rosa pointed out three of the men and greeted them in Italian.

"The rest are Alan's friends," she continued. "They come every Friday and Saturday. Now, what I want you to do is stay here and when anyone asks for a drink, or a sandwich, you're to fetch it for them. If we run out of anything, you'll have to go to the kitchen and make some more. Okay?"

Doreen nodded. How wrong her assumption had been. The evening would prove far from enjoyable. Once again, she was working; at the beck and call of Alan and his friends. It was destined to be a long night too, as Rosa had mentioned that the games often went on until four in the morning.

At times, there were periods of frantic activity, as Doe dealt with requests for food and drink. At others, there were bouts of boredom, when she sat silently in the corner. Occasionally, there would be shouts of satisfaction, as a player won a sizeable hand and then groans of despair, as some gambled heavily and lost. Sometimes the atmosphere was frightening; fuelled by alcohol and disappointment. There were claims of cheating and the potential for altercation. Yet Alan ensured that there would be no violence. With just a word, or a look, he defused all such situations. No one dared challenge his authority. Rosa hadn't mentioned what her husband did, but Doe knew that he was a man it was best not to ask questions about.

Getting to bed at quarter past four, Doreen was exhausted. It wasn't long before Rosa was waking her.

"It's five-thirty, Doreen. It's time to get up."

Too tired to argue, Doe stumbled out of bed, got dressed and made her way down to the kitchen, where she was confronted by more dirty nappies. Her routine was being established. She seemed a prisoner of circumstances. Rosa clearly didn't believe that she was being unreasonable and was under the impression that Doreen was there to work for her keep. Although she was angry, Doe knew how vulnerable she was. She therefore decided to hold her tongue and bide her time and hope that when school started on Monday, the situation would change for the better.

When Monday arrived, the routine continued. When Doreen mentioned that she felt a little tired, Rosa suggested that she stay off school. Her lodger declined, astute enough to suspect that if she did, Rosa would find more tasks for her to do. Doe decided that she would have to talk to her dad. After school, Doreen sat on the wall outside Rosa's, waiting for Jim to come back from work. When he appeared, Doe told him about her situation and how unreasonable it was to be forced to work so hard, when Jim was already paying £2 a week for her keep.

"Don't worry Doe, I'll have a word with Rosa. For the moment, don't say anything and just do as she asks until I can get it sorted out. Remember, I don't know where your mam is and it'll be difficult to find somewhere else for you to stay."

Doreen found his answer confusing. After all, it seemed a simple matter. He was giving them two pounds a week, so other than keeping her room tidy and helping out a little, she should be allowed to come and go as she pleased. Nevertheless, he was right about one thing; there weren't people queuing up to offer her a home. Reluctantly, she continued with the routine. The days passed and the situation got worse. When Alan wasn't working away, he and Rosa would go out in the evening and Doe was expected to babysit. It meant that she couldn't spend time with her friends. A week later, she approached Jim again. Once more he asked her to be patient. He assured her that he would have another word with Rosa and he was confident that eventually, everything would get straightened out.

It didn't and as the weeks passed, Doreen felt that she couldn't go on any longer. She had already stopped going to school, although Rosa didn't know it. Instead, she tried to pick up odd jobs in the shops down Stockport Road, or knocked on doors to ask if anyone wanted her to brownstone their steps. The fact was that Doe still needed money to buy shoes and clothes and it was no good asking her dad. He always told her that he had none. Given how tired she was working for Rosa, when Doe returned from school, she had less energy to work for herself. Wagging lessons seemed the only solution to her problem. Convinced that Jim was unwilling to speak to Rosa, Doreen finally decided that she would do it herself.

It was April Fools' Day, quite apt thought Doe. She was now a teenager and everybody's fool. She had been duped by Rosa's original expressions of kindness; her dad hadn't acknowledged her birthday and her mam was nowhere to be seen. Awoken at five-thirty, she got dressed and went down to the kitchen. Politely, she asked Rosa why she had to work so hard, when her dad was paying for her keep. Having suggested that it wasn't fair, Doreen was in for a rude awakening.

"Paid for your keep! Every other week, if we're lucky! The jobs you do in the house are to pay us back for the roof over your head and the food in your belly. You should be thankful that Alan is good enough to allow you to stay. Betty would have you living out on the streets. You need to be a little more grateful, young lady!"

Doe was crestfallen. There was nothing that she could say. How she despised her dad. He had lied to her once again; let her down. No wonder he hadn't said anything to Rosa. He hadn't been paying her. Effectively, she had been working for her keep. Doreen felt humiliated; she was nothing more than a slave. It was unbearable, but she was helpless. Alan and Rosa were well aware that Doe's only alternative was to live on the street; they would never let up on her.

Doreen was waiting outside Betty's, as Jim returned home from work. As he approached her, it was clear that she was angry.

"Why Dad? Why did you have to lie?"

"What?" asked Jim, seemingly unaware that he had done anything wrong.

"You know what!"

"I don't."

"You lied to me about paying for my keep and that's why Rosa's got me working non-stop. All those times that you said you'd talk to her, you knew full well that you couldn't, because you owed her money. I stuck up for you, dad. I told her that you'd paid them. But you haven't, have you?"

Jim looked at the floor. Doreen knew that he was searching for an excuse. Eventually, he replied.

"Well, it's only a couple of weeks that I've not managed to pay them. Work's been a bit thin and I didn't want to worry you, love."

Doe knew that he was lying. He had plenty of work. He almost always did. Jim had lots of regular customers, who knew that he was cheaper than his competitors and excellent at his job.

"What you really mean, is that you've spent it all in the pub and on the dogs."

Jim didn't answer.

"I'm not staying there," insisted Doreen. "You need to find me somewhere else and this time, pay them the money."

Jim was embarrassed. Once again, he'd been shown up by his daughter. He tried to reassure her that he would put the matter right.

"I'm really sorry, Doe. I promise I'll find you somewhere else. It's probably going to take a few days, so just stick it out for a bit longer. Don't say anything else to upset them. You still need to have somewhere to stay."

"All right Dad, but don't think I'm going to forget about it. I'll be meeting you every night from work, until you find me somewhere else."

True to her word, Doreen was waiting for him every day at teatime on the corner of Hyde Road and Tiverton Place. Doe made sure that she had both the front and side doors covered. There was no way that Jim could avoid her. Yet, as the days passed, there seemed no prospect of change in sight. Finally, on the last Thursday in April, Jim had some better news.

"Get your things from Rosa's, love. I've got Betty to let you stay whilst I find your mam and then the pair of us will find you somewhere to live."

Chapter 39

Betty had been reluctant to take Doreen back and was insistent that it would only be on a temporary basis. It was a tricky situation; given that Betty refused to acknowledge Doe's existence. She wouldn't talk to her and insisted that Doreen stay out of sight. Every morning, the young girl had to leave the house before eight forty-five; the time when Betty got up. Doe was allowed in after half past four, but she had to go straight upstairs and into her room. At teatime, Betty refused her anything to eat, although Jim would sometimes buy some chips on the way home and take them up to her. Doreen was able to leave her bedroom after six-thirty, when Jim and Betty had gone to the pub. She could then do her washing, ready for the following day.

After a couple of weeks, Doreen got the news that she had been waiting for. Jim had found Emily and they would meet her the following evening in Ardwick Green Park. Doe hoped that the sight of her daughter, after an absence of twelve months, would prick Emily's conscience and she would help to find somewhere decent for her to live. It seemed strange that they were meeting in the park, but Jim explained that Betty wouldn't allow Emily to come to the house.

It was with a sense of anticipation that Doe walked through the gates of Ardwick Green Park. She and Jim made for the shelter and saw Emily sat on the bench. Her mam rose to her feet as they walked towards her. Doreen held out her arms and the two of them hugged.

"I've missed you, Doe," said Emily, kissing her daughter on the cheek. "You're growing up, aren't you? You'll soon be a young lady."

Doreen was silent. It would have been easy to take issue with her mam's profession of concern, but this was no time for recrimination. The young girl needed help and she had learned that it was beneficial to keep her own counsel, in situations such as this.

Turning her attention to Jim, Emily invited him to sit down. Doing so, Jim got straight down to business.

"What are we going to do about our Doreen, Em?"

"I'm not sure why you've contacted me," replied Emily. "I thought that you were looking after her."

"I was, but Betty won't have her in the house anymore. She was living with the neighbours, but she didn't like it there. She's going to have to go somewhere, because Betty's had enough. She wants her gone."

Doe couldn't believe her ears. They were talking about her as if she was a piece of luggage that needed storing away. Aware that she could hear every word of their conversation, they clearly didn't care about hurting her feelings. Doreen was convinced that her parents regarded her as an unwanted problem, the responsibility for which, each desired to hand over to the other.

"Well, it's no good looking at me and Sam," continued Emily. "We've only got a bedsit and there isn't any room for her."

"Well, she's got to go somewhere," replied Jim. "We can't leave her out on the street."

Neither Jim nor Emily noticed as Doe walked away. Sitting on a nearby bench, she waited as the argument continued. As her parents raised their voices, the passers-by could hear every detail of the heated conversation. Doreen sensed that she was going to be let down. It seemed that there would be no way out of her predicament.

"Well, you were the one that turned her against me, Jim. I offered to take her before you met Betty and she refused. She's your problem now. You need to sort it out and Betty needs to stop taking it out on an innocent child!"

"If you hadn't knocked on with your fancy man," insisted Jim, "none of this would have happened. It's a mother's job to take care of the kids. It's like Betty says; she looks after her kids, so you should look after yours."

Doreen had heard enough. She wouldn't lose anything by speaking up now and she was determined to say her piece. Jumping up from the bench, she ran over to her squabbling parents.

"Look, I'm not bothered about your arguments; who's to blame and for what. I just want somewhere to live. I know that neither of you want me; that's obvious. But you did have me and so you need to find somewhere for me to go!"

Shocked by their daughter's outburst, the two adults were silent. They both looked at her. Doreen felt her eyes beginning to moisten and suddenly, a tear ran down her cheek. Wiping it away, she was angry with herself. The young girl had her pride and hadn't intended to let them know that she was hurt and upset. Nevertheless, the sight of her distress had brought Emily and Jim to their senses.

"I'm sorry, love. We shouldn't be arguing," said Jim.

"No, we shouldn't," added Emily. "You're wrong Doe, we do both love you. It's just that life can be complicated. You'll understand, when you're older."

'When you get older'. It had now become the phrase used to justify all the hardships she had to go through as a youngster. For a moment, Doe felt like taking her mam to task for saying it, but now they had finally stopped arguing and seemed ready to discuss her problem, she thought better of it.

"Please, can you both just find me somewhere safe to live?"

"We will," said Emily. "I promise you. I'll be in touch with your dad."

Jim nodded. He looked eager to bring the meeting to an end.

"Well, Em. I've got to be getting off. Betty's waiting. We're supposed to be going out."

"Yes. I need to be getting off too. I told Sam that I wouldn't be long."

Getting up, Emily embraced Doreen, gave her a kiss and pressed half-a-crown into her hand.

"Here's something for you, love. I'll see you soon."

Doe watched as her mam walked off to the bus stop, disinclined to spend any more time with her daughter. Doreen thought of calling after her and telling her to keep the money. Was half-a-crown supposed to make amends for abandoning her? Sensibly, she held her peace. Jim had been unable to find a suitable home and Emily now seemed her only hope. Yet once she had gone, would she actually deliver on her promise? It had proved too easy for Emily to forget her in the past; a case of out of sight, out of mind. To shield herself against disappointment, Doe refused to harbour any expectations about the future. She was prepared for her mam to let her down once more. This time however, she was wrong. A few days later, Emily was in contact with Jim. She had found her daughter a place to stay. Doreen was going to Auntie Dora's.

Chapter 40

Dora was actually Doreen's great aunt; her gran's sister. Yet Doe had never met her. She lived in Bennett Street flats, which were a little way up Hyde Road.

Bennett Street flats, or Heywood House as they were officially called, had been built on the site of Manchester City's old Hyde Road ground, where the team had played until they relocated to a new stadium at Maine Road. Heywood House had been built in the 1930s. It was an early attempt by the Corporation to re-house residents of some of the old terraces condemned as slum housing.

As Doreen and her dad walked towards the flats, she was amazed by the size of them. Massive and imposing, they were four storeys high, with access roads passing through two huge archways that were incorporated into the building. Inside the archways were two stairwells, giving access to the upper flats. Between the stairwells, at the top of the building, the words 'Heywood House' were picked out against a white background and set into the tiled roof. Walking through the second archway, Doe could see that there were three, separate blocks of flats beyond. The blocks were arranged around a large open space, creating the impression of a square.

Auntie Dora's flat was on the third floor of the block furthest down Bennett Street. As Jim knocked on the door, Doreen wondered what lay in store for her. She was hopeful that Auntie Dora would be kind and understanding. After all, she didn't have to give her a home, yet seemed willing to do so.

Suddenly, the door opened and Auntie Dora was there. Throwing her arms around Doe, she gave her a kiss on the cheek.

"Come in, love. Don't stand there."

Jim guided Doreen towards the door and into the flat.

"Hello, Jim. Are you keeping well? I can't remember how long it's been since I've seen you."

"Must've been a long time ago," replied Jim.

"Yes, it must."

Doreen looked around the entrance hall. It was a mess. It hadn't been decorated in years and the lino on the floor was old and tatty.

"Come into the front room, love and I'll introduce you to everyone."

Doe followed her through. Her eyes rested on two men, a girl and a 'Lassie dog' called Trixie who ran towards her and licked her hand.

"These are my boys, Larry and Walt and this is my granddaughter, Sally."

Larry and Walt weren't boys, but two young men in their twenties who, not being married, were still living at home. They were employed at the local coal yard, working on the delivery lorries and Doe assumed that this was responsible for their dark complexions. Certainly, they didn't impress her, for she thought that neither of them was particularly handsome. Doreen learned later that the young men were keen on drinking and gambling. Occasionally, the brothers would fight. It would happen when they'd had 'one too many' and argued over the relative merits of City, Larry's team and Walt's heroes, United. Sally, who was a little older than Doe, smiled and said hello when Dora introduced her. It was a reassuring sign and made Doreen feel more positive about her new surroundings.

Dora was certainly intent on making sure that her great niece felt welcome.

"Don't you worry; you'll be fine with us. We're 'rough and ready' but you'll be safe here. I've told your mam that I'll look after you. You'll be sleeping in my bedroom with me and Sally."

Doreen looked around the living room. There were no rugs or carpets; in fact, there wasn't one in the whole flat. There was lino on the floor, but in places it was ripped. Auntie Dora had hardly any furniture and what there was, was very shabby. The curtains were old and full of holes. Yet Doe found comfort in this as she knew that Auntie Dora wouldn't be like Betty and Rosa. There was no chance that she would be expected to spend hours cleaning, dusting and washing. It seemed a reasonable compromise and so Doreen happily accepted her dilapidated surroundings. What impressed her most though, was Auntie

Dora's warmth and sincerity and in Sally, it looked as if she would have a good friend. Doe decided that moving in with them was her best possible option.

Dora and Jim went into the kitchen to talk, whilst Doreen sat with Sally in the living room. Doreen knew that Jim would be paying Auntie Dora for her 'keep'. Jim had tried to give her money in the living room, but Auntie Dora had put up her hand and asked him to follow her into the kitchen. Before they had left the room, Doe had heard Dora whispering to her dad.

"Not in front of the lass, Jim. It's hard enough for her as it is. She's welcome to stay. I don't want her thinking that she has to pay to live here."

Shortly after, Jim came back into the living room.

"Right, Doe. You'll be fine with Auntie Dora. Be good. Your mam will be over to see you soon and you can pop by to see me anytime."

"Betty permitting, of course."

Doreen couldn't help her acerbic response. It irked her that Jim was in denial; making out that everything had been fine at Betty's.

Pretending that he hadn't heard her, Jim made his way to the front door, where he and Dora said goodbye. Doe followed him outside. The two of them were alone and she took the opportunity to remind him to pay regularly for her keep.

"Dad, Auntie Dora looks really poor. You will make sure that you pay her, won't you? Otherwise, she won't be able to afford to look after me."

"Of course, love."

"But you didn't pay Alan and Rosa, did you?"

"Honestly, Doe. I'm telling you. Don't worry. Your mam and I have agreed that we'll both pay her. Your mam wants to help out. She'll be coming to see you and giving you money for shoes and clothes."

"That'll be a first!"

"No, love. Your mam and I have realised that we need to take more care of you. You can be sure that Auntie Dora will get her money."

Having tried hard to reassure her, Jim was gone and Doreen went back into the flat. She soon felt comfortable with Sally and

Auntie Dora, but found out at bedtime that there was only one big double bed and that the three of them would have to share it; 'top and tailing'. Doe took the situation in her stride, but a few days later, she woke up wet through. Sally explained that her gran had a weak bladder and that occasionally, accidents would happen. It was the reason why the mattress was covered with a polythene sheet. Doreen understood, but every time it happened, she washed herself assiduously, fearing that she wouldn't get rid of the smell of wee.

Doe's initial impressions of Dora weren't misplaced. As the days passed, her kindness continued. Unlike Betty and Rosa, she expected nothing in return. Only four feet ten, her grey hair in a bun, Dora had a tired face, but one always ready to break into a smile. Slight and thin, she had a fragile constitution. Only in her fifties, she looked much older; a hard life etched into her features. Dora had lost her husband when her boys were young. A widow's pension was all she had to keep herself, Larry, Walt and Sally. Her sons gave her little and she never asked for more. It meant just enough for food and rent. There was no gas nor running hot water, but for Dora's boys, coal was free. Dora cooked on her coal-fired range and in the morning, everyone washed in cold water.

Yet for all her problems, Auntie Dora never complained. Doe could only assume that she was an angel, put on earth by God to do good works. She often helped those who'd fallen on hard times, letting them sleep on the settee or front room floor. Dora would give anyone her last, but with so little, there wasn't always enough food to go around. At such times, Dora would go without, ensuring that everyone else had something to eat. When Doreen saw this happening, she would decline a meal herself, explaining that she had been to her dad's and had already eaten. It wasn't true, but it eased Doe's conscience knowing that Auntie Dora wouldn't go hungry.

Most importantly, Doreen's new home provided her with a sense of belonging. For the first time since leaving Bright Avenue, she was living with people who cared about her; Auntie Dora and her cousin Sally. Dora had taken Sally in when she was a toddler. Sally's mam, Susan, had divorced her husband and then had taken up working as a prostitute. Concerned, Dora had assumed the responsibility for her granddaughter's upbringing. Sally still saw her mam and as she got older, would visit her once a week. When Doreen arrived, the two girls had quickly become inseparable and through Sally, Doe had made friends with other youngsters who lived on the flats. It wasn't long before Sally asked Doreen to go with her to visit her mam. She had already told Doe about Susan's lifestyle. Sally said that her mam was 'on the batter' and that she was living with a West Indian guy called Eddie.

It was a long walk for the girls, given that Susan lived in a flat in Longsight, but they were happy to amble along, looking in the shop windows along Stockport Road. Eventually, they reached their destination. Doreen didn't know what to expect. She was now old enough to know what a prostitute was and it was something that she found uncomfortable. When friends had talked about women 'on the batter' she believed that Sally, although she didn't show it, must have found it embarrassing and as a result, Doe tried hard never to mention it. Going into Susan's house, Doreen was surprised. It was small, but ever so clean. The flat was spotless; so different to Auntie Dora's. It had a kitchen, living room and bedroom and very nice furniture. The living room had a table, sideboard, settee and chairs, whilst the kitchen had a new electric cooker. On the table there was always bread and butter, 'Adam's best butter', covered up with a cloth. Susan was very particular about flies.

Sally's mam was pleased to see them and made Doe feel welcome. She offered them a strawberry jam sandwich and a drink of orange squash. The two girls immediately accepted. Doreen savoured the fresh, crusty bread and butter. She always seemed to be hungry and was appreciative of any extra food that she was given.

Sally liked to go and see her mam because she knew that Eddie would always be there. Eddie lived with Susan and effectively looked after her, keeping her safe from the 'punters'. He wasn't really a pimp, but he didn't work. Susan earned the money to keep them both. Eddie had been with Susan for a long time and Sally told Doe that he loved her mam. Eddie impressed Doreen. He was good looking, clean and always immaculately dressed, but she wasn't prepared to do what Sally did. Every time they would visit, Eddie would give Sally two bob for scratching his head. He loved it and Sally was happy to oblige; especially for two shillings.

The money certainly came in handy and for Sally, as with Doreen, there could be no clothes or entertainment without it. Even shoes were a luxury, but as usual, the girls learned to adapt. They would buy a pair of moccasins for 3s 11d; the fashionable red ones, with the tassels on top. When the soles wore out, the girls would cut new inners from the edge of the lino covering Dora's kitchen floor and put them inside their shoes. Protecting them from the grit on the roads and pavements, it didn't keep their feet dry when it rained. Yet the girls knew better than to make a fuss, accepting with patience and equanimity, the trials and tribulations that life had dealt them.

Chapter 41

After moving to Auntie Dora's, Doreen continued to avoid going to school. She felt safe in doing so, as she was confident that the school authorities wouldn't know where she was. Her address was still registered as Bright Avenue. Only Mrs Morgan had known that she was living at Betty's and she had resigned, to act as her husband's political officer, shortly afterwards. Now that Doe had moved again, there seemed little chance of her being tracked down, should anyone at Ardwick Girls Secondary be interested in doing so.

What was most important for Doreen now, was to ensure that she had money for food and clothes. Although Jim had told her that Emily would provide her with the latter, she hadn't turned up to see her. The only way that she could have these items, was to earn the money to buy them herself. Doe therefore continued to do as she had in the past. She would brownstone steps, offer to do odd jobs and run errands for people and try to get work in the local shops at weekends.

Of great concern to Doreen was that after the first few weeks of living with Auntie Dora, Jim had stopped coming to the flat. She now feared that he wasn't paying for her keep as he had promised. Knowing that Dora wouldn't want to embarrass her by discussing the matter, Doe waited in the hope that Jim would return. By the middle of July however, Doreen felt that she could wait no longer and asked Auntie Dora if her dad had been to see her whilst she herself had been out.

"Why?" asked Dora.

"I wondered whether he was paying you for my keep."

"That's no concern of yours. I'm not looking after you for the money."

"Oh no, no!" replied Doreen, concerned that she had upset her. "I know that, but it's just so hard for you to manage and my dad should be helping you. I didn't mean anything."

"I know, Doe. You don't need to worry. Your dad comes round in the day when you're out. He always makes sure that he gives me something and your mam helps him out too. Now, there's an end to it. I don't want to hear anything more."

Doe didn't believe her. It was Auntie Dora all over. She wouldn't say a bad word about anyone, even if they deserved it. Doreen also knew that she wouldn't allow her to become concerned; somehow, they would all manage. It was a phrase that Dora used all the time. But Doe did worry. She knew how hard it was for Auntie Dora and so felt guilty that she was adding to the burden of worries that were heaped on the shoulders of such a caring and lovely woman. Doreen therefore realised that she would have to go and see Jim and find out if he had actually been paying any money. In the meantime, she decided that she wouldn't take anything else from Auntie Dora. Doe would use the money that she was earning to buy her own food.

Given Dora's difficulties, both Sally and Doreen couldn't help but feel anger towards Walt and Larry. Auntie Dora waited on them hand and foot and they never went without. Regularly, she would cook them cheese and milk in the frying pan on the Range. It was their favourite dish and they would dip wedges of fresh, white bread into it, unconcerned that their mam hadn't eaten for days. Not once did they offer to give her money from their wages to help. Yet there was nothing that Doe and Sally could do. They were living there because their parents had neglected them and Auntie Dora had come to their rescue. Both of them felt that they didn't have the right to criticise her sons; especially as they knew it would upset her. Yet, they were grown men who should have known better than to treat their mother with such a lack of love and respect.

Doreen's plan soon brought into focus the parlous state of the household finances. A couple of days later there was little to eat and Auntie Dora had served up some fried potatoes. She put four plates on the table and called everyone to come and eat. Doe realised that once again, Dora was neglecting to feed herself. As a result, she declared that she wasn't hungry, but Auntie Dora insisted that she must eat. For the first time since moving in, Doe defied her.

"I don't want it, Auntie Dora. I'm not hungry."

Dora wasn't pleased.

"Doe, you're being silly. Of course, you're hungry."

"I'm not. Honest. You have it. I saw my dad at dinner and he bought me some chips."

Reluctantly, Auntie Dora sat down, took the plate and started to eat.

Larry, with them at the table, asked Doe a question.

"Your dad bought you a bag of chips, did he?"

"Yes, at dinner."

"Well Mam, he can give Doreen money for chips, but he can't give you any money for her keep, can he?"

"That's enough, Larry!"

"No, it's not. You need to go and see Jimmy Brodie and get some money off him."

"I said, enough!"

Larry was shocked. His mother was furious and he knew better than to say anything more.

"Ignore him, Doe. He's stupid," said Dora.

"No, Auntie Dora, he's not. Larry's right. My dad hasn't given you anything, has he?"

Dora paused. She knew that it was pointless trying to hide the truth. Carefully, she responded.

"Doe, you're my sister's granddaughter. You're part of my family. Do you think that I would be bothered about money and turn you away?"

Dora was starting to get upset and Doreen realised that it was only fair to bring the conversation to an end.

"I know that you wouldn't and I'm so grateful for everything that you've done for me."

"Good," replied Auntie Dora. "There's no reason for any of us to talk about it anymore, is there?"

Dora looked at Larry, who nodded his head in agreement.

After washing the tea pots and cleaning the kitchen, Doe rushed over to see her dad. She was able to catch him just before he was leaving for the 'Richmond'. She told him that they had no food at Auntie Dora's and that Larry had complained that his mam had received no money for her keep. Doreen was adamant that she wouldn't stay there if Jim didn't pay; it just wasn't fair to Auntie Dora and she now felt embarrassed in front of Walt and Larry.

Jim, eager to get to the pub, was full of assurances. He told her to return to Autie Dora's and promised her that he would be there with the money tomorrow at teatime. The following day, Doreen waited, but by seven o' clock it was clear that he wasn't coming. He had lied to her. With a heavy heart, Doe packed her rucksack, putting her few items inside it: clean underwear, skirt, jumper, blouse, towel, the tin opener and spoon she'd acquired in case she bought baked beans and her Cliff Richard fan book. In addition, that morning she had bought some candles and matches in case she needed light. Pulling the rucksack over her shoulder, she carried her winter coat over her arm. It would have to be her blanket for tonight. That was it; she was leaving. She had already sworn Sally to secrecy. She mustn't let Auntie Dora know that she planned to leave, for she would only try to stop her. Doreen had her pride and Larry had made her feel that she was living there on sufferance. Doe couldn't stay under such conditions.

That morning Doreen had been walking around the streets looking for somewhere that she could stay and had spied an empty house a few streets away. She was able to work her way round to the back of the property, making sure that she wasn't observed by anyone. Taking a half-brick from the garden, she wrapped it in a piece of sacking, which smothered the noise when she smashed one of the panes in the kitchen window. Lifting the now exposed latch, she was able to open the bottom of the window and climb in. Carefully clearing away the broken glass, Doe climbed back out and found a piece of board to put over the window. Anyone coming to the back of the house, would assume that the window was boarded up to make it secure.

Arriving back at the house that evening, Doreen was pleased to see that the board was still intact. She quietly pulled it off the window and climbed in. Nipping through the kitchen she found that the key had been left on the inside of the back door. She opened it and replaced the board over the window from outside. Back inside, Doreen turned the stopcock on under the sink. Opening the cold tap, Doreen heard the pipes bang and shudder for a moment and then the water came out. She was delighted.

She could have a drink and wash herself and her clothes. As it was summer, she could hang up the latter in the house to dry.

Doe had arranged to meet Sally the next morning at the entrance to Bennett Street flats. Sally told her that Dora was concerned and wanted her to return. Doreen said that she couldn't and again made her cousin promise that she wouldn't tell her where she was. To reassure Auntie Dora, Doe suggested that Sally tell her that she had now gone to stay with her mam, who had managed to rent a house. Doreen didn't like being dishonest, but had no wish to cause her Auntie any distress. Sally agreed and it was now time for the girls to put the second part of Doe's plan into action. She had found somewhere to sleep; now she needed a job.

The girls chose Stockport Road as their location. It was far enough away for no one to know her. Although she was small, Doreen was mature, articulate for her age and felt sure that she could convince employers that she was fifteen and legally entitled to work. Looking at the advertisements on the cards in the newsagents' windows, the girls thought that they would be out of luck, until they saw a notice in a hardware store asking for an assistant. Doe realised that she needed the job, given it was the only opportunity that they had found. She had dressed as smartly as she could that morning, wearing her blouse and skirt. Doreen knew that she needed to make a good impression and so persuade the shop's owner that she would prove to be a reliable assistant. Doe was aware that she was going to have to lie and this made her feel uncomfortable. Nevertheless, she was a hard worker and the shops on Syndall Street and Hyde Road, that she had already worked for, were all pleased with her. Doreen was convinced that she wouldn't let anyone down.

Sally wished her luck and waited outside; her fingers crossed for her cousin. Doreen walked into the shop to see a slightly balding man behind the counter.

"Hello love, can I help you?" asked the man.

"Yes," said Doreen. "It's about the job advertised in the window."

The man looked at her surprised. She seemed so small.

"Are you sure you're fifteen?" he asked. "It's a full-time assistant I'm after."

"Of course," Doe replied, her feigned look of surprise suggesting that she was somewhat put out by his comments.

"All right then," said the man.

Pausing, he turned and called out towards the back of the shop.

"Jean!"

"Yes?" answered a woman's voice.

"Someone's here about the job, love."

"All right. Hang on. I'm coming."

"Jean's my missus. She always makes the decisions about who we take on. She's a much better judge of character than me. Don't worry, she's nice. I wouldn't have married her otherwise," he added, winking mischievously.

"I heard that, you cheeky monkey!"

Doe looked down the aisle at the side of the shop and saw the man's wife coming towards her. She had a smile on her face, brown curly hair and seemed friendly.

"Hello, love. What's your name?"

"Doreen Brodie,"

"You're here about the job then?"

"Yes."

Just like her husband, Jean looked Doreen up and down.

"I hope you don't mind me saying love, but you do look a little on the small side. There's some heavy work involved; lifting boxes of tools and so forth. Will you be able to manage?"

"Yes, I can show you. I've done similar work in other shops I've worked at."

"Oh," said Jean. "So where have you been working?"

Doe had already prepared a response to the question. She told Jean a fictitious name and address of a shop in Salford and said that her parents had just moved to Ardwick and she now wanted to work locally. Doreen had already reasoned that she would get taken on before any new boss would contact her old employer and that as she would soon convince them that she was a good worker, they wouldn't then be interested in asking for any references. It seemed very simple and straightforward. Yet unfortunately, it wasn't. Having satisfied Jean of her suitability, Doe was finally asked a question for which she wasn't prepared.

"What's your National Insurance number, Doreen? Have you got your card with you?"

Doe had to think fast.

"It's with my boss at work. I forgot to ask him for it, but I've got the number written down at home. I can bring it in if you decide to give me the job."

"Well, we do need it, love. Everything has to be official and above board."

Doreen thought that her chance was gone, but luck was on her side. She'd obviously made a good impression on both Jean and her husband.

"Look, I'll tell you what," said Jean. "We need someone urgently. If you come back tomorrow with your National Insurance number, we'll set you on and see how it goes. Mike, my husband, starts getting everything in place at eight-thirty, ready for opening at nine. You'll need to be here by then."

"Oh, thank you," Doreen replied. "Eight-thirty. I'll be on time."

Walking out of the shop, Doe felt elated. Finally, she would be able to support herself; earn the money to buy her own food and clothes. It was just a shame that she couldn't go back to Auntie Dora's, but Doreen knew that she would find out that she was working and would put a stop to it.

Outside, Doreen saw Sally waiting on a nearby bench. Her cousin looked at her and could see that she was smiling. Sally ran towards her, squealing with delight and hugged her.

"You did it, didn't you, Doe?"

"Yes, but you're going to have to help me. We need to find out about National Insurance numbers. They want me to give them one."

The girls thought hard and then Doreen suddenly realised the solution to her problem.

"They're bound to know at the library, Sally. Let's go there."

Carrying on down Stockport Road, the girls headed towards Longsight Library. Once inside, the lady at the information desk pointed them towards the careers section and told them that they should look inside the leaflet entitled 'Starting Work'. Locating the leaflet, the girls opened it and found out that a National Insurance number was issued to all pupils just before they left school and it consisted of a series of letters and numbers. Fortunately, the leaflet contained an example of one, so Doreen carefully copied it down, changing two of the numbers, ready to give it to Jean and Mike on the following day.

Going back to Bennett Street, Doreen spent the rest of the day with Sally and their friends. Doe then returned to the house at eight, wanting to make sure that she got a good night's sleep. Thankfully, the board was still in place; her refuge was secure.

Concerned that she may not wake up on time, Doreen had started to panic. Sally had told her that she was being silly, for she always woke up around six-thirty and that would give her plenty of time to get to work. Luckily Sarah, one of their friends, told them that she could lend Doreen an alarm clock until she could buy one with her wages. After all, it was the six weeks holiday and she didn't need it. Grateful, Doe borrowed it and with the added security of knowing that it would rouse her, she awoke at her usual time, ten minutes before the alarm was ready to go off.

Arriving on time, Mike opened the shop door with a cheery smile and welcomed her in.

"I've got my National Insurance number for you," said Doreen.

Mike seemed pleased.

"Oh, good. We always need to make sure that we do everything properly."

Doe handed him the number on a piece of paper.

"I've asked my old boss to send my National Insurance card to me and I'll give it to you as soon as I get it."

Doreen quickly got into the routine of work. At first, Jean and Mike had her checking and organising the stock; familiarising herself with the items that the customers would ask for. A quick learner and eager to please, Doe had soon impressed and by the afternoon she was already trusted to work on the till and so deal with the money. Jean and Mike were convinced that they had uncovered a real diamond. Doreen, in her turn, was appreciative of the kindness they showed her. At dinner, they told her to go for a break. She declined, saying that she normally didn't have anything before tea. Jean however, insisted that she take two shillings from the till; she had been working hard and so must go and get something to eat. Doreen thus bought some chips and kept one and six to buy three small tins of baked beans to put in her rucksack.

The following day, Saturday, was the store's busiest of the week. Doreen was rushed off her feet, but served everyone with the cheerfulness borne out of a feeling that finally her life was taking a more positive turn. She was in charge of her own destiny; doing something useful and earning the money that meant she could be independent. Thirteen years of age, Doe was proving that she could look after herself and by doing so, she wasn't running the risk of a so-called, responsible adult, ruining her life. When the store closed its doors at six o'clock, Doreen knew that she had put in a good day's work. Her sense of satisfaction increased further, when Jean approached her just before she left.

"Doreen, Mike and I have been really pleased with you over the last couple of days. We're going to give you an advance on your wages. We didn't like the thought of you having to wait until next Friday until you got paid. We know how you youngsters like to go out and enjoy yourselves."

Jean held out her hand. In it was a pound note. Doreen felt as if she had won the pools. She now had enough money to see her comfortably through to the end of next week.

"Thank you," said Doe, smiling.

"No, Doreen. Thank you. You're a credit to your parents. We'll see you again on Monday morning."

Doreen made her way back to the house. She wanted to check, as she had every day since she had moved in, that no one else had been there. Finding the board to the kitchen window intact, she set off to the flats to meet up with Sally and Sarah. Telling them her good news, her friends were delighted. It all seemed to be working out for the best. Sally and Sarah, both a year older than Doreen, wished that they too could be working and earning money. They knew however, that they wouldn't be able to leave school until the following Easter. The authorities, unlike in Doe's case, knew where they lived. 'Wagging' school, wasn't an option.

The following week at work went well and on Friday evening, Doreen received her first wage packet to add to her savings. The following day, she took advantage of her dinner break to buy herself some new socks, knickers, a jumper and a couple of blouses. All of the items were placed carefully in the rucksack that she always carried with her. Reflecting on her good fortune, Doe could almost believe in the promise of a brighter future. Just before she went home however, Jean took her on one side.

"Have you got your National Insurance card back from your old boss yet, Doreen?"

In her enthusiasm, Doe had forgotten all about it.

"Not yet. I'll get on to them again."

"It's just that we need it to get our records straight. The tax and insurance want us to give them the details to work out your contributions. At the moment, we're having to stop your tax at the emergency rate."

Doreen didn't have a clue what Jean was talking about. Only interested in the money on the inside of her wage packet, she had ignored what was written on the outside.

Doe realised that the issue wouldn't go away when, at the end of the following week, Jean again quizzed her about the card. Desperate to allay her employer's concerns, Doreen told her that she had got back onto her old boss and asked him to send it.

"Do you want me to telephone him?" asked Jean.

"No, it's all right. I'm sure that he'll send it to me."

"Fair enough," replied Jean, "but we really do need it, Doreen. We're breaking the law if we continue to employ you without it."

Doreen felt deflated. She knew that everything was on the verge of going wrong. That evening, Doe discussed her situation with Sally.

"I don't know what to do, Sally. Everything was going so well. I can't tell Jean and Mike the truth. They'd have to let me go straight away."

"Can't you just work for them part-time?" asked Sally. "You're thirteen and you wouldn't be breaking the law. It could earn you enough money for food."

"I've thought of that, but I can't face admitting that I've lied to them. I could get them into trouble. They've both been really good to me. It just wouldn't be fair, would it?"

No matter how they looked at the situation, the girls knew that it was hopeless.

"No," said Doreen. "I'll see out the week and then I'll leave. They won't be any the wiser and I'll have earned enough money to keep me going for a while."

It was with a heavy heart that Doreen went to work on the following Monday. She knew that it was going to be her final week. She wanted to thank Jean and Mike for giving her the job and treating her so kindly, but she couldn't. She knew that she would have to leave without telling them. It made her feel guilty, even though she knew that she had worked hard for them. The customers liked her and she had taken on far more tasks than had originally been planned.

Receiving her wage packet on Friday, Doe told Jean that she would bring in her National Insurance card on the following day. This meant that the next morning she was able to say that she had rushed out and forgotten it. As she said goodbye to the couple and walked out of the shop for the last time, Doreen knew that life's challenges were about to begin again.

Chapter 42

Returning to the house, Doreen was in for a shock. The board over the kitchen window had been nailed up and the back door was boarded up too. The landlord had finally got round to securing the property and Doe would have to find somewhere else to stay. The day was turning out badly. She remembered her Gran's favourite saying; that trouble always comes in threes. She had just lost her job and her home, so what else was going to go wrong?

Yet Doreen had learned to be resourceful. She knew how quickly situations could change. Every day when she walked to work and every night when she was out with her friends, Doe was always on the look-out for other empty houses where she could stay. Her friends, knowing Doreen's situation, also kept an eye out and over the coming weeks would provide her with the addresses of other suitable properties. Tonight, Doe would stay in a 'two-up, two-down' on Galloway Street, close to Bennett Street flats. Together with Sally and Sarah, she had previously been down the alley behind the house. Looking through the back gate, they noticed that the back door and window had still not been boarded up. The three girls had waited until it was dark and when everyone in the street was indoors, or in the pub, they crept back. Entering the back yard, they were surprised to find that the back door was unlocked. Doe pushed it open. In silence, the girls entered the kitchen, listening out to make sure that there was no one else inside. After a few moments, Doreen lit one of the candles that she carried in her rucksack. The girls then went slowly through the house. It had been almost emptied of furniture, except for a kitchen table and an old settee, but the upstairs was reasonably clean with lino on the bedroom floors. As usual, Doe would have to sleep on the floor, using her rucksack as a pillow. Going back down the stairs, the girls peeped around the back door. Unable to see or hear anything in the gloom, Sally and Sarah quickly departed. Doreen bolted the door on the inside and checked the locks on the kitchen windows. She felt secure.

Doreen always slept upstairs. Beatles and cockroaches terrified her. She knew that the latter infested dirty houses and near the old empty terraces, the back alleys often contained piles of rubbish which hadn't been cleared away. This provided a perfect breeding ground for them. Doe had seen plenty of cockroaches in the downstairs of empty houses, but relatively few upstairs. She therefore reasoned that if she stayed in the bedrooms, she was less likely to wake up covered in 'creepies'. Yet sleeping upstairs brought a serious disadvantage. It would be far more difficult to get out, should someone come into the property.

Over the next few weeks Doreen found herself moving from house to house. She worried about staying in one location too long. Doe always left the house early in the morning, but she could never be certain that someone hadn't spotted her. People were on shift work and the terraces invariably backed on to one another. If she wasn't careful, she could easily be seen from the upstairs window of a neighbour's back bedroom. Keeping on the move would keep her safe and out of the clutches of the police. Whilst Doe was anonymous, she could stay a step ahead of the authorities. Capture by the police would lead to the juvenile court and accusations of breaking and entering; which wouldn't take into account, her peculiar circumstances. A quick wit, fortitude and an ability to improvise, would hopefully ensure that Doreen kept her independence.

It seemed as if half the kids from Bennett Street flats were scouting around for empty houses. There was no shortage of properties suggested to Doe and her friends. Doreen was amazed at the camaraderie of these young people; they sympathised with her plight and were determined to help out. Doe stayed in a range of properties of varying quality. One house was exceptionally clean. It had an inside bathroom and the electric was still turned on. Doe felt so comfortable, that she risked staying there for a couple of weeks. Gradually, she began to feel that her transient lifestyle could carry on indefinitely. Yet with confidence, came complacency and the young teenager was about to receive a rude awakening.

Doreen had been told about a house in Armitage Street and even though she hadn't checked out the location thoroughly, it seemed fine. At night she returned. As usual, she entered the house and listened carefully for any signs of life. Encouraged by the silence, Doe made her way inside. Examining the back door, she noticed that it had no bolt or keys to secure it, but feeling tired she had no wish to go elsewhere. Ignoring her usual practice, she allowed herself the assumption that she wouldn't be disturbed. Making her way upstairs and into the front bedroom, Doe fell asleep.

In the middle of the night, she awoke with a start. There was a loud bang and the sound of a voice muttering and then swearing loudly. Someone had entered the house and they were clearly stumbling around in the dark. Doreen panicked; certain that the intruder was going to find her. What could she do?

Looking around in the gloom, she was able to make out a door next to the fireplace. She quickly stood up and moved over towards it. Quietly opening the door, she could see that it gave access to a shallow cupboard. With nowhere else to hide, Doreen squeezed herself into the narrow gap, which provided her with just enough room to kneel down. Pulling the door to, it wasn't long before the intruder came into the bedroom and she heard them slump to the floor, swearing and mumbling. Eventually there was silence, followed by snoring. Feeling certain that the intruder had fallen asleep, Doreen slowly opened the door, careful not to make a sound. As her eyes began to focus, she could make out the shape of someone lying in the corner. A whole host of questions raced through her mind: What should she do? Make a run for it and race down the stairs? What happened if she tripped? What would the drunk do if she woke him? Frightened, she decided to stay where she was. She just hoped that in the morning, the intruder wouldn't look in the cupboard. Pulling the door shut again, Doreen sat hunched up. Terrified, but incredibly tired, she finally fell asleep.

A couple of hours later, Doe was awoken by the sound of the intruder moving around. She remained still and held her breath, thinking that it would make her invisible. She prayed: 'Please Lord. Save me. Don't let me be discovered.' Her skin seemed to tighten; she felt sick. And then she heard footsteps going down the stairs. Her heart lifted. She thanked God, but still she waited and waited. It was silent. Finally, she opened the door ever so slightly and peeped through the crack. No one was there. And still no one was there as she opened the door wider and wider. Standing up, she stumbled. Her legs were numb from kneeling in the cupboard. She rubbed them furiously, desperate to get some life back into them. Moving to the top of the stairs, she listened carefully. There was no noise; it seemed safe. But aware of the danger she had only recently avoided, Doe was taking no chances. She slipped quietly down the stairs, peered into the kitchen and seeing no one there, raced to the door. Flinging it open she was out, never to return.

Chapter 43

The episode on Armitage Street had made Doreen wary. She could have no illusions about how dangerous her lifestyle was. To her friends it seemed like a great adventure; an exciting challenge. Yet for Doreen it was a nightmare, but one that she was prepared to continue. It was her stubborn streak. She had been abandoned by her parents and Larry and Walt had only grudgingly accepted her presence at Auntie Dora's. Doe remained adamant that she didn't need anyone else. She was determined to continue looking after herself. Yet a lesson had been learned and unless she was sure that a house was safe to stay in, Doe would resort to finding a sheltered spot in an alley, or even an outside toilet. The latter was often the only option if it was raining, but it wasn't always safe. Once, Doreen had been discovered in the middle of the night. The woman who found her was so startled, that she had failed to react and Doe was able to escape.

One night, in early October, Doe again found herself without a safe house to stay in. Desperately tired, she was preparing to settle down in an alley when it began to spot with rain. Doreen knew that she couldn't afford to get soaking wet and so risk getting ill. Looking down the alley, in the faint light of a distant street lamp, she noticed a stray dog walking into a back yard. Getting up, she went to investigate and found that the back gate was open. Walking into the yard she was surprised to see that there was a shed. Trying the door handle, she found that it wasn't locked. With the rain beginning to fall, Doreen opened the door. Taking a candle out or her rucksack, she carefully lit it and surveyed the interior. Doe could see that there were lots of boxes stacked up against the side of the shed and at the end too, but there was enough room down the middle for her to sleep. Doreen noticed that there were some old blankets on top of the boxes. Closing the shed door behind her, she took some of them and lay them on the floor. Settling down, she covered herself with the rest. As she cuddled into the blankets, Doe heard the rain bouncing off the roof and sides of the shed. It was a comforting sound. She couldn't believe her luck. She felt so safe and warm.

Doreen awoke to the sound of screaming. Startled, she opened her eyes to see a woman stood in the doorway. Springing to her feet, Doe went to push past her but was grabbed firmly. Not wanting to hit out, she was trapped.

Overcoming her shock at seeing someone asleep in the shed, the woman gradually calmed down.

"What on earth are you doing?" she asked.

Doe couldn't speak. She was suddenly afraid. What if someone had heard the woman scream? What if they had called the police? Doreen felt as if her luck had finally run out.

"Come on. Speak up child."

"I'm sorry."

"What for?"

"For sleeping in your shed."

The woman looked at Doreen. Her mood had changed. Her compassion for the lost 'waif and stray' had overcome her initial anger and she released her grip on the young girl.

"Don't be afraid, child. Let's go inside, get you some breakfast and then you can tell me why you're sleeping out."

The woman let Doe out of the shed and the two of them walked towards the kitchen door. Doreen knew that she could have run away, but something told her that it was safe to go inside. Entering the kitchen, Doe was told to sit at the table. Her host went to the hallway and shouted to her husband who was still upstairs.

"Andy. I'm putting your breakfast on. We've got a visitor."

Coming back into the kitchen, she was quick to put her guest at ease.

"Don't worry. My husband's nice. He's called Andy. My name's Dorothy, but everyone calls me Dot. What's your name, love?"

"Doreen."

"Well, Doreen. We'll have something to eat and then we can have a chat."

"Do you want me to help?"

"No, love. You just sit there."

Dot set about preparing some toast and porridge. She had already made Doe a drink of tea, which was something of a luxury for the young girl, as she normally woke up in empty houses with no cooking facilities or hot water. Dot looked to be around the same age as her mam, but she was taller and plump. With medium length, brown hair and wearing glasses, Dot had a kind and friendly face.

"Hello. Who's this then?"

Doe turned to see Andy. He was big and broad. She was a little intimidated by the size of him.

"This is Doreen. I've asked her in for some breakfast."

"Oh. Nice to meet you, love."

Andy smiled. It was a smile of reassurance. It dispelled Doe's earlier misgivings. They were a nice couple. They had come across a young girl in difficulty and they were offering her a helping hand.

Andy and Dot sat down and the three of them had breakfast. Doreen couldn't remember the last time that she had eaten a meal, sat down at a well laid table, like she was part of a proper family. Soon her eyes began to fill with tears. She put her head down trying to disguise her distress and told herself to stop it. Stop getting upset. But both Dot and Andy had seen her and although they carried on talking to one another, Doreen felt embarrassed. She wanted to appear tough; not allow anyone to see her soft centre and so expose her vulnerability. Regaining her composure, she quickly wiped her eyes.

Soon it was time for Andy to set off to work. Dot kissed him at the door and he was gone. Sitting back at the table, Dot began to ask Doe lots of questions: Why was she sleeping rough? Why wasn't she at school? Where were her parents? How did she manage to survive? Doreen answered truthfully. She told Dot that she couldn't go to school as she had to work to earn money for food and clothes; that her parents took little interest in her. She explained how her parents' new partners made it almost impossible for her to live with them and how she was terrified of being sent to a children's home. Dot listened sympathetically. She was shocked; her heart went out to her visitor. She felt that she must do something to help and suggested to Doreen that she stay with her and Andy for a time, so that she could rest and recuperate. Doe agreed. She felt safe and was confident that Dot wouldn't contact either the police or the children's department.

Doe insisted on helping Dot to tidy up. There wasn't much to do, however. Everywhere was spotless; everything in its place. Dot and Andy had a lovely home. Nice furniture and carpets and all of it very well decorated. As Dot chatted to Doreen, she told her that they didn't have any children, but that they had nieces and nephews who would occasionally stay over. Both she and Andy had wanted children but if it wasn't to be, they were more than happy to have each other. It was a lovely sentiment and one that made Doe wonder why her own parents couldn't have appreciated one another more. If they had, they would still be together and their daughter's situation would have been very different.

When Andy came home from work, they all had tea. Dot had made a corned beef hash and Doreen eagerly tucked in. Having eaten breakfast, had a sandwich for her dinner and now a hot meal for tea, she was almost ready to burst. Doe asked if she could help by washing the pots. Dot agreed and asked Doreen if she would excuse her, as she needed to talk privately to Andy in the front room. As Doe was putting away the last of the pots, Dot returned and asked her to sit down at the table.

"Doreen, will you take me to see your dad?"

"Why?" replied Doe, surprised.

"We'll need your dad's permission if you're to stay here."

Doreen was startled. She didn't realise that Dot had envisaged her staying for a long time. She had assumed that it would just be for a few days in order to give her time to get back on her feet.

"I haven't seen my dad for three months. Why do you need his permission?"

"Andy says that as he's your parent, we have to get his permission. If you'd rather, we can ask your mam, but at least one of them will have to agree."

Doreen wasn't convinced.

"But they don't care about me. Neither of them has any idea where I am. For all they know, I could be dead."

"I'm sorry Doreen, but Andy insists on me speaking to one of them."

"All right," replied Doe, somewhat reluctantly.

"Well, when do you think we should go?" asked Dot.

"It's too late tonight. My dad will already be in the pub and so will my mam. Anyway, I'm not sure where she's living. I can take you to my dad's tomorrow. It would be best to go just after tea when he should be home from work."

It was agreed. Doreen felt a sense of relief. She had managed to secure at least one more comfortable night, without having to worry about where she would sleep.

When they had finished talking, the two of them went into the front room and joined Andy. For a time, they played board games and then Dot told Doreen that it was time for a bath. They went upstairs and Dot showed her the bedroom in which she would be sleeping. There was a fire burning in the grate and the room was warm and inviting. Dot left her to run the bath and then returned with a spare nightie.

"When you finish your bath, bring down your dirty clothes and I'll wash them for you."

Getting in the bath, Doreen slipped into the welcoming hot water. Dot had added some salts and the smell was fragrant. She had given Doe some Palmolive soap papers with which to wash her hair. Shaped to the palm of her hand, they had a hole through which she placed her thumb. Dipping her hand in the water, she rubbed it in her hair and felt the soap foaming through her fingers. Lying back, she felt completely relaxed. Tapping on the door, Dot asked her if she was all right. Answering affirmatively, Doreen was grateful for her concern.

Getting out of the bath, there were two big fluffy towels for Doe to dry herself on. She rubbed them all over her. Their softness was comforting and when she had finished, she cleaned out the bath, wiped it dry with the towels, put on her nightie and brought the towels and her dirty clothes downstairs. Dot took them to the kitchen and the two of them returned to the front room. Andy was listening to the radio and so Doreen and Dot sat quietly waiting for the programme to end. Once it had finished, Dot went into the kitchen to make them all a cup of tea and then brought in the drinks on a large tray, along with a tin of biscuits. It seemed that Dot and Andy's life pretty much ran to a routine. They lived well. It was so far removed from what she was used to, even when compared to the time she had lived with her parents in Bright Avenue. And there was the problem. What was she going to do about the request to see her dad? But for one night at least, the young girl could afford to put such thoughts to one side. Going up to her room, she fell asleep as soon as her head hit the pillow.

Dot woke her at ten o'clock. Doreen was still drowsy. She didn't want to wake up. The bed was warm, the pillow was soft and the fire was still alive, Dot having kept it going through the night. Doe wished that it could be like this forever. No worries; everything just perfect. But soon reality returned and Doreen's mind began to wander. Awkward questions began to pop into her head. What if she wanted this to continue? Stay here with Dot and Andy. What could she do to avoid having to take them to see her dad?

Awake, Doe got out of bed and soon realised that she had no clothes. Dot had taken all of them to wash, including the ones out of her rucksack. Dot had however, left her a dressing gown on the bottom of the bed. Doreen put it on and made her way downstairs. Entering the kitchen, she could see her clothes drying on the maiden in front of the fire.

"Hello, sleepy head," said Dot. "You really were tired, weren't you? I suppose you haven't had a proper night's rest for days."

"No, I haven't. It's hard to get comfortable or warm in some of the places I've had to stay."

"Well hopefully, all that could change. Sit down and I'll make you some breakfast."

Dot chatted away as she made some boiled eggs and toast along with a steaming, hot cup of tea.

"There's salt and pepper on the side if you want some," said Dot.

"Thanks," replied Doreen. "You've been very kind. I'm really sorry that I scared you in the shed yesterday."

"That's all right, love. I don't blame you. You didn't have much choice, did you?"

Doe was finding it hard to believe that someone could be so kind to her. After all, she was a stranger and this wonderful lady had no reason to help her. Why couldn't her own parents show just a small amount of the concern and compassion that Dot had?

Yet something was eating away at Doreen. It just didn't seem right for Dot and Andy to take on the responsibility of taking care of her, when it should be her parents' concern.

"Well, Doreen. What time are we going to see your dad?"

Doreen hesitated.

"You don't like the thought of going to see him, do you?"

"No."

"Why not, love?"

"Because he doesn't care. I don't want to see him ever again. He promised me faithfully that he would pay Auntie Dora for my keep and he lied. All he's bothered about is going to the pub with Betty. I don't think that he even remembers that he has a daughter. I don't want to ask him for anything again."

"I understand," replied Dot, "but Andy's right. We can't let you stay without his permission."

"Can't you wait for me to try and find my mam. Someone's bound to know where she is."

"But that could take a long time, Doreen. It's best we go to see your dad, as you know where he is and then we can sort things out quickly."

Doreen agreed, yet she still had misgivings and hadn't told Dot the whole truth. Deep down, she still clung to the belief that eventually, her dad would see the error of his ways. By not contacting him, Doe hoped that he would start to worry about her. It was only then, that he would finally realise how cruel and selfish Betty was, leave her and go back to the life that he and Doreen had shared in Bright Avenue.

Yet experience had consistently undermined such hopes and Jim's attitude was unlikely to change. It therefore seemed sensible to take Dot to see him. The only problem was that Betty would insist on getting involved; just like she had when Mrs Morgan had contacted her dad. Doe had to assume that if they went to the house, Betty would be vindictive. She would insist that Jim's daughter was unruly and disobedient and if Dot and Andy believed her, they would withdraw their offer of help. Even if they didn't, Doreen was sure that Betty would persuade Jim to withhold his permission for her to live with them.

With a growing sense of unease, Doe decided that she had to take the chance. It was Friday lunchtime and she suspected that her dad may have knocked off early from work, as he often did at the end of the week and was with Betty in one of the pubs around Syndall Street. Together with Dot, Doreen looked in the 'Clarence', the 'George', the 'Rutland' and the 'Richmond'. Jim wasn't in any of them. By now, Doe was becoming increasingly anxious; dreading the prospect of a confrontation with Betty. Finally, Doreen took Dot to Betty's house on Hyde Road. As they waited outside the front door, the young girl was silently praying that there would be no answer. There wasn't; thankfully her dad and Betty were out.

Returning to Dot's, Doe was relieved and hoped that she would be allowed to remain without her dad's permission. After all, they had tried. It wasn't their fault if they had been unable to contact him. In the afternoon, Doreen and Dot got on with the cleaning and prepared the tea ready for Andy's return; lamb chops, potatoes, peas and gravy. The food was lovely and Doe suddenly realised how long it had been since she hadn't worried about having enough to eat. She was safe and secure; Dot making sure that she was properly cared for. The young teenager was tantalisingly close to a situation where her lifestyle would change completely. Yet the problem remained. After tea, Andy was adamant; they needed Jim's blessing if Doreen were to stay.

"I know it's probably just a formality," said Andy to his wife. "Especially given what Doreen's told us and the fact that we saw her sleeping rough for ourselves. I suspect that he probably won't object to Doreen staying here, but we have to be certain. It's Saturday tomorrow, so we can all go round to the house to see him."

That night Dot asked Doreen more about how she had managed to survive on her own and get away with not going to school. Doe explained that lots of part-time jobs could be found in the local stores and at times, some shopkeepers would let her work all day. Dot was surprised. Surely, they knew that she was too young? Doreen told her that they didn't care; that they were prepared to pay her eight shillings and with this she was able to buy her food. School hadn't been an option for months; food and clothing had to come first.

Dot was visibly shocked that a young girl could simply avoid going to school and that local shopkeepers, knowing that she was truanting, were still prepared to give her work. She could see however, the fierce pride that shone in the young girl's eyes. She felt independent; able to stick up for herself. It was an impressive achievement that she had survived alone against the odds, adamant that she would never end up in a children's home, scrubbing floors and being beaten. If ever anyone needed help and deserved it, it was Doreen and Dot was desperate to give it.

Later, as she lay awake in bed, Doe realised that the conversation with Dot had provided food for thought. She had been let down by people in the past and wondered if she could ever feel comfortable relying on anyone else again. If she did stay with Andy and Dot, could she be certain that everything would remain as it was and if it did, was it really what she wanted? She had to admit that to some extent, it was appealing. For the first time in ages, she had no real worries. She had food, warmth, a bed, clean clothes, everything that she had dreamed of. Yet Doreen was well aware that they would expect her to go back to school and would discourage her from working. It would mean that she would become dependent and that was a situation that ultimately, she wasn't prepared to accept. So, whilst Dot contented herself with thinking about how they would improve Doreen's life: getting her back in the grammar school; buying her new clothes and taking her on holiday, in her own mind, the young girl had already gone. Doe decided that she would leave tomorrow. Before that however, she would appreciate her last, comfortable night; safe and happy, before reality came stealing back into her life.

Next morning, Doe made sure that she packed all her clothes and her few possessions into her rucksack. Whilst Dot and Andy were talking in the front room, she sneaked out to the shed and hid it behind some boxes. At ten o'clock, Doreen took Andy and Dot back to Betty's. She asked them if it was all right for her to wait outside, saying that she didn't want to go in and see her dad. Dot, who knew of her dislike for Betty, assured Andy that it was fine. Doreen said that she would wait at the corner of Tiverton Place and from there watched as Andy knocked on the door. There was no answer. He knocked again. This time the door opened. Doe heard Andy introduce himself and saw him disappear through the door, followed by Dot. It was Doreen's cue to leave. As quickly as she could, Doe made her way back to the house, picked up her rucksack from the shed and set off to find Sally and Sarah.

Doreen couldn't help feeling guilty at leaving without a word of explanation, for Andy and Dot had been so kind to her. But for all her misgivings, Doe knew that she had to move on. It was time to make her own way again.

Chapter 44

Having collected her rucksack, full of clean clothes, candles, matches and her tin opener, Doreen resumed her nomadic lifestyle. Her first priority was to find herself shelter for the night, which meant locating an empty house and then to secure herself some employment. Working at Jean and Mike's hardware store had shown her that she would be able to work without cards for a short period of time and that she could then disappear and find employment elsewhere. Doreen also knew that she could sometimes find employment at 'Scotts', a shop on Hyde Road, that would pay her seven shillings for working on a Saturday. They often had cleaning to do and stock to organise, so were always eager to see her. Yet it wasn't regular work and as they knew Doreen's age, she couldn't 'work on the books' for them. Doe knew that she needed a more regular income if she was to continue to take care of herself, so there was no option but to keep applying for full-time jobs in shops and factories when she saw them advertised. Doe knew that it was risky, but it was a case of 'needs must'; she had no alternative.

Sally and Sarah continued to help as best they could, keeping an eye out for empty houses and staying quiet about her whereabouts. The school system had lost her. As long as she stayed anonymous, there was little chance of her being taken into care. Auntie Dora refused to give up on her though and had walked around the flats after hearing that Doreen had been seen there. Sally noted how difficult it was to lie to her Gran, but she had told her that as far as she knew, Doe was living safely with one of her aunties and that none of her friends had seen her. Dora wasn't convinced and insisted that Sally was to bring Doreen to see her, if she did return to the flats.

For several weeks, Doreen's new routine continued. She found regular work and managed to buy herself some jumpers to help keep her warm as the weather turned colder towards the end of October. One Thursday evening, having finished work in one of the factories behind Ardwick Green, Doe was walking along Stockport Road. Glancing across the road, she spotted a familiar figure. It was Jimmy. Doreen waved her arms and shouted, but it was rush-hour and the noise of the traffic meant that he couldn't hear her.

"Our Kid! Our Kid! Jimmy!" shouted Doe, even louder.

He stopped and looked around, but still didn't see her. She shouted again.

"Our Kid! It's me, Doreen!"

Doe jumped up and down and waved her arms above her head, finally grabbing his attention.

Doreen walked to the edge of the pavement, waited for a gap in the traffic and then moved to the middle of the road. Eventually, another space opened up and she was able to race to the safety of the other side. Jimmy was waiting for her.

Doe was shocked. Her brother looked a gaunt and forlorn figure. He was stooping forward slightly, the result of the injuries to his back which he'd sustained in the beating he had taken outside Betty's. He was surprised, but pleased to see her. Doreen wanted to hug him; but she held back. She was older now and perhaps he wouldn't like it.

"I can't believe I've seen you," said Doe. "It must be two years. How are you?"

It seemed a ridiculous question. One look at her brother told her that things weren't going well. He looked so unhappy. But what else could she say? She had to break the ice and start the conversation somehow.

"I'm alright, Doe. What about you? Are you still living with Dad and Betty?"

Doreen explained how she had been forced to leave. How their dad had effectively washed his hands of her, just as their mam had done. Doe told him that she had been living with Auntie Dora, but was now looking after herself.

Jimmy listened intently, then replied.

"I've not seen Dad since getting beaten up at Betty's. I'm on my own at the moment. I've got a bedsit on Stockport Road. You can come and stay if you like. There's enough room."

"What about your girlfriend?"

"I don't have one."

Doreen was surprised. Her brother had always been popular with the girls. She found it hard to accept that he was living alone. Nevertheless, it was an opportunity to have a stable home for a time.

"All right then. Thank you. It'll be safer than the places I usually stay."

Doreen walked with Jimmy past the junction with Brunswick Street and on down Stockport Road until they turned into Polygon Avenue. Almost immediately, Jimmy cut into the alleyway behind the shops that fronted on to Stockport Road. His bedsit was above the greengrocers. Doe followed him through the door at the back and up some stairs. It was gloomy and it didn't smell very nice. Doreen hoped that his flat was going to be better. Approaching a door on the first landing, the stairs continuing upwards, Jimmy stopped, took a key from his pocket and let them into the bedsit.

"Here we are Doe. It's not much, but it's home."

He was right. It was dilapidated like Auntie Dora's. There was a threadbare rug on the floor, an old, battered settee, a sideboard, wardrobe, a table and a couple of chairs, a bed and two televisions stacked in the corner of the room. Doreen was surprised to see the latter. Televisions were a luxury, why would Jimmy have two? Looking at the kitchen area, Doe saw an Ascot boiler above a sink with a draining board. A gas cooker stood to the side and on top of it was a tray with an electric kettle and a couple of mugs. A gas fire completed the picture on the other side of the room. The bedsit was located at the front of the building and tatty old curtains covered a window looking out over Stockport Road.

"I don't use the cooker or the fire," said Our Kid, noticing his sister looking at the latter. "I don't pay for the gas because I'm not in that often and I usually get some food out."

"Oh," replied Doreen. "I'm not bothered about that. Where I stay, I don't have heating or hot water. I'm used to keeping lots of clothes on to keep warm"

Jimmy nodded.

"Why don't I go and buy us some chips from Chiappe's," she continued. "I've not had anything to eat today."

Doe noticed a concerned look on Jimmy's face.

"It's all right, Our Kid. I've got money. I've got plenty enough to get them. Let me buy them."

Going back out and down the road, Doe returned with two portions of steak and kidney pudding, chips and gravy. It was still her favourite meal.

Eating their tea in the paper, the plates in the cupboard being full of dust, the siblings sat talking at the table.

"What are you going to do, Doe?"

"What do you mean, Our Kid?"

"Well, you should be at school. You shouldn't be wandering the streets."

"I'm not. I find work most days and the money I earn keeps me. I'll be okay until I'm fifteen and then I can work properly. I'm not going in a children's home. If I went to school, they'd find out I wasn't living with Mam or Dad and so that's where I'd end up."

"Yes, I can see that," noted Jimmy. "You're welcome to stay here as long as you like. I'll give you my spare key and you can come and go as you please. I go to the pub or the dogs most nights, but you'll be safe here."

Doreen was pleased. The bedsit wasn't much but she was reunited with her brother and that made her feel better. She was no longer alone. Jimmy's presence provided her with a sense of belonging which she hadn't felt for a long time.

When Jimmy left to go to the pub, Doe set about cleaning up the sink and washing the pots. At least there was an electric kettle to provide hot water. Cleaning the table and using an old hand brush and dustpan that she found under the sink, Doreen was able to give some semblance of order to the room. Having finished, she turned on her brother's transistor radio and sat on the settee, which was to double up as her bed. Tired, she took a couple of blankets from the sideboard and lay down, the drone of the radio sending her to sleep.

Doe was awoken by the sound of the door being opened. Still drowsy, she heard two voices; one her brother, the other belonging to another man. Jimmy switched the light on. It was bright. Doreen squeezed her eyelids tight and burrowed her head into the cushion that she was using as a pillow.

"Who's that?"

"My little sister. She's staying with me. You don't need to worry about her."

"Oh. All right."

"It's over here, look. It's a belter, isn't it?" continued Jimmy.

Doe didn't move. She thought it was best for her brother if she pretended to be asleep.

"It's a Philips; nineteen inches. I can let you have it for fifteen quid," said Jimmy. "That's a bargain. They'll set you back forty in the shops."

There was silence, then a sharp intake of breath.

"I'm not sure, Jimmy. That's a lot."

"Look. I'll take twelve quid. I want it off my hands, but I won't go any lower."

"Go on then. You're twisting my arm, but I'll have it," said the voice. "Here you go."

Doreen assumed that the money was changing hands.

"Take care down the stairs," said Jimmy. "Wait, let me get the door."

Doe heard the man grunting. He was obviously finding it difficult to carry the television. Opening her eyes, Doe saw him struggling towards the door, before Jimmy moved past him and out on to the landing. From there, he led his visitor downstairs to the outside door. As he came back up the stairs, Doe closed her eyes and pretended that she was asleep. Coming into the flat and closing the door, Jimmy turned off the radio and got into bed.

Doreen was woken by her alarm clock at six-thirty. She could hear the noise of the buses outside, as they travelled along Stockport Road. Sitting up on the settee, she wiped her eyes. It was gloomy, but she could make out the shape of her brother under the covers in the bed across the room. Occasionally snoring, Jimmy was still fast asleep.

Doe quickly got washed and changed and ready to go to work; back at the factory behind Ardwick Green. She'd been there almost two weeks and was due her wages. Doreen knew that today would have to be her last. She couldn't risk staying any longer. The awkward questions over her National Insurance card were becoming persistent. Filling the kettle, Doe prepared to make herself and Jimmy a brew. It was now close to seven and she would soon have to get off to work. Waiting for the water to boil, Doe found it difficult not to think about last night. Where there had been two television sets, there was now just one. She wondered if there had been more. Doreen knew that after Jimmy had moved in with Val, he'd been involved in burglaries with her brothers, for which he had spent time in Strangeways. It seemed likely that he hadn't learned his lesson. Having finished the drinks, she walked over to the bed.

"Our Kid," said Doreen, softly.

Getting no response, she gently shook his shoulder.

"Umm. Yeah?"

"It's seven o'clock. I thought you'd have to get ready for work."

"Yes. Thanks, Doe."

Jimmy slowly roused himself and sat up in bed, his sister handing him a mug of tea.

"Where are you working, Our Kid?"

"The top of Lewis's. Painting the outside in the cradle. You wouldn't fancy that much, Doe. It's pretty high up."

"I don't know how you can do it."

Doreen had been afraid of heights, since feeling dizzy when she had tried to climb her dad's ladder, in the days when he had taken her to work with him.

"Well, I can't say it's ever bothered me and besides, it pays well. Lots of lads are afraid to do it and so that means they pay more to those of us who will."

Doreen wondered why her brother needed to sell 'knocked off' televisions, for that's what she assumed they were, if he was earning such good money. But again, she decided to stay silent, not wanting to say anything that could upset her brother. Yet she knew that if Jimmy was involved in criminal activity, there was little chance that her new living arrangements would have any permanence.

Arriving at work, Doe received her wages but was told to see the boss about her National Insurance card at the end of the shift. Her usual excuse of having left it at her previous employer and blaming them for not forwarding it, was wearing thin. Ignoring the request, Doreen left the factory, never to return. It would mean searching for another job but as there seemed to be plenty available, she didn't expect it to be much of a problem.

When she arrived back at her brother's flat, it was time for tea. Doreen had bought some bread, butter, potted meat and jam with which to make some sandwiches. Jimmy was already home. He had knocked off early and was in a good mood, given that he'd received a bonus from his boss. It was 'danger money' he explained and tonight he was off to the dogs at Belle Vue, hoping that his luck would continue.

The two were together for about an hour before Jimmy left. It gave them a chance to have a proper conversation. Doreen asked him about the breakup with Val. He told her that he had taken responsibility for planning the burglaries, when it had actually been Val's father. He received a longer sentence for that and whilst he had been in Strangeways, Val had cheated on him. Doe couldn't help thinking that it seemed so much like what had happened to her dad. How foolish the pair of them were. Since leaving prison, her brother had not had a steady girlfriend and had lived alone. Underneath a seemingly carefree exterior, Doe could see that her brother was desperately unhappy.

After Our Kid had left to go to the dogs, Doreen went to the flats to see Sally. She told her that she had found Jimmy and that she was staying with him. Doe wasn't sure how long it would last and expected that at some stage she would find herself back in an empty house. But Doreen noted that she was prepared for that; knew that she could cope with whatever life would throw at her. Spending time with Sally, Sarah and her friends provided Doe with a period of respite. It enabled her to be a teenager again; enjoying a laugh and teasing the boys. The girls were at an age where boys were assuming a prominent role in their lives. Doreen, a year younger than her friends and focused on everyday survival, was less concerned about them than either Sally or Sarah. Still, she enjoyed spending time with the lads and was becoming aware that they found her attractive. For the moment, she turned down the requests to 'go out' with her. It was something that would have to wait until later.

Doe returned to Jimmy's flat at around ten o'clock. She turned on the radio and settled down on the settee under the blankets to keep warm. Falling asleep, she was woken by her brother, returning from his night at the dogs. She sat up, rubbed her eyes and called over to him as he was filling the kettle.

"Did you have any luck, Our Kid?"

"No, Doe. Down all night."

Jimmy asked her if she wanted a brew. Doreen said yes. She knew that she didn't have to get up early. Tomorrow would be about searching for vacancies; trying to find another job. Jimmy, having finished making the drinks, put the mugs down on the table and Doe came across to join him. He was quiet, seemingly lost in thought.

"Are you all right, Our Kid?"

"Yes."

Suddenly, without any warning, Jimmy started to cry. Doreen was shocked and upset. Getting up from her chair, she moved around the table and put her arm around him, squeezing him tightly. Although she was only thirteen, Doe felt a powerful maternal instinct; she was determined to protect her brother. As his tears began to subside, Jimmy spoke of his despair.

"No one cares about me, Doe. They don't care if I live or die."

His words cut deep. Doreen knew exactly how he felt. She carried with her the same thoughts too, but she fought against them, always trying to put them out of her mind. It was the way to survive; forget the misery of the past, move on and put your faith in the future. Doe believed that one-day, everything would be all right. It was what had kept her going.

Taking her arm from around his shoulders, Doreen fetched her chair and placed it beside him. Sitting down, she put her hand on his knee and attempted to reassure him.

"I love you, Our Kid. I care about you. I always have."

Jimmy looked up. His eyes were red; his cheeks smeared with tears. He sniffed, took out his handkerchief, wiped his face and took a couple of deep breaths.

"I know and I feel bad. I should have made sure that you were all right, Doe. I've never even been to see you. If I'd been round to Betty's, I would have known that you were in trouble."

"That's okay. It's not your fault that Mam and Dad aren't interested in me. Anyway, I can always go back to Auntie Dora's. There's a place there for me if I'm really desperate."

Jimmy was quiet. Doreen sat waiting. She wasn't sure if he was comfortable unburdening himself to his younger sister. Finally, he continued.

"Dad never cared about me. You remember, when I was a kid, that he never gave me anything. I had to rely on you giving me money."

"Yes, Our Kid, but I always did."

"That's why I feel guilty for having ignored you."

"It's all right. I told you that."

"Mam's the same. I saw her a couple of weeks ago in the 'Waggon and Horses' at the top of Plymouth Grove. I'd gone in there to meet a couple of the lads from work. I went over to her and at first, it was as if she was pretending not to know me. I could tell that she didn't want to speak to me."

Doreen was surprised at the mention of her mam. She now had a location; a pub. Perhaps she would be in there again. Maybe she and Sam lived in Longsight.

"You know, Doe. Mam could have stopped Dad forcing me to become a decorator. I loved it at Dewhurst. I would have been someone. I could be married now and have kids. Instead, I'm on my own in a bedsit. Thinking back, neither of them wanted me to be happy. Dad doesn't even think I'm his kid."

"No, that's not true."

"It is, Doe. Do you remember how he used to look at your hands and say how your fingers were just like his: that anyone could tell that you were his kid? Well, he never said that about me, did he? He thinks Mam carried on behind his back and that I'm some other bloke's kid. That's why he's always been so nasty to me."

Doreen didn't know what to say. It was true that her dad had always mentioned her hands and fingers and thinking back, she remembered her brother often being there. She had never, as she was young, thought anything of what he had said, other than to be childishly pleased at her dad's obvious approval of her. Now older, Doe could understand how Our Kid had felt. When she thought about how Jim had stopped him from working at Dewhurst and then forced him to push the handcart around the streets, it did seem as if he was being vindictive. Perhaps he really did believe that he had brought up another man's child. Nevertheless, Doreen sensed that Jimmy was looking for reassurance. She knew that he'd had quite a few pints and although he wasn't drunk, it had probably made him feel depressed. Quietly, she sought to put his mind at rest.

"Honestly, it's not true. Dad knows you're his son. He and Mam are just selfish. They only care about themselves. That's why they ignore me too. Come on, drink your tea and let's get some sleep."

Doe grabbed his hand and gave it a squeeze.

"You'll feel better in the morning, Our Kid. Don't worry."

Jimmy was calming down. He took a couple of sips from his mug and started to tell his sister about his 'bad luck' at the dogs. For all that he was angry with his dad, he was just like him in wasting his money on drinking and gambling. Furthermore, whilst his friends were settling down and taking on responsibility, Our Kid had no inclination to start his own business and so offer a promising future to a prospective wife. Doe suspected that in the morning he would have forgotten their conversation. Nevertheless, she still realised that he was unhappy; his whole demeanour told her that. Humorous and good company when he was out with his friends, deep down he felt sad and unfulfilled. Doe remembered when her brother had involved her in his choice of Val over Valerie. As a young child she had approved. Now she realised that Valerie could have been the making of him. Older and wiser, she also understood that it had been his choice, not hers and he had to live with the consequences.

Next day, Doe went out early. Jimmy was still asleep and she didn't disturb him. Looking in the windows of the newsagents along Stockport Road, she was able to find employment. This time it was as a trainee machinist; taken on after a brief interview on the following Monday morning. Once again, her excuse about her National Insurance card was accepted. As usual, she stayed for two weeks, picked up her wages and disappeared. As November arrived and with it, the onset of winter, she was still at Jimmy's. It had provided her with some stability and her brother had not shown any signs of the emotional frailty that had been apparent earlier. Yet Doreen was unsure how long she would be remaining, for it seemed as if Jimmy was looking to move on.

The change in her circumstances was quicker than she expected. It was the following Tuesday and Doe had been making her way home down Stockport Road after finishing work. As she approached the junction of Polygon Avenue, she saw a group of people gathered on the pavement. When she got nearer, she was surprised to see that they were looking at her brother. He was holding the television set that had been in the flat. Stood with him were two men.

"Don't you want to put that down, Jimmy? It must be getting heavy," said one of them.

"Yes. Here, can you help me," Our Kid replied.

The man grabbed hold of it with Jimmy and the two of them bent down and put the television carefully on the ground.

"There. We don't want to damage it, do we?" asked the man.

Both of the men were tall and well built. They were wearing suits with overcoats. The one who had helped her brother, was wearing a hat. CID thought Doreen and she was right.

"Fancy us driving down the road and seeing you struggling with that telly," said the man in the hat. "We had to stop to give you a hand with it. Don't you reckon, Harry?"

He turned to his partner, looking for a response. Unlike Jimmy, both of them could see the funny side of the situation.

"Yes, of course. Only too glad to help," said Harry, turning towards Our Kid. "I tell you what, Jimmy. Let's put the television in the car."

Whilst the two of them picked up the television, the man in the hat opened the back door of a car which was parked by the side of the road. The television was safely loaded away.

Doreen felt that she should do something to help, but her brother was with the police and it was best for her to remain in the background. Yet Jimmy was in trouble and she couldn't just ignore him.

"Are you all right, Our Kid?"

Jimmy looked at her. His eyes told her to go away; to keep quiet.

"Stay back, young lady," said Harry.

"It's all right. It's just my sister," said Jimmy. "She was coming to see me."

The other policeman looked at Doreen.

"It looks like your brother has been a naughty boy. That's right isn't it, Jimmy?"

"Yes, Detective Sergeant Butler. I won't lie to you. You would be passing right at this exact moment. Couldn't you have driven past a couple of minutes sooner? It's just my luck!"

"Well, there you go Jimmy," replied Butler, with a smile. "You'll never be much of a villain. You ought to pack it in. Go straight."

By this time the crowd of people had dispersed. There wasn't going to be any further excitement. Jimmy was the type who always came quietly and as Doe soon found out, always admitted his guilt as soon as he was questioned.

"Well, Detective Sergeant Butler, I can't say that you're not right. I suppose if I own up to some more of those unsolved crimes, you'll have a word with the judge for me."

"Seeing as last time you got let off, I don't think it's going to stop you getting sent down. But if you co-operate with us, I'm sure the judge will give you a shorter sentence."

"All right," replied Jimmy. "Never mind, I'll be in Strangeways over Christmas. It's always good in there then. You get Christmas dinner and good company."

Harry and Butler laughed. It was clear that they liked Jimmy. He was a bumbling criminal; he showed no malice and provided no problems. Doe realised that her brother had been in and out of trouble since coming out of prison. More concerning, was that Butler was now turning his attention towards her.

"Well, I'm afraid that we're going to have to take your brother with us, love. What did you say your name was?"

"I didn't," replied Doe.

"Well, what is it?" asked Butler.

"Doreen."

"Are you going to be all right, Doreen? Were you supposed to be staying with your brother?"

"No," said Jimmy. "I couldn't have her staying with me. I can't even look after myself! No, she was down here on a visit; a bit earlier than I expected. She likes to keep in touch, but since I went to prison, Mam and Dad won't bring her to see me. That's why she's here on her own."

Jimmy was lying for his sister's benefit. He knew that Butler was searching out information; looking for new lines of enquiry. If he had any inkling that Doe was living with him, she'd be put in the back of the police car and taken down to the station.

"Yes," explained Doreen. "Mam and Dad have never forgiven him. They won't allow him to come to the house and they don't like me coming to see him. That's why I have to come on my own."

"I can see why," replied Butler. "Your dad's Jimmy Brodie, the jewel thief, isn't he? It's good to see that he's kept out of trouble. He's probably angry with your Jimmy, because he hasn't."

Doe was becoming concerned. Butler seemed to know far too much about her family.

"Where are you going home to, Doreen? Is it on our way?" asked Butler.

"No," replied Doe, careful not to give any details.

"She lives over in Greenheys," said Jimmy "and she should be getting off now. Go on Doe, I'll be in touch when all this is over."

Jimmy stepped towards the car and got into the back seat beside the television. Taking his lead, the two police officers got into the front of the car and closed the doors. Pulling out into the road, the car executed a 'U' turn and headed back towards Longsight Police Station.

Doreen watched as the car disappeared down Stockport Road. She was shaking. Not only had her brother been arrested, but she'd almost been taken away herself. What if they'd insisted on driving her home? How could she have got away from them? She was frightened. Only her brother's quick thinking had kept her out of trouble. Although she had the key to Jimmy's bedsit and he had paid the rent in advance, there was no way that she was going to stay there. The police would be bound to return; they would be looking in the flat for more stolen goods. Once again, she was going back on her travels. After entering the bedsit one last time, Doe picked up her rucksack and headed back towards Bennett Street flats. She would meet up with Sally and Sarah and they would find another empty house where she could stay.

Chapter 45

It was November and the weather was getting seriously cold. It was a month that Doe had loved as a young child. It meant bonfire night, fireworks, baked potatoes and roast chestnuts. Now trying to find shelter from the bitter winter weather was what dominated Doreen's life. Still, there were plenty of empty homes in which to stay, as she continued to support herself by all means possible. But it was getting more difficult and she was becoming more aware than ever of the danger of being caught working underage. Her brush with the police outside Jimmy's flat had certainly heightened her fears of being discovered. It was possible, she reasoned, that she was worrying too much; that she had developed an exaggerated fear that ultimately, she would be caught. Yet prospective employers did seem less inclined to believe her story. Two factories turned her down following her work as a trainee machinist. No card; no job. That was what she had been told. Finally, she found employment in a meat processing factory. The boss, who was short staffed, prepared to wait for her card.

After her first week in the job, Doe was getting nervous, even though she knew that she would be leaving once her pay packet arrived on Friday. On Thursday, whilst she was working on the conveyor belt, Doe noticed two men in suits being taken into the manager's office. Pointing the men out to Alice, who was working alongside her, Doreen asked who they were.

"They're the factory inspectors. They come every few months."

"Why?"

"They're probably getting their brown envelopes," said Gladys, opposite them.

"Brown envelopes?"

Gladys and Alice laughed.

"Yes," said Alice. "It's a 'pay off', so they don't report us for putting out food unfit for human consumption."

Doe was shocked, yet had been at the factory long enough to know that it was probably true. After working there, she wouldn't eat sausages again. The vats and troughs that they put the meat into, were full of rust and if any sausage meat fell on the floor, they were ordered to pick it up and put it back on the conveyor belt. Doreen had actually seen one woman vomit onto the conveyor. The foreman had stopped the belt to remove the affected portion, but had left the rest. It was meat for the sausages that were being sold to the education committee for school dinners.

"They're supposed to check up on safety too and that the bosses are following all the correct regulations. But I don't believe that for a minute. They're not bothered about us," added Gladys.

Doe was worried. What if the boss mentioned that she was working without her card? What would the inspectors do? Her worst fears seemed to have been realised when the works supervisor came over to them.

"Doreen, the boss wants to see you in his office"

"What, now?"

"Yes, now," replied the supervisor, sharply.

Doe sensed that he intended to accompany her to the office. She realised that if she went with him, the door would be closed behind her and she wouldn't be able to get away. Doreen appeared calm, but she was terrified; afraid that the police had already been called to come and collect her. She needed an excuse to get away.

"I need to go to the toilet," said Doe. "I've been hanging on, but I need to go. I'll come as soon as I've been."

It was perfect. He wouldn't be able to follow her in there.

"All right, Doreen," replied the supervisor, "but you should have gone before. I'll see you in the office."

The toilets were away from the factory floor, together with the lockers. Doe made her way out to them. She looked around. No one was following her. Doreen had done it; she could escape. In the toilet she took off her overalls, hat and gloves. She dressed back into the clothes from her locker and united with her rucksack, she made her way out of the building by the side entry, so avoiding the woman on reception. She then ran like the wind, determined to put as much distance between the factory and herself as possible. Finally stopping and gasping for breath, she felt numb. She had just lost a whole week's wages, but at least she was safe. Doe knew that working full-time had become too dangerous. She couldn't risk doing it again.

Walking the streets, Doe was at a loss. What should she do? There was Auntie Dora, but how could she go back there unless her parents paid for her keep? Then she remembered that Jimmy had told her that he'd seen Emily in the 'Waggon and Horses'. Doreen decided that she would go there that evening and see if she could find her. Perhaps there was a chance of staying with her for a while. Sam was a concern, but Doe realised that she could no longer afford to be choosy.

The 'Waggon and Horses' was a huge building on the corner of Stockport Road and Plymouth Grove. It was 'half-timbered' with mock Tudor panelling on the outside walls painted black against the white render. Doreen had seen it many times when, as a youngster, she had travelled with her dad down to his decorating jobs in Stockport. Doe arrived there at seven o'clock. She knew that she wasn't allowed to go in, so waited by the door of the lounge bar, craning her head around it as people opened it, to see if her mam was there. She found that it was no good. The room was huge and her visibility was seriously restricted. The noise and the smoke didn't help either. As the customers came in and out, Doreen began to ask them whether they knew Emily, who came in with Sam. The first few couples didn't, but then an old man acknowledged that he did. Doe asked him if he would look to see if she was in there and if she was, tell her that Doreen, her daughter, was waiting outside. About five minutes later the door to the lounge opened and stood there, was her mam.

"What are you doing here?" asked Emily, a look of surprise on her face.

Doe was irritated.

"Oh, great Mam. You're really pleased to see me, aren't you," she snapped. "I'm not allowed to see my mother then? I suppose I'm not, seeing as you never bothered to come and see me at Auntie Dora's, or help my dad pay for my keep."

"Don't be like that, Doe. I didn't mean it that way."

"No, you never do, do you?"

"Alright, Doe. I'm sorry. What do you want?"

Doreen explained to her about why she had been forced to leave Auntie Dora's, had started working without a National Insurance card and how she had nearly got caught. She was worried. What would happen if they did catch her? Would she go to prison?

"No, Doe. You're too young to go to prison, but you can't keep doing it. If they catch you, you'll be taken into care and put in a children's home."

"That's as bad as prison."

"Why can't you go back to Auntie Dora's?" asked Emily.

Doreen ignored her. She had already explained why and it seemed obvious that her mam wasn't taking her seriously enough.

"Couldn't I stay with you for a couple of days?" asked Doe. "Just until I get something sorted out."

"I'd like to, but there's a problem. Me and Sam only have a bedsit and there's no room for you. What about your dad?"

Doreen couldn't believe it. She'd not seen her mam since she moved in with Auntie Dora. She had told her that she was living rough and yet Emily didn't seem to care. It hadn't bothered her brother that he only had a bedsit. He'd made her more than welcome.

"Forget it, Mam. I'll sort something out for myself."

Doreen turned and walked away.

"Doe, let me give you something."

Doreen stopped and turned around. She had her pride and wouldn't accept a meaningless handout, offered in order to salve her mother's conscience.

"No, it's all right, Mam. I've still got a little money from working. I can manage on my own. I don't have any alternative, do I?"

And then she was off, speeding up as she walked down Stockport Road. Once again, she'd acted tough; determined to avoid giving Emily the impression that she needed her. If her mam wouldn't help, then so be it. Yet Doreen couldn't ignore the pain of rejection and it made her feel angry. Why had she been so foolish as to believe that her mam would show her any compassion? After all, it was so long since she had done so. Doe felt a fool. When would she ever learn?

As Doreen made her way back to Bennett Street, she wondered what she would do. The decision was effectively made for her. Afraid that Doe would be picked up by the police after Jimmy's arrest, Sally had finally told her Gran that she knew where her cousin was. When Doreen arrived at the flats, Dora was waiting to meet her.

"Doreen. You're coming back with me. You'd no right to leave like that. I didn't want you to go."

"I know."

Doe wasn't in any condition to argue. She needed security. If Detective Sergeant Butler was checking up on her and she wasn't living with a responsible adult, Doreen would be taken into care. Once in a children's home she would no longer be anonymous. If she tried to run away, the police would find her, just like Robert. For the time being, living with her auntie was the best option.

"I was told that you've been on the flats," continued Dora. "I've been out looking for you, to see if you were all right. I don't know why you left in the first place."

"It wasn't fair for you to have to look after me without any help from my mam or dad."

"Well, that's not your fault, love. You can forget about that now. I don't want to hear any more about it. You're always welcome."

Back with Auntie Dora, Doreen had some semblance of stability. Furthermore, she was able to secure a regular weekend job working for a greengrocer on Hyde Road. She was paid ten shillings and gave the money to Dora. A paper round brought in another four shillings and finally, Doe got a cleaning job in a factory at the end of Bennett Street. The job was five days a week, from four till six and paid her another ten shillings. Doreen kept her paper round money and gave the rest to Auntie Dora. Best of all, her jobs were part-time and legal; there was no chance that she would get into trouble. Most importantly, her contributions meant that they all ate well and shamed Larry and Walt into handing over some of their wages too. Doe had little money for herself, but she had no regrets. She felt independent, knowing that she was paying her way.

Chapter 46

Doreen's life now settled back into some kind of routine. She was no longer nomadic. She didn't have to worry about finding a roof over her head and risk the dangers of sleeping in empty houses. But there were drawbacks. She no longer had the money that she had previously earned and it meant her being unoccupied during the day, as she had no intention of going back to school. Doe felt that education had nothing to offer. She had already proved that she could hold down a variety of jobs, all of which required simple common sense and an ability to learn. By returning to school, she would face a host of difficult questions: Why wasn't she living with her parents? Who was Auntie Dora? Was she being cared for properly? Perhaps they would take her away from Dora's; after all, she hadn't been to school for almost a year. It just wasn't worth the risk. The dreams that Mrs Morgan once had for her, could never come to fruition. Yet Doreen didn't care. 'Here and now' was all that mattered. Doe knew that after Easter 1964, she could work full-time. That would be in less than eighteen months and Doreen kept reminding herself that each passing day brought her one step closer to freedom.

Life certainly wasn't easy. Doreen could save just enough money to buy herself shoes and underwear, but her other clothes would have to last. Nevertheless, she got by. Occasionally she would go to see her dad, despite the fact that he still hadn't given anything to Auntie Dora. Surprisingly, he did remember her birthday and she was pleased when he gave her five bob. She was also interested to learn that Jim had seen her mam in the 'Shakespeare', a pub on Stockport Road and had mentioned to her that Doe was back with Auntie Dora.

Doreen hadn't thought very much about what Jim had told her but a couple of weeks later, one Friday night in March, Emily turned up at Dora's. Doe hadn't seen her for a few months; not since the night outside the 'Waggon and Horses'. Auntie Dora had answered the door and brought Emily into the front room, where Doreen and Sally were getting ready to go out. Older now, Doe was more conscious of her appearance. She had scrimped together the money to buy some eye makeup, which she and Sally were now applying.

"Doe, look who's here," said Auntie Dora, as she came into the room.

Doreen and Sally took their eyes away from their small hand-held mirrors and looked up. They saw Emily emerge from the doorway. Doe was shocked. It was Friday night. Booze night. Why was she here? Where was Sam? They must have had a row, thought Doreen. Why else would she have come?

"Hi," said Doe, with more than a hint of indifference.

She stayed seated on the settee, determined that she wouldn't get up and make a fuss of her mam.

"How are you?" asked Emily.

"Fine."

"I've missed you."

"Really?"

"Yes, really," insisted Emily.

Doreen didn't react. She didn't believe her. There was an awkward silence. Emily stood, waiting for her daughter to respond. Finally, she did.

"Where's Sam?"

"I've left him in the 'Hyde Road'."

"Does he know that you've come here?"

"Yes, of course he does."

"Oh, that surprises me. He usually doesn't want you to acknowledge that you've got a daughter. Anyway, why are you here?"

For a moment, Doreen wished that she hadn't said it. To be so hostile to her mam, whose love, deep down, she really wanted, seemed silly. But Doe was hurting and she wanted Emily to suffer too.

"Like I've said Doe, I've missed you. I've come to see if there's anything that you need."

"Other than a roof over my head, food and clothes, which costs money that you obviously don't want to give, what else is there that I could possibly need?"

Doreen's biting sarcasm and the withering look she cast at Emily, shocked Dora and Sally. Doe usually saw the best in everyone and could forgive most things. It was clear to them that Emily had wounded her daughter deeply.

"Don't be like that, Doreen. I worry about you all the time."

Doe affected a laugh.

"I'm sure, Mam."

"I've given Auntie Dora some money," continued Emily, hoping that her daughter would accept it as an olive branch.

It was no good. Doe was about to release the pent-up emotions that she had harboured for so long. Doreen didn't want her mam to go, but she couldn't stop criticising her. Perhaps it was because she believed that Emily wouldn't return for another six months and this would be the only chance to vent her anger.

"What have you given her? Six months keep?"

"All I could afford."

"Mam, do you really think that you could possibly pay Auntie Dora enough for what she's done for me?"

"No, I don't."

"Well, I'm pleased that you've given her something."

Again, there was silence. Emily, still standing near the doorway, shifted uneasily on her feet. Trying to reach out to her daughter, her comments only increased Doreen's anger.

"I'm sorry that I've not had the chance to come before," said Emily. "I often work six days a week and long hours. I have to spend Sundays trying to catch up with all the washing and cleaning."

"I'm sorry too, Mam. I'm sorry that you haven't had the chance to come and see your only daughter. Life must be so very hard for you."

"Don't be like this. I've come to see you. I want to help."

"Well now you've seen me and done your bit, you can go and come back in another six months!"

Auntie Dora had heard enough. Increasingly uncomfortable, she understood why Doe was angry, but she now felt that Emily had been adequately criticised. It served no useful purpose for Doreen to keep on attacking her. What could Emily do? Perhaps she was genuinely trying to make it up to her daughter and Dora had seen enough of life and people to know that Doe didn't really wish to upset her mam. The reality was that Doreen simply wanted her mam to love her; to care for her. The last thing she wanted was never to see Emily again. Perhaps there could be a new beginning. Surely it was worth trying to build some bridges between them.

"Doreen, don't speak to your mother like that," said Dora.

"Why not?" asked Sally. "She's telling the truth."

"Sally. It's nothing to do with you. Please be quiet," replied her gran.

Dora's intervention had a sobering effect. For a time, Doe had thought that only her mam existed; she'd forgotten that her words may make others feel uncomfortable too. Doreen had no wish to upset Dora, who had done so much for her. Calmly, she tried to explain herself.

"I'm sorry, Auntie Dora. I don't want to upset you or cause any trouble. But don't you think that she should have been to see me before now? Does she realise how you've gone without food to feed the rest of us on your pension? She doesn't care; no matter what she says. Why has she come today? What's so different about today? I just don't understand why she's here. There has to be a reason. There's always a reason for doing something."

Doreen's frustration was evident to see and she was determined that Emily wasn't going to have an easy ride. Sally's contribution had stiffened her resolve. Ever since she first moved in at Dora's, Sally had explained to her that for kids like them, you had to accept that your parents didn't give a damn. They were only concerned about themselves and their partners. Yet Sally had never known love from her mother, whereas Doe had been doted on by her father and loved by her mam until the arrival of Sam and Betty. Doreen couldn't simply discard her feelings where her parents were concerned. She still had the happy memories of living with them in Bright Avenue and still hoped that those days could return. Part of wanting to wound Emily, was to bring her to her senses; get her to leave Sam and start living with her daughter again. To Sally, her gran was the only one who genuinely cared, hence the only one she had true affection for. The two girls were so similar in the rejection they had faced, but so different in what they hoped for in the future.

Emily wasn't giving up. She could have left, but she didn't. Doe was right. Emily hadn't bothered to visit her for months. In fact, she hadn't shown any real desire to see her since Jim moved in with Betty. If she had wanted to, she could have found a way. It had been too easy for her to accept Betty's hostility and Sam's indifference to her daughter. Therefore, it shouldn't have proved difficult for Emily to walk away from Doreen's withering and wounding comments. Yet it was, for Doe's question had hit home. Why was she there? There has to be a reason. Emily began to realise that it was guilt. She had started to think beyond herself; recognise that there was a child out there, her own flesh and blood and she had let her down. Emily needed to do something for her daughter. Acknowledge, at last, some responsibility for her.

"It's coming up to Whitsun and I thought I would take you to get some new clothes," said Emily.

"Why? Have you won some money?" asked Doreen.

Emily could see her defiance and was reminded of the little girl who had sat all night on the toilet roof in protest at Rex having to be put down. Her daughter was proud and stubborn all right. When she believed in something, she couldn't be easily moved. Emily also knew that she couldn't be bought. It would take far more than a few new clothes to gain her approval.

"No. I've been saving up."

Doreen was unconvinced. She had never known her mam to save money and since she met Sam, most of her earnings went in the pub.

"I wanted to have enough to get you something nice," continued Emily, "especially as I missed your birthday."

"All right, but I need some shoes as well," replied Doe. "So does Sally. Because Auntie Dora uses her money to feed me, Sally hasn't got anything decent to wear either."

"I'll buy outfits for both of you," replied Emily. "I'll come back tomorrow morning and take you both into town. I don't have to go to work this Saturday."

Emily said goodbye and left. Doe didn't believe her. She had no faith in Emily returning the next day. Her record of keeping promises was hardly inspiring. Yet return, she did. At nine-thirty she was at the door, ready to collect the girls. Catching the bus to Piccadilly, they headed down to Market Street and went in

'Pauldens', where Emily bought each of them a Navy-blue suit with white trim and a pair of matching, Navy-blue shoes. Having got the girls their outfits, Emily took them to a small Italian cafe. Doreen had a Horlicks, Sally a milkshake and Emily a cup of tea. It was a real treat for the girls. Not having any money, they rarely ventured into town.

In the cafe, the three of them enjoyed a pleasant conversation. The girls talked about Auntie Dora, Larry and Walt and some of the boys they were friendly with. It was as if a truce had been called and Doreen wasn't going to criticise her mam again. Finishing a cigarette, Emily reached into her handbag. Taking out her purse, she drew out a five pounds note and offered it to her daughter.

"Doe. Take this."

Doreen was surprised. She hadn't expected to get anything more.

"Why are you giving me this?"

"So that you have some money to tide you over. Buy yourself some underwear, makeup, magazines if you want them."

"Just give it to Auntie Dora."

"No, Doe. I gave Auntie Dora some money last night. You need this."

Doreen was intrigued. Where could all this money have come from? She just had to ask.

"You can't have saved all this money up, Mam. You don't earn enough and you're always in the pub. Where's it come from?"

"I have been saving but I have to admit, I've also had some good luck."

Doreen knew it. She had been right all along. Now though, it didn't seem to matter. She realised that her mam didn't have to share her good fortune, but had chosen to do so.

"What good luck?"

Doe and Sally leaned across the table, eagerly anticipating her answer.

"The other day I took Sam's bet to the bookies. When I was in there, a chap I've seen a few times and who often chats to me, gave me a couple of tips. He said they were from his brother-in-law who works for a trainer and they were dead certs. He told me to have them as a double and bet as much as I could afford and not tell anyone else."

"Why shouldn't you?" asked Sally.

"Because if too many people bet on them, then the odds go down and so do your winnings," explained Doreen, who thanks to her dad and brother, knew far more about gambling.

"That's right," said Emily, nodding. "Anyway," she continued, "I believed him and so put five shillings on and they both came up; ten to one and sixteen to one. It brought me 40 quid plus my five bob back. As usual, Sam's bet went down. I couldn't believe it when I went in the next day! I didn't tell Sam and kept all the money for myself. That's why I've got it spare. I'll never have this much again, so I wanted to treat you. I know I've let you down Doe, but as I've said, it's just a little something to help out."

"All right," replied Doreen, "but I'll share it with Sally."

"That's up to you, Doe."

Emily's revelation was the first indication that all may not be well between her and Sam. Yet Doreen knew that most women tried to secrete a little money away from their husbands, or the men they lived with. But this was an awful lot of money and it was clear that Emily didn't want Sam to find out about it. It was enough to persuade Doe that her mam didn't really trust him. Perhaps there was hope that in the future Emily may leave Sam and she would be able to live with her again.

Having made their way back to Piccadilly, Emily and the girls got a bus back to Hyde Road. As they said their farewells, Emily attempted to reassure Doreen of her ongoing concern for her.

"If you need me, Sam and I often go in the 'Shakespeare'. We'll be moving soon and I'll let you know my new address."

Walking back to the flats, Doe wondered how long it would be before she saw Emily again, for she knew better than to put too much faith in her mam's promises. Nevertheless, Doreen had enjoyed their day together and at the very least, it had provided a happy memory for her to look back on.

Chapter 47

Doreen and Sally decided that they would save their new suits until the Whit Walks. They would wear them when they went into town to watch the processions go through Albert Square. Whit Monday was slightly later than usual, June 3rd, but it didn't make any difference to the number of churches and bands parading through the town centre. Dressed in their new, matching outfits, the girls were delighted. They had spent time on their hair and makeup and felt like a million dollars. Doe had started dying her hair black and piling it up into a beehive to follow the fashion of the time. It made her look older and quite elegant. Calling for Sarah, the girls then caught the bus on Hyde Road to make their way into town. As soon as the girls sat down, they attracted the attention of a group of boys who were already on the bus. Doe wasn't keen on any of them but Sally and Sarah were happy to chat to a couple of lads who were more forward than the rest.

Arriving at Piccadilly, Doe was eager to be rid of the boys. They were immature and had become somewhat irritating; childishly running up and down the bus in a vain attempt to impress them. Sitting with her friends on a bench in the gardens, Doreen told the boys that they were waiting for her parents to arrive. It did the trick, as the lads quickly disappeared. Pausing for a while, to make sure that they had gone, the girls then made their way down to the Town Hall in Albert Square, where they could watch the procession. Using the money that Emily had given her, Doreen was able to buy sweets and drinks for the three of them. It wasn't long before another group of boys came along. They were older and more sensible and Doe found herself talking to a well-dressed and pleasant young man called Edward. Two of Edward's friends soon began conversations with Sally and Sarah, as they all watched the procession together.

Wearing a smart black jacket, shirt and tie, Edward was very well spoken. He told Doreen that he was sixteen and at Manchester Grammar. Doe was a little put out. She was only fourteen. But to Edward, she looked older than that; quite the young lady in her fetching new outfit. He was struck by how pretty she was. Petite with a smiling face and sparkling green eyes. Her black hair, tightly in place, was her crowning glory. In his young and rather innocent way, he thought that she was lovely. Doreen didn't tell him her age; in fact, he never asked her. As they talked, Doe found that she quite liked him. His hair was a little unkempt and his nose a little too big and she suspected that his eyesight wasn't all it should be, given that he squinted as he looked into the distance. Probably he needed glasses, yet didn't want to wear them. But he was all right. What she actually liked about him was his quiet manner and his attentiveness. He wasn't like so many of the pushy, often aggressive lads from her neighbourhood. It was probably because he came from a more comfortable background and lived in an area where he didn't face the challenges that everyday life often presented in Ardwick. Edward could thus view the world in a more positive and less cynical light.

"Where are you from?" asked Edward.

"Ardwick. Bennett Street flats," replied Doreen.

"I'm not sure I know that."

"It's off Hyde Road."

"Oh, near the ABC. I've been to see a couple of groups there."

"Yes, it's up from there. Where are you from, Edward?"

"I live in East Didsbury."

"You're lucky. It's nice there. My dad's worked there quite a bit."

"Oh, what does he do?"

"He's a painter and decorator."

Doreen wasn't going to tell him that she didn't live with her dad, but was proud of the job that he did.

"What does your dad do?"

"He's a manager with Lloyds Bank," replied Edward.

"That's good."

Having introduced themselves to one another, they watched the procession for a while before discussing their musical tastes.

"What's your favourite group, Doreen?"

"I love Cliff."

"What about the Beatles?"

"They're okay. I like Paul, but I prefer Cliff."

She sensed that Edward didn't approve, but she knew that he didn't want to tell her that and risk upsetting her. Doreen was growing up quickly. Relatively inexperienced with boys, she was learning to understand them and their behaviour. Furthermore, she sensed that boys found her attractive. Those on the bus had not wanted to leave her alone and now Edward was paying her such close attention. Yet for the moment, Doe was content to enjoy their company and nothing more. She wasn't ready for a steady boyfriend. Edward was nice, but he was too old and lived in a different part of Manchester; a different world in fact, so far removed from her life on Bennett Street flats.

"It would be nice to see you again, Doreen," said Edward, as the procession was ending and people were slowly drifting home.

"Yes," she replied. "Maybe I'll see you at the ABC sometime."

Her answer was noncommittal and Edward knew that Doreen didn't want him to follow it up. It had been an enjoyable afternoon with a very pretty girl, but Edward knew that was all it was going to be.

The girls said goodbye and set off to catch the bus home. On the way they chatted about the boys they had met.

"Doe, that lad was really keen on you," observed Sarah. "He couldn't keep his eyes off you, could he?"

"I don't know," replied Doreen, with more than a hint of embarrassment.

"Oh yes, you do," said Sally. "Don't come it."

"Well, I suppose he was."

"What was he like? Where was he from?" asked Sarah.

Doe told them all about him and mentioned that he seemed keen to see her again, but that she didn't want to.

"Why?" asked Sally.

"Well, there's no real point. He lives miles away. Anyway, he's too old for me."

"Yes, Doe," observed Sarah. "You've got to watch the older ones. Some of them are only after one thing."

"Well, they're not getting it here!"

Doe had enjoyed the attention but knew all too well what Sarah was referring to. There were girls on the flats too eager to please the boys; she would never be one of them. Such things could wait until she was much older and married. Relationships for her had to be true. She had seen the destruction of her own life through her parents' failure to honour their commitments to one another. Conscious of her changing body and with a developing awareness of the possibilities of sexual pleasure, Doe decided that emotions and desires had to be held firmly in check. She would wait for the right time and the right one. For now, Doreen was content to spend her time innocently with boys, safe in the company of her friends.

Chapter 48

It was July and the weather was scorching hot. The kids had finished school and the flats echoed to the sound of their voices through the long, lazy days. Auntie Dora had managed to get hold of a cheap record player. Sally and Doreen were over the moon. They could have their own music at last and not be reliant on listening to what the radio chose to play.

The only problem was that they didn't have any records. But they soon found a solution. Doreen ran errands for Mrs Evans who lived a few doors away. Mrs Evans had a daughter called Katie who shared a flat with Joan. The latter worked in a record shop on Hyde Road which specialised in selling cheap, ex-jukebox records. Doe and Sally went to see Joan and asked her if they could borrow some records to have a dance with their friends. Joan agreed and lent them a box of singles. It included songs by the Beatles, Gerry and the Pacemakers, Frank Ifield, Cliff and the Shadows, Billy Fury, Andy Williams, Buddy Holly, Eddie Cochran; in fact, lots of different artists.

Next morning, at eleven, Sally and Doe went round to their friends to tell them that they were going to open the windows and play some records, which they could dance to outside. Returning home, the pair of them placed the record player on the window sill and took turns to act as the deejay. More youngsters began to arrive as news spread about the music and dancing. There were lots of boys and girls that they didn't know, but everyone was happy and friendly. The neighbours could see that everyone was enjoying themselves and no one complained about the noise, as the music continued into the night. Twice more that week, the girls provided musical entertainment and dancing for the teenagers of Bennett Street flats and beyond. Eventually though, the records had to be returned; the entertainment was at an end. Significantly, new friendships had been formed; in particular with four boys. All were sixteen and working: Jack was an apprentice plumber, Paul worked on a fruit and veg stall and their best mates Bob and Mark, worked on the roads. It wasn't long before Sally, Sarah and Doreen were spending increasing amounts of time with them.

That summer also provided a significant turning point. Since visiting her daughter at Dora's, Emily had been true to her word. She had seen Doreen every couple of weeks and even given Auntie Dora some money. Doe began to think that her mam really was trying to turn over a new leaf. At the start of August, Emily's visit brought with it an unexpected offer.

"Me and Sam have rented half a house in Harpurhey. There's room for you to move in, if you like."

Doreen wasn't sure. Harpurhey was a fair distance from Bennett Street. It would mean being further away from her friends. She knew that she could come back, but it would be awkward and time consuming. Yet what concerned her most, was how she would get on with Sam. As a young girl, he had scared her. He made her feel uncomfortable. Would she be able to cope with him now? Would he seem different to her, now that she was older?

Ultimately, Doe had to acknowledge that her mam was finally accepting some responsibility for her. As such, she didn't feel that she could refuse, regardless of her misgivings about living with Sam. Nevertheless, her world had been shattered too many times for her not to take precautions. After Emily had left, she spoke to Auntie Dora and asked her if she could return if it didn't work out with her mam. Doe explained her misgivings about Sam and how he had frightened her when she was young. Dora was quick to reassure her.

"Don't worry, Doe. You know where I am if you need me. You can come back to stay anytime. We'll always manage."

Doreen squeezed Auntie Dora and gave her a kiss, relieved that she was providing her with a safety net.

The house in Harpurhey was on three floors, large enough to split in two. The ground floor was occupied by Tom and Patricia, who were the owners of the house. They were both in their fifties and their children had grown up and moved away. They had divided the house in order to make an additional rental income, now that they didn't need as much space. They seemed friendly, but Doe didn't see them that often. Emily had rented the top floors. There were two bedrooms, but Doreen's was very small. It was built into the roof and accessed by a small flight of stairs leading up from the hallway. It had a camp bed that just fit into the room lengthways and still allowed the door to open. At the side of the bed was a space wide enough to fit in a chest of drawers and a small wardrobe, but with little space to move around in.

Doreen found out that her mam worked long hours and as she herself didn't go to school and could only get part-time jobs after four o'clock, she had to spend much of the day indoors by herself. This was fine because at least she was sheltered from the elements. Yet she soon had other concerns. In particular, she didn't like the way that Sam looked at her. His eyes seemed to follow her around the room, creating the same impression as when she had first met him. He usually didn't say very much and depended heavily on Emily to look after him. When he'd been drinking however, Sam was loud and aggressive. His behaviour upset Emily, although Doe hadn't seen him threaten her and felt sure that Jim would have mentioned it, if he'd heard that Sam had done so.

The first Saturday after moving in, Emily took her daughter into town. Before they left, Doreen noticed that her mam had put a brown paper package into her shopping bag. She wondered what it was, but said nothing. Getting off the bus, they headed to the second-hand bookshop, where for a small charge customers could exchange books and magazines for something new to read. Doe thought it was peculiar when her mam asked her to wait outside, but did as she was asked. As the time passed and there was no sign of Emily, Doreen began to get bored and her natural curiosity began to get the better of her. What was taking so long? Entering the shop, she was shocked to see her mam handing over some adult magazines to the female shop assistant. She then picked up another pile from the counter, ready to put into the empty brown paper bag that she'd brought with her. Doreen understood why she had been asked to wait outside; her mam didn't want her to know. As Doe was stood behind her, Emily hadn't realised that she had come in. Before putting the magazines in the bag, she quickly flicked through the pages. Doreen could see the pictures. They were of women with large breasts. She was shocked. Not so much by the magazines, as Doe knew that they existed, but the sight of her mam openly looking through them in the shop. Embarrassed by the magazines, Doreen quickly departed.

Outside, Doe was stunned. It was her mam and she felt uncomfortable. Since leaving Bright Avenue, Doreen had lost much of her innocence. She had learned that her parents put a higher value on satisfying their personal desires than they did on caring for her. Older now, she tacitly accepted the sexual nature of the relationships they had forged with their new partners. But to see her mam dealing with 'dirty books', was a step too far. It may be all right for others, but Emily was her mam and it just didn't seem right. Such magazines were for teenage boys to snigger at and dirty old men, perverts, to drool over. It was 1963 and in public, that was what everyone said and Doe was conditioned to accept it. When Emily came out, the magazines safely stored away in her shopping bag, she just couldn't stay quiet. Doreen wanted answers.

"Why were you exchanging those magazines, Mam?"

"What magazines?"

"I saw you. I came in the shop. You've got new ones in your bag, haven't you?"

Emily wished that she hadn't brought Doreen with her. She should have known that her daughter wouldn't wait outside. Emily said nothing. It was left to Doe to continue.

"I suppose they're for Sam, aren't they?"

"Yes," replied Emily.

"Why can't he change them himself?"

"He doesn't like coming into town. He gets nervous in big crowds."

"He doesn't want to be embarrassed more like. He doesn't want people in the shop to think he's a pervert."

"No, it's not like that, Doe. Lots of couples have these magazines. It's just that no one talks about it. If they didn't have them, how do you think the shop could survive? You'll find out it's true, when you're older."

Emily was being as honest as she could. She would have preferred her daughter not to have found out, but she wanted her to understand that there wasn't anything 'dirty' about these magazines. Yet Doe wasn't convinced.

"But it must embarrass you to have to bring them in for him. What would happen if it were a man in the shop?"

"It never is," replied Emily. "The woman understands. It was embarrassing the first time, but it's soon all right. It's just like buying anything else. The woman in the shop's not bothered, she's just pleased to make the money."

There was something else bothering Doreen, but a matter she felt unable to discuss with her mam. The magazines contained pictures of women with large breasts. Emily was thin and she had a small bust and Doe assumed that the magazines must upset her. It must make her feel inadequate that Sam wanted magazines of women who had attributes that she didn't. Doreen wondered if he really appreciated her mam, if he wasn't happy to accept her as she was. It wasn't long before the knowledge of the magazines began to play on Doreen's mind.

During the following week she was pleased that Sam was out at work, for she was becoming convinced that his eyes were following her around the room. It was a school holiday so she could have been working, but as yet she hadn't managed to find a job and as her mam was looking after her, there was less pressure to do so. However, on Friday morning, Sam was home in bed. His contract had finished early and his new one didn't start until Monday. After her mam had left for work, Doreen was left alone with him. Last night, he had been blind drunk and Doe hoped that he would be incapacitated for the rest of the day.

Nevertheless, Doe decided to take precautions. The magazines had made a huge impression on her and she was worried. It was clear that Sam was obsessed with big breasts and unlike her mam, Doreen was still physically developing. She didn't have a huge bust, but she feared that it was big enough. She felt that Sam had become more talkative lately and she began to fear that maybe his interest was focused on her chest. As a result, Doe went into her bedroom and moved the camp bed across the room and located it in front of the door. There was no chance that anyone could get in. The door was jammed shut; the bottom of the bed wedged against the back wall.

Doreen lay down on the bed and started to read a couple of teenage magazines. Doe enjoyed keeping up to date with all the new fashions and reading interviews with pop stars and film idols. Suddenly, she was disturbed by a noise. Someone was stumbling around in the living room on the lower floor. It had to be Sam. Listening carefully, she heard him muttering away to himself and then there was a loud crash, as if he had fallen against the table and chairs. There was a pause and then the sound of a cupboard door being slammed shut. Doreen assumed that he was after the whisky, as her mam always kept a couple of bottles in for him. Doe carried on reading. She heard nothing further and assumed that Sam had gone back into the bedroom.

About half an hour later, Doreen heard steps outside her room. It was Sam. She heard him stop at the door and then he tried the handle. The door opened a few inches and then hit the frame of the bed. It could go no further. He pushed again, assuming a greater effort would overcome the obstacle to the door opening. The bed held firm, just as Doreen knew it would. Although she felt a little nervous, Doe knew that she was secure. There was no chance of Sam getting in.

"Open the door. I want to talk to you."

Sam's voice sounded hoarse as he stumbled over the words. He was clearly drunk.

"Get lost, Sam. I'm reading," replied Doreen, loudly.

Sam fumbled with the handle a little longer, then stopped. She heard retreating footsteps and then it was quiet. Doreen assumed that he had gone back to his whisky.

Doe waited for half an hour. The house was silent. Carefully, she got off the bed and ever so quietly turned the handle and opened the door a few inches before it would move no further. She looked through the gap, but it was too narrow for her to see anything. There was no alternative, she would have to move the bed. It wasn't possible to stay there until her mam returned. Besides, although Sam had left her alone, he'd continued drinking and she didn't want to be there if he returned to her room.

Lifting the bed as quietly as possible, first at the head, next at the bottom, Doreen moved it away from the door. Carefully turning the handle, she slowly pulled the door open. Pausing, there was silence. Getting braver, she opened it fully and moved out down the stairs and into the hallway. Off it lay the front room with the kitchenette, the bathroom and her mam's bedroom, to which the door was slightly ajar. Doe could hear snoring. Pushing the door open a little further, she saw Sam sprawled out on his back across the bed. There was a whisky bottle, almost empty and a glass with a little liquid still in it, on the bedside cabinet. To all intents and purposes, he appeared dead to the world.

 Doreen breathed a sigh of relief. Quickly, she washed her hands and face and brushed her hair. She could wash her hair and put on her makeup later, when she arrived at Auntie Dora's. Making a jam sandwich to take with her, she hurriedly wrote a note to her mam and put it under the teapot on the table. Doe told her that she was going to see Sally and her friends and that she would stay a couple of nights at Auntie Dora's and return on Sunday. Doe was well aware that Emily and Sam would be out drinking over the weekend and she didn't welcome the prospect of having to suffer Sam's antics when he returned from the pub. Grabbing her rucksack, Doreen left the house. Wanting some fresh air to clear her head, she decided that she would walk the three miles to Bennett Street.

 Arriving at Auntie Dora's, Doreen washed her hair and did her makeup. As usual, the water was freezing, but Dora was pleased to see her. She wondered why Doe had come back so soon after moving in with her mam.

 "I just wanted to see you," said Doreen. "Make sure that you're all right."

 Dora suspected that it wasn't true. After all, if everything was fine at her mam's, then she wouldn't have rushed out without washing her hair and putting on her makeup. Dora was well aware of how much importance teenage girls attached to their appearance. She understood Doreen too and knew that her great niece wouldn't want to worry her. Dora would have to tease the information out of her.

 "Is everything all right at your mam's, Doe? How are you getting on with her?"

 "Fine," replied Doreen. "She's been good to me."

 "How's Sam?"

 Doreen paused.

"He's all right."

"You don't trust him, do you?"

The question took Doreen by surprise. She was silent; unable to respond.

"I met him once," continued Dora. "Your mam came here with him to give me some money before she took you and Sally into town. What do you think of him?"

Doreen was sure, by the way she'd asked the question, that Dora felt that there was something not quite right about him. Yet Doe didn't want to add to her Auntie's worries. She already had enough of her own.

"Come on, Doe. I can tell something's wrong. Tell me. I might be able to help."

Taking a deep breath, Doreen talked about the visit to the second-hand bookshop and then recounted the morning's events.

"He didn't touch you, did he?" asked Dora, her body stiffening.

"No, no," replied Doreen. "I just don't like the way he looks at me. Knowing about the magazines hasn't helped. I feel he's looking at my chest all the time."

"He's just a pervert, Doe. A disgusting pervert. I've heard stories about him. They say he got thrown out of Ireland. That they deported him. He's probably a sex fiend! I thought he was shifty when I saw him."

Doreen thought that Dora was going too far. After all, Sam was from Belfast in Northern Ireland and she knew that it was only the southern part of Ireland that was a separate country. Sam couldn't possibly have been deported from Belfast to Manchester. Nevertheless, Dora's words had made it clear that Doe wasn't alone in suspecting that he had a sinister side. Others thought so too.

"You need to keep well clear of him, Doe. Don't allow yourself to be with him on your own. Make sure that your mam's there with you at all times."

Although Dora only intended her words to be reassuring, in reality they only served to cause Doreen further concern.

"I don't know why your mam's stayed with him, but I'm sure he won't try anything when she's around. Anyway, just remember that you're always welcome to stay here if you feel that you might be in danger."

Auntie Dora paused in order to emphasise the fact that she would always provide Doreen with a place to stay.

"You have to remember," she continued, "there are some really bad men out there and boys for that matter, too. All they think about is sex and if you allow them to, they'll take advantage. Find yourself a nice, young man; someone who truly loves you and proves it. You're very pretty, Doe. You're going to get all kinds of attention. Treat them mean; that's the only thing men understand. Be the boss. Don't end up like most of the women around here; unpaid slaves to drunken husbands."

Doe knew that she was safe with Auntie Dora. She had never seen her so animated and she was clearly angry with Sam. Doreen suspected that as Emily continued to stand by him, she had lost respect for her too. Nevertheless, Dora had no wish to upset Doe and refrained from criticising her mam. For the rest of the day, Doreen helped Dora clean the flat and washed the net curtains for her. When Sally arrived home, they went to the chippy and then spent time with their friends on the flats. Doreen stayed over for two nights and at teatime on Sunday, she returned to Harpurhey. Emily was pleased to see her. Sam was now sober and Doe assumed that he didn't remember any of Friday's events. Doreen decided it was best not to mention anything to her mam. As long as she wasn't alone with Sam, then everything should be all right.

Chapter 49

It wasn't long before Doe realised how peculiar the relationship between Sam and Emily was. Sam wasn't the man who Doreen remembered from Bright Avenue. Now, he was completely lacking in self-confidence. Unable to travel to jobs on his own, Emily had to accompany him on the bus, before setting off to work herself. When Emily had said that Sam didn't exchange his own magazines because he didn't like crowds, Doreen hadn't believed her. Having assumed that it was just an excuse, she now knew that it was true. Yet once he'd had a drink, Sam was far from shy and retiring; a completely different character. Working as a plasterer on building sites around Manchester, he would always have 'a couple' with the lads at dinner and that was enough to perk him up. He was a good worker and didn't go short of employment. He also earned good money, although Doe saw no evidence that he gave any to her mam. Emily was expected to take care of the food and the bills. It appeared to Doreen that her parents had partners who took their earnings and gave them little in return. Doe was determined that when it came to men, she would follow Dora's advice. She would never end up with a husband like Jim or Sam.

When Sam and Emily came back from the pub, particularly on Friday and Saturday nights, they would often be arguing. Doreen didn't like it, but stayed in her room. As far as she was aware, it was just words. There was no sign that Sam had laid a finger on her mam. Nevertheless, the arguments often became very heated and when he was drunk, Sam would make some vicious and hurtful comments.

Living with Emily provided mixed blessings. Sam bothered Doe and although he hadn't touched her, the magazines and his staring eyes, made her feel uncomfortable. Yet she was back with her mam, who finally seemed to want to look after her. She had enough food and a reasonably nice house to live in. Importantly, the fact that one of her parents was supporting her, meant that

Doreen no longer felt beholden to anyone else. Although, as a last resort, she could go to Auntie Dora's, Doe always felt guilty about staying there. The last time, when she had contributed to the family budget, Doreen had felt better, but she could never forget Larry's comments and the fact that he had made her feel like an outsider. Although the arguing between Sam and Emily was unpleasant, Doe had lived in far more difficult situations and for the moment, felt confident of being able to tolerate it.

For Doreen however, life was never straightforward. Wherever she went, it seemed that something had to go wrong. In early September, she received bad news. Patricia had been up to see her mam. The previous night, there had been yet another blazing row and Patricia wasn't happy. The upshot was that she and Tom had had enough. The constant arguing was upsetting them and they'd had complaints from the neighbours. Patricia told Emily that they would have to leave, but as they had Doreen with them, she would give them a week to find somewhere else. Emily took the news in her stride, rather nonchalantly telling her daughter about their landlord's demand. Doe sensed that it was a situation that her mam was used to. She suspected that their arguing had led to them being evicted elsewhere. As her daughter had begun to resign herself to moving, Emily informed her that there was worse to come.

"It's going to be awkward, Doe. It's hard to find anywhere with two bedrooms. This was cheap, it will take me a while to get another like it. I think Sam and I will have to take a one bedroom place this week and then look for somewhere bigger. I'm sorry love, you're going to have to ask Auntie Dora to put you up again for a while."

Doreen didn't know what to say. She was angry and frustrated. If her mam and Sam didn't argue, or better still, if she didn't live with him, Doe knew that there wouldn't be any problems. Why on earth did she stay with him? What did she see in him? To Doreen, he was simply awful; disgusting. Yet just like Jim, who insisted on standing by Betty, her mam would stay loyal to Sam. Doreen was convinced that both of her parents were determined not to admit that they had made a mistake; neither of them prepared to lose face by being the first one to leave their partner. In the recriminations that surrounded their separation, both were adamant that they had gained someone better. Doreen thought it pathetic that they continued to live unhappily, rather than admit that they'd chosen badly. Not only had she suffered from their separation, but they had too. Doe knew that it would have been easy to criticise Emily, but she decided not to. Her mam had wanted to give her a home and had proved it. Doreen would give her another chance to find somewhere else. She would wait and see.

Moving back to Auntie Dora's wasn't an easy option. The situation there had changed. Walt and Larry were now unemployed and money was exceptionally tight. Moving to Harpurhey, Doe had given up her part-time jobs and needed time to get new ones. She couldn't make an immediate contribution to the family budget. Furthermore, as Emily was looking for a new flat, she wouldn't be giving Dora much either. Doreen was sure that her return to Bennett Street would be met by Walt and Larry's displeasure.

Doreen wondered what she could do. She didn't want to 'put on' her Auntie Dora and had no intention of asking her dad for anything. She was at a loss. It looked like she would have to resort to living in empty houses again. Then, unexpectedly, came an opportunity. Doe was staying overnight with Sally and the two girls had been asked to babysit for a couple who lived in a terrace house opposite the flats. It wasn't the first time that they had been there and the couple, Bill and Mary, seemed quite friendly. Their children were twin boys and four years old. Mary had only recently started her recovery from a serious road accident. She was still having to move around with the aid of a stick and she was finding it hard to cope. The couple had asked Doreen how she was getting on with her mam and when Doe mentioned that she was going to have to move out for a time, offered her the chance to stay with them. The condition was that she would help Mary to look after the children and assist her with the household chores. For this, they would give her five shillings a week on top of her board and lodgings. Doreen had been in a similar situation with Alan and Rosa, so she knew that it would be hard work. Nevertheless, it seemed the best option available and perhaps it would only be for a short time if her mam found a two-bedroom property for them to live in.

Doe moved in the following day, having returned in the morning to see Emily and tell her that she was leaving. Emily gave her a pound and told her that she would be in touch as soon as she had located somewhere suitable. Returning to Bill and Mary's, Doreen quickly found it as tough as she had expected. She wasn't just helping; effectively she was doing everything herself. Whether Mary was still genuinely weak from the effects of the accident, or just downright lazy and using her walking stick as a passport to an easy life, it made no difference. Doe had to graft continuously from seven in the morning, until seven at night. From then, the time was her own; as it was after dinner on Saturdays and Sundays. Then she would eagerly leave the house to spend time with Sally and Sarah.

At the end of the first week, Doreen became aware of another problem. The small bedroom she occupied was in the attic above Bill and Mary's room. The walls and floors weren't particularly soundproof and Doe could often hear them talking and moving about. It was a situation that she wasn't particularly comfortable with and not wanting to invade the couple's privacy, albeit through no fault of her own, she would often bury her head deep into her pillow so that she couldn't hear them. On Sunday, Doreen had spent the afternoon and evening with her friends. Given a back door key, she returned at ten o'clock and let herself back into the house. As there was no one downstairs, she made her way up to her room. Passing Bill and Mary's bedroom door, Doreen could hear that they were still awake. Going up the attic stairs and into her room, Doe got ready for bed. As she lay under the covers, trying to get to sleep, Doreen was disturbed by voices from below. She could only assume that Bill and Mary thought that she was still out, for she had never heard them talking this loud before. Bill, in particular, was becoming quite animated and whether Doe liked it or not, she couldn't avoid hearing what they were saying.

"You've not let me for ages now. How long is it going to be? I know you've not been well, but I need you, Mary."

"That's all you think about, isn't it? Just so long as you're all right. You aren't bothered about me."

"That's not true. If I didn't love you, I wouldn't keep asking, would I?"

"I need more time. Another couple of weeks and I should be all right. You're going to have to be patient."

"You said that last week. You don't mean it."

"I do. You'll see. I'll be all right by then. I want you to enjoy it. It'll be worth the wait."

"But it's like you're asking me to book an appointment. You're my wife; I need you."

"Get off! I've told you! I need more time."

From the fierce tone of Mary's voice, it was clear that she was firmly in control of their relationship.

"Get over on your side and shut up! Doreen's going to be back soon. I don't want her to hear you carrying on," continued Mary.

There was a short pause. Doe felt embarrassed. She had overheard their conversation and was in no doubt about its content. As Doreen became more aware of sexual intimacy, she wondered why something that was talked about as being so wonderful, often led to arguments and misery. Doe was thankful that their disagreement wouldn't affect her. Or so she thought, until Mary continued with a comment that shocked her to the core.

"And whilst we're on the subject of Doreen, I've seen the way you look at her. And you can just pack it in."

"What do you mean?" asked Bill.

"You know very well what I mean. All the attention that you give her. Trying to laugh and joke with her. Remember, she's only sixteen. Now let me get to sleep."

Doreen wasn't sixteen, she was still fourteen, but she hadn't told them that. She felt a little guilty. Would Bill have acted as Mary claimed, if he'd known her true age? Was it her fault that he and Mary were arguing? She thought carefully about the events of the past few days. She hadn't thought anything about Bill's pleasant nature. Yes, he did joke with her and always seemed to have a smile on his face, but she had never felt uncomfortable when she was with him, like she did with Sam. Doe certainly didn't feel that Bill had acted inappropriately.

The following day Doreen tried hard to put the conversation between Bill and Mary out of her mind. She was irritated and confused though and couldn't stop thinking about it. Perhaps she should have shouted through the bedroom door that she was back and then their conversation may not have taken place. Yet it was useful to know what Mary was thinking. At least it may explain why she was sometimes short with her. Yet Doreen also wanted to be fair to Bill and wondered whether Mary had only made the comment in order to stop his advances. Significantly, the incident left her with a problem. How would the two of them react to her after Mary's claim and how was she to deal with Bill? Was his attention harmless, or was he another Sam? How many men could really be trusted?

It was with some difficulty that Doreen worked her way through the rest of the day. She felt relieved when it was finally seven o'clock and she could leave for the flats and talk to Sally. She told her cousin about the conversation she had heard the previous night. At first Sally made light of it, then realising Doreen's unease, tried to give her the best advice that she could.

"I'm sure you needn't worry about Bill. He's just being friendly. I can't imagine him ever trying it on. If I were you, I'd try and avoid talking to him too much. Get on with your jobs and take the kids out to the park more."

"It's not just Bill though," replied Doreen, "it's Mary too. She's got more demanding lately and now I understand why. I'm worried that it's going to get worse. She'll have me working even harder, just like Rosa did. I won't stay if that's the case."

"Why don't you come back to us, Doe? You know my Gran will always make you welcome."

"No, Sally. It's tough enough for Auntie Dora with Larry and Walt being out of work. I'll stick it out as long as I can. Hopefully, it won't be too long before my mam gets in touch."

But Emily didn't contact her and over the next fortnight, Doreen experienced an increasingly strained atmosphere at Bill and Mary's. Reluctantly, Doe went with Sally to see her dad, to find out if he knew where her mam was. She was in luck. Jim told her that he'd heard that she'd been seen in the 'Shakespeare'. Doreen waited until Friday night and went down there. Looking through the door and into the lounge, she saw Emily sat in the corner. Doreen shouted to her across the noise of the room. Her mam looked up and made her way outside. Although surprised to see her, Emily immediately threw her arms around her daughter and kissed her on the cheek.

"I'm sorry I haven't been to Auntie Dora's yet. I'm hoping to have somewhere for you to stay in a few days."

"I'm not at Auntie Dora's."

Doe told Emily about how she was living with Bill and Mary and how hard it was for her. How, for her keep, she was expected to do all the washing, cooking and cleaning, as well as looking after the twins.

"I can't stay at Auntie Dora's, Mam. It wouldn't be fair. She's got hardly anything with Larry and Walt out of work. You can't help out and it's no good asking my dad. I lost my part-time jobs when I moved in with you, so that's why I'm with Bill and Mary. It'd be good if you could find somewhere."

Emily recognised that she and Sam had placed Doreen in her current predicament. Having managed to reconnect with her daughter, she was determined to put things right. It was the only way to maintain their new relationship.

"Come back here next Saturday, Doe. I'll make sure that I find somewhere for us all to stay. Try and stick it out until then."

Doreen said goodbye and set off back to the flats to spend the rest of the night with Sally and her friends. She would give it a week to see what, if anything, her mam came up with. Even if she didn't, Doe knew that she would definitely leave Bill and Mary's. If necessary, she would simply live rough again, until she could get enough part-time work to go back to Auntie Dora's.

The following week, Doreen returned to the 'Shakespeare', unsure whether Emily would be there. Fortunately, she was and had brought some good news.

"Me and Sam have found somewhere to live in Salford. It's a house and it's got two bedrooms. We'll be moving in tomorrow. I'll meet you here tomorrow night at six and I'll take you there."

Doe was delighted. After finding Sally and telling her the news, she spent time with her friends before returning to Bill and Mary's. She told them that her mam had found a new house and that she would be moving in the next day. Rather than being pleased for her, the couple were angry. Vindictively, Mary demanded that she leave there and then; effectively putting her out on the street. Doreen went up to her room, gathered her few possessions and put them in her rucksack. Without a word of complaint, she left the house and ventured out into the night.

Too late to go to Auntie Dora's, Doreen managed to find a sheltered spot in one of the back alleys. It wasn't raining and she was reasonably warm, but she couldn't sleep. Doe didn't understand why Bill and Mary had reacted with such hostility to her news. Unanswered questions raced through her mind. Hadn't she worked hard for them? Wouldn't Mary be happy that she would no longer be there to distract her husband? Why did they have to be so awful to her? It just didn't seem to make any sense. Why did there seem to be so many evil people in the world?

Eventually, Doreen nodded off. Woken early by the sound of the milkman on his rounds, Doe made her way to Auntie Dora's in order to wash and change. Dora was annoyed with her for not coming to them in the night, but was pleased that Emily was standing by her. Having spent the day with Sally and Sarah, at six Doreen went to the 'Shakespeare'. Emily was waiting for her. After bus rides to Piccadilly and then Weaste Depot, Doreen and Emily took a short walk and then they were there. A new chapter in her life was about to begin.

Chapter 50

Doreen had been a little concerned about moving to Salford, but was reassured by the fact that there were regular bus services back to Piccadilly. She knew that she would be able to visit Sally and her friends, as long as she could afford the bus fare. The new house, 78 Guide Street, was a two-bedroom terrace. It was in Weaste, just around the corner from the bus depot. It was a location much like the terraced streets she had been used to in Ardwick. It seemed strange that her mam had relocated in Salford. It was possible that the house was cheaper, although Emily and Sam's reputation for arguing may have left landlords in Manchester reluctant to rent them a property. After her negative experience with Bill and Mary, Doe hoped that her accommodation would prove more satisfactory. Her room was bigger than it had been in Harpurhey and her bed was far more comfortable than the small camp bed that she had slept on there. In addition, she had a wardrobe and a chest of drawers. The latter was located next to the door and could be moved across it should she feel the need to do so. As ever, Doreen was thinking ahead.

The first week went well. Doreen got to know the area and managed to get a Saturday job, helping a local hairdresser. Doe was paid eight shillings which would enable her to visit Sally a couple of times during the week. As yet, she hadn't met any new friends in Weaste. The situation would have been easily remedied if she attended school, but Doreen had no wish to do so, given that in a few months she would be working anyway. Emily certainly didn't seem too concerned that she did. In fact, her mam had other matters weighing on her mind. Her relationship with Sam had begun to take a turn for the worse. The drink was having a serious effect on him. He had begun to experience terrible mood swings and was becoming increasingly hostile towards her when he was drunk. Conversely, he was ever more dependent on Emily to get him ready in the morning and take him to work.

Doreen's first weekend at Guide Street was similar to her last in Harpurhey. On both Friday and Saturday night, Sam had been shouting and swearing at her mam. Doe had come out of her bedroom but Emily had told her to go back in, insisting that everything would be all right; Sam had just had too much to drink. She had told him not to mix whisky with his bitter, but he had taken no notice. Reluctantly, Doe did as she was told, but felt uncomfortable. She didn't understand why her mam was putting up with it. Only once had she seen Jim show any aggression towards her mam and that was because Emily had smacked her. At the time, Doreen had protected her mam and her dad had never done it again, no matter how much he had been drinking. So why did Sam have any reason to do it? Doreen supposed that Emily liked Sam's vulnerability; that he depended on her in a way that Jim never did. Perhaps too, her mam even believed that she could change him. Yet if that were the case, she would have to stop him going to the pub and in reality, she enjoyed going out just as much as he did. Doe remembered how different Emily had been when she was married to Jim. She rarely went out at night and stayed with her daughter. Now, it was as if she had been let off the leash; determined to catch up for lost time. Yet Doreen sensed that there was something darker too. At times she feared that her mam actually liked being mistreated by Sam. That in some perverse way she enjoyed his negative and ultimately destructive attention. Doreen could see that Sam's hostility towards his partner was increasing. She knew that it would only get worse and was well aware of the sufferings of similar women who lived on Bennett Street flats. She feared that Emily would become another 'battered wife', regularly and systematically abused. When she had tried to raise the issue with her mam, Doreen was ignored. Emily wouldn't hear a word against Sam.

    Matters came to a head the following Saturday night. Doreen had been working at the hairdressers and felt a little tired. She therefore decided that she wouldn't go to Sally's until the following morning. Settling down in her room, Doe read some magazines and listened to the radio. There had been a television set in the room, left behind by the previous tenants. Doreen had tried it but it didn't work and so it had been put on a small table on the landing at the top of the stairs. Emily had asked Sam to put it in the back yard, but as yet he'd failed to do so.

Reading her magazines on the bed and listening to the drone of the music, Doreen's eyes began to close and she fell asleep. Sometime later, she was awoken by the noise of shouting coming from downstairs. It was her mam and Sam, rowing yet again. Back from the pub, it was the usual weekend routine. Doreen pushed her head under the pillow in a vain attempt to drown out the sound. But it was no good; the voices were just getting louder. Suddenly, there was a crash, followed by a scream. It was her mam. Doe jumped up and made for the bedroom door. She opened it. It sounded like pandemonium downstairs. Sam was swearing and shouting. Emily was pleading with him to stop. There was another bang, then the sound of smashed crockery. Appearing at the bottom of the stairs, Emily scampered up them towards her daughter.

"Oh, Doe. Help," she cried, weakly.

Reaching the landing, Emily clung on to Doreen like a scared and hurt child. She was sobbing and her top was torn. She had a trickle of blood coming from the side of her mouth. Appearing at the bottom of the stairs, Sam was shouting and swearing at them. It was clear that he wasn't going to calm down. Doreen had to think quickly. She expected that at any moment he would try to climb up the stairs and reach her mam. Pushing Emily into her bedroom, Doe pulled the door shut behind her. She screamed down at Sam.

"Clear off, Sam! Leave my mam alone!"

For a moment Sam was quiet before shouting back.

"Come out you bitch! I'll get you!"

Slowly, he started to climb the stairs, but it was obvious to Doreen that the excess of alcohol had befuddled his senses. He staggered forward, but slipped back down the first couple of stairs. Cursing and swearing, he grabbed hold of the handrail. Tentatively, he began again. Unsteady on his feet, Sam balanced precariously on the edge of each stair in turn, as he laboriously made his way up towards the landing.

Doe watched him as he slowly got nearer; his face red with drink and the strain of the climb. He was foaming at the mouth and his eyes bulged. He was evil and she hated him. Doe always had and now he'd gone and hit her mam. She wanted revenge; she wanted to get even. He had broken up her family and ruined her childhood. She was going to make him pay. Halfway up the stairs, but stumbling as he went, it seemed unlikely that Sam would reach the top. But Doreen wasn't going to wait and see. Turning to the table at the top of the stairs, she stepped behind it and pushed with all her might. Table and television hurtled through the air. There was an almighty bang as the TV hit the stair above Sam; a shower of glass as the screen imploded and slivers embedded themselves into her nemesis who, shocked, fell back down the stairs.

Emily opened the bedroom door. The noise of the imploding television had shocked her into silence. She stepped over to Doreen and looked down. She saw the crumpled and pathetic figure of her would be persecutor lying at the foot of the stairs. Her heart went out to him.

"Oh, Sam! Are you alright?"

Sitting up slowly, Sam moaned and then sobbed. He had absolutely no idea of what had just happened to him. Doe was pleased. He'd got what he deserved. But Doreen just couldn't believe her mam's reaction. It was pathetic.

"Sam! What about you, Mam? You were the one he was trying to kill!"

"I'm all right," replied her mam, dismissively. "We've got to help Sam!"

Doreen quickly grabbed Emily's arm.

"Careful, Mam. There's glass everywhere. You don't want to cut yourself."

"What happened?" asked Emily, looking at the scene of devastation.

Seeing her mam's concern for Sam, Doe had no intention of telling the truth. She wouldn't stand by and let him gain any more sympathy. Her response came quickly.

"Sam pulled the TV set on himself when he was trying to get on the landing."

Carefully, the two of them made their way downstairs. Sam was no longer a threat. The exertion of getting up the stairs and the tumble back down them, had left him a spent force. He was now sat up on the floor and in a complete daze. His face was full of small cuts; trickles of blood all over it. His hands were too, as he had used them to attempt to sweep away the tiny fragments of glass that were covering his clothes.

"Mam, be careful. Don't try to touch his clothes. Leave them on. You'll just get cut."

Emily grabbed Sam's hand and tried to pull him to his feet, but she couldn't move him. Seeing his distressed state, she began to sob.

"Go to the phone, Doe. Please. Get an ambulance."

Doreen didn't want to, but before she could complain, a loud knocking came to the front door. Probably the neighbours thought Doe, come to complain about the noise. She went to the door and opened it. She was wrong. It was a policeman.

"Hello, young lady. Is everything all right? We've had a report that you've had some trouble."

"Yes, my mam's boyfriend attacked her."

"Where is he now?"

"At the bottom of the stairs."

The officer moved past her and drew out his truncheon. Doe followed behind, hoping that he would use it on Sam. Seeing the sorry figure of the assailant, slumped bewildered on the floor, the policeman put his truncheon away. Crouched down beside Sam, Emily was trying to get him to talk. Noticing the cut on her mouth and the slivers of glass all over her boyfriend, the officer turned to Doreen.

"Have you got a pair of scissors, love?"

"Yes."

"Can you get them for me, please?"

Doreen went into the kitchen and took a pair of scissors out of the drawer. Returning, she handed them to the policeman. Carefully he cut away at Sam's jumper, removing it without having to pull it over his head. He turned to Emily.

"Can you get him another pair of trousers, love?"

Emily slowly got up and went to fetch a pair from the ironing basket in the kitchen. The officer again asked for Doreen's help.

"Can you go to the phone box, young lady and call for an ambulance. Say that PC Lawrence has asked you to phone and give them your address. Don't worry, your mam's fine. I'll be staying right here with her."

Doe went to the phone box at the end of the road and within ten minutes she was back in the house. Sam's trousers had been changed and the policeman had moved him on to the settee in the front room. His face and hands were still bloody and there were bits of glass embedded in his skin. Concerned, Emily was about to remove a piece of glass.

"No, leave it," said Lawrence. "You might make it worse, or more to the point, cut yourself. We don't want that now, do we?"

Emily stopped. Doreen looked at her. She had a bruised right eye, as well as a cut mouth. Sam had obviously hit her more than once and the bruising was only just starting to come out.

"Your daughter's phoned an ambulance, Emily. We need to take you and your boyfriend to hospital. You need to be checked out too. That's a nasty looking bruise you've got there. How did it happen?"

"He punched her," answered Doreen. "Didn't he, Mam?"

Doe was looking for confirmation from Emily, but her mam wasn't listening.

"Emily. Emily."

PC Lawrence spoke quietly, yet insistently.

Emily turned to look at him.

"We need to know what happened, love."

"Nothing," replied Emily.

Lawrence had been here before. Battered wives who defended their man to the hilt. He hated to see it but there were a host of reasons why they did so. Many were afraid of what would happen to them if the police charged their husbands and insisted on using them as a witness. They worried about whether they could be protected and if they would still have a home to live in. The husband's name was always on the rent book, so in retaliation he could throw his wife and children out on the street. Most women doubted that the courts would act. Judges seemed to write them off, regardless of the evidence. Mostly elderly, upper middle-class men, they had no sense of responsibility to working-class women. After all, they reasoned, the working classes didn't know any better. Police officers often shared that point of view and felt that it wasn't worth the effort to pursue a prosecution. Lawrence though, was different and tonight, he was determined to push a little harder.

"It can't be nothing, Emily. You didn't get a cut mouth and a shiner from nothing, did you?"

"We were just arguing, being silly and I fell over against the table. I banged the side of my head. Sam would never hit me."

"Don't lie," said Doreen, hopeful that Sam would be arrested. "Sam hit you. Didn't he?"

"No," insisted Emily. "I fell. You weren't there, Doe. You don't know what happened."

It was true. She hadn't been there, but Doreen knew that her mam was lying. She had seen the panic on Emily's face as she rushed up the stairs. She had been terrified of him.

"Come on, Mam. You can let the police charge him. Tell the truth."

"I am," said Emily. "He never touched me."

Lawrence realised that it was no good. Even if he did persuade her to support the bringing of charges, she would probably withdraw her evidence the next day, as many women did. He turned to Emily.

"I'm just going into the kitchen with your daughter. I don't think we'll get any more trouble from your boyfriend now. Just shout if you need me."

Emily nodded.

Lawrence beckoned to Doe and she followed him out into the kitchen.

"What's your name, love?"

"Doreen."

"Right, Doreen. Tell me exactly how Sam ended up with a shattered TV screen all over him."

Doe told him how Emily had run up the stairs and that she had pushed her into the bedroom. Sam had followed, but as he reached the landing, he'd tried to grab her, but instead had pulled the TV on top of him and had stumbled backwards down the stairs. The television had then shattered as it tumbled down behind him.

Lawrence watched closely as she related her story. He noticed the gleam in her eye and the obvious satisfaction she felt when she told him about the glass showering all over Sam.

"Are you sure that you didn't push it down on him, Doreen? I don't care if you did. He's a bully. He deserved it."

Doreen was silent.

"Just be careful, love. It was a dangerous thing to do. All that glass could have been fatal. He'll get over this; we don't want you to get into serious trouble for wounding scum like him."

Lawrence wasn't supposed to take sides but coppers usually did. He wasn't at all interested in pursuing a charge of GBH against a young, teenage girl. To Lawrence, she was a hero. She'd stood up to a drunken bully and should get a medal, not face the juvenile court. Lawrence asked Doe if Sam had attacked Emily before. She told him no. He warned her that it could well happen again. After one assault, others invariably followed.

"Do you have to live here, Doreen? Isn't there anywhere else that you could go?"

"No. I haven't got a choice."

"Okay, let's get back to your mam. The ambulance should be here soon."

The pair of them returned to the front room and sure enough, a few minutes later, the ambulance arrived to take Sam and Emily to hospital. Doreen had no intention of going with them, especially as Lawrence would be accompanying them to ensure that her mam was safe. Doe told Emily that she would stay to clean up the mess before she returned.

"Be careful of all that glass," said Lawrence.

He was a decent copper, thought Doreen; one of the best she'd come across. She watched them get into the ambulance and closed the front door. As Doe set about cleaning the house, she went over the night's events. She felt sorry for her mam having been on the receiving end of Sam's aggression, but angry that she had put up with it. If Lawrence was correct, it was only going to get worse. It was so frustrating. Doreen knew that Emily could find a man far better than Sam. Why couldn't she see that? Staying with him made no sense.

Doreen was proud of what she'd done to Sam and would have loved to have taken the credit for it. Yet Emily's concern for her boyfriend, even after he had attacked and terrified her, told Doe that she wouldn't appreciate her actions. Doreen decided to say nothing. It was clear that her mam was going to stick by Sam regardless of what he did. The only thing she now had to consider, was how she felt about it. If she acted emotionally, as she usually did, Doreen would have given Emily an ultimatum. She would have insisted that she leave Sam and then have walked out herself, when her mam refused. Yet her head told her that this would achieve nothing. It wouldn't help Emily and once again, Doe would be homeless and at the mercy of the streets. Doreen therefore decided that she would stay. She'd put up with everything else and this was just another scenario that she would have to deal with. More importantly, Doe was maturing; accepting that sometimes it was necessary to compromise some of her principles in order to survive. She loathed Sam, but for the time being, she needed a place to live. Doe could at least comfort herself with the knowledge that whilst she was there, she would at least afford Emily some protection. Nevertheless, Doreen wasn't naïve enough to believe that she could do so forever.

Chapter 51

Emily returned early on Sunday morning. She had been checked over by the medical staff at the casualty department who had, but for her black eye, given her a clean bill of health. Sam had been kept in longer for observation, after having the glass removed from his face and hands. It seemed that he hadn't remembered anything about the TV set falling on top of him, so Doreen wouldn't face any recriminations. As far as Emily and Sam were concerned, he had pulled it down on himself. When Emily had told her that Sam wouldn't be back until Monday, Doreen had gone to see Sally. She knew that she needn't have any concerns about her mam's safety for the rest of the weekend.

Sam came back on Monday and by Tuesday he was back at work. As usual, in the evening he and Emily went straight out to the pub. It didn't seem to bother either of them that Emily still had a black eye, her attempts to disguise it with makeup, failing miserably. The unpleasant fact was that she wasn't the only woman who suffered at the hands of her partner. Although abusive men weren't respected, society hadn't moved to the point where such individuals were shunned and publicly shamed. Sam was, for all his faults, a worker and like in Harpurhey, he managed to drink moderately when he knew that he was working the following day. It was Friday and Saturday nights, the work-free weekend, when he drank to excess and lost control. By Thursday, Doe was starting to feel a sense of trepidation. She realised that it was because the weekend was coming and potentially, her mam would be in danger. Nevertheless, Doreen decided that she would go to see Sally, as she had arranged, on Friday. Doe believed that her mam would be all right, as long as she caught an earlier bus home. It would enable her to arrive back before Emily and Sam returned from the pub.

Doreen set off in the middle of the afternoon to get the bus to Piccadilly and then on to Bennett Street. She arrived shortly before Sally arrived home from work. Doe was looking forward to spending a few hours with her friends. It was a relief to get back to the flats after the tension of living with Sam. Together with Sally and Sarah, they could spend time with the lads. By now Doreen was becoming very friendly with Jack. He had brown curly hair and a mischievous smile and always made her laugh. Her only concern was his familiarity with lots of the girls on the flats. Wherever they went, girls she didn't know would come up to him; many suggestively. Pauline Campbell knew Jack too. She always smirked when she saw him and Pauline had a reputation, it was said, for being 'easy'. 'The introduction', Bob had told Sally and when prompted, had indicated that she was the one to whom the boys would go to learn about sex. Nice though he was, Doe wondered whether Jack would ever become more than just a friend.

It was Jack who walked Doreen to the bus stop at nine-thirty. She'd been enjoying his company so much that she had lost track of time and had nearly forgotten that she needed to return to her mam. Yet the buses were regular and she was sure that she would comfortably manage to get back for eleven. Reassuringly the bus arrived almost as soon as they had reached the stop on Hyde Road. Jack, seeing Doreen distracted, darted forward and pecked her on the cheek. His action took her by surprise and she didn't know what to say. Jack smiled. Doe couldn't be annoyed and secretly, she was quite pleased.

"Bye, Doe. Are you coming again tomorrow?" asked Jack.
"I can't. I'm working. I'll be back on Sunday though."
"I'll call for you at Sally's, around twelve."
"All right."

Doe got on the bus and sat down. She was tingling. It was Jack's kiss. How stupid she thought. Don't be daft! But she couldn't help smiling. Doe knew that she liked Jack and she sensed a certain chemistry between them.

The bus made its way rapidly to Piccadilly and then disaster struck. The next bus, waiting to take her to Weaste, had a large queue of people beside it. Surprised that they weren't waiting on board, Doreen was told that the bus had broken down and they would have to wait until the next one arrived. Concerned by the delay, Doe hoped that Emily and Sam stayed in the pub longer than usual; that she would get back before they arrived at the house and Sam became argumentative.

The situation became worse with the arrival of an Inspector. Suitably attired with his imposing cap, he was insistent that the bus remain at Piccadilly. There were additional fares to collect and the conductor needed time to get this done before the driver could set off. He was one of those individuals who was determined to do his bit for the bosses. That's why he was an Inspector. Frustrated by his actions, Doe found it hard to understand his mentality. What did it matter to him, she reasoned, if some passengers got off the bus before the conductor could take their fares? He wasn't going to get any of the money and the bosses wouldn't appreciate him for it. Couldn't he see that he was working late-night shifts for low wages? What a fool. Despite the mutterings of many of the passengers, sick of the delay and desperate to get home, the Inspector dismissed their complaints, seemingly pleased at the unpopular exercising of his authority. A little man, with a greying moustache, the Inspector was probably ex-army thought Doe. She could almost imagine him breaking out with a rendition of: 'I fought a war for you buggers.' How many times had kids of her generation been regaled with that one? The man was consistent though, he was unpopular with everyone, including the conductor who whispered to Doreen that he was 'a complete tosser'; 'a little Hitler'.

Eventually, the conductor was allowed to give the two rings necessary to start the journey and they were on their way. With a full bus and more people than usual waiting at the following stops, the journey was painfully slow. The bus seemed to be groaning as it made its way uncertainly from stop to stop. When they finally made it to Weaste Depot, it was almost twenty past eleven.

Stepping off the bus, Doreen walked quickly down the main road. Turning left, she made her way to the top of Guide Street. She saw a couple of police cars come past her in the opposite direction. Doe noticed someone walking quickly towards her. As the figure got nearer, she was surprised to see that it was Sam. He had his haversack on his shoulder and he was clearly in a hurry. Doreen called to him.

"Where are you going, Sam?"

Sam looked straight past her, mumbled something unintelligible and rushed on.

His behaviour seemed strange, but Doe felt relieved that he wasn't going to be at the house. As she continued towards number seventy-eight, she noticed Phyllis, one of the neighbours, waiting at her front door. She shouted to Doreen and motioned her over.

"It's terrible, love. It's your mam."

Doe felt a sickening feeling. Looking at Phyllis, it was clear that she was holding something back. It was bad news and she didn't know how to say it.

"What, Phyllis? Tell me."

"She's been taken in an ambulance to Hope Hospital. She's in an awful state, Doreen. I've got the keys to the house for you."

Phyllis handed them over.

"What's happened?" asked Doe, desperate to find out more.

"It's Sam. It seems they had a row in the pub earlier on and your mam left him. About half an hour ago she came home in a taxi and when she opened the door to get out, he was waiting for her. He dragged her to the floor and started kicking her on the pavement. At first, the taxi driver didn't realise what was going on, but then he jumped out of the cab and went to pull him off. Sam ran away before he could get hold of him. I came out to see what all the noise was and saw to your mam the best I could. The taxi driver radioed for the police and an ambulance."

"I've just seen Sam, heading up to the main road."

"Typical," replied Phyllis. "Where are the police when you need them?"

"I saw a couple of police cars when I got off the bus. I never realised that they were looking for him. I should have got back before now. I would have done if the bus hadn't broken down."

Doe felt guilty; convinced that it was her fault. She should have kept an eye on the time and left Bennett Street sooner.

"Doreen. It's not your fault, love. You didn't hit your mam," said Phyllis.

"But I still should have been back earlier."

"No, love. There's lots of men like Sam. They're evil in drink. If not tonight, he would have done it another night. You can't be there all the time, can you? He could just as well have done it outside the pub. You mustn't blame yourself. Your mam should leave him; she shouldn't put up with it."

Phyllis's words had given Doe some degree of comfort, but she still couldn't help feeling guilty.

"I'll go back down the street and try and find one of those police cars and tell them that I've seen him."

Doreen walked to the main road, flagged down a passing police car and told them that she'd seen Sam earlier. They explained that they hadn't found him yet, but assured her that they would. They told her to return home and wait for her mam and that an officer would be calling in the morning to take more details.

Back in the house, Doreen waited nervously. A couple of hours later she heard a car pull up outside and she ran to the front door. Opening it, she was confronted with an awful sight. Emily was almost unrecognisable. Her face was swollen, her lips split, her eyes puffed up and almost closed. Doe stood aside to let her in.

"I need money for the taxi driver," mumbled Emily.

She moved past Doreen, heading for one of the places where she kept money hidden from Sam. Like many men, he believed that whatever was in his partner's purse was his to use whenever the need arose.

Doe walked over to the taxi. The driver, a man around her dad's age, was shocked.

"They should string the bugger up for that."

Realising that his language was inappropriate, he apologised.

"Sorry for the language, love. Still, nothing's too much for the animal that did that."

Doe was well aware that decent men didn't swear in front of women or children. His words had been an indication of just how disgusted he was by the attack on her mam.

"It wasn't your dad, was it?"

"Not likely! It's my mam's boyfriend. He's disgusting. I hate him! I don't know why she stays with him."

Re-emerging from the front door, Emily slowly made her way to the taxi and passed some money to the driver.

"Thanks, love. Get inside now and let your daughter take care of you. Remember what I said. You've got to let the police charge him. Don't let him get away with it."

Emily thanked him. It was clear that she was in agony. Every attempt to speak was a real effort. The taxi pulled away and she and Doreen returned inside. It was now three o'clock and Emily was utterly exhausted.

"You need some sleep, Mam. Don't worry about Sam coming back. I'll bolt the front and back doors. The police are out looking for him. It won't be long before they pick him up."

Emily nodded weakly and made her way upstairs, with Doe following closely behind to make sure that she didn't stumble or fall. Emily was hurting both physically and emotionally. Seeing the state of her, Doe forced back the tears. Her mam needed her; she had to remain strong. Once upstairs, Doreen prepared the bed. She pulled back the eiderdown, sheets and blankets and piled up the pillows so that her mam could sleep sitting up. It was the best way to stop any pressure on her face. Emily went to take off her top, but she was finding it painful to move her arms. They too must have taken the brunt of Sam's kicks as she had tried to protect herself.

"No, Mam. Leave your top on. You'll only hurt your face more by taking it off and you need to keep warm under the covers."

Emily did as she was told and lay against the pillows. Doreen pulled the covers back over her. Painfully, Emily pulled out her left hand and put it on top of the eiderdown. Doe held it softly, feeling the faintest of squeezes from her mam. After a short time, Emily's fingers relaxed. Her head had settled slightly to the left and into the soft pillow. She was asleep. Carefully, Doreen replaced Emily's hand under the covers.

As her Mam slept, Doreen looked at her face in the light of the bedside lamp. Her eyes were black, her lips swollen and she had a deep cut on the top of her nose. She was black and blue. Doe was amazed that she had been sent home for surely the hospital should have kept her in. Yet here she was. Only later did it emerge that Emily had slipped out of casualty when a nurse had left her alone in order to fetch her a drink.

Going downstairs, Doreen again checked that she had secured the front and back doors. She doubted that Sam would return, but wasn't taking any chances. He had taken his rucksack and with it his plastering trowel and he knew that the police were after him, no matter how much he'd had to drink. She decided to sleep downstairs on the settee. Sam would then have to come through her to get to her mam. Doreen found some covers and then went into the kitchen. There she took out the carving knife from the cutlery drawer. She carried it with her into the front room and put it on the floor beside the settee. She would have no hesitation in stabbing Sam if he tried to get in.

However, just as Doe had thought, Sam didn't return. It meant that she had the chance to sleep a couple of hours before getting up and deciding whether or not she could work at the hairdressers. Waking up at seven, she had a quick wash and started to get ready. She would wait and see how her mam was before making a decision. Doe needn't have worried as Gillian, who owned the hairdressers, had been in the local newsagents and the incident with Emily had been the topic of conversation. At eight, Gillian knocked on the door and told Doe not to come into work, but to stay with her mam. Doreen was relieved. Not having wanted to lose her job, nevertheless she was determined to do what was best for Emily. Having spoken to Gillian, she went back upstairs to check on her mam. She was sleeping peacefully. Hopefully, the police wouldn't come too early and disturb her.

They didn't. At ten o'clock, Doreen went upstairs after hearing the noise of Emily's feet on the bedroom floor. She knocked on the door.

"Can I come in, Mam?"

"Yes," came a weak reply.

Doe opened the door and saw Emily struggling to get her top off.

"Mam, leave it. You'll hurt yourself."

"No, Doe, I want to get washed and put some clean clothes on. I feel dirty."

"Let me help. You're going to hurt yourself. Your face is badly damaged. You don't want to knock it."

Emily was wearing a top over a blouse. The latter could be removed without too much discomfort but the top would have to be taken off over her head.

"Mam, I'm going to have to cut your top. I can't lift it over your head. You're too bruised. The top's covered in blood anyway. I don't think you'll be able to get it clean. Just wait and let me get the scissors. We can get you another blouse and cardigan to put on."

Emily agreed and Doreen went to fetch her mam's dress making scissors and filled a bowl with warm water, soap and a flannel. Returning, she cut away at the side of the top and pulled it off. Removing the blouse, she could see that her mam's arms were black and blue. She had been incredibly lucky that there were no broken bones. Emily washed herself carefully and Doe helped her to dress.

"The police will be here soon," said Doreen. "Come on, I'll make you a brew."

The two went downstairs, Doe going first in case her mam felt dizzy. Reaching the kitchen, Emily sat down at the table. When Doreen had finished making the tea, she suggested that they go and sit in the front room.

"Let's stay here," replied Emily. "The police will probably come to the back door anyway."

About half an hour later, a police officer arrived. Introducing himself as DC Barnes, he sat down with Emily, whilst Doreen made him a drink.

"You've been in the wars, haven't you, love? We came out last week as well, didn't we? We need to do something about this, don't we?"

DC Barnes spoke quickly. He didn't want to give Emily too much time to reconsider the matter of Sam's prosecution.

"I've got some good news for you," he continued. "We picked up McLaughlin last night making his way into Manchester. Your daughter's details about him carrying his rucksack made it far easier to stop and identify him. If you remember Emily, we took photos of you last night at the hospital. We can show these as evidence to the court. I don't think you'll need to appear as a witness. I'm sure he'll plead guilty anyway."

"Do you have to charge him?" asked Emily.

Doe couldn't believe what she was hearing.

"Mam!"

Before she could say any more, DC Barnes placed his hand on Doreen's arm and looked sternly at her. For once, Doe was quiet. She understood that if she continued to criticise, it would make Emily less willing to co-operate. She would simply have to control her frustration.

"I'm afraid that we do have to charge him," continued Barnes. "You see, there are other witnesses, especially the taxi driver and he came in and gave us a statement after finishing his shift this morning. We can't allow him to get away with what he's done. So, you might as well give me a statement."

Slowly, Emily told Barnes what had happened. He wrote down her statement carefully, read it out and then handed it back to her. Reluctantly, Emily signed it.

"Don't worry, love. He won't be released until Monday morning. He knows that he's not allowed to come anywhere near you. He'll be dealt with at the Magistrates Court. We'll let you know the date. Putting the paperwork safely away, Barnes said farewell and was gone.

Now that she had her mam to care for, Doe realised that she wouldn't be able to see Jack as she had promised. In fact, it was likely that she wouldn't be visiting Bennett Street for some time, as she had no intention of leaving her mam alone until after the court case. Doe was determined to do her best to ensure that Emily's resolve didn't waver. Once Sam was in prison, Doreen was convinced that her mam could make a fresh start and find a new partner who wouldn't beat her.

The police contacted them a few days later. Sam had been charged with assault and battery. His case would be heard in a couple of weeks at Salford Magistrates Court in Bexley Square. They were sure that Sam would plead guilty but still wanted Emily, as well as the taxi driver, to attend in case he didn't. Doe was worried that Emily might decide to stay away. To her surprise, when the day arrived, her mam took little persuading.

The police were right. Sam did plead guilty. He looked a pathetic sight as he stared down at the floor throughout the proceedings. Finally, he was reprimanded by the lead judge, who ordered him to look up in order to receive the final verdict.

"Sam McLaughlin, you are a pathetic coward. I have no doubt that if you were confronted with a man of your own size, you would run a mile. You think it's acceptable to use your strength to bully and intimidate women. Well, you are going to pay the price. You will serve no less than three months in prison."

Doe was pleased, but Emily let out a gasp. It seemed as if she hadn't quite believed that he was going to be sent down. For a moment, Doreen was concerned. Yet the pleasure she felt, almost a sense of euphoria, at the knowledge that Sam would be out of their lives, led her to push any negative thoughts aside. As Sam was led away, Doe was full of optimism; she was sure that a new chapter was opening in their lives. Finally, they could be a family again.

Chapter 52

Emily decided that she and Doreen would stay in Salford. She was working locally and it was easy for Doe to catch the bus back to Ardwick in order to see her friends. She also made another significant decision. Her daughter would finally go to school. Doreen wasn't happy.

"No, Mam. I don't see any point in going. I'll be leaving soon anyway. I won't be staying on to take any GCEs. I just want to get a full-time job."

"But Doe," replied Emily, "you're the one who wants us to be a proper family again, so I have to try and put things right. Your dad and I should never have ignored your education. We've let you down. If you're living with me, then I'm responsible for you going to school. Just do it for me. You never know, you might end up wanting to stay on to take your exams."

Reluctantly, Doe agreed. Yet she had no intention of staying on at school beyond next Easter and knew that she wouldn't change her mind. It was the beginning of November 1963 and Easter was less than six months away. Doreen was enrolled at Tootal Road School. Unlike the other senior schools that she had attended, this one was mixed and joining it was surprisingly straightforward. Emily had assured her that the school would simply accept her as they had moved into the area. It was extremely unlikely, she insisted, that they would be checking any records from Manchester. After all, Salford was a different authority. And she was right. Emily told Tootal Road that her daughter had been in the GCE class at her previous school and Doreen was told to arrive on the following Monday when she would join 4A.

Before then, Emily and Doe were in for a major surprise. On Friday night, Doreen had decided to stay in with her mam, rather than visit Sally and her friends. After all, it was a night when Emily was used to being in the pub and Doe didn't like to leave her on her own. At about eight o'clock, when they were watching their newly rented television set, a knock came to the back door.

"Who's that?" asked Emily.

It seemed rather late for visitors or for someone to be trying to sell them something.

"It's okay Mam, I'll go" said Doreen, getting up from the settee.

Walking slowly to the door, Doe opened it and there, stood in front of her, was Jimmy. For a moment, she was too shocked to react and then she bounded down the steps and threw her arms around him. Almost bowled over by her enthusiasm, Jimmy felt her holding him tightly. She seemed afraid that he may run away.

"Mam. It's Our Kid!"

Emily, hearing Doreen's excitement, quickly rose from the settee and made her way to the door.

"Oh, Jimmy!" said Emily, taken by surprise. "Come in!"

Emily began to cry. The realisation that she had excluded him from her thoughts for so long, had suddenly hit home.

"Don't cry, Mam. I've not upset you that much by turning up, have I?"

Jimmy smiled and Emily put her arms around her son, hugging him until finally, her sobs began to subside.

"Come on Mam. Let's go and sit down. Doe can make us all a brew. Can't you, Doe."

"Yes. Of course."

Jimmy led his mam towards the settee. Having calmed down, she sat quietly sipping her tea, as Our Kid began to explain how he had been able to find them.

"It was in the *Evening News*," he explained. "Sam's case. Johnny Cooper showed it to me. It mentioned your name, Mam and it gave the address that Sam lived at. Guide Street. I assumed that you must still live here, so I decided to come and see. And here I am."

"Where are you living now, Our Kid?" asked Doreen.

She hadn't seen her brother for a year, not since she had stayed with him in the flat on Stockport Road.

"Nowhere in particular. I've not had a proper flat for a while now."

"There's room for you here, Our Kid. Isn't there, Mam?"

"Yes. We've got a couple of bedrooms, Jimmy. Doe and I can share. You can have her room if you like."

Emily, like Doreen, seemed keen to have Jimmy move in. It would be like getting their family back together again and it would give Emily the strength to get over being on her own. Doe and Jimmy couldn't be expected to understand, but Emily had always felt that she needed a man. Except for the time that Jim had been in prison and before Sam had arrived, she had never been alone. She had always had a partner to share her life with and importantly, to take her out. Emily knew that as a working-class woman, she couldn't go out on her own. She would be shunned; all separated, widowed or divorced women of her age were. In a pub on their own, a woman would be seen as nothing more than a 'prostitute'; on the lookout for someone else's husband. But for Emily, there was more to it than that. She desired a partner who could meet her physical needs; those of a mature woman who desired pleasure and satisfaction. Emily couldn't explain this to her children. To them, she was a mother, not a sensuous and passionate woman. They wouldn't have understood and to try and explain it to them would have been embarrassing. Perhaps, thought Emily, if she recovered her family, for the time being it would be enough to get by without satisfying her other needs.

Jimmy hesitated. He couldn't accept that finally, he was being offered a chance of stability. He'd gone through far too much to believe that it was a possibility.

"I don't know, most of my work's in Manchester. It's a bit far out here."

"No," said Doe. "There are loads of buses into Piccadilly. The bus depot's just around the corner. I go back to Ardwick all the time. You'll get to work easily, Our Kid."

"That's right, Jimmy. You've nothing to worry about. We'd love to have you stay with us," said Emily.

"All right then," said Jimmy. "I'll give it a try. I'll bring my things tomorrow night. I haven't got a lot, so it won't take up much space."

"We'll have the room ready for you," said Doreen.

It was all agreed. Jimmy stayed for another half an hour and then he left.

The next day, Doreen went to work at the hairdressers, pleased to be kept busy. It meant that her mind couldn't wander too far, worrying about whether her brother would actually turn up or not. Both Doe and Emily were eager for him to stay and hoped that he'd not had second thoughts.

At five-thirty, the last customer having departed, everywhere swept up, the sinks and chairs spick and span, Gillian told Doe to get off home. Particularly pleased with Doreen's efforts, she gave her another five shillings on top of her wages. If only Jimmy turned up, thought Doe, it would turn out to be a wonderful day.

Doreen needn't have worried. Arriving home, she was delighted to open the back door to see Our Kid sat drinking a mug of tea at the kitchen table with Emily.

"Hi Doe," said Jimmy, cheerily.

A beaming smile covered Doreen's face.

"You're early," she replied.

"Oh, in that case I'd best go away and come back later," joked Jimmy.

"Don't be daft, Our Kid. You're puddled."

"Jimmy's going to take me out for a drink tonight," said Emily. "I'm looking forward to it and so there's no reason for you to stay here. Why don't you go to see Sally and your friends."

"No, it's fine, Mam. I'll go again next weekend."

"But by then, it'll be a couple of weeks since you've seen them."

"It's all right," replied Doe. "They understand that things come up. They'll still be there next week."

That was how it was. There was no telephone for Doe and Sally to contact one another; neither Dora, nor Emily could afford one. Sally would expect Doreen whenever she turned up and Doe knew that her cousin and friends would be pleased to see her when she did. Reunited with Jimmy and her mam, Doreen wanted to make sure that everything ran smoothly. Desperate for Our Kid to stay, she hoped that if he settled in over the weekend, he would.

Chapter 53

The weekend went perfectly. Emily and Jimmy had enjoyed themselves at the pub and Sunday saw Emily cook a roast dinner in celebration of Jimmy's return. It filled Doreen with optimism and meant that she could just about face up to the fact that on Monday morning she would be going back to school.

It was a strange situation, that hardly seemed real. Doe didn't feel like a schoolgirl anymore. How could she? She had looked after herself; held down a succession of full-time jobs and lived on her own. She was an adult before her time. Doreen knew that unless the school was prepared to recognise her maturity and independence, she would be liable to walk away.

Class 4A seemed pleasant enough. The form teacher, Mr Buchan, was friendly. He understood that the young people in his charge would soon be going out into the world of work and he treated them with respect and kindness. A young man, just in the job, he was one of the new generation of teachers, many of whom were keen to communicate with their charges, find their level and relate to them. The students in the class made Doreen feel more than welcome and it wasn't long before she had been invited to turn up at the local cafe, 'Kazim's', where teenagers went to hang out. Particularly attentive, was a young man called Ray Lacey. Ray was a year older than the others. Twelve months ago, he'd been involved in a bad road accident and having missed so much school, he'd been held back a year to catch up. Ray's parents had insisted on it. They had ambitions for their son and this involved him staying on to take his GCEs. It was obvious that they had money. Ray was immaculately turned out. As it was a non-uniform school, he would always wear the latest fashions. A handsome lad, with more than a passing resemblance to Billy Fury, he was a smooth talker and it was clear that most girls in the class were desperate to go out with him. The problem was, that Ray knew it and so there was a clear arrogance evident in the way that he would talk to them. Such an attitude didn't endear him to Doreen; he was the type of lad she couldn't stand.

Doe's indifference to Ray, made him all the more eager to win her round. She was a very pretty girl. She had large green eyes, high cheekbones, a lovely smile and a fashionable black beehive. She was bubbly, warm and promised to be great fun. Ray wasn't used to her reaction, not understanding why she ignored him. All the girls fancied him; he could have who we wanted. Doe had become a challenge and one that he was determined to win.

Unfortunately, Ray's desire to impress had unforeseen consequences. The day had been going fine. Doreen had attended science and maths lessons and the teachers had been friendly towards her. The maths teacher, Mrs Brown, was particularly impressed. Doe had quickly completed all the tasks that she'd set for the group. Not wanting to be seen as different, Doreen told the teacher that she had just covered the work at her old school. She purposely kept quiet about the fact that it had been extra work set by Mrs Morgan, just before she had stopped going to school. It reinforced to Doe just how able she was at maths. Yet she had no regrets about the direction her life might have taken if her parents hadn't split up, or Betty hadn't stopped Mrs Morgan from looking after her. That was in the past; Doreen lived for the future. Leaving school, getting a job and a place of her own, would give her true independence. Having regrets, thinking about what might have been, wasn't any part of Doe's agenda.

Dinner time had come and Doreen had chatted to the girls, Ray hovering in the background. Afternoon was English and Miss Charles. The girls had told her that Miss Charles was new to the school. She was young, tried to be strict and they didn't like her. Miss Charles however, fancied Ray; or so the girls thought. She would always smile and speak nicely to him. The girls were quite cruel in their comments. They had dismissed Miss Charles as unattractive and claimed that she couldn't get a boyfriend. Who would possibly look at her? asked one of them. She had 'a face only a mother could love'. She had no figure, said another, who explained that her nickname was 'two backs'. It was clear that Miss Charles was hated. Doreen however, would reserve judgement. She knew how spiteful teenage girls could be and she would wait and see how the teacher responded to her.

As Doreen entered the English classroom, Miss Charles was stood waiting at the front. Doe walked towards her to introduce herself. Charles was dismissive.

"Oh, you're the new girl, Doreen Brodie. Go and sit down. I'll talk to you later."

Slightly put out, Doe decided to give her the benefit of the doubt. She moved to a desk at the back of the class and sat down. The desks in the room were all single. Miss Charles had moved them apart. It seemed clear that the young teacher didn't want any of the students distracting one another. They were here to work, not talk. After Doreen had sat down, there was a disturbance to the side of her. Ray had told the boy who was sat there to move forward to another seat and the lad had objected.

"Move, Bill. Let Ray sit down," ordered Miss Charles from the front.

"But I was here first, Miss!"

"I'm not interested. Do as you're told or I'll send you to Mr Yates!"

Reluctantly, Bill moved. He had no wish to go and see 'Thrasher Yates'. Roy took his seat and smiled at Miss Charles.

"Thanks, Miss."

"That's all right," replied Miss Charles, smiling at Ray. "Now," she continued to the rest of the class, "let's get on with some work."

Work was composing a letter to a prospective employer asking for an interview. Miss Charles wrote out the letter's format on the board and the class got on with copying it down. They were then told to start writing the main body of the letter, in which they were to outline their educational achievements and interests. Doreen had enough employment experience to write several pages but of course, she couldn't admit to it. She therefore got on with writing a standard, yet dishonest letter, about her schooling and mentioned a couple of legal, part-time jobs that she had held. Trying to concentrate and avoid any kind of confrontation with Miss Charles, Doreen became increasingly annoyed with Ray. It was clear that he was intent on using the lesson to attempt to chat her up. However, like any typical teenage lad, he was doing it in the most immature fashion possible; flicking paper pellets at her and smirking as she motioned at him to stop. It never ceased to amaze her that boys like Ray actually thought that acting like an idiot could possibly make them an attractive proposition.

Suddenly, Miss Charles's voice cut across the classroom.

"Doreen Brodie. You're here to work," she said, fiercely. "That's what we do in this school, no matter what you may have done in your last. Get on with it!"

Doreen looked at her. She couldn't believe it. Surely the woman had seen what Ray had been doing. She remembered what the girls had told her; that Miss fancied Ray. Well, it was certainly looking that way. Charles had made Bill move for Ray, allowing him to sit at the desk near to her and now, she was ignoring the pellets that Ray had been flicking at her. Surely, she could see them littered all over the floor around her desk. Nevertheless, Doe worked hard to control her sense of injustice. There were only ten minutes to go, she reasoned. So far, the day had gone well. Doreen would see the lesson out and ignore the teacher's comments.

That would have been fine, except for Ray. Unable to grasp the simple truth that Doreen was too mature to be attracted by his schoolboy pranks, Ray continued to flick pellets at her, convinced that it was the only way to win her over. Finally, Doe had had enough. When one hit her on the cheek, she turned to him.

"Pack it in, Ray. Grow up!"

Miss Charles was on her like a shot.

"Doreen Brodie. I've already told you to get on with your work. What do you think you're doing?"

Doreen had no intention of backing down. She had already given this obnoxious woman far too much respect and now she went on the offensive.

"You saw what he did, Miss. Look on the floor. I suppose I've done that, have I? Why aren't you shouting at him? He's been messing around since we came in. Why is Ray so special?"

There was a sharp and collective intake of breath, as the rest of the class waited to see how Miss Charles would react. They didn't have long to wait.

"How dare you!" screamed Charles. "You'll go and see Mr Yates, right now!"

"No," replied Doreen, firmly. "I won't."

Defiant. She glared back at the teacher. Determined to stand up for herself, Doe had no intention of becoming a victim. She certainly wasn't going to let any teacher lay a hand on her again; hit her like Gale had done at Ross Place. Getting to her feet, Doreen moved out from behind the desk. She was alert; ready and waiting.

"You will. You'll go right now!"

Charles was so angry that it seemed as if she was about to explode. Her face, contorted by rage, was getting redder by the second.

The two stared at one another. Charles was still at the front of the class. There was almost a chasm between them. Fortunate, as it meant that Doe wouldn't have to physically defend herself and could therefore avoid the difficulties that such a course of action would bring.

Saying nothing, Doreen stared ahead of her. Charles realised that her authority was hanging by a thread. The new girl was standing up to her and if she succeeded, the students would never fear their teacher again.

Desperate to regain control, Charles launched a scathing attack on her adversary. It was an ill-judged move, as her words only convinced the girls that they were correct in their belief that 'Miss' fancied Ray.

"You. You, Doreen Brodie. You came into the classroom wearing your tight jumper, purposely flaunting your tits at Ray and the rest of the boys. You're disgusting. You're nothing but a trollop, distracting the boys from their work. Get out of my classroom, now!"

Refusing to move, Doreen resolutely dismissed her comments.

"You're pathetic. Ray Stacey? You can have him. Why are you trying to please him, anyway? He's a student. Are you really that desperate?"

A couple of the girls sniggered. They and their classmates were taking satisfaction in witnessing Doe's demolition of their teacher.

"And how dare you refer to my body," continued Doreen. "If you want to get personal, ask yourself why your nickname is two backs!"

A spontaneous burst of laughter erupted from the class. Doreen was pleased. Charles's comment had upset her. It had made her out to be 'easy' and nothing could be further from the truth, as Ray had found out. It was his behaviour that had brought about this situation; it wasn't anything that she had done.

"I wouldn't stay in your class another minute. You're the worst teacher I've ever come across. You're a nasty, frustrated bitch. You've no right to take it out on the kids. You're nothing but a bully."

The class cheered and burst into applause. As Doe walked towards the classroom door, it opened and Mr Buchan came into the room. The applause died down as the students noted his presence. Doreen continued on towards the door.

"Excuse me, Mr Buchan."

Buchan stepped aside.

"What's happened, Doreen?"

"Ask her," Doe replied, pointing at Charles.

"Where are you going?"

"Home and I'm not coming back."

Doreen strode out of the classroom, down the corridor and headed outside. She had returned to school for her mam's sake, given it a go and it hadn't worked out. At dinner, she had felt able to get through the few months until Easter. But Charles had now made that impossible. Doe knew that she couldn't remain a student. She was too independently minded and wouldn't allow anyone to treat her unfairly. School brought her into contact with teachers who were nothing but bullies and she had no intention of allowing them to mistreat her. She remembered a saying of her dad's when she was young. How he had told Emily that when he worked for someone too demanding, he would simply pack up his equipment and tell them to "stick their job." Doe hated school because it was different. You were expected to put up with the punishments and humiliations and if you were prepared to risk wagging it, you were breaking the law and in serious trouble. Yet Doreen wasn't worried too much about the latter. Close to leaving school, she had got away with not going for so long.

Surely no one would be interested in her now? As far as Doe was concerned, today would definitely be her last day at school. She wouldn't be going back.

That evening Doreen had gone to 'Kazim's' to meet up with some of the girls that she'd met in her class. Kazim's was a coffee bar, with a jukebox. It was a great meeting place for teenagers. They could chat, listen to music and there was even room enough to dance. It was simple fun and they loved it. First to approach Doe was Ray. He had been waiting for her to turn up and as soon as she'd arrived, he was over to greet her, eager to apologise for his part in the day's events.

"I'm sorry, Doreen. I shouldn't have been so daft. Can you give me another chance?"

"What do you mean, Ray?"

"Well, will you go out with me?"

"No, Ray. I've already got a boyfriend."

"Who?"

"A lad in Manchester."

Doreen hadn't quite told the truth. She knew that Jack was keen to go out with her, but Emily's problems with Sam had meant that she'd seen little of him recently. Anyway, she hadn't quite decided whether she wanted him as a boyfriend yet.

"What's his name?" asked Ray, not entirely convinced.

"Jack."

"Well, you can't see that much of him living here. Why don't you go out with me, instead?"

"Because I don't want to Ray. You've got plenty of girls who want to go out with you."

"But they're not like you."

"Flattery won't get you anywhere, Ray. I've told you. I'm not interested."

"Why not? It's like you said, Doreen. Lots of girls want to go out with me. Why don't you?"

"You just said it, Ray. Lots of girls want to go out with you. You think your God's gift. You're too full of yourself."

Ray hesitated, unsure of what to say next. He was working hard. He never did that; he didn't have to. Ray became irritated with himself; why couldn't he just forget her? There were plenty of other girls to go out with and some of them prepared to let him do anything he wanted. So why should we care what Doreen thought? But he did. Ray realised that he'd met his match. With his girlfriends it was a case of 'treat them mean, keep them keen'. He now felt that Doreen was doing the same to him. Perhaps he would just have to grovel a little bit more. After all, she was worth it. All the lads fancied her.

"I didn't mean to sound big-headed. It came out wrong. I was just put out that you didn't like me."

"I didn't say that I didn't like you, I just said I wouldn't go out with you. You're just not my type. Let's forget it. I want to go and talk to the girls."

Doreen had gone up in everyone's estimation following her confrontation with Miss Charles. She found out that Mr Buchan had been asked to take the rest of the class. Charles had left and hadn't been seen again. Mr Buchan had questioned them all about what had happened. Later on, Mr Yates had visited the classroom to talk to Mr Buchan and the students could clearly hear that the latter was supporting Doreen. Although interested in what they had to say, Doe still made it clear that she had no intention of going back. In fact, she hadn't mentioned anything about the incident to her mam when she had returned home from work. Doe didn't want Emily going to the school or persuading her to return.

About a week later Cynthia and Lorraine, two of her new friends, told her that Mr Buchan had asked them if they knew anything of her whereabouts. They had feigned ignorance, but he hadn't believed them. Buchan asked them to pass on a message to Doreen. He said that Miss Charles had been warned about her conduct and that Mr Yates understood how badly Doreen had been spoken to. Mr Buchan had said that she should come back to school and that there would be no recriminations. He also asked the girls to warn Doe that she would get herself in serious trouble if she kept truanting.

Doreen took no notice but began to think that it would be best to try and persuade Emily to move back to Ardwick. That way she could stay a step ahead of the truant officer. Yet her mam seemed settled in Guide Street and so did Our Kid. Doreen feared that everything may change if they were to move elsewhere and so decided to say nothing. Staying at the house, Doe would occasionally pick up a casual day's work in one of the local factories. As the days passed into weeks, Doreen felt sure that the school had now given up on her. Everything would be fine.

Chapter 54

Christmas came and went and as the new year began, Doreen had every reason to feel optimistic. Sam was no longer around and she was back with her mam and Jimmy. Once more, she was part of a happy family. The future seemed bright. Soon, she would be fifteen and after that, it would be Easter, when she could finally start working.

At the end of January, early on a Wednesday evening, Doe returned home after helping out in a local machine shop. She had been collating orders and generally cleaning up. She was in a good mood, having just received six shillings from the boss. As Doreen opened the back door and entered the kitchen, she saw Emily sat at the table reading a letter.

"You're back early aren't you, Mam?"

"Yes."

Emily seemed distracted; her eyes still trained on the letter. She was gripping it in her hand and didn't look inclined to let it go. Whatever the letter contained, it seemed that it wasn't good news and Doe could see that her mam was concerned.

"What's the matter, Mam? Is it Sam?"

It was the obvious thought that came into Doreen's head, yet Emily's response caught her by surprise.

"Why didn't you tell me that you weren't going to school, Doe? You agreed that you would."

Doreen hesitated. She suddenly felt guilty. She hadn't been honest with her mam. She should have been. The fact that Emily had let her down dozens of times in the past, made no difference. Doe had made a promise and as such, she now felt that she had failed in her responsibility to keep it, or at least to explain to her mam why she hadn't done so.

"I'm sorry, Mam. I thought of doing, but you seemed settled and happy and I didn't want to burden you with my problems. I'm entitled to leave soon anyway, so it doesn't really matter that I'm not going, does it?"

"But why haven't you gone?"

Doreen proceeded to tell Emily about the incident with Miss Charles and what she had said. She pointed out that some of the girls from the school had told her that Miss Charles had been reprimanded by the headmaster for her behaviour.

"Doe, you should have told me."

"I didn't want to, Mam. You had enough on your plate without dealing with that. I didn't think that the school would be bothered with me being so close to leaving. It won't be a problem, will it?"

Doreen waited for Emily's reassurance, but she was silent.

"Well, there can't be, can there?"

Slowly, her mam responded.

"The letter's from the Juvenile Court in Salford. I've got to take you there next week. They want us to explain why you've been truanting. The school have obviously contacted them and reported you for not attending."

Doe now remembered the conversation in 'Kazim's' shortly after she'd walked out of school. Cynthia and Lorraine had told her that Mr Buchan had asked her to return in order to avoid getting into trouble. Their words were now coming back to haunt her.

"But surely, there's nothing that the court can do?"

Doreen's question was asked with more than a hint of trepidation. In no way was it a statement of certainty.

"I'm not sure," replied Emily. "You're still only fourteen. You forget that, Doe. You should have told me about what happened. I could have sorted it out."

"I sorted it out. I left and I'm not going back."

"You can't say that to the magistrates, Doe. If you do, there's no telling how they'll react. They'll think that I've got no control over you."

"Well to be honest, Mam, you haven't."

Doreen had responded bravely, but she was concerned. Emily had impressed the seriousness of the situation upon her and it was clear that her mam wasn't simply trying to scare her into going back to school.

In the coming days, Doe thought long and hard about what she would tell the court. She needed to gain their sympathy by making them understand how Miss Charles had tried to humiliate and embarrass her in front of the class. Perhaps she would then escape with a warning and avoid any chance of her mam getting in trouble for not ensuring that she had been at school. Jimmy had made it clear to his sister that her actions had compromised Emily too. Even though their mam hadn't known that Doe was truanting, the law would still hold her responsible.

Jimmy was a wealth of information as far as the courts were concerned. After all, he'd been up before them on many occasions.

"It depends on who you get," he told Doreen. "We all know that. You get the nice ones and the evil sods. The nice ones show you understanding; more likely to tap you on the wrist, give you a suspended sentence and a fine. The nasty ones send you down. They'll never listen; whatever you say."

"But surely, Our Kid. I can't be up for a prison sentence."

"No. I'm just telling you. Judges or magistrates, whatever court you're talking about, fall into those two types."

"Well, what can I do? I don't want sticking in a children's home."

"You tell them the truth, just like you usually do. I always do. I don't try to lie. You've got a very good reason for not going to school. You went and the teacher was trying to bully you. She embarrassed you, a teenage girl, in front of all those lads. She was personal and made sexual comments. She can't do that. No wonder you haven't been back. You can't face seeing the other kids after what she said."

"But the other kids have been all right about it. I see them at 'Kazim's'. It's teachers that I have a problem with. Not all of them, but there's always at least one and I'm not accepting it. Especially when I've worked and looked after myself. I'm not the victim that they think I should be."

"I know," said Jimmy, "but you can't tell the court that. Like Mam said; you're fourteen. We both know that you're grown up. Crikey, you're more sensible than any adult I know! But to the court, you're still a girl; like it or not. So, what you need to do, is tell the court what I've told you. If you get a decent judge, they'll understand and you and Mam will get off with it. Just for once, take some advice. Please, Doe. I know what I'm talking about."

Doreen thought carefully. She knew that he was right. She was a crusader; always eager 'to tell it how it is'. But this time, just for once, she wouldn't. There was too much at stake for both Emily and herself. She would do as Jimmy advised.

Waiting outside the court room, Doreen and Emily were nervous. Doe felt uncomfortable. She was short of breath, her head ached and she felt a sickening sensation inside her stomach. Was this it? she asked herself. Had the authorities finally caught up with her? She had just one positive thought; thankful that the court was in Salford. It meant that they would have no knowledge of her school record, or lack of it, in Manchester. Doreen knew that in a couple of hours, she would either be taken from her mam, or reprieved. She now knew how her brother must have felt whenever he appeared in court. How on earth could he go through it more than once?

"Doreen Brodie!" The voice boomed down the hallway, rousing Doe from her thoughts.

Emily tapped her daughter on the arm.

"It's us, love," she said, quietly.

As the two of them stood up, Doreen saw an attendant moving towards them.

"Doreen Brodie?"

"Yes," replied Emily.

"This way, please. Court room number two. The magistrates are waiting," said a stout, balding man, who smiled reassuringly at Emily.

Doreen fastened her hopes on that smile. It was a promise that things weren't going to be too bad. She drew herself up and strode purposefully after him. Following the attendant down the corridor, they turned right into an entrance, beyond which was a large door. Court Two was written in bold letters above it.

"Through here, please," said the attendant, as he opened the door.

Emily and Doreen followed him in. It wasn't as Doe had imagined. She had seen trials in the movies and had been to the magistrates' court to see Sam sent down. That room had seemed official and intimidating. There were raised seats and benches for the magistrates and officials, a dock for the accused and rows of seats for spectators. This room was nothing like that. There were just three tables with seats behind them. Two separate ones close by, as they entered the room and a much longer one beyond, behind which was stood a man in a suit. The man must have been in his late forties but to Doreen, given the gravity of the situation and her relative youth, he seemed much older. Tall, bespectacled and with a trim beard, distinguished by flecks of grey, the man had a friendly appearance. Sat on either side of him was another man, along with two women. All of them had a mass of paperwork in front of them. The man motioned to the seats in front of them.

"Hello. Mrs Brodie, I presume. Please take a seat."

Emily and Doe sat at the table on the right.

Sitting down himself, the man looked closely at the mother and daughter in front of him. They were a pleasing sight. Emily had bought new two-piece suits for both of them; black for herself and blue for Doreen. With new blouses and their hair immaculate, the two of them were smart and well-presented.

"Hello, I'm Justice Dawson and I'm leading the meeting today. As we proceed, Mrs Brodie, if there's anything that you don't understand, please stop me and ask. Remember, we're here to do what's best for Doreen."

Dawson looked kindly at Doreen and gave her a smile. Doe's spirits rose. She remembered what her brother had told her. This was a nice judge. Perhaps everything was going to turn out all right.

Dawson looked to the left of them and noted the empty table.

"It seems that the Education Committee, in their wisdom, have decided not to turn up for the case today. I have to say Mrs Brodie, that I'm not impressed with them. It hardly lends substance to the seriousness of the claims that they have brought against you. Not only that, but we don't seem to have received any paperwork from them either. I am right, aren't I?" he asked, turning to one of the ladies to the side of him.

"Yes, that's correct," she replied.

"Well," he continued, looking back at Doreen, "according to the information we have got, it seems that you haven't been going to school, young lady. Is that right?"

Doe sensed from the tone of his question that Dawson was kindly disposed towards her. She looked at him straight in the eyes and replied.

"Yes, that's true."

Dawson waited, but Doreen didn't continue. It struck him as unusual. Normally the youngsters who came before him would immediately try to proclaim their innocence. Dawson recognised that this girl was different. She had accepted the fact of the statement made against her. He was impressed with her honesty; he knew that he would be inclined to believe whatever she told him.

"So, Doreen," continued Dawson, "are there any reasons why you haven't been to school? You certainly look healthy, so I assume that can't be the issue."

After a short pause, Doe replied.

"Yes, I do have a reason. But I'd rather not have to tell you about it."

"Why is that, Doreen?"

"Because it's embarrassing for me to talk about it."

Dawson took a deep intake of breath.

"Hmmmmm."

Doe could see that he was thinking.

"The problem is, Doreen," he continued, "that we have to know the reason in order to come to a decision. If we believe that your reason justifies you not attending school, then we'll deal with the matter differently. So, to be fair to you, we do have to know just why you felt that you couldn't attend school, like all the other pupils did."

Dawson paused. Leaning closer to the woman on his left, he whispered something. This prompted a quiet conversation between the two of them. After they had reached agreement, Dawson turned his attention back to Doreen.

"My colleague, Mrs Smith, has made a suggestion. If you write down your reasons on a piece of paper, then you can wait outside whilst she reads it and then tells me privately about what you've written."

Looking at Emily, Dawson continued.

"That seems the best way forward. Wouldn't you agree, Mrs Brodie?"

"Yes," confirmed Emily. "Come on, Doe," she continued, turning to her daughter, "that seems a fair way to do it. The judge does need to know."

"I suppose so," replied Doe, albeit reluctantly.

Handed a pen and paper, Doreen began to write down what had happened in the classroom. Doe had told Dawson the truth. She couldn't bring herself to say out loud the words Miss Charles had used; that she had been "flaunting her tits" and was "a little trollop." Writing it down was still difficult, for she felt that it was demeaning to have the words brought to the attention of an old, male judge. Doreen wasn't quite fifteen. She knew that boys found her attractive, but that was as far as it went. She hadn't had a proper boyfriend yet and comments about her body and suggestions about her sexuality, were extremely embarrassing. The last thing she wanted was to have the incident talked about openly in front of people she didn't know. It was an ordeal that Doe didn't want to go through. After all, she hadn't even told her mam about the incident until the court summons came.

Having finished writing, Mrs Smith came and collected Doreen's statement and led her and Emily to the door. Opening it, she motioned to some chairs against a wall outside.

"If you and Doreen wait there, Mrs Brodie, I'll read your daughter's statement and talk to the judge. We'll call you back into the court room once he's made his decision."

When she had gone, Doreen looked nervously at her mam.

"Don't worry, Doe" said Emily, trying to reassure her. "The judge seems a nice man. I'm sure he'll understand."

But Doreen could see that Emily was worried too. She couldn't hide it.

"Whatever the judge asks you to do, just agree. Let him know that you'll co-operate. That way everything should be all right."

Doreen didn't need telling, for she understood the seriousness of the situation. She was terrified of being carted off to a children's home. Having vowed that it would never happen to her, it now seemed possible that they would soon be calling the police to collect her from the court. Doe considered whether she should make a run for it, trying hard to remember the way out of the building. If she could get outside, then she could get away; but for how long? Any attempt to escape would bring far worse consequences than those she could face today. Before Doe could decide, the door to the courtroom opened and Mrs Smith approached them.

"Can you come in now, please. The judge is waiting for you."

Emily grabbed Doreen's hand and gave it a reassuring squeeze.

"Come on, Doe."

Doreen got up and followed her mam into the court room. Dawson was stood behind his desk waiting for them.

"I'm sorry we took such a long time," he said.

Doe, who'd been lost in thought, hadn't noticed.

"I think we've got a good picture now," he continued. "From what you've written down for my colleague, Doreen, I'm not surprised that the Education Committee haven't sent anyone here today. There are too many difficult questions that they would have to answer."

Doe sensed that everything was going to turn out fine.

"I can fully appreciate why you wouldn't want to go back to school after what happened, Doreen and yes, it was very embarrassing for you. But you are required by law to go to school and it's my job to make sure that you do."

Doe nodded in acknowledgement and Dawson turned his attention towards Emily.

"I understand from Doreen's statement that you knew nothing about her truanting. As there's no evidence that the school tried to contact you about her absence, I don't feel that you, Mrs Brodie, have been negligent as a parent."

Doe's confidence rose. She knew that children were taken into care when they were 'beyond parental control'. Dawson clearly didn't believe that.

"I do hope though," continued Dawson, now looking at Doreen, "that you confide in your mother, young lady, if anything like this ever happens again. These problems can be addressed, but only if you make us all aware of them. Simply walking out, isn't something that you can do again."

As Dawson paused and looked sternly at her in order to reinforce the importance of his words, Doe felt certain that she was being reprieved. This time he would forgive her; but not in the future.

"So, young lady," he continued, "you have to go back to school. I know you'll be leaving at Easter, which is only a couple of months away, but the law has to be obeyed. You will go back and continue your education."

Dawson had spoken firmly but by now, Doe knew that he was a kind and decent man. Confident that he would continue to be understanding, she spoke up.

"May I say something, please?"

"Of course," replied Dawson.

"I can't face going back to the same school. I would like, if I can, to go to school in Manchester. That's where all my friends are. I still see them regularly, even though we live in Weaste. There are plenty of buses that I can catch to get to school on time."

"Which school do you want to go to?"

"Ardwick Girls Secondary."

Dawson turned to Mrs Smith and the two of them again engaged in a hushed conversation. Finally, the judge gave his response.

"Given all the circumstances I'll agree, but only on the condition that you make sure that you attend regularly and on time."

"I will," replied Doreen.

"And Mrs Brodie, I don't have to remind you that it's your responsibility to make sure that she does."

"Yes, I understand," confirmed Emily.

"Don't forget, young lady," warned Dawson, looking straight at Doreen. "You can rest assured that I'll be checking up on you, so make sure that you keep going to school."

Dawson paused for effect and then concluded the hearing.

"We're finished now. You and your mother are free to go."

Emily and Doe thanked Dawson and said goodbye. He couldn't help but smile as the two of them got straight to their feet and left the courtroom as quickly as they could. He was sure that he'd made the correct decision. In fact, he felt that the case should never have been brought. The teacher hadn't acted professionally and he had seen no evidence that either the school or the education committee had taken any action against her. With only a few weeks of formal education before Doreen could officially leave school, the court had no intention of checking on her again. However, as she wouldn't know that, Dawson felt that he had fulfilled his legal responsibilities.

Outside, Emily and Doe breathed a sigh of relief. Both had been worried; neither telling the other just how much. Fortunately, everything had turned out all right. Doreen wasn't going to be taken into care and she wouldn't have to go back to school. Doe guessed that the court wouldn't bother to check on her. It was now the beginning of February and Easter fell early, on March 29th. It meant that the school term had only about six weeks left; one of which would be half term. Doreen knew that by asking to go to Ardwick Secondary, she was returning to a different education authority. It would take time for all the paperwork to be transferred across to Manchester and by then it would be pointless to organise any checks on her. Doreen felt confident that she would soon be able put all her concerns about school behind her and concentrate on making her way in the world of work.

Chapter 55

With the court case over, Doreen was as content as it was possible to be. She had her mam and brother beside her and she felt part of a real family again. In all, there seemed much cause for optimism. Yet she refused to allow herself to get carried away. Experience had taught her that happiness was a precious and finite commodity; that at any time, her life could be turned upside down. It was as well that she was prepared, for everything was about to change.

The Friday after Doreen's court appearance, Emily and Jimmy had been out to the pub. On their return, Emily was feeling cold and had asked her daughter to go upstairs to fetch her cardigan. Entering the bedroom, Doe picked it up off the bed and noticed some paper sticking out of one of the pockets. Investigating further, Doreen found that it was an envelope. Turning it over, she received a shock. Printed on the top left-hand corner in bold letters, were the words 'HM Prisons'. Doe immediately knew what it meant. Without stopping to think, she ran down the stairs and into the front room.

"What's this, Mam?"

Emily looked round and saw Doreen holding out the envelope towards her. The atmosphere was charged as Emily tried to grab the letter from her daughter.

"That's mine, Doe. Give it to me."

Jimmy, realising that something was amiss, looked towards his sister.

"He's written to you, hasn't he?" asked Doreen.

She backed away from Emily and held out the envelope behind her. Jimmy, moving closer, took it from her grasp. Pulling out the letter, he began to read it out loud. There was nothing that Emily could do but listen. It was from Sam and it was obvious that Emily had written to him previously. Sam was responding to a number of questions that she had asked him. Emily had promised that she would never have anything to do with Sam again. He had beaten her senseless and yet she was writing to him and it seemed that she would welcome him back with open arms once he was released. Doreen was incredulous; too stunned to take it in. Jimmy, lubricated by alcohol, was furious. He despised Sam and couldn't believe Emily's stupidity.

"What's wrong with you, Mam? How can you write to that bastard. You enjoy it, don't you? You do, you enjoy it."

"What do you mean?"

"Being beaten. You must do. Otherwise, why are you writing to him?"

Doe was worried. Her brother was getting angry. She had seen her dad turn nasty in drink and now it was happening to Jimmy. She tried to calm him down.

"Leave it, Our Kid. It's my fault. I shouldn't have mentioned the letter until tomorrow. Let's get to bed. We'll talk about it in the morning."

"No, Doe. She's going to tell us now. We deserve to know. She's hardly been the best of mothers, especially to you. We stuck by her when she needed us. I want to know why she's going back with that arsehole."

Doreen could see her brother losing control. He always tried not to swear in front of her. With the drink inside him and furious with Emily, he wasn't holding back.

"Come on, Mam. Tell us. Tell us why you're going to let that evil sod come back."

Upset, Emily attempted to answer.

"It's not like that, Jimmy. Please don't be like this."

"Don't be like this?" shouted Our Kid. "What should I be like? Jumping up and down and cheering because my mam wants to live with a bastard that beats women."

Slowly, Emily began to edge away. She moved behind Doreen and towards the bottom of the stairs. Doe could sense that her mam felt threatened. Jimmy was enraged; his language menacing. She tried to calm her brother down and bring him to his senses. How she wished that she had paused to think before bringing the letter downstairs.

"Please, Our Kid. Calm down. You're scaring Mam. You're acting just like Sam."

But it had gone too far. Fearful, Emily had now reached the bottom of the stairs, ready to scramble to the safety of her bedroom. As Jimmy moved towards her, Doreen blocked his path. Her brother was in a rage, oblivious to anything but his mam. He was determined that she would hear him out and as Emily turned to get up the stairs, he clumsily reached out to stop her. Unsuccessful, he only succeeded in striking his sister in the face. It felt just like a punch and completely unexpected, it caused Doe to stagger back. With a loud bang, Emily shut and locked her bedroom door.

Jimmy was distraught. He had hit his sister, his little Doe. The shock of it immediately quelled his anger.

"Oh Doe, Doe. I'm so sorry. Please be all right."

He reached forward to his sister, putting his arms around her.

"Please forgive me. I'm so sorry."

Our Kid started to cry.

Her head buzzing, Doreen tried to collect her thoughts. Slowly, her mind began to clear. Good, she thought, Mam's safe and Jimmy's calmed down. But her right eye, which had taken the main force of the blow, really hurt.

"Jimmy. It's okay. Don't worry. Let me sit on the settee. Get me a cold cloth. My eye hurts."

Jimmy didn't answer. He was sobbing uncontrollably and leaning heavily against her. She tried hard to get him to respond.

"Jimmy, stop. Please. Help me. I need to sit down. It's all right. Come on. You're too heavy. You're hurting me!"

Finally, Jimmy began to stir. His sobs subsided and he lifted his weight off Doreen, who slowly moved over to the settee and sat down.

"Can you get me a cold, wet tea towel, Our Kid. I need it for my eye."

Jimmy did as he was asked. Moving into the kitchen, Doe heard him run the cold tap. He was quickly back with a cold, damp cloth to put on her eye. Applying the cloth, Doreen finally got some relief, but her brother didn't. Seeing her eye closing up and the bruising beginning to appear, he again started to cry.

"It's okay, Our Kid, I know you didn't mean it. It was an accident. Sit down."

Jimmy sat beside her and Doreen held his hand.

"It's not your fault. You couldn't help being angry. I am, too. I can't believe how stupid she is. I know that you didn't mean to hurt me."

"But what about your eye, Doe. It's a right mess."

And it was. A real shiner.

"Don't worry, Our Kid. It'll heal."

Doe patted his hand and the two of them sat quietly for a moment.

"Do you know Jimmy, I really believed that she'd seen sense. I honestly thought that she wanted rid of him."

"Well," replied Our Kid, "maybe she'll listen to us."

"Perhaps, but I wouldn't pin your hopes on it. I just don't have a clue what she sees in him. He makes my skin crawl."

"Well, if she wants him to come back here, then I'm moving out, Doe. I won't stay where he is. What will you do?"

"Well, I kind of feel responsible for her."

"Responsible for her?" asked Jimmy, surprised. "You're the kid, not her."

"No, that's not quite what I meant. What I want to do, as far as I can, is to help protect her from him. To be able to do that, I'll probably stay around."

"But you can't protect her, Doe. You couldn't last time. You can't be with her every minute of the day. You can't go out to the pub with them, can you? That's where it's going to start kicking off."

"Well, I'll just wait and see how things turn out. I'll have a proper job soon and I know that once I'm earning, I'll feel okay staying at Auntie Dora's. I'll be able to pay my way. Working gives me some options."

"It was nice while it lasted Doe, wasn't it?" observed Jimmy, reflecting on their time together. "Just for a short time we were almost a family again, weren't we? What did you and I do to deserve parents like ours?"

"I don't know, Our Kid, but I'll tell you what, when I have kids of my own, however tough it gets, they won't go without. They'll never have to walk the streets."

"Yeah, I know, Doe. You care too much. I love you. You're my little sister, but I know that if I ever need you, like when those men attacked me, you'll be there for me."

Jimmy started to cry again.

"I'm so, so sorry, Doe. I just wish that I'd never hit you. How could I have done it? The only person in my life who's ever cared about me."

Doreen put her arm around Our Kid and cuddled him. She sensed that once again, her brother would be moving out of her life. Just a week later, on Friday night, Jimmy told her that he was leaving. He had spoken to Emily who had insisted that Sam had changed; that he was truly sorry and that she was determined to give him another chance. For Jimmy, that was it. Doe wasn't surprised by her mam's decision and now, until Sam returned, there was just the two of them again.

Chapter 56

As Doreen's fifteenth birthday approached, she felt a mixture of emotions. She hoped that it wouldn't be long before she was working and on her first steps towards true independence, but she was also concerned that Sam would soon be released from prison, with the resultant impact that it would have on her life. After Jimmy had left, disgusted by Emily's decision to have Sam back, her mam had become reticent about the subject of the latter's return. Although Doe had asked her when Sam would be released, Emily was evasive, giving her no dates or details. When pressed, she had insisted that nothing had been decided. Doe found it hard to believe her and suspected that Emily was already well prepared for Sam's release. Doreen was also aware that her own position, when that occurred, was by no means certain. Doe had therefore spoken to her Auntie Dora, who was happy for her to stay but wasn't sure that she could provide her with regular meals, given that Larry and Walt were still out of work.

On the Tuesday morning before Doreen's birthday, Emily left for work at seven-thirty, as usual. She said farewell and was gone. Doe, who had arranged to do some casual work in one of the local shops, left an hour later. By mid-afternoon, Doreen had finished and with cash in hand, decided that she would catch the bus into Manchester and go and see her friends.

Doe arrived at Auntie Dora's just after tea. She and Sally worked on their hair, put on their makeup and went to meet up with Sarah before joining up with Jack, Paul, Mark and Bob. The boys were all working, but as they were still under eighteen, the pub was forbidden to them and they were happy to spend their time with the girls. Doreen had become very fond of Jack; captivated by his kiss. Doe had sensed an affinity between them and felt frustrated when she had been unable to see him after her mam had been assaulted. Yet Jack had been disappointed too and Sally had told Doreen, that he was desperate to see her. Tonight, the two of them would finally meet again.

The girls went to Jack's home to call for him. Once there, they found that Jack's mam had gone out. Jack was in the house along with Mark and Paul. Jack's face lit up as soon as he saw Doreen and he quickly invited the girls inside. Entering the living room, Sarah went straight to the settee, Paul and Mark moving over to let her sit down. She leaned over and kissed Paul. Doe could see that they were clearly an 'item'. Sally however, chose to sit on one of the chairs. As yet, she hadn't decided on a boyfriend and had no intention of giving Mark any ideas.

Standing just inside the living room, Doreen looked to see where she could sit. Behind her, Jack stretched out his hand and tapped her on the shoulder. Surprised, it made her jump.

"Oh, I'm sorry," said Jack.

Doe took a deep breath and smiled.

"It's all right, Jack. I just didn't expect it."

Reassured, Jack smiled back. He was eager to make a good impression on her. When Doreen hadn't turned up at her Auntie's, he immediately thought that she had no interest in him. He felt that he'd acted too rashly; too quickly. He had taken a liberty by giving her a kiss and she'd not appreciated it. But the fact was that other girls hadn't objected in the past. Jack's experiences had made him confident that he knew what they wanted. Now, he wasn't so sure.

Doreen had made a huge impression on Jack in the time that he'd spent in her company. She was fun, feisty, independent and pretty. Now he wanted to go out with her, but expected that he would have to work hard to win her over. Most importantly, she would expect commitment and respect and Jack hadn't given that to any of his girlfriends before. He'd always been eager to take advantage of 'easy' girls and had boasted to his friends that some of them had let him go 'all the way'. Now, if he was serious about Doreen, his attitude would have to change.

"I'm going to make us all a brew. Do you want to come and help me, Doe?" asked Jack.

"All right," replied Doreen, smiling.

Entering the kitchen, Jack went to the cupboard and got out the mugs, tea and sugar, then filled the kettle and put it on the gas cooker. He reached over the sink and grabbed the bottle of sterilised milk off the window sill, the coldest place for it, given that his mam had no fridge.

"Sit down," said Jack, motioning to the chairs beside the table.

Doreen sat and Jack pulled up a seat opposite her.

"Is everything all right, Doe? I came round to your Auntie Dora's that Sunday, but you weren't there."

"Yes, I'm fine. I've had some problems with my mam. She was hurt that weekend, so I had to stay with her."

"Oh. She's better now, I hope."

"Oh, yes. For the moment, at any rate."

Doreen said no more. She didn't feel that she knew Jack well enough yet to tell him her personal business.

"I did worry that you might have been annoyed at me for kissing you," continued Jack. "I'm sorry if you thought I was a bit cheeky."

"No. It's fine Jack, but from now on, I'll decide whether I want to kiss you or not."

"Yes. Of course."

Even though she had been willing to come into the kitchen, Jack had still needed the reassurance of knowing that she wasn't displeased with him.

Sat there, the two of them began to talk. The tea was soon forgotten as they discussed their favourite music and film stars, before the conversation turned to Jack's job and Doe's hopes for the future. Lost in conversation, the two were interrupted by Sally.

"Are we getting a brew then, or do you two intend to yap all night?"

"Oh. Right. Sorry." said Jack.

Doreen and Sally noticed his face going red. Scarlet in fact.

"We'll do it, Jack. You just go and sit down," suggested Sally.

"Oh, all right then. Everything's there, you just need to re-boil the kettle."

Jack went back into the living room. Sally walked over to the cooker and relit the gas under the kettle. She turned to Doe who was still sat at the table.

"He fancies you. It's obvious. Did you see how embarrassed he was?"

"No."

"Yes, you did," replied Sally, smirking. "You do know that he's got a reputation, don't you?"

"Well, so people have said. He's not tried it on with me though and I think he knows that if he does, he'll be gone."

"Oh, so are you going to go out with him then?"

The question took Doreen by surprise. She hadn't really gone out properly with anyone, other than the childish encounter with Freddie Newton when she was eleven. Life's difficulties had meant that the subject of boys rarely entered her head. She had her ongoing crush on Cliff, but that was an unattainable fantasy and not part of the real world. Now Sally was confronting her with thoughts about a young man whose company she found pleasant and reassuring. Furthermore, Doe was well aware of Jack's interest in her.

"I do like Jack," replied Doreen. "He kissed me at the bus stop; only on the cheek, but he made me feel all tingly."

Sally smiled, touched by her cousin's reaction.

"Well, it's quite obvious he's taken with you, Doe. He's good looking and fun too, but just make sure you keep your eye on him."

When Sally and Doreen returned to the living room with a tray of drinks, Doe settled on the arm of the chair in which Jack was sat. Unconsciously, she found herself leaning against him, as they and their friends chatted, laughed and joked. When it was time for her to go home, Jack insisted on walking with her to the bus stop, suggesting that if they wanted, Sally and Sarah could stay with Mark and Paul in the front room. Doreen signalled her agreement to her girlfriends and the two of them set off.

On the way, Jack had wanted to reach out and take hold of Doe's hand, but he had resisted the temptation. Jack was sure that she liked him, but he was determined that he wouldn't take her feelings for granted. Reaching the bus stop, they found that they were waiting alone. Talking quietly together, their words were warm and tender. These were precious moments but they couldn't last forever. Soon they could see the bus heading towards them and Doreen turned to Jack.

"Are you going to kiss me good night then?"

Softly, Jack pecked her on the cheek. He was desperate to kiss her properly; square on the lips and feel a response. Yet for now, that would have to wait.

Stepping on to the bus, Doreen said goodbye. She would be returning to see Jack on Saturday night.

Chapter 57

Sat on the bus, Doreen's mind wandered over the day's events. She felt strange; a sense of anticipation. She knew that it was because of Jack. She couldn't help herself. She felt charged in his company; alive in a way that she had never felt before. Was it love? Possibly. Yet love wasn't something that she really wanted to consider. Love suggested trust and Doe's whole life had been one in which trust had been denied her. She still hoped for a future where her personal and family relationships would be honest, open and secure, but her unspoken fear was that this was impossible. Love would, she suspected, let her down. True love, she mused. Where was it with her mam and dad, her mam and Sam and her dad and Betty? Their relationships were based on deceit; on abuse. Doreen therefore wondered if any loving relationship could truly exist. But now she had found a young man who made her happy and who was funny and considerate. Yet Sally had warned her of his chequered past. All the girls knew of Jack's reputation. Was he just leading her on? Did he really intend to change? Doe therefore decided that she would have to take their relationship slowly. She would stay in control and ensure that he never took her for granted.

Arriving back at Weaste Bus Depot, it was half past eleven. The streets were empty and quiet as Doreen walked the short distance to Guide Street. She was surprised to see no light on in the house, as Emily usually stayed up late, especially when she knew that her daughter had been to see Sally. Approaching the front door, Doe pulled the key out of her pocket and turned it in the lock. Pushing at the door, it didn't open. She was confused. She turned the key a few more times and pushed on the door, but it was all to no avail. Taking the key out, she wondered if there was a problem with the lock. Reinserting the key, she again got the same result. Opening the letterbox she shouted into the house, so that her mam would hear her and come down to let her in. Yet her shouts were in vain. Nothing moved. The house was silent as she bent down to listen through the letterbox. Calling out once more and again receiving no reply, she stood up and saw the light come on in the front room next door. Doreen realised that her shouting was likely to wake up the street.

Going to the neighbour's, Doe tapped on the front door. The curtains to the front window were drawn back slightly, light shining out onto Doreen's face as she turned towards it. Phyllis opened the front door. She seemed surprised.

"Doreen. What are you doing here?"

"I've come home. I've been visiting my friends in Manchester. My key won't work. My mam must have gone out. Do you know if she's had a problem? Somehow, she seems to have locked me out."

"Oh no, love," replied Phyllis. "Didn't she tell you? Surely, she did."

Doe felt a familiar sinking feeling. What could have happened now?

"Your mam's gone."

Doreen couldn't take it in. What did Phyllis mean?

"Gone? Where?"

"I can't believe that she could do that to you."

"Do what Phyllis? Tell me, please!"

"I assumed that you'd gone with her. She's done a flit. Moved her things out and left. The landlord came round today and changed the locks."

"When?" asked Doreen. "Why?"

"This afternoon," replied Phyllis. "Apparently, she's not been paying the rent and today he was coming to evict her, but she was gone before he got here. I'm sorry, love. You won't be getting in there."

"Oh."

"I suppose she'll have gone back to Manchester," said Phyllis. "You'll have to go and find her there."

Phyllis closed the door. The light went out in the front room. She had gone to bed.

Doreen tried to collect her thoughts. It was late and she was tired. Phyllis hadn't invited her in and was unconcerned about where she would go. Yet Doe was resourceful; she didn't need to rely on others. Perhaps the landlord hadn't secured the back door and windows to the house. They often didn't, as she knew only too well. It was late and there was no chance of anyone seeing her, as Doe quietly opened the back gate and crept into the yard. Holding her coat against the back door, she slammed her elbow into the small window pane above the door handle. Having muffled the main sound of the break, Doreen winced as the shards of glass tinkled as they fell onto the floor behind the window. She looked around her. No lights came on; she had got away with it. Reaching through the broken window, she was in luck. The key had been left in the lock and she was able to turn it. She then tried the handle, pushed on the door and it opened. Going into the kitchen, she went over to the light switch. Pushing it down she was relieved to see that the electricity had been left on. Going quickly through the house, she was shocked to see that almost everything had gone. Nevertheless, she could still sleep on the floor and fortunately a couple of chests of drawers had been left behind and they still contained some blankets.

Over the next three days, Doreen decided that she would stay at the house. After all, she had found work cleaning in a local factory and the money would allow her to buy food and clothes and a new rucksack to keep them in. She didn't want to go to Auntie Dora's until she was working properly and could pay her way. Doe tried hard to hide her presence in the house from the neighbours, but on the fourth day she exited the back gate to see George, Phyllis's husband, in the alley. George said hello but was clearly surprised to see her. Nothing more was said between them, but when Doreen returned to the house late that night, it had been secured. The back gate had been padlocked and after climbing over it, Doe found that the back door and window had been securely boarded. It seemed that George and Phyllis had contacted the landlord. It was obvious that they didn't want her around. Although she tried, she knew that without heavy tools and making a great deal of noise, she wouldn't be able to gain access. Given her appearance in court, Doe couldn't risk the chance of anyone calling the police. There was no alternative; she would have return to Ardwick. That was where Jack and her friends were and no doubt, where Emily was too. Salford hadn't provided a positive experience for her and if Phyllis was anything to go by, people there weren't going to be any less vindictive than many of those she had dealt with in Manchester.

Having only earned a few days wages, Doreen knew that she would have to manage her money carefully. She therefore decided that she would walk to Manchester and save the bus fare. It was late though and Friday night, with plenty of drunks about. And with them came the police, on the lookout for trouble and no doubt concerned if they were to see a teenage girl alone on the streets. Doe's journey was therefore a nervous one, hiding in doorways and nipping down alleys whenever she saw an approaching vehicle, or heard the sound of raucous, drunken men. She was aware of how she had physically changed. Men looked at her very differently now and when they were older, or under the influence of drink, she often felt intimidated.

Gradually, Doreen made her way into Piccadilly and then on to London Road. Reaching Ardwick Green Park, Doe knew that it wasn't far to the flats. Relieved, she began to relax, but as she passed the far entrance to the park, Doe was grabbed from behind. Startled, she tried to pull away, but to no avail. Looking at her assailant, Doreen could see that it was one of the 'down and outs' who hadn't made it back to the railway arches. Ragged, with a matted beard and long, straggly hair, he stank of sweat, dirt and alcohol.

"What's a pretty girl like you doing out? It's late. Do you want some fun?"

Turning his head away, he shouted behind him.

"Boys, come here. Got a little darling for us."

Doe struggled hard to pull away, but his grip didn't loosen.

"Ah, don't be like that. You know you want to"

Moving his face towards her, he smiled; his rancid breath making her nauseous. Behind him, another figure emerged from the gloom. She knew that they would drag her into the park where, in the darkness, no one could help her. She had to think. What could she do? It was no good trying to pull away, for the tramp held her firmly. Quickly, Doe moved towards him. Surprised, he relaxed. She remembered what Jimmy had told her when he had taught her to fight. If it's a big lad, kick him, punch him, knee him in the groin, as hard as you possibly can. Distracted, her assailant wasn't ready. Doe brought up her knee as sharply as she could. He groaned, slumped forward and relaxed his grip. Stepping back, she took her rucksack and brought it down on top of his head. Containing the tins of baked beans, it laid him out on the ground.

Galvanised, Doreen turned to his friend. Startled by what she had done, he hesitated. Doe was prepared; ready for anything. How dare they think they could rape her.

"Come on, you bastard!" she heard herself say. "I'll kill you!"

She spat the words out with real venom. She was emotionally charged. Where had the word come from? She had never used it before. She breathed heavily, ready and waiting for the inevitable attack. But it didn't come. The second tramp had dropped to his knees attending to his friend.

Doreen stepped back and her mind quickly recovered. 'Boys'; she remembered that the first tramp had shouted 'boys.' There had to be more of them. She had to get away. With that realisation, she began to run as fast as she could. Up to the corner and left up Hyde Road. Quickly! Quickly! Doreen didn't stop until she reached the depot on Devonshire Street. Short of breath, she bent over and gulped the air into her lungs. She had got away! The lights were on and the main doors were open. Mechanics were inside and working on the buses.

"Are you all right, love?"

Startled, Doe looked up to see the amused face of an elderly, bespectacled, bus conductor.

"Yes," she replied, still panting.

"You must have been trying to break the four-minute mile. You did know that Roger Bannister's already done that love, didn't you?"

Doreen smiled. She felt calmer. She had nothing to fear.

"Seriously, love. You are certain that everything's all right, aren't you?"

"Yes, I'm fine. I just need to get to my boyfriend's house. I want to see him before he sets off for work."

Doe had no intention of telling him the truth; no desire to relive the episode at the park or have him call the police.

"All right. As long as you're happy, I'll get on then. Bye, love."

"Bye," replied Doreen.

The conductor walked into the depot ready for work. Doe looked at the clock on the front of the building. It was quarter past five. Not far to go she thought, as she secured her rucksack on her shoulder and continued down Hyde Road. A few people were beginning to emerge now, setting off for their early shifts.

It wasn't until just after five-thirty that she arrived at Bennett Street flats. She made her way to Jack's and sat down outside, exhausted, waiting for him to leave for work. At half past six the door opened and Jack came out. Noticing Doreen he stopped, a look of disbelief on his face. Getting to her feet, Doe rushed forward, threw her arms around him and began to sob. Jack tried to comfort her, but she wouldn't stop. He was shocked; his girlfriend was usually so tough. Stroking her hair, Jack softly kissed the top of her head.

"Come on Doe, it's okay. You're safe now."

Doreen's sobs began to subside. Finally, she spoke.

"Jack, don't ever let me down. I need to trust you. Promise me."

At first, Jack didn't know if it was something that he'd done. He was confused. But she'd flung her arms around him and sought comfort. Surely, he reasoned, she wasn't blaming him for anything. Slowly and calmly, he responded.

"I won't, Doe. I promise. I'll always protect you. Come into the house. You can stay here until you're ready to go to your Auntie Dora's."

Jack led Doreen inside, sat her in the front room and then went upstairs to wake his mam. Coming down, he gave her another hug.

"I've got to go to work now, Doe. I'll see you at teatime. Mam says you're welcome to stay as long as you want. Lie down and have a sleep, you look done in."

Doreen didn't attempt to argue, she was exhausted. Lying down, she fell asleep almost immediately. Jack covered her up with a couple of coats and set off to work.

The journey from Weaste had taken its toll and in Jack, Doe had finally found someone to believe in. Furthermore, she had allowed him to see just how lost, lonely and vulnerable she really was. The tough persona that she presented to the world, so crucial to her survival, had been exposed. After her ordeal, it had been Jack who she had reached out to. Her intuition had told her to trust him and in return he had shown her love and understanding. It was enough for Doe to reassess her attitude towards him. Having been reluctant to allow their relationship to develop too quickly, Doreen was now prepared to take a leap of faith. She would believe in Jack, for Doe understood that if she were ever to find true happiness, it could only be through sharing her life with someone else.

Chapter 58

Doe slept until dinner. Maureen, Jack's mam, kept a close eye on her, aware that something unpleasant had occurred. She was fond of Doreen; grateful for her positive impact on Jack. After the two had met, her son seemed more mature and was even willing to help around the home. Maureen hadn't had an easy life. Jack's father had left when he was a baby; no one knew where he'd gone. Life had been a perpetual struggle; a hand to mouth existence, with no family to fall back on. As Jack got older and attended school, Maureen had gone out to work and with more money, life was a little easier. Yet Jack had proved a difficult charge. Influenced by his wayward friends, he was soon in trouble and warned by the police. Caught breaking into a warehouse, he was sent to borstal. Out a year later, the institution's strict regime had the desired effect. Jack was determined to stay out of trouble. His mother thanked God for the miraculous change in his behaviour.

A devout Catholic, Maureen felt genuine Christian charity towards Doreen, but when her son had, that morning, suggested that his girlfriend come and live with them, she was appalled.

"No, Jack. I can't allow that."

"Why? I pay for my keep and I'll give you extra for Doe. In fact, she'll soon be working herself."

"You know I can't, Jack. As God is my witness, Doreen is always welcome to visit, but she can't stay. A young man and his girlfriend sleeping under the same roof. What would Father O'Hara think about that? It's not right."

Jack knew that there was no point arguing and he was well aware that Doe would agree with his mam's sentiments too.

Waking up in the middle of the afternoon, Doreen had a quick wash, got changed and then, having thanked Maureen for her hospitality, set out for Dora's. As usual, her great aunt welcomed her with open arms.

"Of course, you can stay. I told you that."

"I know, but it's tough for you with Larry and Walt still out of work."

"You need to go to your dad's, Doe. Make him give you something. He shouldn't be getting away with it. After all, you're still his daughter."

Doreen nodded in agreement but she had no intention of going to see him. She had far too much pride now. And unlike when she was younger, she had no intention of trying to shame him into helping her. In reality, she no longer cared. Why should she? She would be working soon and could then pay Auntie Dora herself. Until then, she felt confident that she would be able to pick up some part-time jobs. She would go back to the shops and factories she'd worked at prior to moving to Salford.

With that in mind, Doreen decided to approach Scott's. Mr Scott had always been kind to her. He owned a shop on Hyde Road, selling just about everything. In the past she'd done general tidying and worked in the stock room for him after four o'clock and on Saturdays she had often helped serve at the counter. Mr Scott had daughters of his own and Doe was sure that was why he was so generous towards her. She recalled how, when she'd only worked for him a few days, she had turned up at work in a cardigan with holes in the sleeves. Looking at it, Mr Scott had told her to take it off. Doreen hadn't reacted, but he was insistent and she had done as she was asked. Mr Scott had then handed her a new red cardigan and told her to put it on. Doe had assumed that he wanted her to look smart for his customers and at six o'clock when the shop closed, she took off the cardigan, folded it neatly and gave it back to him.

"No, Doreen. Put it back on. It's yours now," he had said.

It was the first of many items of clothing that he had given her. He never said anything about it though. Probably, thought Doe, as he had no wish to embarrass her by drawing attention to her obvious poverty. She received a number of cardigans, skirts and blouses from him. They were items that he had been unable to sell, or so he told her. It helped Doreen to know that there were people out there like Auntie Dora, Mr Scott, Dot and Andy who were good Samaritans. It made her feel that there was hope for the world after all.

Mr Scott was pleased to see Doreen and he had plenty of jobs for her. The stock room needed a good tidy out, everything reorganised and he wanted her to help out in the shop. Doe told him that it would only be for a few weeks. At Easter she would be leaving school and looking for a full-time job.

"Oh," said Mr Scott, surprised. "You passed the eleven plus, didn't you?"

"Yes," replied Doreen.

"Well, I thought in that case you aren't allowed to leave until you're sixteen and have finished your GCEs."

Doe was shaken, but she was sure that he was wrong.

"No, Mr Scott. If you don't want to stay on to do the exams, you don't have to."

"Oh, I must have got it wrong then."

"Yes" replied Doreen, with as much certainty as she could muster.

Back at Auntie Dora's, Doe was becoming concerned. Mr Scott's comment had come like a bolt from the blue. For so long now she had believed that she was close to starting work. Perhaps it was going to be denied her for another year. The consequences, if it were true, were unthinkable. She couldn't keep on avoiding school, especially as she had been to court for truanting. The judge hadn't been aware that she had passed the eleven plus. If he had, perhaps he would have acted differently. Confused, Doe needed an answer. She couldn't approach the Education Committee and Auntie Dora wouldn't know. All her older friends had left school at fifteen, but had also failed the eleven plus. She feared approaching her dad. Betty was vindictive and would thoroughly enjoy reporting her. No, there was only one person who would be able to help her. She would have to find her mam.

Chapter 59

For two weeks, during which time she reached her fifteenth birthday, Doreen unsuccessfully tried to find her mam. She had been to see Jim, but he'd heard nothing and after checking in the pubs that Emily usually frequented, she was no further forward. Doe was surprised, because she'd assumed that her mam had made her way back to Ardwick and was now living with Sam. Doreen was resigned to the latter's return and with a boyfriend of her own and working life to look forward to, she simply accepted her mam's decision. After all, true to form, Emily had put her 'boyfriend' first. Doreen had been forced to cope with it in the past, but she was now in a much stronger position to deal with it. Doe no longer felt any anger towards her mam. She still cared about her and was concerned by the thought of Sam beating her, but she now had Jack to worry about. He was the future and the past was being slowly put behind her.

Not only worried about whether she'd be allowed to leave school, Doreen was also aware that she still had no National Insurance number. Without that she knew she couldn't begin work. Sally, employed for almost a year, had received her National Insurance card through the post. Given that Doreen hadn't turned up to school in Manchester, the relevant authority didn't have an address to send her card to. Doe desperately needed Emily's help.

Doreen was beginning to despair. It was mid-March and Easter was less than a fortnight away. She just had to find Emily. Intensifying her search, she revisited all the pubs that her mam and Sam frequented and others that she knew they didn't. Finally, she was successful. Enquiring at the 'Polygon', she found one of her mam's old friends. She had seen Emily at the MRI in the casualty department at the weekend. She'd been there with Sam, who had been beaten up by a couple of men who had taken exception to him arguing with Emily on Oxford Road. Emily told her friend that she was living close to Whitworth Park and was working at a machine shop off Rusholme Road. It was sketchy information, but enough for Doe to work with. The following day, starting at the top of Rusholme Road, she worked her way up and down the side streets, searching out all the little machine shops. Enquiring at each one, she finally had success on Garden Street. The boss sent for her mam who, coming quickly, told her daughter to come back at dinner. When Doreen returned at twelve-thirty, Emily was waiting outside. She was full of apologies.

"I was about to come and find you, Doe. I thought that you would probably be at Auntie Dora's."

"I am."

"I waited for you. You didn't turn up. Didn't Phyllis give you my new address? I left it with her. I thought that you didn't want to live with me and Sam and had made arrangements to stay with Auntie Dora."

Doreen knew that her mam was lying, but she didn't care. It no longer mattered. She just needed help. Knowing that Emily was feeling uncomfortable and guilty at leaving her stranded in Salford, Doe decided to play along.

"It's okay, Mam. I'm fine at Auntie Dora's, but I need your help."

Doreen watched Emily's reaction change from relief, at the word 'okay', to concern, at the word 'help'.

"Don't worry, Mam, I don't need any money or want to move in with you and Sam."

Unconsciously, Emily let out a sigh. Clearly relieved, she could continue to play the role of the concerned parent.

"What is it that you need, Doe?"

"I haven't got my National Insurance number, Mam. Sally said that she got hers through the post, but they haven't got an address for me. I don't know what to do. I'm worried about something else too. Mr Scott thought that I couldn't leave school until I was sixteen, as I'd passed the eleven plus. Is he right?"

Doreen waited nervously for her mam to respond.

"No, Doe. Mr Scott's wrong. Of course, you can leave at fifteen. What we need to do, is go down to the National Insurance Office and get your card. We'll have to take your birth certificate and then they should be able to issue it to you."

"But I don't have a birth certificate."

"I do. I've got it. I've always kept it with me, Doe. I've got Jimmy's as well."

For a moment, Doreen was impressed. Keeping the certificate suggested that Emily really did care about her. Quickly though, she came to her senses. Her mam had let both of her children down; Doreen most of all. The certificate was probably a way to salve her conscience; a trick of self-delusion to kid herself that her children were close to her heart. But in reality, it just wasn't true.

"I'll have a quick word with the boss and see if I can have a couple of hours off on Monday morning," said Emily. "If you meet me here at half past eight, we can go to the offices on Aytoun Street."

Nipping in quickly to see the boss, Emily re-emerged to confirm the arrangements.

Although Emily had spoken with conviction and had given her the reassurance that she would be able to leave school, Doreen spent an uncomfortable time waiting for Monday morning to arrive. Sat with Jack at his home on Saturday night, it was clear to her boyfriend that she was worried.

"What's up, Doe? Something's bothering you, isn't it? What is it?"

"Nothing."

"No, Doe. It's something. I can tell. Please, tell me. Perhaps I can help."

Jack carefully took her hand in his and squeezed it ever so softly.

"I'm being daft, Jack. I know I am."

"But?" asked Jack, invitingly.

"Well, I've managed to get through all these years where I stayed ahead of the police and the education and welfare services. I stayed out of the children's home, I've avoided going to school and I've looked after myself and just when everything seems to be all right, I'm dreading that it will all go wrong on Monday."

"You mean when you go for your National Insurance card?"

"Yes."

"Why?"

"Because the judge in Salford said he'd keep an eye on me going to school, even though there were only a few weeks to go. I haven't gone, so what happens if they've attached a note to my file at the National Insurance office?"

There was a short pause before Jack replied.

"They won't have done that."

His response was unconvincing. Her point had hit home.

"If they have," she continued, "they could arrest me and put me in a home."

"No, that won't happen," said Jack. "They don't know that you'll be turning up there on Monday, so when you've given them your details, why don't you let your mam stay to get your card. You can get out of the building and wait outside. That way, if they call the police, you won't be there to get arrested."

Jack paused to consider the situation further.

"Anyway Doe," he continued. "Why do you have to work? I'll look after you. We can move and live off what I earn. They can't find you. They don't know that I'm your boyfriend."

Jack looked into Doreen's eyes. Her heart was touched by his deep concern. She couldn't help but smile.

"You daft thing. You're potty!"

On Monday morning, Doreen arrived outside the factory to find Emily waiting for her. The two set off. It was a relatively short walk to Aytoun Street and the nearer they got to the National Insurance office the more nervous Doe became. Reaching the building, they entered through the main doors and Emily headed straight to the reception desk. Doreen hesitated as she entered, but she was drawn almost unconsciously towards her mam and soon found herself stood at the desk, facing a rather elderly grey-haired woman. Emily explained why they were there and after looking Doe up and down, the woman directed them to the first floor. Taking the stairs, they reached the first landing and walked into a large waiting area. At one end was a long counter, behind which was a door. Placed on top was a shiny button and a sign inviting visitors to press it. Having done so, Emily and Doreen waited.

It wasn't long before a young woman emerged. Smiling, she asked them how she could help. Emily explained that Doreen had moved address and changed schools and so hadn't received her

National Insurance card. She then took out her daughter's birth certificate to verify her identity and show that she was fifteen. Looking at it, the young woman told them to take a seat whilst she went to locate Doreen's records and issue her with a new card.

"Come on, Doe. Let's sit down. It might take a while," suggested Emily.

The two of them sat at the side of the room and to pass the time, Emily asked Doreen about the types of jobs she was interested in.

"You know Doe, you might not have taken any GCEs, but you've always been a quick learner and anyone can see that you're clever. I'm sure that once you get a job, you'll soon be able to move on to better things. What have you thought of doing?"

"Well, I enjoyed working in the hairdressers and once I've qualified and have saved up, there's no reason why I can't run my own salon. I talked to Gillian and although it's been hard work, she's done well out of it. She told me that if I'm good and I can get into one of the top salons in town, I could build up a group of personal clients and then could set up my own business and take them with me."

"Maybe," replied Emily. "I think you'll find though, that you have to work for a long time before you get to that stage. I've known a few hairdressers. Most of them give it up. It's long hours and pretty poor pay. Not much use if you have a family. Then again, you're a way off that, aren't you?"

Emily could see that Doreen wasn't really listening to her. She was agitated; staring at the floor and tapping her feet.

"What's wrong, Doe?"

"It's taking too long."

"What is?"

"My card. Where is she?"

"It hasn't been long," said Emily, surprised at Doreen's comment.

"It has."

"Well, they've got to go through the files and make sure they copy the details down correctly. You don't want your contributions, once you're working, going to someone else, do you?"

"I'm not sure about that. I'm worried. The judge in Salford told us that they'd be keeping an eye on me. Maybe that woman has called the police. She's trying to keep us waiting here until they arrive."

"Don't be silly," said Emily, "calm down. They're not concerned about you anymore. The judge knew that you only had a few weeks of school left. He was just trying to frighten you into going. The court has better things to do than waste their time checking up on you."

"No, Mam. You wait here and collect the card. I'm going. I'll wait outside. They're not getting me now!"

Doreen had started to panic and was on the verge of leaving, when the door behind the counter opened and the young lady emerged. Emily rose to her feet and walked over but Doe, fearing the worst, seemed unable to move.

"I'm sorry for the delay, your daughter's records got mislaid. Never mind, we found them, eventually. Now," she continued, handing Emily some documents, "here's the birth certificate back and of course, Doreen will need this to give to her new employer."

It was the National Insurance card. Having thanked the young lady, Emily turned towards her daughter.

"Come on. Let's go."

Doreen just sat there. She could feel the tears coming, but she fought them back. It was impossible for her to describe just how she felt. Her head throbbed. She had been so afraid that everything would go wrong. After all, it usually did.

Looking at her daughter, Emily could see that she was in a state of some distress.

"Come on Doe, get up. Let's go and find a cafe and have a drink and something to eat."

Emily put her arm around Doreen and slowly stood her up and led her on to the stairs and outside into the fresh air. As she exited the building, Doe felt as if she had been handed a last-minute reprieve. She also appreciated that Emily was responsible for resolving her difficulties. Without her mam's support, she knew that she couldn't have done it alone. Doreen hoped that it would be possible to build more bridges with her mam, despite Sam's troubling presence in the background.

Her ordeal over, Doe began to calm down and she felt her positive mood returning. Sat with her mam, drinking a cup of tea and eating a bacon barm, she felt a real sense of freedom. She no longer had to live in the shadow of the children's home. Now she could work and finally be in control of her destiny.

Chapter 60

With her National Insurance card secured, Doreen immediately began to look for work. As in the past, she knew that it was easiest to walk down Hyde and Stockport Roads, looking in the shop windows for vacancies. It was 1964 and jobs were plentiful; there were lots of openings for all types of work. She decided however, that she would like to train as a hairdresser. It was a job that would, when she was qualified, allow her to do something creative and in time, she hoped that she would be able to open her own salon.

An opportunity soon arose to work for a hairdresser on Hyde Road. The business catered mainly for older women, yet this didn't concern her. Her new employer was eager to restyle the salon, in order to attract a younger clientele. Doe was taken on, joining an existing trainee called Janet. They would eventually become the new, young stylists. Doreen was attracted to the job by the fact that she was sent to college to attend a weekly half-day release course. This would enable her to obtain a City and Guilds qualification. It seemed an ideal situation and at first, Doe was content. The salon was owned by a married couple, Ted and Rita. Rita was a woman in her late thirties. She was very attractive, her long auburn hair framing a pretty face. She had large brown eyes, an hourglass figure and a winning smile. Her husband, an accountant, idolised her and had invested heavily in the stocks and premises in order to establish the business. Ted helped Rita by keeping the books and paying the suppliers. Doreen liked him. He was kind, older than his wife and he looked it. Grey and balding, he always seemed to be in good spirits. On Saturday nights, when the salon had closed, he would often, unbeknown to his wife, give the girls an extra five bob, to thank them for their efforts.

It was after a couple of weeks, that Doe became aware that Rita was cheating on her husband. On Friday morning a man arrived at the salon. Waiting at the reception desk, Janet quickly attended to him. Doreen, washing a customer's hair, glanced over towards them.

"Hello, is the boss in?" asked the man, cheerily.

"Yes, she's in the back," replied Janet.

"Okay then, I'll go through."

The man moved behind Doreen and past the sinks and dryers. He walked through the strip curtain and into the room behind. A few minutes later, Rita emerged and called over to Janet.

"You'll be able to deal with Mrs Porter, won't you, Janet? It's just a set that she wants. I'm a bit busy with Mr Adams at the moment; new supplies I need to sort out. You and Doreen can take care of things. Don't disturb me."

"Yes, of course."

Rita disappeared back through the curtain. Janet looked towards Doe and rolled her eyes.

"What?" asked Doreen, clearly intrigued by her reaction.

"I'll tell you later."

It was a fairly quiet morning. They only had a few customers in and whilst a couple of the old ladies were under the dryers, Janet took the opportunity to speak to Doe. Having been at the salon for nearly a year, she knew all the gossip.

"What did you think of him?"

"Who?"

"Keith. Mr Adams. The man who went in the back."

"Oh."

"He's good looking, isn't he? I certainly wouldn't mind if he showed me his supplies!"

Doreen couldn't help laughing at Janet's cheeky grin, yet had to admit that she was right. Keith was handsome. He looked a bit like Sean Connery, she thought.

"Janet. You've got a one-track mind."

"Well. He's not here to sell supplies. I can assure you of that."

"What do you mean?"

"They'll be upstairs," continued Janet. "There's a flat up there. A bed, bathroom, everything. They'll be at it right now. I can guarantee it."

"No, you're kidding," said Doreen, clearly surprised.

"I'm not, Doe. It's been going on for six months. I found out when I had to go into the back because Ted wanted to speak urgently to her on the phone. I couldn't see her but the door to the stairs was slightly open and so I went up thinking she'd be up there. Wasn't she! Bang at it, the pair of them! I told Ted that I'd remembered that she'd had to go to the bank. She never knew I'd seen them. I'm sure I'd have been sacked otherwise."

"Poor Ted."

Doe was shocked. Aware of Ted's devotion, surely Rita appreciated what he had done for her.

"It's a shame for Keith's wife, too. He's got a wedding ring on, Doe. He and Rita are a pair together. I have to say though, I can understand what she sees in him."

Doe didn't. She thought that Keith was nothing but a cheat and a liar. Made aware of the illicit liaison, Doreen felt uncomfortable.

"He comes every fortnight," continued Janet. "He owns a hairdressing supplies company. I think she wants a bit of excitement. Ted's a nice guy, but too old I suppose. She's after a bit more energy. We women have needs."

And Doreen felt sure that Janet herself was getting them met regularly. She'd already mentioned going out with three different lads during the short time Doe had been working there. Doreen didn't judge her, but felt that she was silly. If Janet gave these lads what they wanted, which of them would ever respect her?

Doe wasn't sure that she wanted to continue working at the salon. She had started a City and Guilds course however and if she left now, would have to find another employer willing to sponsor her and then wait until the course started up again. Reluctantly, she decided to stick it out, but found it difficult facing Ted. Doreen felt uncomfortable with the knowledge that he remained unaware of his wife's betrayal, but she knew that if he found out, he would be devastated. Over the next few weeks, she tried to have as little contact with him as possible. In the meantime, Keith turned up regularly. He would always go through into the back and then emerge about an hour later, supposedly complete with his order. He'd not spoken to Doreen on his first few visits, but had finally turned up when she was alone in the salon. Rita was in the back, probably preparing for his arrival, whilst Janet had nipped out to get some change from the bank. Approaching him, Doe pointed towards the rear of the salon.

"Rita's in the back."

Assuming that he would be eager to reach his lover, Doreen was somewhat surprised when he stopped to talk to her. It wasn't long, before they were deep in conversation.

"I've not said hello to you, have I? That's very rude of me. My name's Keith. What's yours?"

He held out his hand and smiled.

"Doreen," she replied, shaking his hand.

Doe noticed his eyes wandering over her face, quickly dropping to her feet and weighing up the rest of her, before returning. It was as if he hoped that she hadn't noticed him checking out her physical attributes. Doreen felt that she should be angry, but she wasn't. Actually, she felt flattered. Keith was in his early thirties, handsome and immaculately dressed in a made to measure suit. He was charming and knew how to treat women in order to make them feel appreciated. Fifteen years old, it was easy for Doe to feel special when receiving attention from someone like him.

"How long have you been working for Rita, Doreen?"

"Just over a couple of months, Mr Adams."

"Call me Keith," he replied, smiling. "Are you enjoying it?"

"Yes, Keith."

"How old are you, Doreen?"

"Fifteen."

"Oh, I thought you were a little older than that. You do look it."

Keith sounded disappointed. He was. He thought that Doreen was a very pretty little thing but for him, she was too young. Nevertheless, he found himself continuing the conversation. She interested him.

"So, what are you hoping to achieve, Doreen? What do you think working here will lead on to?"

Keith made her feel comfortable and Doe was soon telling him about her ambition to own her own salon.

"Well, Doreen. I wouldn't bet against you doing it. You seem to be a very sensible young lady."

At that moment, their conversation was interrupted by a loud cough from the rear of the salon. It was quite obviously false, but it had alerted them to the fact that Rita had emerged from the back room.

"Oh, Rita," said Doreen, turning towards her. "Mr Adams has just arrived to see you."

It was clear by her reaction that Rita wasn't impressed. With a frown on her face, it seemed that she had been stood there for a while. Why hadn't Keith noticed her? After all, he was the one looking in her direction.

"It was nice talking to you, Doreen," said Keith. "I'd better go and negotiate with the boss. Let's hope she doesn't give me a tough time."

Keith gave Doreen a big smile and then moved towards Rita, who wasn't bothering to hide her displeasure. She was glowering at him. Doe watched as she turned round, Keith quickly moving behind her and smiling as he patted her softly on her behind. It seemed that he was enjoying her jealousy; her anger at him having stopped to talk to one of the girls. It told him that he was in charge. That she wanted him; was desperate for him. Keith knew that there was little chance that these enjoyable encounters, without commitment and kept secret from his wife, would be ending any time soon. In fact, Rita's jealousy would act as a spur to their lovemaking; she would be more eager than usual to please him. As the two of them disappeared into the back room, Rita glanced towards Doreen.

"I'm sure that you can be getting on with something. Can you clean the sinks please?"

The request was terse, not the type that Doe would normally like responding to. Before she could say anything however, the two were gone. When, shortly after, Janet returned, Doreen told her about Keith's arrival and Rita's reaction.

"Oh, don't worry," said Janet. "She's just frustrated. Once she's had a romp with Keith, she'll be all sweetness and light."

"Janet!" replied Doreen, with a reproachful sigh.

"Well, it's obvious, isn't it? Poor old Ted can't help out, can he? It's probably stopped working," said Janet, laughing. "You'd be desperate too, if you were Rita."

"No, I wouldn't."

"How do you know, Doe? Don't knock it until you've tried it. Everyone can't save themselves for Mr Right, like you are. Anyway, don't tell me that boyfriend of yours hasn't tried it on and you've not thought about letting him."

Doreen was silent. That was her business and she wasn't about to discuss it with Janet.

Yet Janet was right. The older Doreen got, the more she found herself experiencing the stirrings of sexual awakening. She had been forced to stop Jack going too far, when kissing and petting had threatened to get out of hand and she herself had felt emerging desires that were threatening to run out of control. But Doreen wasn't like Janet. She had no intention of being disrespected like the 'easy' girls on the flats; good for what the lads could get, but not good enough to be considered as steady girlfriends. No man would ever be allowed to treat her like that. Furthermore, she knew where unbridled sex could lead. In some ways it had helped to devastate her life. Her mam's relationship with Sam had destroyed her marriage and family. Her dad's obsession with Betty had led him to give her all his money and attention, whilst ignoring his daughter. It would have been easy for Doe to develop deep emotional issues from such experiences, but she remained balanced and in control. She didn't feel negatively about sex or agonise about its place in her life. Doe embraced it, accepted that it was part of human experience and that, if she was in a truly loving relationship, it would be the final piece of the emotional jigsaw. Doreen believed in God and said her prayers silently every night. Yet, except for attending Sunday school, she had experienced no real religious instruction. Nevertheless, she had a true Christian perspective on sex outside marriage. She honestly believed that if she were to give herself to someone completely, it had to have emotional meaning. That would make it special and a force for good. Only marriage could provide a framework in which Doreen could feel the necessary commitment to experience the joys of making love completely.

It seemed that Janet's reassurances about Rita's reaction to Doe's conversation with Keith were correct. After he'd left, Rita seemed fine. Yet the following week, although Doreen couldn't quite put her finger on it, Rita seemed to be more reticent in her communications with her. Conversations were short and tended to be instructional. There was no longer any small talk between them. Everything focused on the job and Rita projected an image of herself as the boss. That was fair enough thought Doreen, she was, but it wasn't how Rita had been previously and she certainly seemed to be treating Janet in a far more friendly fashion.

Doreen asked Janet if she'd noticed Rita acting any differently towards her.

"You could be right, Doe" replied Janet. "She hasn't really spoken much to you over the last few days."

"Good. I thought that I might have been imagining it."

"No. I'm sure things will settle down though," continued Janet. "Just ignore Keith when he comes in next time. I'll talk to him. Rita can't get funny then, can she?"

"Well Janet, I'm not sure that I want to stay on. I thought of trying to get a job in another salon. It's just that it'll make it awkward with my college course and I can't afford to pay for it myself. At least Rita's doing that."

"No. You mustn't leave, Doe. It'll be boring around here without you. It's going to be all right. You'll see."

Doreen decided that she would stay, but the following Saturday the relationship between her and Rita got worse. It all revolved around Mrs Higgins and her appointment for a perm.

Mrs Higgins was in her early seventies and a difficult customer. She never tired of telling the two girls and Rita that she had been born in the last century and had lost her first husband in the Great War. She was part of the old generation; moaned about the new teenagers, their blaring music and ridiculous fashions. She never tipped and would complain at the least perceived mistake that she claimed Doreen and Janet had made. The two girls hated dealing with her but if the salon was busy, Rita would make one of them wash her hair. It was a traumatic experience. Not just for Mrs Higgins, but for the girls too. If just one bit of shampoo or water ran down her face, there was hell to pay and the inevitable cry of 'stupid girl' would reprimand them in front of a packed salon. When Rita indicated that she would have to deal with Mrs Higgins, Doe felt a degree of trepidation.

"Doreen, I want you to see to Mrs Higgins. Wash her hair and I'm going to trust you to give her a perm. You've learned how to do it at college, so there's no reason you can't do it now."

"Are you sure?" asked Doreen, hoping that Rita would change her mind.

"Of course, I am, or I wouldn't ask you to do it," replied Rita, sharply. "I'm here if you need me."

Doe realised that she would just have to get on with it. Anyway, she reasoned, she had done it at college successfully and at some stage she knew that she would have to do it alone. If she could deal with Mrs Higgins, then she could deal with anyone. So, asking the old lady to follow her, she took her to the sink, washed her hair without incident and then sat her back in the chair ready to prepare her for applying the perm. However, as she carefully combed through Mrs Higgins hair, ready to receive the perm rollers, she noticed that its condition was very dry and brittle.

"Mrs Higgins, have you had a perm anywhere else since you last came to see us?"

"No," insisted Mrs Higgins.

"Are you sure?" asked Doe, continuing to run the comb through her hair.

"Yes, I've told you. Are you deaf, you stupid girl!"

Mrs Higgins was becoming irate.

Doreen didn't believe her. She was concerned because the college tutor had told her class that they should never apply perms in quick succession. It could lead to disastrous consequences. Leaving Mrs Higgins waiting in the chair, Doreen approached Rita, who was about to start on a cut and set for another customer. Quietly, she told her about Mrs Higgins. Rita went over to see her and ran the comb through the old lady's hair.

"Just checking, but have you had a perm recently, Mrs Higgins?"

"What's wrong with you people? Are you deaf? I've told your girl that I haven't."

"All right then. I have to check, because when you've had a perm, your hair needs time to recover. If we do it again and it's too soon afterwards, it can damage your hair."

"Well, you don't need to worry," replied Mrs Higgins.

Satisfied, Rita left and gave her instructions to Doreen.

"You can go ahead. She insists that she's not had one."

"But you've seen the condition of her hair, Rita. I'm sure she has. The college told me that you can't do it again that quick."

"Let me worry about that, Doreen. Just do it. I don't want her shouting the odds with all the other customers here."

Reluctantly, Doe did as she was told. She put damp cloths all around the back of Mrs Higgins neck after applying barrier cream to stop the chemicals coming into contact with her skin. Getting out the perm solution, she then applied it to the strands of hair and began to wrap them around the rollers. Everything seemed to be going fine, but when Doe was half way through the task, she noticed that the areas covered by the rollers were slowly turning green. It was exactly as she had been told at college. Mrs Higgins had recently had a perm; her hair was too full of chemicals and the additional peroxide had led to a chemical reaction. Immediately, she alerted Rita, who came to deal with the problem.

"Neutraliser, Doreen. Quickly!"

Doreen fetched some and handed it to Rita, who applied it liberally over Mrs Higgins hair, but as they waited, there was no change. Applying more made no difference and soon Mrs Higgins was starting to sense that something was wrong. As yet, no perm solution had been applied to the front of her hair, so as she looked forward into the mirror, it wasn't obvious what the problem was. Fortunately for Rita, the old lady was one of her last appointments, so there were only a couple of customers left in the salon when she finally had to tell her the bad news.

"You didn't tell us the truth did you, Mrs Higgins? You have had another perm," said Rita.

"So what?"

"Well, I told you that it could lead to problems. There are too many chemicals in your hair. They've caused it to go green."

Mrs Higgins almost exploded off the chair.

"Let me see!" she demanded. "Get me a mirror!"

Rita got the hand-held mirror and positioned it behind Mrs Higgins head. She could now see the green hair reflected in the main mirror in front of her. Immediately, the old lady directed her anger at Doreen.

"It's your fault, you stupid girl. You put on the wrong perm."

"No, I haven't," replied Doreen, firmly. "I told you that it would be a problem if you'd had a perm recently and you didn't tell the truth. There's no way that it's my fault."

Mrs Higgins got out of the chair.

"If I was younger, girl."

Mrs Higgins raised her arm and moved towards Doreen.

Rita restrained her as gently as possible.

"Please, Mrs Higgins. We need to get the rest of the rollers out."

Sitting her back down, Rita quickly took out the remaining rollers and rinsed off the neutraliser. Having dried her hair, Rita told Mrs Higgins that she could leave.

"Hopefully, it's going to settle down soon and start to fade."

"You wait till I tell my son. We'll sue you for this. I've never been treated so badly in all my life!"

Putting on her coat. Mrs Higgins strode towards the door, opened it and then slammed it shut behind her.

Doe was annoyed. It wasn't her fault. She had warned Rita not to go ahead with the perm, but her advice had been ignored. She had been proved right and now Mrs Higgins was blaming her and she suspected that Rita would too. However, when Doreen returned to work on Monday morning, nothing was said about the incident, nor was it for the rest of the week. Yet Mrs Higgins was true to her word and a couple of weeks later, Rita received the inevitable solicitor's letter demanding compensation. Contacting her insurers, Rita was told that they would have to make a payment to the customer and consequently her future premiums would be increasing. Angry, Rita looked disapprovingly at Doe as she told her the news. It seemed clear that Rita had quickly forgotten her own responsibility for the incident. Doreen knew that she had no long-term future at the salon. She therefore decided to start looking for a similar position elsewhere.

It wasn't long before Doe was no longer working for Rita, but it wasn't because she had secured another job. The catalyst for her departure was another visit from Keith. He had arrived early and once again he had turned up just when Janet had been sent to the bank. Try as she might to direct him towards the back room,

Keith insisted on talking to her. Doreen felt frustrated, for she didn't want to appear rude by simply ignoring him.

"My Doreen, you're looking lovely today."

He smiled and winked at her.

"Rita's in the back, Keith. She's expecting you."

"Oh, I'm sure she can hang on for a bit, Doreen. I've missed having our nice chats."

Doe was starting to feel irritated. At any moment she expected Rita to emerge and it wouldn't help matters if she was talking to her 'fancy man', as Janet called him.

"Well Keith, I'm busy and I'm sure you want to get on and sell Rita some supplies."

"Yes," said a voice from behind her.

It was Rita.

"Doreen. I don't pay you for idle chit chat. Make sure you get those dryers dusted down."

It was the wrong thing for Rita to say. There and then, Doe knew that she wouldn't be working for her any longer.

"It's my fault," said Keith. "I interrupted Doreen from her work."

He seemed shocked at Rita's reaction and quickly walked towards her and into the back room.

Doe was finished. No one ordered her around. Rita could stick her job, but first she would wait to say goodbye to Janet.

But where was Janet? She should have been back by now, ready to prepare for the first customers. However, there was no sign of her. Having waited twenty minutes, Doreen decided that she would just go. She took off her overall, put on her coat and walked towards the door. Before she got there, it opened. It was Ted. Doe was surprised to see him.

"Hello, Doreen. Are you going out?"

"Yes, Ted. I've decided to give up the job."

Ted was shocked. He thought that Doreen enjoyed working at the salon and he had seen for himself that she was a grafter. She was definitely someone who was an asset to the business.

"Why?"

"I'm not good at being ordered about, Ted."

"Oh!"

Ted didn't know what to say. Something had obviously happened, but Doreen had no intention of saying what it was.

"Does Rita know?" asked Ted. "I'm sure that she'll want to talk to you."

"No, she doesn't. You can tell her I'm leaving. I'm sure she won't be sorry. Anyway Ted, I'd like to go now, please."

Stepping aside, Ted watched Doreen as she made her way outside.

Confused by Janet's absence and still angry at how Rita had spoken to her, Doreen's mind was in a whirl. Walking away from the shop, she made her way along Hyde Road and back towards Bennett Street. Getting closer to Auntie Dora's, she stopped. Doe had suddenly realised that she'd left Keith alone with Rita. If Ted walked in on them, he'd be devastated. Running back to the salon, Doe hoped that Janet had turned up to distract Ted or if she hadn't, he'd stayed in the shop and hadn't gone upstairs. But when she got there, her hopes were dashed. At the front of the salon there was a crowd of people. Keith was getting into his car and Ted was sat on the pavement crying. Rita was stood between them, pleading for their attention.

Doreen turned and walked away. At first, she felt a sense of guilt. If she had kept a clear head and not been so angry, she could have distracted Ted and have somehow warned Rita. Yet slowly, she began to reconsider. Rita and Keith had cheated on their partners, just like her parents had done. Perhaps Ted deserved to know. After all, Rita had played him for a fool. Doe couldn't help feeling sorry for Ted, but it wasn't her fault. It was his wife who had let him down; not her. Perhaps, if Janet had been there, it would have turned out differently. Yet it wouldn't have changed Rita's behaviour and sooner or later, she was bound to be caught out. Like so many others, Rita failed to appreciate what she had; a spouse who was loving, faithful and gave her unwavering support. Doreen wondered why anyone could think that it wasn't enough. It certainly would be for her.

Chapter 61

Over the next few weeks, Doreen had a succession of jobs. She couldn't continue her training at college, as there was no employer who would pay for the course. Emily had told her that the wages in hairdressing were poor and it was true. Doe had received two pounds and fifteen shillings a week plus tips, which were few and far between given that the elderly clients were poor. Sally was earning an extra pound a week working in a food processing factory. Although it was a 'dead end job', Doreen didn't hesitate to work alongside her cousin, when a vacancy became available.

Money was crucial. Doe needed it to pay her way. She couldn't afford admission to the emerging 'swinging sixties'; the 'fab' age of the Beatles, new fashions and so-called liberation. It was for the sons and daughters of those who were comfortably off. The families where parents could subsidise their teenagers through A levels at school and see them pick up their government grants when they went to university. Those youngsters who'd left school and had money in their pockets to spend as they pleased. Fortunate to have parents who took a small contribution from their wages and allowed them to go out and have fun. For them, there was pleasure without responsibility. They could go into Manchester and see new, exciting groups at clubs like the 'Oasis', the 'Three Coins', or 'The Twisted Wheel'. In 1962, before 'Beatlemania', you could see the 'Fab Four' for three and six and Manchester's teenagers were queuing down the street to get in. There was an explosion of Manchester's own bands: The Hollies; Freddie and the Dreamers; the Mindbenders; the Dakotas and Herman's Hermits. It was an exciting time for the city's youngsters.

Yet Doreen couldn't be part of it. She, Jack, Sally and most of their friends, weren't privileged enough to enjoy it. There was the odd visit to the cinema, an occasional match at Old Trafford or Maine Road and they could go on the local pub or club's annual trip to Blackpool. Reality for them was tough. Parents to support, if they had them, wages eaten up by rent, food and bills, with little left for the new 'hip' fashions and records. Yet they were happy. On the cusp of adulthood, they made their own entertainment. Just hanging out together, on the flats or in each other's homes, was enough. And they could look forward to the future. To getting married, having their own home and getting better jobs and prospects. It was the optimism that kept them going, but it didn't alter the fact that life was extremely tough.

When Petula Clark's 'Downtown' hit the charts at the end of 1964, Sally and Sarah raved about the song. Doe disagreed, dismissive of the naivety of the lyrics. 'When you've got worries things will be great when you're Downtown'. 'Neon signs', 'where the lights are much brighter', dancing 'to the rhythm of a gentle bossa nova'. It was for the privileged; a dream straight out of the movies. For Doe and her friends, living in a different reality, it could never be true. The 'Sixties' were a myth. In Ardwick they didn't exist. Women's liberation, gender equality, an affluent society; none of it was there. But it didn't mean that Doreen wouldn't fight for them. For as long as she could remember, she had always been a fighter and no boss, no man would ever tell her what to do if she didn't believe it was right. Doe was optimistic; convinced that the world could become a better place, regardless of the traumas in her past. More than anything, she was determined to find happiness.

Doreen found it incredibly boring working at the food processing factory. In fact, it was soul destroying. She had visited Emily a few times in her flat near Whitworth Park and at the end of August told her about her frustration at work.

"The thing is, Mam, I need a reasonable wage and the factory pays quite well, but I can't stand the monotony."

"Auntie Dora doesn't take too much off you, does she?"

"Well, I like to make sure she has enough. Larry and Walt still aren't working, so I have to make sure I'm paying my way."

"Well, I'd like to be able to ask you to come and live with me, but we've only got one bedroom. It's a shame that you can't stay somewhere else."

"I'm planning to Mam. I've opened a savings account at the TSB and every week I try to put five shillings in it. I'm going to use it towards paying the advance on the rent and buying what I'll need for a new home."

Emily was impressed but also aware that her daughter was being too optimistic.

"You do know, that you need to be at least eighteen to rent somewhere and landlords won't let properties to women on their own, no matter how old they are."

"Why?" asked Doreen, surprised.

"It's because unless they're widowed, women on their own are considered trouble. Landlords assume that they're on the batter; that they'll be out trying to attract punters and the neighbours will want them evicting. No, at your age especially, a landlord would never take the chance."

"What you're saying Mam, is that I can't have my own house until I'm married."

"Well, not unless you buy some premium bonds and get lucky and win enough to buy your own place," replied Emily, with a wry smile.

As Doreen thought about it, she could see that Emily's words were true. Where were there women living in houses on their own? Doe knew that her mam had always told landlords that she and Sam were married, even though they weren't. Doreen thought hard, but could only think of old widows alone in houses, not younger women. She realised that she would have to think very carefully about how she was going to go about getting her own place.

Mindful of her daughter's monetary concerns, Emily suggested that Doe try her hand at machining. The small factory she worked at was looking for trainee machinists and they were good employers. Emily explained that it was all piecework. The prices were fair and if she could work quickly, regardless of her age, once she had ceased to be a trainee, she would earn good money. Emily had made as much as £7 a week and was sure that Doreen would soon be taking home more than she was doing in her current job. Desperate for a change, Doe decided to give it a try.

"Can you have a word with your boss then, Mam?"

"Come along tomorrow morning at nine o'clock," replied Emily. "It'll give me time to talk to him."

Doreen arrived bang on nine. It was the same machine shop that she had found in Garden Street when she needed Emily to sort out her National Insurance. Her mam was waiting outside and took her in. The building was full of rows of machines, rattling away as women bent over them, eager to complete their tasks as quickly and efficiently as they could. Doe marvelled at the speed of their work and the apparent danger of it. Industrial machines were nothing like Emily's old Singer sewing machine that she had made Doreen's clothes on in Bright Avenue. They made a thunderous noise and looked well able to take someone's hand off.

"How can they work so quickly? Isn't it dangerous?" asked Doe.

"Not if you know what you're doing. Everyone has slipped and had the needle go through their hand or finger," replied Emily. "It's happened to me a few times, but I'm all right. Don't worry."

Emily took Doe to an office at the back of the shop. She knocked on the door, paused and went in, followed by Doreen, after hearing a voice calling out for them to enter. In front of them was a desk and behind it was a youthful looking man who appeared to be in his late twenties. He had a pleasant face and brown, collar length hair and straightaway, he smiled at them.

"My dad's left to see a new supplier, so I'm in charge at the moment. I assume this is your daughter, Emily."

"Yes," she replied. "Doreen."

"Hello," said Doe, looking the man straight in the eyes.

"This is Mr Steyn," said Emily.

"Robert," replied Mr Steyn, smiling at Doreen once more. "We don't need to be so formal, except perhaps with my dad," he continued, with a laugh.

Emily was surprised. She'd always had to call him Mr Steyn. She hadn't realised. Her daughter was growing up. She'd obviously made a pleasing impression on the young man.

"Well, Doreen, your mum says that you haven't done any machining before, but you've worked part-time in shops and warehouses and you've trained as a hairdresser. Is that right?"

"Yes."

"Your mum also says that you're a quick learner. It will certainly help if you are. My dad believes in treating our machinists well; it's good for them and good for us. We get some big orders and tight deadlines. We need women who are really prepared to get stuck in. If you can do that, it will certainly be worth your while."

Doe nodded. She liked Robert. He was friendly, enthusiastic and seemed fair. He was very well spoken, Doreen noticing that he referred to Emily as mum and not mam.

"You can start right now if you want to, Doreen. In fact, your mum can take you to join the other trainees right away."

"Yes, I'd like to. Thank you, Mr Steyn."

"Robert," said Mr Steyn, emphasising the point by smiling and wagging his finger at her.

Emily and Doe turned to leave. Shutting the door behind her, Emily led Doreen to an area off the side of the machine shop. It was here where the trainees learned their trade. Before leaving, Emily gave her daughter some key words of advice.

"Be careful, Doe. Don't mention to any of the other girls about Mr Steyn telling you to call him Robert. I don't know anyone else here who calls him by his first name. Some of the others might get annoyed, or get the wrong idea if they hear you doing it."

"Wrong idea?"

"Yes. They might think that you're carrying on with him."

"That's ridiculous," said Doreen, in disbelief. "He's far too old and there'd be no chance of it anyway."

"Trust me, Doe. Women can be really bitchy. Watch what you say and you won't have a problem."

Wishing her daughter luck, Emily was gone, eager to get to her own machine and start earning some money for herself.

Over the next few days Doe learnt the basics of operating her machine and was soon trusted enough to do some of the simpler work unsupervised. She'd always picked up new skills quickly and with little fuss and it wasn't long before she was taking her place among the experienced machinists in the main shop. The work suited her. It was well paid and she had to perform quickly, so that the day seemed to go by much quicker than it had in her previous job. Her bosses were pleased with her. Old Mr Steyn, a kind, bespectacled man with white hair and whiskers, complimented her on how quickly she had settled in, when he was making one of his occasional rounds of the shop floor. Robert, who was in the shop every day, always stopped to talk to her, a fact, as Emily had warned her, that wasn't lost on some of the other women. But, as yet, Doreen had received no adverse comments from any of her colleagues. In fact, they seemed fine with the additional attention that young Mr Steyn seemed to be giving her.

By mid-November, Doreen had been working at Steyn's for nearly three months. Arriving for work one Monday morning, Robert asked her to come into the office. Surprised, she followed him in. Sat at the desk was his father, old Mr Steyn.

"Sit down, Doreen," said Mr Steyn, motioning to a chair in front of his desk.

Doreen sat down and watched Robert take a seat at the side of his father. She wondered what they could want. Surely, they weren't unhappy with her. Feeling nervous, Doe considered asking them if her mam could be present, but it wasn't necessary. Mr Steyn, noticing her look of concern, quickly offered her words of reassurance.

"Don't worry, Doreen. There's nothing wrong. In fact, on the contrary, we've got you in here because we're happy with your progress and want to make you an offer that we think will interest you."

Doe was intrigued.

"We've been watching you," continued Mr Steyn. "You're a quick learner and a clever girl. Emily told us that you passed your scholarship and both Robert and I think that your talents are wasted if we only use you as a machinist. You get on well with everyone and we've noticed how you're always prepared to help the newer girls. Not many would do that Doreen. They wouldn't stop their own work and lose money to help others. Taking all that into account, we've decided that we want to offer you more responsibility. Robert has some good ideas and I want to back them. He thinks we can start designing our own range of clothes, rather than just subcontracting work from others. It's going to take time, but it could take the business in a whole new direction. It means that Robert is going to have to give up some of his current jobs in the office and we think we can train you to do them. We want you to help with the ordering and accounts, because Robert will be doing less of that from now on. I'll need you to help me keep an eye on production too and make sure that all the new machinists are settling in all right."

Doreen was stunned. The offer was completely unexpected and she didn't know what to say.

"Well, Doreen?" asked Robert.

Slowly, she responded.

"It sounds very interesting but if I'm not machining, then I won't get the chance to put in any overtime to boost my wages."

"Oh, don't worry about that, Doreen. If you accept the job, you'll be given a regular wage," explained Mr Steyn. "We intend to start you on seven pounds a week. The most you've earned so far, is five pounds and of course, your new wage will be guaranteed every week."

Mr Steyn paused to let the figures sink in.

"You're a sensible young lady," he continued. "Why don't you go and find your mum. Tell her that you can both have half an hour's break. Here's half-a-crown"

Mr Steyn reached into his pocket and handed Doreen the money.

"Go to the Cafe and have a cup of tea and talk to your mum about it."

Doe looked at him, but didn't move.

"Go on! We'll see you in half an hour."

Doreen and Emily were soon sat in the cafe discussing the offer. Emily was convinced that her daughter shouldn't hesitate.

"Doe, you should be grabbing his hand off. You can't go wrong. He's going to make you part of the management if things go well. You'll learn all about the business. It'll set you up."

"But I'm not sure, Mam. How will the rest of the women react? I get on well with everybody. They might not like it."

"That doesn't matter. You need to do what's best for you," advised Emily. "You'll always have to deal with jealousy. You just have to learn to get on with it."

That was easy for her mam to say. Although she was always prepared to stand up for herself, Doe also wanted to be liked. Rejected by her parents and having striven to please the many people she subsequently lived with Doreen had no wish to find herself back in a hostile environment. She was enjoying coming to work and was friendly with everyone. Doe feared that if she accepted the offer, the situation would change and she would find it difficult to manage. Nevertheless, she had been offered a great opportunity and it would be foolish not to take it. Despite her misgivings, she found herself agreeing with Emily.

"Yes. I suppose you're right, Mam. I'll just have to learn to cope."

"Remember, love. It's just a job. You work to earn money so you can have a decent life with your family. It doesn't matter if people are awkward. You're going home at the end of the day and leaving them behind. Ignore their jealousy, because that's all it is. There's no reason you can't do that, Doe. Your dad and I messed things up, but you needn't."

Doreen was surprised. Rarely did Emily acknowledge that she and her dad had let her down. If she was going to be cynical, Doe could say that it was easy now for her mam to accept her shortcomings. After all, Emily wasn't expected to take responsibility for her anymore. Yet Doe sensed that her mam's remorse was genuine and it suited her to accept it as such.

Returning to work, Doe went straight to the office. Knocking confidently on the door she entered. Mr Steyn and Robert were sat behind the desk going through some papers.

"Well, Doreen?" asked Mr Steyn, looking up at her.

"I'd like to take you up on the offer please."

"Congratulations, Doreen," said Robert, smiling.

Getting up, he walked around the desk and held out his hand. She took it and the pair shook hands, just like they were sealing a business deal.

"You'll be based in here now, Doreen. That's your desk."

Robert pointed to the side of the room where there was a small desk and chair.

"We'll have to familiarise you with all the records and files, but you'll soon get the hang of it."

Out of the blue, Doe was, as her mam pointed out, moving 'onwards and upwards'. She had certainly made a sound decision. There were a few murmurings of discontent among the machinists, but not many. A couple of suggestions that she owed her elevation to Robert, but Emily soon silenced those! In fact, Robert was the perfect gentleman. Married with two young daughters, he clearly loved his wife and although he thought Doreen pretty, not once did he act inappropriately. He loved her infectious and bubbly personality and was amazed at how quickly she effectively took control of the office. She had a maturity well beyond her years, forged by years of adversity and hardship. There had been just one point when Doreen had faltered. A couple of weeks after moving into the office, Robert had noticed that she was unusually quiet after she had been out on the shop floor.

"What's the matter, Doreen?" he had asked.

"Nothing."

Robert pressed her. She was distracted; subdued. It just wasn't like her.

"Just a couple of comments. It's nothing."

"From who?"

"It's all right. It doesn't matter."

"If it's upset you, then it does," insisted Robert. "Tell me who it was. I'll sack them, if they've been causing you any trouble. I won't have bickering and jealousy."

"No! I've told you, Robert. It's nothing. I can deal with it. You mustn't do anything."

She was insistent, but Robert wasn't prepared to let the matter drop.

"I won't have anyone criticising you, Doreen. You work hard for my dad and I. We don't want you getting upset and leaving us."

"I'm not going to. Please, Robert. Promise me that you'll forget it."

Robert shook his head. It was Doreen all over. He might be the boss, but she was the one telling him what to do. He couldn't help but smile.

"Fair enough, Doreen, but you must tell me if it doesn't stop."

"I will."

She was a wonderful girl, thought Robert. Forever putting others before herself, even if they didn't deserve it. Doreen had proved a real asset to the company and he and his father were delighted to have her.

Chapter 62

Just before Christmas, Doreen decided that she would go to see her dad. Doe hadn't seen him since just after she had returned from Salford and had sought his help in locating Emily. As usual, she had to stay outside and talk to her dad at the door. Betty's hostility was clear when she shouted to Jim to tell Doreen to 'get to the bitch'; that it wasn't his place to support her. After that, Doreen had left, more determined than ever to make her own way without him. Now that she had a new job and real prospects, she was determined to go back. Doe intended to show them how she had succeeded on her own and would take great pleasure in letting Betty know that she could no longer regard her visits, as an attempt to get money out of her dad.

Doreen turned up one Wednesday evening at six-thirty. She'd assumed that Betty and Jim would be in and she was intent on walking straight into the house. Knocking on the front door, she waited. It wasn't long before it was opened, but she was in for a surprise. Standing there was Kevin. It was a long time since she had seen him. He still had the shock of red hair, but his freckles seemed less noticeable. Perhaps it was because she was older and less concerned about such things. Almost eighteen, Kevin had grown into quite a handsome young man.

"Doe!" said Kevin, equally surprised. "I can't believe it! I haven't seen you in ages. Come in," he said, excitedly. "Come in."

Doreen entered, overwhelmed by the warmth of his welcome. It wasn't what Doe had expected, for she had assumed that her visit would be greeted with hostility. She could sense that Kevin wanted to give her a hug, but he was holding back. Doe realised that it was because she was older now. Kevin was worried about how she would react. Taking the initiative, Doreen threw her arms around him. Carefully, he squeezed her in return, the two embracing as long, lost friends, who'd shared a host of difficult challenges together. Both of them had suffered at the hands of Betty and it had given them a common bond.

As the two slowly separated, Doreen spoke.

"You look great, Kevin. How are you? What have you been doing?"

"They're not here, Doe," said Kevin, failing to address her questions. "Mam and Jim are in the pub, as usual."

"It's a bit early, isn't it?"

"Not lately. It stops them having to face reality. Let's go and sit down and I'll tell you all about it."

Kevin led Doreen into the front room and they sat down at opposite ends of the sofa.

"Hold on, Doe. There's a bottle of port wine in the cupboard. Do you fancy a drink?"

"I don't think your mam will be pleased."

"Who cares. Go on, have one."

"I don't drink alcohol, Kevin. I'd rather not."

"Go on, just have one. It's on Betty," he replied, smirking.

"Okay, but just a tiny bit."

Doe wanted to be sociable but she couldn't help recalling the time when Betty had got her drunk. The memory made her shudder and she decided that she wasn't going to drink the port when Kevin had poured it out for her.

Kevin's attitude towards his mam had surprised Doe. She appreciated that he was older, but she remembered how terrified he had been of her when she had lived with them. Doreen was finding it hard to accept just how unconcerned he was about the consequences of drinking Betty's booze.

"How's Trevor?" asked Doreen.

"He's married now. He moved out shortly after you left. He's never been back. I still see him from time to time. He's living in Stockport and his wife has just had a baby."

"What does Betty think?"

"She's no idea where he is. She doesn't even know he's married and I've never told her. When he left, he said that he was never coming back. He hated her for how he treated you and me, Doe."

"What about you, Kevin? What are you doing now?"

"I'm working for an insurance broker in town. It's good money and I get some useful bonuses. I'm going to be off myself soon, renting a flat in Levenshulme off my boss. I can't wait."

"Have you told Betty?"

"Yes, but she's got other things to worry about, so she's not said very much."

"Oh. What's happened?"

"She's been threatened with prison by the Corporation for not paying her rates."

"Prison? They can't do that, can they?"

"Yes. I heard her talking to Jim a while back and she left a letter last week on the table. I read it. She's got a court appearance coming up in January. Happy new year, hey!"

Kevin laughed. He'd had a couple of large port wines and was becoming a bit 'merry'.

"Do you think they might let her off?" asked Doreen.

"Apparently, she's not paid the rates for about three years and the Corporation have got fed up of her promises. You know what she and Jim are like. All the money in the pub or on the dogs before any bills are paid. Even if she goes to prison, she'll still have to find the money. She was talking to your dad about having to give the house to the Corporation in exchange for the debt."

Doreen was shocked. She didn't care about Betty, but the latter's misfortune didn't provide her with any sense of satisfaction. Nevertheless, Doe couldn't avoid thinking that Betty was being paid back for how evil she had been to Kevin and herself. It seemed that the saying was true: 'what goes around, comes around'. Betty was finally getting punished.

"What about you, Doe?" asked Kevin. "What have you been doing?"

Doreen told him about her job and then recounted just some of her experience since leaving to live at Alan and Rosa's. Kevin was fascinated and eager to listen. Before long, Doe was lost in the details and finally, looking at the clock, saw that it was just gone ten. She suddenly remembered that she had arranged to meet Jack an hour earlier outside the Wellington Hotel on Hyde Road.

"I'm sorry, Kevin. I've got to go. I'm supposed to be meeting my boyfriend. Can you tell my dad that I've been to see him and tell him about my job. I want him to know that I'm doing well."

"I will," replied Kevin. "You showed them, Doe. Just like me. We've done it without them."

"Yes," said Doreen. "I knew that you'd understand."

The two said good bye, knowing that it was unlikely that they would ever meet again. They hugged and wished each other good luck.

Outside, Doreen was confronted by an eerie scene. There was a thick, Manchester smog and she could hardly see more than a few yards in front of her. With the darkness too, Doe felt uncomfortable. The pubs would be letting out soon and in these conditions she felt vulnerable. The drunks would be out on the streets and after her experience coming back from Salford, she had become very conscious of her own safety. In the day, she felt flattered by much of the attention that men gave her; the cheery shouts and wolf whistles amused her. She usually didn't take offence. As Sarah said, you needed to worry when they weren't doing it to you. But at night it was different. She'd learned that drink brought out the dark side in men and robbed them of their judgement. It was so easy for women to fall prey to their predatory instincts.

As she crossed the road, Doreen was conscious of the silence. She could hear no traffic. Cars were staying off the road. Eventually, there was the noise of an occasional bus making its way slowly down Hyde Road, its lights invisible until a hazy glow emerged out of nowhere to slowly move past her. Doe knew that it was only a short distance to Bennett Street, but she was feeling uncomfortable. She wished that she had set off earlier. Jack would have been waiting for her. Now she would have to walk past the 'Wellington' on her own. Hopefully she could get beyond it before it closed and the men would still be inside drinking. Doreen continued on and realised that she was getting close to Blucher Street; the location of the 'Wellington'. Gradually, the noise coming from inside the pub began to increase and the lights of the 'Wellington' slowly came into view. Walking faster, Doe was startled as a figure emerged into the hazy light and advanced towards her. Her heart jumped into her mouth. She stopped, standing to the side in the hope that the figure would walk on by. Clenching her fists, Doreen prepared to defend herself.

"Doe. Where have you been? I've been worried sick."

The figure rushed the last few steps towards her. It was Jack. He flung his arms around her and kissed her on the cheek. Doreen felt a huge wave of relief flow over her. She was no longer alone and was touched by Jack's display of emotion. Quickly, she pulled herself together. She had no intention of letting Jack know how worried she had been.

"I'm sorry, Jack. I stayed longer at my dad's than I intended. He wasn't there and I've been waiting for him and talking to Kevin."

"Oh," said Jack. "Who's Kevin? I've not heard you mention him before."

Doreen sensed a touch of jealousy. His question sounded like the start of an interrogation. She didn't like it and she was surprised at him.

"He's Betty's son," she replied. "I lived with him and his brother when I was with Dad and Betty. He was treated as badly as I was."

"Well, I've been waiting outside here for over half an hour," said Jack. "I was beginning to think that you'd forgotten about me, so I went back to your Auntie Dora's. She told me that you had definitely gone to your dad's, so I was on my way back to find you. You had me worried, Doe. Especially with this smog."

"I hope you're not being jealous, Jack," replied Doreen, sharply. "I won't have anyone telling me where I can and can't go."

Jack looked at the floor, his head bent like a naughty schoolboy's.

"I'm sorry Doe," he muttered. "I didn't mean it that way. Honest. I was just worried about you."

"All right. Don't worry. Let's go. We need to get out of this awful smog."

As they walked away from the 'Wellington', Jack realised that he had been too quick to ask about Kevin. He had sounded too abrupt. But it was only because he'd been concerned about her, especially with the smog. It was a relief to know that Doe had been safe, but irritating to learn that she'd been chatting to Kevin whilst he'd been worried sick. Yet that was Doreen. She would give her time to anyone and it was something he would have to accept. Jack certainly didn't want to risk losing her and his actions had taught him a lesson about the tolerance and understanding that Doe expected from her boyfriend.

Reaching Bennett Street, they continued on towards the flats. Jack had placed his hand in Doreen's and felt reassured when she grasped it. They were both silent and everything was still as they walked through the smog. Jack was desperate to say the right thing, going over the words in his head before he risked opening his mouth. He didn't want Doe to go to sleep that night with any lingering doubts about him. Finally, he summoned up the courage to speak.

"I'm sorry for before, Doe. I didn't mean to suggest anything. I was just so worried and so relieved to see you. If we didn't have this horrible smog, I wouldn't have got myself into a state."

"It's all right, but you need to understand. No man will ever tell me what to do. I'll talk to who I want, when I want. If you can't trust me completely, then I'm not the girl for you. I've watched my mam and dad being pushed around by Sam and Betty; their lives controlled. I never want to be like them and I won't be. It's up to you, Jack. I'm not going to change one bit."

"I know, Doe. I don't want you to."

"Good."

Having cleared the air, Jack realised that they were getting closer to Dora's. He didn't want the night to end just yet. He'd been thinking a lot over the last few days and there was something that he wanted to ask his girlfriend. Tonight, having found the words to apologise to her, he felt that the time was right. It had to be now.

"Do you want to come and have a drink before you go home?" he asked. "We don't seem to have had much time together."

"All right," replied Doreen, "but I can't stay long. We've got work tomorrow."

Arriving at Jack's, the two found that they were alone. Maureen had already gone to bed. Jack quickly made a brew and they settled down on the settee in the front room. Doe could tell that her boyfriend was agitated. It was clear that he wanted to tell her something. She waited patiently for him to summon up the courage to speak. Finally, he was ready and looked into her eyes.

"I wanted to ask you something, Doe."

"Well, go on."

"It's about us," continued Jack. "I think we get on really well together. I know that I love you. You're like no girl I've ever known. I know how I feel about you; how much I care. Just like tonight. The thought of anything happening to you, or of losing you, upsets me and it hurts. It's hard to explain, but when I'm worried about you, I feel strange inside; as if I can't breathe. Helpless."

Jack paused. He'd never been articulate and he'd spent several days working out what he was going to say and rehearsing it in the privacy of his bedroom. Now he needed to steady himself, as he prepared to deliver the most important words of all.

"If you feel the same way, Doe, I'd like us to get engaged."

Doreen was taken by surprise. The last thing she was expecting was a proposal of marriage. Jack's words were powerful and she had no doubt that his sentiments were sincere.

"Doe, I'm almost eighteen and you'll soon be sixteen. We can get married then, put our wages together and have a house of our own."

Jack fell silent and looked away, glancing down towards the floor. He was mentally exhausted and now dreaded that Doreen would reject him.

It seemed an age as Doe considered the implications of what he had said. Questions flooded into her mind. Most importantly, did she love him? Yes, she believed that she did. Over the last few months their relationship had become close, warm and tender and she had developed a deep and lasting affection for him. She enjoyed his company, appreciated his cheeky demeanour and he was very handsome. Most importantly, he had been faithful. Nevertheless, Doreen was aware that there were other, more practical considerations, that had to be taken into account. They were young and it meant that they would need parental permission to marry and it would be hard to find a landlord prepared to rent them a home. Yet Doe believed in following her heart; it's what she did. Life's difficulties could be overcome.

She had proved it again and again and was positive that she and Jack could build a happy, new life together.

Turning towards Jack, Doe put her hand under his chin and lifted his head.

"Jack," she said, quietly. "Look at me."

Jack turned his head towards her.

"Yes, you big softy. Of course, I will."

Jack sidled up to her on the sofa and put his arms around her. He kissed her firmly on the lips and felt Doreen respond warmly. Gently, she pulled herself away.

"And I want a nice engagement ring. Don't think that you can get me any old rubbish."

The pair of them laughed.

"Come on Jack. You'd better walk me home. I'll see you tomorrow after work."

Chapter 63

At Christmas, Doreen had her ring. Yet it was never going to be an expensive one. Doe knew that they needed to save money. Jack had wanted something grander, but Doreen reminded him that possessions weren't important; commitment was. Buying an expensive ring didn't mean that he would love her any more. Besides, the money saved would buy items for their new home and that would prove far more beneficial.

Once Doreen was wearing her ring, she had immediately shown it to her mam at work. Emily was shocked, for she knew very little about Jack. That was hardly surprising, given that she had always lived too far away to have had a chance to meet him. Emily had doubts about the engagement, but could see that Doe was level-headed and held no illusions about the difficulties that she and Jack would face in the years ahead. Importantly, Emily realised that she had been given the opportunity to have a positive influence on her daughter's life. That would be achieved by ensuring that when Doreen and Jack were married, they would be able to move into a home of their own.

"Am I going to meet Jack then?" asked Emily.

"If you want," replied Doreen. "You could come to Auntie Dora's and see us there."

It was arranged for the following Saturday morning, the first of 1965. Emily liked Jack, he was cheerful and polite. Yet he was just a lad and Emily realised that Doe was going to have to provide the maturity necessary for their relationship to succeed. Given that her daughter was such a strong character, Emily was sure that she would pull him through. It was obvious that Jack idolised Doe. He sat close to her on the settee, held her hand and hung on her every word. Emily could still remember how it felt to be in love. But that was in the distant past and for her, it no longer existed. Nevertheless, she couldn't help but be lifted by the sight of two young lovers who clearly meant so much to one another. Momentarily she wondered why, for her, it had all gone wrong, but quickly she returned to the present. Nothing could be gained by raking over the ashes of her failed relationships.

"If you like, Jack," said Emily, "I can help you get somewhere to live. I've already told Doe that because you're young, landlords might be reluctant to rent you a house. If you want, I could stand as a guarantor."

To Doreen, who knew that her mam hadn't proved the most reliable of tenants, the idea seemed quite amusing. The departures from Salford and Harpurhey had shown that and there were many others. However, new landlords might not know this and Doe knew that her mam's presence and support may be the deciding factor in getting someone to accept them.

"Thanks Emily," said Jack, smiling. "Doe's going to sort out a house. I'm sure she'd be glad of your help."

Jack wasn't sure what a guarantor was, but had felt too embarrassed to ask.

"Well, when it's Doe's birthday and you've applied to get married at the register office, you're not going to be able to hang around," continued Emily. "You'll need to have somewhere to live and I'm sure that you wouldn't want to start married life lodging in someone else's home."

Doreen agreed. It was something that had been bothering her, so if her mam was prepared to help, she certainly wouldn't refuse.

The weeks that followed, leading up to Doe's sixteenth birthday, seemed to go quickly. Doreen hadn't told Mr Steyn or Robert about her plans to get married. Emily had advised her against it.

"Wait a while, Doe. They'll probably think you're planning to start a family. Keep working and show them that you're serious about keeping your job. You don't want to give them a reason to reconsider keeping you on."

Doreen thought that her bosses were unlikely to react like that, but decided that she would tell them later and not take any chances. After all, she was working hard and taking on an increasing amount of responsibility. She was learning all aspects of the business and Robert had been working on new clothing designs that they could produce themselves and attempt to sell to the big stores in Manchester and beyond. Nothing concrete had come of it yet, but Doe couldn't help feeling that exciting times were on the way. Certainly, her bosses were pleased with her. She was hard working, purposeful and showed initiative. They could hardly believe that she was still shy of her sixteenth birthday.

As that day approached, Doreen went with Emily to the register office at All Saints. She picked up the forms that she and Jack would have to fill in. Maureen would have to countersign for Jack and in Doe's case, her mam suggested that she get Jim to sign. Emily hoped that it would encourage him to save up the money for a wedding present.

Doreen was pleased that her birthday fell on a Saturday. It meant that she could spend the day with Jack and take the form to her dad to sign. She knew that Jim and Betty would be in the pub as soon as they opened at dinner, so she and Jack set off for Betty's at ten o'clock. The two of them were in for a shock. As they crossed over Hyde Road at the junction of Devonshire Street, Doe looked down past St. Matthew's Church towards the corner of Tiverton Place and Betty's house. As they approached, they could see that there were boards placed over the bay windows.

"Is that Betty's?" asked Jack. "The house at the end?"

"Yes," replied Doreen.

"What's happened?"

The two of them quickened their pace and were soon at the front steps. They could now see that all the other front windows were boarded up. Doe walked around the side into Tiverton Place. The back was boarded up too. Suddenly it dawned on her. She remembered what Kevin had told her about Betty, the rates and the threat of eviction. It seemed that he had been right. She quickly explained this to Jack and suggested that they go and ask the neighbours if any of them knew where her dad had moved to. This they did and found out that Jim and Betty had left about three weeks ago. No one knew where they had gone. The bailiffs had come and boarded up the house, but there hadn't been anything for them to take away, as it seemed that Betty had already sold everything beforehand. One of the neighbours had seen Jim a couple of times since. It was therefore possible that he was still going in the local pubs. Doe decided that they would return at dinner to see if they could find him in any of his usual haunts. Doreen still wanted to tell him that she was getting married and if she did see him, wondered if he would remember that it was her birthday. She suspected that he wouldn't.

Having gone back to Jack's for a couple of hours, the two of them ventured back down Hyde Road. They tried the 'Clarence' first and then the 'Rutland' and the 'Richmond', but without any luck. Walking down to the bottom of Syndall Street and on to Stockport Road, they reached the 'George'. Doreen popped her head into the Vault. She spotted her dad at the far side of the bar. Waiting until Jim looked up, she shouted over to him.

"Dad! Dad!"

Everyone in the Vault turned round but Jim, who clearly hadn't heard her. An elderly man sat at a nearby table looked over at her.

"What's up, love? Can I help?"

"It's my dad. Jim Brodie. He's stood at the other bar. I can see him, but he can't hear me. Can you ask him to come outside please and tell him that Doreen wants to talk to him."

The man walked over to the bar and shouted across to Jim. Doreen could see that he'd got his attention. Her dad looked over and she waved. Closing the door, she joined Jack outside and they waited for Jim to appear. He wasn't long. He was soon outside, immediately throwing his arms around her.

"Doe. It's good to see you."

Jim gave Doreen a kiss and stood back to look at her.

"You're quite the young woman now. I can't believe just how you're growing up."

"Did Kevin tell you that I came to see you, Dad?"

"Yes. He told me that you're working now and doing well for yourself."

"Yes, Dad. Kevin mentioned about Betty having problems with the rates. Is that why you've moved out?"

"Yes, love. She could have gone to prison if she'd stayed, so we left the house for the Corporation to sell off to pay the debts. It should stop them from trying to find us."

"Oh," replied Doreen.

"We've got a place in Longsight now. It's not too far away. We're not letting anyone know where we are, until things settle down a bit. Anyway, what brings you here and who's this?" asked Jim.

"It's my boyfriend, Jack. He's a plumber, a tradesman like you. I seem destined to be surrounded by them, don't I? You, Our Kid and now, Jack."

Jim laughed. He and Jack smiled and nodded towards one another.

"I've come to tell you that we're getting married," said Doe.

"Married!"

Jim was taken completely by surprise.

"I am sixteen now, Dad."

She waited to see if he'd realised that today was her birthday. If he had, he wasn't acknowledging the fact.

"It goes so fast," said Jim, after a pause. "It only seems like yesterday when you were sat on the toilet roof upset over our Rex."

It certainly hadn't gone fast for her, thought Doe. She wished it had. Never mind, that was in the past now. They had come to get her dad to sign the marriage papers.

"Yes, Dad. I understand now that the court forced you to have Rex put down. It wasn't your fault. He was a lovely dog though."

"Yes, love. He was."

"Dad, I'm here because I need you to give your permission for me to marry, as I'm not twenty-one. I've brought the paperwork along. Could you sign it for me, please?"

Jim was glad to be asked. It was like he could be a real dad again. With a stern look on his face he turned towards Jack.

"Do you promise that you'll look after my daughter properly? I'll be after you if you don't you know."

Jim glowered at Jack who appeared concerned. Doe couldn't help laughing.

"You daft thing," said Doreen, looking at Jack. "Can't you see that he's joking?"

Once again, Doe started to laugh, this time joined by her dad. Eventually they settled down and turned their attention back to the paperwork.

"Of course, I'll sign it, Doe. Have you got a pen?" asked Jim.

"Yes, here."

Doreen took the form and a pen out of her bag and showed Jim where to sign it. He quickly nipped back inside the pub to rest the form on a table and with the job done, he returned.

"Here you are, love."

Jim handed the form to his daughter.

"Can you come to the wedding, Dad? It'll be at All Saints Register Office. I can let you know the date once I've given the forms in."

"I'll try, Doe. Things are a bit difficult at the moment though, as you can appreciate."

Doreen suspected that Betty wouldn't want him to come.

"Where can I find you, Dad. Will you be here?"

"We usually come here, but sometimes we go to the 'Waggon and Horses'. It's a bit nearer for us."

"Oh," said Doreen. "Is Betty with you now?"

"Yes. I'll tell her about the wedding later. She's still feeling down over losing the house. I'd better be getting back to her, love."

"All right."

Jim gave his daughter a kiss, shook Jack's hand and went back inside.

Later on, as she thought about her meeting with Jim, Doreen realised how strange it had been. For the first time since leaving Bright Avenue, she had felt no strong emotions, of either love or anger, towards him. Finally in charge of her own destiny, Doe had drawn a line under the past. Whether or not Jim turned up at her wedding, didn't concern her. It would be nice if he did, but of little consequence if he didn't. Like he had recognised, she was a young woman now and soon she would be a wife and in time have a family of her own to look forward to. Now, all that concerned her, was the future.

Chapter 64

It was her mam's suggestion. Doreen should stay with her for a few weeks prior to the wedding.

"It makes sense, Doe. You've put my address on the wedding form and as me and Sam have got a house now, there's a spare bedroom for you to stay in. You can save all your money until the wedding. You'll need it to help you move in."

Doreen agreed. It seemed to make sense. It would only be for a short time and it was getting difficult at Auntie Dora's. Larry and Walt had become very bitter. Unable to find work, they didn't seem too happy that she and Sally were earning and helping out with the bills. It was best for everyone if she moved out. Doreen wasn't looking forward to being near Sam, but as they both worked and she would be spending most nights and weekends with Jack, only coming back to sleep, she wouldn't have too much contact with him. Doe hadn't noticed any marks or bruises on Emily's face or arms since they had been working together. Perhaps Sam had finally learned to control his temper.

Doreen and Jack's wedding had been arranged for Easter Saturday; April 17th, 1965. Doe had let her dad know, finding him at the 'George' and he had promised that he would try to see her on the day. Most important of course, was finding somewhere for her and Jack to live and that was proving difficult. As soon as landlords knew how old the couple were, they were immediately turned down. As such, Doreen was grateful to Emily who, at the end of March, found a house on Donnison Street. Technically it was in West Gorton, but it was off Hyde Road and near its end joined with Clowes Street, which was close to Bennett Street flats and all their friends. It was an ideal location. Before arranging to look at it, Emily suggested that they go on their own, without Jack.

"It's a young chap, Doe. He owns the Sportsman Club not far away. He's inherited the property off his father and I think he'll give you a chance. You're a little charmer. You'll be able to persuade him that his rent's safe."

"No, I'm not!"

"Not what?" asked Emily.

"A little charmer."

Doreen felt insulted.

"Don't be daft, Doe. Use the fact that you're pretty. You want the house, don't you? Once you start talking to him, he'll realise that you're sensible and responsible. He'll listen because he likes looking at you. You're not doing anything wrong. It just gets you a foot in the door and you need somewhere to live, don't you?"

"But shouldn't Jack come too?"

"If he wants to see Jack, we can return later. You can't make the same impression if Jack's there too."

Doreen understood the point, but it certainly didn't make her feel comfortable.

On their arrival at Donnison Street, Doreen could see that it was a tired looking area. She wondered how long it would be before the houses were being knocked down. They'd already started demolishing the terraces in the streets near to where she worked and the Corporation had announced that they intended to clear most of the older housing in Ardwick and Chorlton-on-Medlock. No doubt, West Gorton would soon follow. The house, number 80, was a typical two-up, two-down. It faced straight on to the pavement, had a back yard and its own outside toilet. To Doreen though, it held out the promise of being her first proper home.

After about ten minutes, the landlord arrived. He drove up to the front door in a brand new, racing green MGB. Impressive, thought Doreen, especially on this street where there were so few cars. Inevitably its presence attracted a gang of young lads who quickly crowded around it.

"Can we watch your car, Mister?" a couple of them asked, as a young man dressed in a sharp suit emerged from the vehicle.

"Go on then," he said, smiling. "I'll give you sixpence each."

The man was quite tall, thin, with sandy hair and green eyes. His teeth were even and white, giving him an attractive smile. Emily walked towards him.

"Hello, Mr Joyce. This is my daughter, Doreen."

She turned and motioned towards Doe at the side of her.

"Hello. I'm Ed. Ed Joyce," said the young man.

He stretched out his hand towards Doreen who grasped it firmly. Shaking it, she looked him straight in the eyes.

Ed looked closely at Doe. She was wearing a pretty blue skirt, a white blouse and matching blue jacket. Her hair was black and piled up in a fashionable beehive. She had high cheekbones and piercing, green eyes. She was indeed, a very pretty girl and clearly, by the strength of her handshake, a confident young lady.

"Let's go in," said Ed "and I'll show you around."

Ed put the key into the lock and opened the front door. He held it open whilst Emily and Doreen walked through.

"It's just a standard two-up, two-down, Doreen, just like any other. But it's a sound property to start off in."

Doe looked around. There was new lino down on the floors and the walls had been walloped. No doubt it had been spruced up after its last tenants had departed. They went into the kitchen. There was an Ascot boiler, a sink, a drainer and a newish gas cooker. There was a table and four chairs, but no other furniture on the ground floor. Upstairs there was no real landing, just a small area with bedroom doors off to the right and left. Both bedrooms had a wardrobe, but that was it. The walls had been walloped and there was newish lino on the floor. Standing in the middle of the front bedroom, Ed looked at Doreen.

"You're about to get married then?"

"Yes," she replied. "On Easter Saturday."

"And both you and your husband are working?"

"Yes. I've brought you a couple of wage slips. One for each of us."

"That's all right. I believe you."

Ed smiled. He was pleased that she'd brought them. It indicated to him that Doreen was someone who appreciated the fact that at her age, most landlords wouldn't have rented her a property. She was determined to prove that she would be a reliable tenant who importantly, would pay her rent on time.

"What does your fiancé do?"

"He's a plumber."

"I'm looking to get someone in right away," continued Ed. "I know it's three weeks until you get married, but I'd like to rent the house out from next Saturday. I'm prepared to give you a couple of weeks rent free, till you get everything moved in. But in return, I'd like your husband to finish off a couple of decorating jobs for me. I want the window frames on the ground floor painted inside and out, if that's all right."

"Yes. I'll tell him. He'll get it done."

"I'll be able to see when I come to collect the first weeks rent," said Ed. "But with you behind him, I've no doubt that it will be." He smiled broadly.

"I haven't told you how much the rent is yet," he continued.

For a moment, Doe was concerned. Given her unusual situation, she worried that the rent may be higher than usual; an attempt to profit from her desperation to find somewhere. Yet Ed seemed decent and he had been so friendly.

"It's sixteen shillings a week," said Ed. "Are you still interested?"

"Yes," replied Doreen.

She felt relieved. It was more expensive than the rents paid by the older tenants on the road, but much cheaper than it could have been. If it had been too high, Doe would have faced the choice of either turning it down, or moving in and going through the daunting prospect of approaching the Corporation to determine a fair rent. She felt that Ed had been reasonable.

"If you like, you can pay me your first week's rent today and I'll give you your rent book. You can come next week and I'll have your keys ready for you to move in. We still need to put a new lock on the back door."

Emily took out a couple of pounds from her purse and handed it to Ed.

"Doe, have you got eight shillings?"

"Yes."

"Well give it to Ed and you're paid up for three weeks after your wedding. That means from next Saturday, with your two free weeks, your rent is covered for the first five weeks."

Doreen was taken by surprise. She hadn't expected Emily's gesture. As quickly as she could, she recovered her composure, searched in her purse for the eight shillings and handed over the money.

"Let's go downstairs and I can sort out your rent book," said Ed.

Back in the kitchen he took out a new rent book from a folder he had left on the kitchen table. Sitting down, he looked up at Doe.

"What's your husband's name?"

"Jack," she replied, "Jack Cassidy"

Ed began to write Jack's name across the front of the rent book.

"Ed. Can you put my name on there as well, please?" asked Doreen.

Ed stopped and looked up.

"It's usual just to put the husband's name on it," he replied.

"That's right," added Emily. "That's the way it's always done. I've never had my name on the rent book. It's always your husband's."

"Well," Doe continued, "this will be my house as well as Jack's. It's the first home I've had of my own, so I'd like my name down as a tenant too."

Ed looked at her. He could see a gleam in her eyes; a look of determination on her face. She was a strong character and attractive with it. He took the book and put it back in his folder.

"It's lucky I've got a spare," he said, smiling. "I'll tell you what, Doreen. I'm happy to just put your name on the front. After all, you're the one who's convinced me that I can safely rent you the house. I'm sure that you won't let me down."

Emily looked in amazement at her daughter. She couldn't believe it. She'd never been equal to her husband or partner. Men were considered the head of the household and so always had their names on the front of the rent book. Women were effectively residents on sufferance. It was the man who was the 'king of his castle'; that was what the law decreed. But Doe had changed all that and she had been given legal control over the property. Ed may be part of the more 'liberated' younger generation, but Emily was sure that he hadn't done it for any of the other married women who occupied his houses. The fact that he'd started to write Jack's name on the original rent book, proved that. Emily knew that Ed had been captivated by Doreen as he had shown them around the house. The little glances that he thought neither of them had noticed. Emily knew that her daughter was pretty, but men beyond their social background, such as Ed and Robert, recognised her vitality and intelligence too. When allied to her warm and engaging personality, it meant that they could not fail to be utterly charmed by her.

Travelling home on the bus, Doe explained to Emily just how important it was to have her name in the rent book.

"I wouldn't have minded if both our names were down as tenants, but if it was only one, it had to be mine. Since Bright Avenue I've never had a proper home. Wherever I've lived, I've always felt that I didn't belong; that people didn't really want me to be there. I've had to clean, cook and look after kids just to get a roof over my head. Now, it's going to be my house. No one can tell me to get out, or that I can only stay for as long as I do as I'm told. It might be a little terrace and the Corporation will probably pull it down in a couple of years, but it will be mine and that means more to me than I can possibly explain."

Silent, Doe turned to look out of the window as the shops and buildings passed them by. When Emily glanced back towards her, she could see the tears in her daughter's eyes. It had been an emotional day, but one that had secured Doreen's future. She and Jack would be starting married life in a home of their own. With Emily's help in finding Ed, they had defied the odds. Everything was falling into place.

Chapter 65

Emily was living with Sam at 46, Parkfield Street. It was off Moss Lane East, facing towards Whitworth Park and technically in Rusholme. It was within walking distance of work and for Doe, Hyde Road and Bennett Street weren't too much further.

On her first night, Doreen went to bed early. Staying in the front bedroom, she always slept with the window slightly open. At eleven o'clock Doe was woken by the sound of knocking and realised that someone was at the neighbour's front door. Although it was late, the visitor was persistent and the knocking intensified. Eventually, the door was opened and Doe heard a woman's voice.

"Shush! I heard you! Give me a chance to get to the door. I don't want any more complaints from the neighbours."

"Oh, sorry," replied a man's voice.

"Come in then. Don't hang about," replied the woman.

Doreen heard the sound of the door shutting behind them and soon drifted off to sleep.

Over the next week Doe found that this was no isolated incident. Every night, at various times, she was awoken by the sound of knocking on the neighbour's front door. Each time it signalled a man visiting the house. Intrigued, she mentioned it to her mam on their way to work.

"It's Doris. She's on the batter."

"What, like Sally's mam?"

"Yes. She has men round all times of the day and night. Sundays as well," continued Emily.

It was true. The following Sunday, Doreen had waited until after dinner before going to see Jack. When she set off, at around two o'clock, she saw a young man being let into the front room by Doris, who was holding the door open.

"Go in love," she said, as the man squeezed past her and into the house.

Doe glanced over and halted when Doris called out to her.

"Hello, you're living next door, aren't you, love?" said Doris, smiling.

"Yes," replied Doreen. "I'm staying with my mam and Sam."

"I thought you were. I've seen you going to work in the mornings with Emily. My name's Doris by the way."

"Doreen."

Approaching her, Doe could see that Doris was about her mam's age. She had brown, wavy, shoulder length hair. It was framing a pleasant face. She was wearing a cardigan, skirt and blouse and high heels. Strange footwear for inside, thought Doreen, but probably for the benefit of the punters.

"You should come round and have a chat, love. You're getting married, aren't you? Your mam told me. I'm usually on my own after tea. You can come round any night."

"All right. Thank you."

A voice shouted from inside.

"I'd better go," said Doris. "I can't keep him waiting."

"Is he?" asked Doreen, hesitantly

"One of my clients?"

Doe nodded.

"Yes."

"But he's young."

"So?"

"Well, I don't mean any offence, but why does he come to you? He's quite good looking, isn't he?"

"Yes, he is, but he's not the only one his age, I can assure you," replied Doris. "Look, I'll tell you all about it if you come round to see me. I'll have to go now, love."

Smiling, Doris closed the front door.

On Monday evening, Doreen decided that she would go and see Doris. She was fascinated. Doe knew that Sally's mam was a prostitute, but she and Sally knew little about her lifestyle. Curiosity had got the better of her. Doe couldn't get over the fact that a handsome young man was paying Doris for sex. She wanted to know why and hopefully Doris would enlighten her.

When she knocked on Doris's back door, it was opened by a man in a suit. He looked to be in his mid-thirties, was immaculately groomed and with his moustache, cut quite a dashing figure. He reminded her of Errol Flynn, whose picture she had once seen in her mam's movie magazines in Bright Avenue. He was wearing aftershave and it smelt exotic.

"Hello. Who have we got here then?" he asked, with a smile. He looked Doreen up and down. She felt him taking in every detail. It was enough to make her feel uncomfortable.

"I was looking for Doris," she said, hesitantly.

"Is that you, Doreen?" asked a voice from inside.

It was Doris.

"Yes."

"Come in, love."

The man stood aside and Doe entered the kitchen. Doris was sat at the table.

"Hello," said Doris. "Have you come round for a chat?"

"Yes, before I go to meet my boyfriend."

"Sit down, love. Do you want a brew?"

"No, it's all right, thanks. I've only just had one."

Doreen sat down across the table from Doris.

"I'll be off now, Doris. I'll be back before ten," said the man.

"All right, Mike."

Mike shut the door behind him and the two were alone.

"That was Mike," said Doris. "He looks after me. Arranges the punters and makes sure that I'm safe."

"Oh," replied Doreen.

"You're going to be married then?"

"Yes, on Easter Saturday."

"Is he a good 'un?"

"I think so. I wouldn't marry him otherwise."

"Is he handsome and has he got a good heart?"

"Yes."

Doris nodded and murmured her appreciation.

"You're very pretty, Doreen. I hope he realises how lucky he is."

"He does," replied Doe, with a smile.

"It's what all women want," continued Doris. "A good husband who loves them and who'll never let them down. I'm afraid it's too late for me though."

"Why?" asked Doreen.

"Because it can't happen now. I've been through too much and known too many men. I've seen all their failings; their foul tempers and their selfishness. I could never trust a man like you can. If I did find the right one, I'd never feel completely certain about him. It just wouldn't work."

Doris paused. Doreen was fascinated and eager to know more. She prompted Doris for further details.

"If you don't mind me asking, why do you do it?"

"It's good money, if you do it right and I've been saving up. Mike takes his share but I often get extra off the punters which he doesn't know about. I've managed to open a couple of savings accounts and I've got the pass books hidden away. Soon I should be able to stop doing this and retire."

Doris laughed.

"It makes it sound just like a regular job. Doesn't it, Doreen?"

Doe smiled.

"That young man who came yesterday," continued Doreen. "Why does he visit you?"

"You really are quite innocent, aren't you?"

Doris looked closely at her young visitor.

Doe nodded. She had to admit that she was. Mature well beyond her years in so many ways, sex was one area in which she certainly lacked knowledge.

"It can be for many reasons," continued Doris. "Some have girlfriends or wives who won't let them have sex, or who won't do certain things for them."

"Such as?"

"Well, dressing up, or beating them, or other things that I'd rather you found out about as you go along."

"Oh."

Doreen decided that she wouldn't pursue the point. It seemed clear that Doris didn't wish to make her feel uncomfortable.

"Others are shy and I make it easy for them and don't cause them any embarrassment," continued Doris. "I get some young men who think that they need to learn what to do; how to please a woman before they get a chance to make love to their girlfriends. Some just want a shoulder to cry on; someone to talk to. They're not even bothered about having sex. They're all different. Men are."

Doreen looked at the clock on the wall. It was time she was getting off to see Jack, who she'd arranged to meet outside the ABC on Stockport Road.

"I'm sorry, but I'm going to have to get off."

"That's all right. You're welcome any time, love. It's been nice talking to you."

Walking to the ABC, Doe thought about her conversation with Doris. She wondered if she'd done the right thing talking to her. Had it just raised unnecessary doubts about men and marriage? Doreen thought not. Doris had readily admitted that she had been unsuccessful in her relationships with men. As such, she possessed a sense of bitterness that she struggled to disguise through her friendly and outgoing personality. Doris operated within a complex situation. Was she exploiting the punters, or were they exploiting her? To Doris, it was business, yet did her clients consider it something more? Did they believe that for a price they could experience real affection; if only for the briefest of times. One thing that Doe was sure of however, was that Mike was exploiting Doris. Doreen still couldn't understand why any woman would give their bodies to men they didn't know and found unattractive. Yet she had a grudging respect for Doris. At least she was being paid, whilst many girls on the flats were far too eager to give away their favours for free.

The Saturday before the wedding Doe, Emily and Jack had been at the house on Donnison Street. Emily had made a deal with a furniture shop on Stockport Road for a bed, settee and chairs and a couple of cupboards. Whilst waiting for them to be delivered, Jack was finishing off the work on the window frames. Doreen and Emily were ensuring that the house was as clean as possible, by disinfecting and bleaching the skirting boards, door frames and floors. At the end of a tiring day, they had all returned to Parkfield Street. Whilst Emily went to the pub with Sam, Doreen and Jack relaxed on the settee and watched the television that Emily had recently rented. The two had fallen asleep and had woken around ten. They arranged to meet at Jack's the following morning, before finishing off the work on their new home. After Jack had gone, Doreen went straight to bed.

She was awoken by shouting. As she struggled to clear her head, Doe's first thoughts were for Emily. She began to reproach herself. She should have stayed downstairs and been there to protect her. It must be Sam. That could be the only reason for the commotion. It had been foolish to believe that Sam, who'd not lost his temper since she'd been there, had actually changed. As she swung her legs out of bed and quickly pulled on the slacks and jumper that she'd worn the day before, Doe suddenly realised that the noise was coming from outside. She moved over to the window, pulled aside the curtain and from the light of the streetlamp, saw Doris on the street below shouting at a couple of men.

"You dirty swine. We're fed up with you. Can't you go before you come out?"

One of the men was bending forward and urinating against the wall. His friend was stood by and looking at Doris as he adjusted his trousers. It seemed that he'd already finished the deed.

It was a problem. The men coming out of the clubs did it frequently, especially as they'd been drinking too much. Often, they did it in the doorways and the women were sick of having to clean away the foul mess the following morning. Doris was furious, obviously having caught the two men in the act.

Rather than just move on, the man facing Doris began to shout back. Doe became concerned as his language became threatening and abusive.

"If I was a man I'd give you a good hiding," replied Doris.

They were the last, clear words that Doreen heard before the other man, who'd now finished against the wall, suddenly rushed at Doris. Punching her in the face, he knocked her to the ground. The other man quickly moved in, kicking out at Doris whilst she was on the floor.

Doe rushed to the bedroom door and out on to the landing. She wanted to help Doris, but at that moment, her mam appeared from the bedroom opposite.

"What's going on?"

"It's Doris. She's getting beaten up. I need to go and help her, Mam."

Emily blocked her route downstairs.

"No, Doe. She knows the risks. I don't want you getting hurt."

"It's not one of her punter's, Mam. Get out of the way!"

Doreen forced her way past Emily and ran down the stairs. She raced into the kitchen looking for a weapon. Picking up a sweeping brush she went into the front room. Opening the door, she stepped outside ready to attack the two men, catch them unawares and hopefully save Doris. But it was too late, the men were off down the street and Doris, curled up in a ball, was groaning on the pavement. Doe went over and knelt down beside her.

"Doris. Are you alright?"

It was a silly thing to ask, but what else could she say?

Slowly, Doris took her arms away from the top of her head and looked up at Doreen. Her face was covered in blood; she had been struck on her nose and mouth. Doe had no doubts that her nose was broken.

At that moment, Emily was beside them.

"I'll check that someone's phoned for an ambulance. We'll get one here soon, Doris. Hold on, love."

Emily went across the road to where a group of neighbours had gathered outside in response to the disturbance. After a brief conversation, she returned.

"Don't worry, Doris. Mrs Johnson has already called for one. They're on their way. Can you move at all? It's cold on that pavement."

"I'll go in and get a blanket, Mam."

Doreen got to her feet and as she looked around, noticed that Mike was stood at Doris's open front door. He nipped back inside and came back with a blanket, which he handed to Doreen.

"Here you are."

Doe took it. She was confused. Had Mike been there all the time? If so, why hadn't he helped Doris? And why hadn't he been over to comfort her? Returning to Doris, Doreen covered her carefully with the blanket.

Slowly, Doris straightened up. She was clearly in a lot of pain, but was slowly regaining her senses. Thankfully, the ambulance soon arrived. Doris was checked over, to see that it was safe to move her, then she was lifted on to a stretcher and into the back of the ambulance.

"Will she be all right?" asked Doreen.

"Yes, I think so," replied the ambulance driver. "She's got a broken nose, black eyes and lots of bruising on her arms and legs, but she seems to have managed to avoid anything more serious. It doesn't look like it now, but she's actually been very lucky."

Doreen got into the ambulance. Doris seemed settled, although still in pain. Doe tried to reassure her.

"You're going to be all right, Doris. Do you want me to come with you?"

"There's no need for that," came a voice from behind. It was Mike.

"I'll stay with her."

Doris nodded weakly and tried to smile.

"Thank you, Doreen."

Her voice was barely a whisper. Doe touched her hand and got out of the ambulance. The doors closed behind her and the vehicle was soon gone, its lights flashing on the short journey to the MRI.

Doris was kept in a couple of nights for observation and by Monday, she was back home. Returning from work, Doreen went round to see her. Doris was on her own. Mike was out. Doe was surprised that he'd left her alone. Doris had a bruised and battered face, but was in surprisingly good spirits. Mentally, she seemed to have taken it all in her stride and was clearly pleased to see her young neighbour.

"Thank you, Doreen. You were the only one who came out to help."

"But I was too late, Doris."

"That doesn't matter. I saw your sweeping brush. You could have done some damage with that!"

Doris started to chuckle and then groaned slightly as she clutched at her side.

"I mustn't laugh," she continued. "I'm bruised all over and it hurts if I do."

Doris tentatively pulled up the sleeves on her top and showed Doreen the bruises on her arms. Pulling up her skirt, Doe saw the heavy bruising on her thighs. It was these areas that had absorbed the impact of the kicks aimed at her by the two men whilst she was on the floor. Doreen winced at the sight of the bruises.

"Sam did that to my Mam," said Doe. "I hate him. I wish she wasn't with him."

Doris looked at her.

"I didn't know, love. I can tell you one thing though; he'll do it again and there's nothing you'll be able to do to stop it. Your mam's a fool, Doreen. If your husband ever raises a hand to you, you leave him. Do you hear? No second chances. It'll be worse the next time."

Doe nodded. She didn't want to contemplate such a thing ever happening. She reminded herself that not all men were like that; there were those you could trust.

"You seem to be in good spirits," remarked Doreen.

"I am and do you know why?"

Doe shook her head. How could Doris possibly be so positive after such a terrible thing had happened to her?

"Because tomorrow I'm off. I'm out of here. I've finally got enough to live comfortably. I'm going to Somerset. I'm buying into a seaside cafe with my sister. She lives down there."

"I don't think that you mentioned having a sister."

"I didn't, Doreen. No one knows. Especially Mike and he never will. He doesn't know I'm off. He thinks I'll stay here and keep tipping up money for him. He'll get a big shock tomorrow when I disappear. Won't he?"

"Well don't worry, Doris. I won't tell him anything."

"I know that, Doreen. If I thought you'd tell anyone, then I would never have mentioned it to you."

Doe was pleased that Doris felt that she could confide in her.

"I wanted to ask you," continued Doreen. "Was Mike here when you were attacked?"

"Yes. He was in the house and he didn't lift a finger to help me. He was scared. He was supposed to protect me. That's what I pay him for."

"I thought so."

"Well, I'm not his meal ticket anymore. I've no doubt that he'll be round asking you and Emily if you know where I've gone."

"Well, we don't know anything, do we?" replied Doreen, smiling.

When Emily and Doe returned home from work the next day, there was an envelope pushed through the door. Addressed to Doreen, she opened it. Inside was a five pounds postal order and a short note.

'Thank you', it said. 'Please buy something for your new home. Good luck on your wedding day. Doris xxx.'

Within a few minutes of their return, a knock came to the door. As Doris had predicted, it was Mike.

"Have either of you seen Doris?" he asked.

"No," said Emily. "Why?"

"She's gone," replied Mike. "She's not here. She's not left a note or anything."

"Oh," said Emily. "Well, there's a mystery."

"I thought she might have mentioned something to you or Doreen. You'll let me know if you hear anything, won't you?"

"Of course," said Emily. "You must be worried, especially after her getting hurt," she added, with convincing sincerity.

"Yes, I am."

Mike left and Emily shut the door behind him.

Well, she's done it, thought Doe. Doris had escaped. She would now experience a completely different lifestyle and like herself, would hopefully have a bright new future to look forward to.

Chapter 66

It was six in the morning and Doreen was lay in bed. She had been awake most of the night. It was Saturday April 17th, 1965. Easter Saturday. The day that she was getting married. She couldn't help but feel nervous, but she wondered why. Her Mam had helped to arrange everything. The house on Donnison Street was ready to move into, the register office was booked for eleven o'clock, the witnesses and guests were already prepared and Emily had arranged for a reception afterwards.

It was a huge step that she was taking and Doe knew it. It was one fraught with risks. Could she really, truly know Jack until she had lived with him twenty-four hours a day, seven days a week? She thought that she did, but how many unhappily married women had she already come across; how many failed marriages? Yet marriage would finally give her full control over her life. She would be in her own house with a secure roof over her head and answerable to no one. With Jack she could build a partnership based on love and trust. Who knows where that could take her? Marriage gave her a feeling of excitement; yet trepidation too.

Doreen didn't wait for her alarm to go off. She just had to get up. It would give her longer to do her hair and makeup and ensure that her clothes were ready. She had bought a lovely two-piece suit; a jacket and knee length skirt that were a light shade of blue. A white hat, handbag, high heels and gloves completed her outfit. Emily needed to be up early too. She had arranged to collect the carnations from the florists on Oxford Road that the small group attending the register office would wear. The witnesses were Margaret, a friend Doreen had made at work and Mark, Jack and Doreen's friend from Bennett Street. Sally and Sarah would be there, but not Auntie Dora who never left the flats. Maureen and Emily, plus Paul, Bob and Mark's girlfriend Yvonne, made up the remainder of those who would be attending.

Once out of bed, the morning sped by. Doe feared that she wouldn't be ready in time and started to panic, believing that something would go wrong. Her mam had ordered two taxis for quarter past ten. It would give them plenty of time to get there. She'd arranged for one of them to go and pick up Jack, Mark, Yvonne and Maureen. Although Emily had covered everything thoroughly, Doreen was still worried. Her early morning doubts had disappeared and she was now becoming concerned that something would happen to stop the marriage from taking place.

Just before the taxi was due to arrive, Doreen announced that she was ready. Emily, wearing a smart, pink two-piece suit, declared that her daughter looked lovely.

"I hope Jack realises just how lucky he is," remarked Emily.

But there was no time for reflection as the whirlwind of a day raced on. The taxi had arrived and it was time to go. Doe got into the back of the car with Margaret and her mam and they were off.

"Take some deep breaths," said Emily, turning towards her daughter. "You're starting to panic, aren't you?"

Doreen nodded. She certainly was. She looked out of the window. Up Moss Lane East, left on to Oxford Road and then past the university and on to All Saints and the register office. As the people and buildings slid past, Doe was finding it hard to focus. She was feeling a funny sensation in her stomach.

"Don't worry," said Emily, "it's just nerves. You'll be fine. It's normal. I was worried myself on my wedding day, but everything went well."

"What if he's not there, or if he's late? Will they wait?"

"Of course, he'll be there," said Emily. "He'd be daft not to be. He'll never get anyone as good as you. I'll tell you now. Jack's already worried sick that you're not going to turn up!"

Doreen smiled.

"That's better," said her mam.

Doe didn't understand why she was so worried. Perhaps it was because so much had gone wrong in the past. Could it be that the fates were finally going to let her be happy? She closed her eyes and prayed silently. If ever she needed God's help for everything to turn out right, it was now. Approaching All Saints, the taxi came slowly to a halt. She opened the door to get out and saw

Jack running towards her. She smiled to herself. Her mam had been right.

"Doe. There you are. I was getting worried," said Jack.

"Why? We're not late."

"I know. I was just getting nervous. You look beautiful, Doe. I'm so lucky."

Jack leaned forward and kissed her. Taking Doreen's hand, he led her towards the register office. The rest of the party were already assembled and Emily went round pinning on their carnations. Doe looked at Jack. He and Mark were wearing black matching suits, white shirts, black ties and black, pointed shoes. They looked fashionable and smart. They had done her proud.

It was time to go inside. Emily had gone ahead, informing the reception of their arrival and they were ushered into the waiting area ready to go in. Soon, the party before them were on their way out, accompanied by the good wishes and merriment of their guests. It was now Jack and Doreen's turn. They went in through the doors, the Assistant Registrar beckoning them towards the rows of chairs at the front of the room. Doe felt short of breath; there were butterflies in her stomach. She was concerned that she wouldn't be able to get the words out once the ceremony had begun. She sat down next to Jack on the front row, with Mark and Margaret on either side of them. Everyone else filed into the row of chairs behind them and sat waiting expectantly.

Walking towards them, the registrar welcomed the couple. He solemnly reminded them of the importance of the declarations that they were about to make. Doe felt even more nervous than before. Jack, perhaps sensing her unease, softly squeezed her hand. The registrar asked them both to stand and called on Jack to affirm that he knew of no lawful impediment to the marriage. His voice rang out, loud and true. A ringing declaration of his love. It was just what Doreen needed. From that moment, she knew that everything would be all right. All her doubts had been dispelled. She knew that Jack loved her; was committed to her beyond any doubt. Doe followed his declaration with a clear and measured response of her own and looked deep into his eyes, as she responded to his vows with her own. Jack placed the wedding ring on her finger and they kissed. It was now time for them to sign the marriage certificate and with their own copy safely in Doreen's handbag, they left the room.

The rest of the party were already outside waiting for them and as they emerged from the building and into the fresh air, they were inevitably showered with confetti. It was a joyous scene. Everyone smiling, laughing, and it was time for the photographs. Doreen and Jack alone, with Mark and Margaret and then the whole party together. As the photographer departed, there was a final surprise. Jim had turned up. He'd been waiting for them to emerge from the register office and had stood aside during the photographs.

"Hello, Doe. Congratulations."

He kissed Doreen and gave her a hug, before warmly shaking Jack's hand.

"Dad. You should have come in."

"Well, I was a little late and I wasn't sure whether Sam would be here. I didn't think you'd want him to be, but I didn't want to ruin your day by causing any trouble."

"No, he's not here. I wouldn't allow him anywhere near, Dad."

"I can only stay a few minutes, love. I've got to get back, but I've brought you a little something."

He handed Doreen an envelope. She opened it and inside was a card containing a ten pounds note.

"It's not that much, but at least it'll get you a few things for your new home."

Doe thanked him. Jim threw his arms around her and hugged her again.

"Doe, you make sure that you and Jack make a go of it."

"We will, Dad."

As he stood back, Jim suddenly realised how sophisticated his daughter looked in her fetching two-piece suit. Despite all the difficulties she had been forced to endure, many due to his own selfishness, he was proud to see that she had turned out to be a confident and beautiful young woman.

"Well, I'm going to have to get off, Doe. I'll see you again soon. If you want to find me, you can try the 'George'."

"You can always come and see us. We're in West Gorton. Donnison Street. It's just a little further up Hyde Road."

Doreen opened her handbag, took out a pen and a piece of paper and wrote the address down. Putting it in his pocket, Jim said goodbye and was gone. Emily, who'd stayed at a respectful distance, now came over.

"Come on you two. I've got us a couple of taxis to take us to the 'Wellington'. I've booked a room for some drinks and sandwiches."

The party made their way to the taxi cabs and set off to celebrate. The bar at the 'Wellington' was already open by the time that they got there, so the opportunity to buy alcohol meant that the celebrations went along merrily. Doreen was excited, chatting away to her friends, Emily and Maureen. She felt a huge sense of relief, satisfied in her conviction that she had done the right thing. Jack sat next to her, holding her hand and smiling. She had never seen him so happy. Doe felt that anything was now possible; she was in a state of utter contentment.

The time seemed to fly by. Doreen hoped that she would always remember today; every little detail. She never wanted to forget. It seemed no time at all before Emily told her that she had called for a taxi to take her and Jack home to Donnison Street. It would arrive in ten minutes. 'Home'; 'Donnison Street'. The words had such resonance for her. She had been preparing for this moment for the past three weeks, ever since she had been given her new rent book. Although she and Jack had been to the house, working, cleaning and moving in new furniture, it wasn't until this precise moment that the thought of living as a married woman in her own home, had become a reality. Just, for the briefest of time, she began to feel overwhelmed. Her eyes began to moisten, her lip began to quiver. Doe took a deep breath and held back the tears. They weren't right. She was happy, not sad. Yet it was the final outpouring of the sadness of everything that had gone before; the misery and hardship of the bad times, finally remembered and cast adrift.

"Come on," said Emily. "The taxi's here."

Doreen quickly regained her composure. She and Jack were surrounded by their guests, wishing them well. Kissing them both, shaking their hands and slapping Jack on the back. Swept outside on a wave of enthusiasm, they got into the taxi. It was only a short drive and they were soon in Donnison Street, the taxi depositing them on the pavement outside number eighty.

"Well, Mrs Cassidy, are you going to open the front door?" Jack turned towards Doe and smiled.

'Mrs Cassidy'. Doreen couldn't believe the words. They sounded so strange. She knew it would take some time to get used to them. Opening her handbag, she located the key and placed it in the lock. She turned it and pushed. The door opened.

"You go in first, Jack."

Jack nodded. He understood how emotional a moment this was for his wife and walked through into the house.

Alone, Doreen stepped back and looked up and down the street. There were children playing in the distance; boys kicking a football and girls skipping rope. Just like her in Bright Avenue she thought. Doreen would have children of her own. She was sure of that and would never desert them or let them down. It had been a long and difficult road, but Doe had reached its end; finally in control of her destiny. Fighting against the odds, she had won. Turning back towards the front door, she took out the key from the lock and replaced it in her handbag. Striding confidently into the front room, she shut the door behind her.